MW00904681

The

Letter

Dustin Wolski

First Printing: 2014

ISBN 978-1502973474

For my friends and family, who helped me along the way.

You guys rock!

The horse ran through the street; its rider swaying from side to side, holding the arrow that protruded from his leg. The darkness of the night consumed his vision, leaving him blind to the forest just outside of the village. Without any notice, he was thrown off the horse by an overhanging branch. The arrow in the man's leg pushed deeper beneath the flesh as he landed on the ground, snapping the missile in twain. He dragged himself to the side of the trail, hiding behind a tree as he slowly pulled on the arrow. Suddenly, he heard the hoof prints of the pursuing horses, snapping his head to the side, watching as they ran past, deep into the forest. The man held onto the tree, using it as a crutch to help him stand to his feet. He looked on in the direction of the two horsemen, as well as his own horse, before looking back at the village. He knew it was stupid to follow them, but even just as stupid to return to the houses behind him, for the men would surely look there upon finding the horse without its rider. The man instead turned in a completely different direction, heading further through the woods. He hobbled from tree to tree, trying to see through the blackness. The ground suddenly became damp beneath his feet, but he didn't think that this would be his end. As he walked, his feet sinking into the wet grass, he began to hear the voices of his pursuers. His slow creep quickly changed to a sprint, dashing through the forest. He had no time to react as he slipped on the rock, falling off the edge of the small cliff. He looked up before letting out his last breath to see the tiny man pulling on his leather pouch, running off into the night. The man laid motionless, dead upon the rocks; the storm looming ever closer.

*   *   *

As the sun slowly crept over the horizon, shining through the window of the country home, Kailan awoke, placing his hand in front of his eyes to block out the sun's rays. He shot up, out from under his covers and hopped to his feet beside the bed. Before scrambling around, looking for his clothes, Kailan walked over to the window, taking in a deep breath. The air that came in through the opening was warm to the touch, filling the room with a fresh aroma. The boy made his way to the lower level of the house, making sure as to not wake his father. Rounding the corner, he grabbed a small bun from a bowl on the kitchen table, and ran out the door.

"Kailan!" yelled his father from behind, inside the house.

"I'll be back soon!" Kailan responded, with the bread hanging half out of his mouth, running towards the forest. "Blart, come!" Behind him, Kailan could hear the rustling of leaves in the bushes as a dog darted out, tackling the boy to the ground. The dog smiled, licking Kailan's face as he tried to push the dog off. "We're going to look at the tower today." The large dog pleasantly hopped off of Kailan, and began wagging its tail.

Kailan lived just on the outskirts of a forest that

[2]

bordered the kingdoms of Helforth, Freltus, and Arad. Together, with the kingdoms of: Achland, Letania, and Thoria, they made up the country of Arlbega. Ruled by the Arch Chancellor, Arlbega covered the north western portion of the eastern hemisphere, bordering with the countries of Takash and Korchetska. The rest was surrounded on the north and western coasts by oceans, most notably the Gardaign Ocean, named after one of the great explorers to map it.

      The boy walked with the large dog, into the forest. Small twigs crunched under Kailan's feet as he strode through the passage, constantly moving off the trail, but never leaving sight of it. Even though Kailan knew most of the forest inside and out, he still didn't trust leaving the trail. The forest constantly seemed to change if Kailan wasn't paying attention. There were some days when Kailan would spend hours in a certain spot, memorizing nearly every detail. He would return the next day to find trees in different places than he had remembered, stones upturned, but with moss growing on the tops of them. Kailan knew of the magic beyond his area, but had never experienced it. There was something about the forest that seemed to give Kailan that sense of magic, separating him from his regular life. Almost all of the forest was imprinted in his mind; a visual map that he created over the years. The only part that wasn't, was the area which was situated next to the small mountain range that lay along the border of Helforth and Arad. This area was home to the town of Duskerlin. It was a strange place that Kailan had hoped to never venture to in his life. After hearing many stories throughout his childhood, Kailan grew a slight fear of the town. Besides Duskerlin, the only place within the forest that other people really knew about was the tower of Vlarinor. Named after the elf that lived there for many years, the tower was now abandoned and left decaying in the middle of the forest. Kailan lived just on the outskirts of a small town, filled with some of the most superstitious people in all of Helforth. They had stories and tales for nearly every place within a day's travel. Many of the older men in the village believed that Vlarinor was killed, and his killer was still living in the tower. Others told stories that Vlarinor was driven out by demons, and the building is still cursed. Either way, no one had set foot in the tower in the thirty years that Vlarinor had disappeared.

Kailan, being the adventurous young man that he was, decided that he might as well explore the tower. It took him a while, over hills, under fallen trees, and crossing streams, but to him it was all mere enjoyment. As he closed in, he could begin to see the clearing ahead, with the light making its way through the trees. It passes through the leaves, leaving a bright patch in front of the boy. The trees began to gain distance from one another as Kailan neared ever closer to the tower. Upon reaching the clearing, Kailan stood back in awe as he gazed upwards at the tower. It leaned slightly to the side, with most of the outer wall covered in moss, but the tower was otherwise in great shape. The grass around the tower was thick and tall, but there was a small path that led directly to the door, separating the grass in two parts. Kailan was surprised by the base diameter of the tower. It was nearly the same size as his house, maybe just a little smaller. As he stepped closer to the doorway, Blart made sure to stay behind Kailan. Something about the house bothered the large dog, but Kailan ignored his actions. The small wooden door was about Kailan's height, the wooden boards almost rotted through. He took in a deep breath as he slowly extended his arm, knocking his fist on the door. Kailan and Blart stood motionless as the waited for a response from inside the house. After a moment or two, Kailan looked down at the dog and smiled.

"I guess that no one is home," said Kailan, smiling. He placed his hand on the door handle and slowly pushed on it, opening the door. With little effort, the door swung open, nearly banging against the wall behind it. Blart slowly poked his nose forward, sniffing the air as Kailan pushed ahead. It was when he noticed the burning oil lamp that Kailan stopped dead in his tracks. Sitting on the table as the lamp burned, was a bowl of fresh fruit, and fresh bread cooling next to that. It was quite a shock to Kailan that someone actually was living within the tower. Blart quickly darted underneath the table, grabbing something with his mouth.

"What is it, boy?" said Kailan, intrigued by the dog's actions.

"Let me go, you damn beast!" said a voice from underneath the table. Blart shuffled backwards, revealing a small man.

"A dwarf?" chuckled Kailan as he knelt to the ground, pulling Blart back as the little man pulled his shirt free from the dog's jaws.

"I'm not a dwarf!" yelled the man as he stood to his feet. "And just what are you doing in my home?"

"I'm sorry about that," replied Kailan. "I didn't think that anyone lived here anymore."

"Well, you thought wrong!"

"Wait a second, if you aren't a dwarf, then what are you?"

"I'm a gnome," replied the little man. "And it is not *what* that matters, it is *who*. My name is Gleeble."

"My name is Kailan."

"Kailan?" Gleeble questioned as he rubbed his chin. "Why does that name stick out so much?" The gnome slowly began to pace back and forth.

"I'm sorry?"

Gleeble stopped and looked up, away from both Kailan and Blart, staring off into the distance. The boy watched as a smile quickly grew on the gnome's face.

"Wait here," said Gleeble as he ran towards the stairs.

Kailan looked down at the dog, giggling to himself. "What a strange little man, Blart." It was then that he noticed something strange about the dog. He was staring directly at the door, tilting his head from side to side. "What is it?"

Blart raised his back legs, standing up on all fours as he slowly began walking backwards, growling.

"Blart, stop!" demanded Kailan.

"They're in here!" shouted a raspy voice from outside

the door.

Blart began to bark, the hair on his back standing up as he began to bare his teeth. The door swung open as a small, greenish skinned monster charged in. It was wielding a small sword, riddled with dents and holes, waving the blade back and forth.

"He's in here!" yelled the goblin.

Out of the corner of his eye, Kailan saw a broom, leaning against the wall. He grabbed it and held the broom in front of him, ready to fight.

"Stupid boy!" yelled the goblin, taking a step forward.

Blart did just the same, showing his teeth to the goblin as he growled fiercely. The goblin stared at the dog, who was nearly as tall as him, and stared into Blart's eyes.

With one clean swing, Kailan knocked the blade from the goblin's hand. Blart ran over to the sword, guarding it as the goblin backed up. Three more goblins ran up behind him, their swords just as tattered as his. Even though Kailan only had a broom, the blades were so worn down that they wouldn't be able to cut through easily.

"What's going on down there?" demanded Gleeble, slowly making his way back down the stairs.

"I think you'd better hurry," Kailan retorted.

"One of you go back and get the others," said the first goblin. The one farthest in the back frowned as he slowly turned around, but quickly began sprinting into the forest.

As Gleeble came upon the sight, he stumbled

[7]

backwards, nearly falling down the stairs. "Not now!"

The first goblin lunged for his sword, only to have his arm grabbed onto by Blart's teeth. The other two quickly made their way for Kailan, swinging their swords above their heads.

Kailan thrust the broomstick forward, knocking one of the goblins back, but not enough force to send him to the ground. The other goblin, however, continued to advance on Kailan, running forward as he raised his sword into the air. It was the first time that Kailan had ever had to fight for his life. Sure, he had been in fights before, but not one that meant life or death. A weight began to grow in his stomach, a pain that welled inside. As the beast swung at Kailan, the boy parried the weapon away and struck the goblin's jaw with the other end of the broomstick. He looked over for a second to see Blart thrashing the goblin around like a rabbit. Gleeble quickly jumped from the stairs with a sword and sheath in hand.

"Kailan!" Gleeble yelled. "Use this!" He threw the sword up in the air. Kailan caught the sword with one hand, while releasing the broom from the other hand.

"Now we can do this properly," Kailan chuckled, with a grin on his face. He pulled the sword from its scabbard and raised it up in the air as he smiled. The pain in his stomach seemed to disappear now. As he brought the sword down against the goblin's, Kailan pushed, using his strength to bring the creature to its knees. He lifted the sword away from the goblin's weapon, striking the green man in the side of the head. With one clean motion, he hacked his sword into the remaining goblin's

[8]

stomach, spilling the dark coloured blood onto the floor. As the goblin fell to the floor, Kailan stepped back and looked up as Blart slowly stopped shaking the goblin. Its neck was broken in several places as its head slumped to the side, turning in a way that one's head never should. A pool of blood formed on the ground, the dark liquid dripping from Blart's mouth. Kailan turned to face Gleeble, smiling, but out of breath.

"Better than I expected," said Kailan.

"Where did you learn to fight like that?" questioned Gleeble, his mouth wide open.

"You don't think I spend all of my time just barging into people's homes, do you?" Kailan laughed. "Sure, I've never handled a real sword, but I've gotten the just of it from swinging sticks around."

Gleeble stood motionless, amazed, before snapping back to reality. He held out his hand and revealed a rolled up piece of tattered paper. "You must read this," said Gleeble, no longer amused by Kailan's ability with a sword. The wax seal on the letter was ripped off, most likely by Gleeble.

The young man unravelled the paper and began reading the words imprinted on it:

THIS LETTER IS TO BE KEPT SECRET AND OUT OF SIGHT. ANY KNOWLEDGE OF THE WORDS ON THIS PAGE COULD MEAN DEATH.

By the power entrusted in me by the six kingdoms and peoples of Arlbega, I, Arch Chancellor Orpeth Armenen, have requested that these children be brought to me: Thorstein Volfkin of Schtein in Achland, Lena Harkonen of Kril Haven in Thoria, Kailan Gallot…

Kailan stopped reading the letter for a moment after noticing his own name. He looked up at Gleeble, who did not say a word as he watched the boy's confusion dance around his mind. He looked down and continued reading the letter:

…Kailan Gallot of Hapreth in Helforth, Guin Pelerin of Alandra in Arad, and Viktor Svetlenka of Dratana in Letania. Bring these children to me immediately. They and their families are in immense danger. They will be given shelter and protection in Freltus.

Kailan stared at the paper in his hands as he looked down upon the Arch Chancellor's crest at the bottom of the page. To his shock, underneath that was his signature as well. "Where did you find this?" Kailan said as he moved the paper out of Gleeble's way.

"I found a dead body a number of years ago," said Gleeble. "The man had this inside a pouch, wrapped around his waist. Naturally, I took it, seeing as he wasn't going to use it. I thought about throwing the letter away, but it looked better as an ornament with the red seal and all. I just didn't think that you would actually come knocking at my door."

"I think that I'm going to take my leave now," said

Kailan, slowly making his way for the door.

"Not a smart idea, dear boy," said Gleeble, stepping over one of the dead goblins.

"Why not?" Kailan asked as he turned around.

"I've seen these goblins before. They're not your average roaming goblins," said Gleeble. "These are soldiers, and they don't fight alone. Your best bet is to go to Freltus and figure out what this letter is all about."

"Why not stay and fight?" questioned Kailan. "You saw how easily me and Blart killed these three."

"Because, my boy, they will return, with greater numbers, and with something much nastier than just a couple goblins." Gleeble quickly ran up the stairs again, returning in a matter of seconds with a map in hand. "There is a boat, by the riverbank in Duskerlin, just north of here. I suggest that you take that and make your way down the river to Freltus. It will take you a couple of days, so remember to sleep on the opposite side of the river as the forest."

"Won't they come here first?" questioned Kailan.

"Most likely, but don't worry, I have all of that covered. I'll make sure that your dog gets back to your house, and I'll try to explain as much as I can to your parents."

Just then, Kailan heard sounds coming from outside. There was a loud thud, shaking the ground as Kailan and Gleeble ran to the door.

"See what I mean?" said Gleeble, rushing to Kailan's side. "You need to leave now. Take the map and run." Kailan

[11]

ran out the doorway, looking back as Gleeble and Blart ran towards Kailan's home. He could hear the goblins talking behind him as he ran, but he didn't want to take a chance to get a glimpse of them. He knew they were after him, and not Gleeble, because the sounds of their voices never seemed to dissipate or get further away. It was only after what seemed like an hour of running, that Kailan could finally no longer hear the goblins, and their large companion. He slowed his pace, being ever watchful of the area behind him. Never once did he make any unnecessary noise while on his way to Duskerlin, nor did he stray from his bearing. Upon reaching the small town, Kailan remembered the fear that he had of it. The stories seemed to be true as Kailan slowly stepped through the archway, into the main square. There was a thick fog that covered the town, keeping most of the light out. It was strange for Kailan to actually find out that one of the stories that he had heard as a child was actually true. He quickly attached the sword's scabbard onto his belt with the frog. A cold wind blew through the town, tossing dead leaves around, scattering them across the square. It didn't take long for Kailan to realise that the town had been completely deserted. Not as single soul was living in the village anymore. As he slowly and cautiously crept towards the dry fountain in the centre of the small town, the wind began to blow again, picking up the leaves just as before. This time, however, the leaves did not just blow to the other side of the square. This time, they made their way to the centre, just next to the fountain, in front of Kailan. The leaves bunched up tightly as hundreds more flew in from outside the main square. As they swirled around, Kailan slowly began to make out a familiar shape within the leaves. It wasn't until they started to slowly separate that Kailan realised it was a face. He stood frozen, quivering. The leaves fell to the ground as the beautiful woman stepped out and smiled at Kailan. Her long, straight black hair hung down almost to her hips, partially waving in the wind. She held out one of her long slender hands to Kailan, caressing his cheek with one of her fingers.

"Don't be afraid," she said with a smile on her face. "I'm not here to hurt you."

In his mind, Kailan kept telling himself that he needed to leave, but there was a strange force, compelling him to stay, to listen to the woman. His cheek began to turn red, blushing as the young woman's finger swept along it. She slowly moved in closer until she was close enough to kiss him. She moved in, rubbing her nose up, and along his neck as she placed one hand on his shoulder, the other above his heart.

"You know, Kailan, I can do anything you wish of me." She pulled back slightly, showing Kailan her seductive smile. She blew on his neck before rubbing her cheek against his, kissing it tenderly.

Kailan couldn't tell if it was her beauty that was captivating him, or her seduction techniques. Either way, it was working very well, for Kailan couldn't even hear as the goblins caught up to him, standing just on the edge of the town.

"There he is!" one of the goblins called out.

Kailan was pushed to the ground as the woman showed

her true form to him and the goblins, shooting up in the air like a cloud of smoke.

"This is my town!" screamed the witch with her piercing voice. Kailan watched as the flesh on her face quickly rotted away revealing the bone beneath.

"You have something we want, witch" said one of the goblins, stepping forward.

"You will not touch this boy!" the witch cried as she raised her hand, throwing the goblin back with one of her spells.

"Get her!" yelled the goblin after picking himself up from the ground. Just like before, Kailan could hear the loud thud coming from the forest as the goblins' ally made its way through the trees. As the ogre crashed through the final branches, he charged the witch at full speed.

Kailan looked up at the advancing ogre and quickly made a dash for one of the houses, hiding behind the corner wall. He watched as the giant beast crashed through the arch way, past the goblins, and into the village. The witch laughed as she floated out of the ogre's way, patting it on the back.

"You could try and give a little more effort than that," said the witch, smiling.

"Just give us the boy and no one gets hurt," said the lead goblin.

"Oh no, I can't do that." The witch giggled as she flew higher into the air, dodging the ogre's second attack.

"Spread out!" yelled the lead goblin to the others.

Kailan began slowly making his way to the back of the

house, but only to find a goblin waiting for him there.

"He's here, Captain!" said the goblin, turning his head to look behind.

Kailan unsheathed his sword and quickly thrust it through the goblin's chest, pulling it to the side and then out. He charged after the remaining goblins, holding his sword in front of him at all times. The first few were easy to kill as Kailan used his forward momentum to slice through them with ease. It was the remaining six that he had to actually pay attention to on how he fought. With each swing of his sword, Kailan began to feel more and more attached to the witch, as though she was compelling him to fight, forcing him to. He slashed one of the goblin's necks, severing its head clear from its body, launching it into the air. He disarmed another, grabbing it by the hair and throwing it to the side and out of his way. Before long, Kailan had killed four more of the goblins, covering the forest floor with blood. He watched as the witch continued to toy with the ogre in the town square, dodging every one of its attacks. With many of the goblins dead, the remaining few retreated, running away from the village, leaving the ogre behind. Kailan turned around and looked up to see the witch, showing the same face as she did before, smiling down at him. When she looked at him this time, Kailan could no longer feel her magic pulling him close. There was something about her though that Kailan could not resist. Even though he knew what she truly was, Kailan found her to be warm, and inviting. Her smile seemed to create a glow within Kailan, making him feel as though he was being held softly.

The ogre jumped into the air, plucking the witch from her sanctuary, and smashing her against the stone floor below.

Never before had Kailan felt so much anger within himself before. With its back turned, he darted towards the ogre, stabbing it in its side with his sword, pushing it as deep as he could. As the beast slowly stumbled to the ground, it reached an arm behind, swatting Kailan to the side like a fly. He was thrown to the other side of the square, watching as the ogre made its way towards him. There was a bright flash of light, causing Kailan to put his hands in front of his eyes. It was like staring directly into the sun as a child. As the light dissipated and his eyes adjusted, the boy removed his arms, watching as the ogre slowly blew away in the wind, like ashes floating above a fire.

"Kailan," whispered the young woman, the pool of blood next to her body becoming bigger by the second.

Kailan hurried over to her still body, limping across the square. "Did you kill the ogre?"

"Yes, but there will be more soon, Kailan," she replied. "I'm sorry Kailan."

"Sorry for what?" replied Kailan, placing a hand on the young woman's shoulder. "You protected me."

"Yes, but only because you tried to protect me," said the woman, holding her arm out again cupping Kailan's chin, rubbing his jaw with her thumb.

"We need to get you out of here then, if more are coming," said Kailan, trying to gently pull on her arm.

[16]

"It's no use Kailan," said the witch. "My time has come. There are no spells that can heal me, no herbs within the forest. No magical bandage that can heal my wounds." She pulled her hand away from his face and placed it on her chest. "My wounds are inside, deep within me."

"I can't just let you die, even if you are a witch," Kailan protested. "You saved me from those creatures. I'll try to do what I..."

She placed one of her fingers in front of Kailan's mouth. "All that I ask from you is a kiss, and that you run from here."

"A kiss?"

"Just one."

Kailan leaned in as what felt like a tear, dripped from his eye, landing on the cheek of the witch. She smiled, bringing her head away from his. She then tilted her head back and let out a long breath as she changed back into the leaves, dancing through the air.

Kailan watched as they lifted up, into the sky, past the tree tops. He felt a pain in his gut, but it wasn't from the ogre. It was a strange pain that Kailan had never felt before. He slowly hobbled over to the pile of ashes on the ground, brushing them away to reveal his sword. He picked the blade up from the ground and placed it back in the scabbard. As he headed towards the river, Kailan took a quick look back at the town, noticing the sunlight slowly break through the fog.

[17]

Kailan had never really had to deal with the magical world outside of his small village, but all in the course of a day, he found out just how dangerous it really was. He spent the first night with the boat turned over on top of him, hiding from any pursuers that he might have trailing behind. The entire night, Kailan was awake. Neither exhaustion, nor the sounds of the night could put him to sleep. His mind was racing back and forth. He never once thought that he would be caught by the goblins; his mind was set too heavily on his family and the events that had just occurred as he played them over and over again in his mind.

The next morning, Kailan's mind began to settle as he began down the river again. His mind was still spinning, but he was able to focus more on the task at hand. He stopped once, to pick apples from a tree, before moving on again. He actually slept the second night, but his dreams kept causing him to wake up. As he looked up at the stars, he let out a long breath.

"*Why me?*" he thought to himself. The more that he began to think of the situation, the more it bothered him. It was by sheer misfortune that the goblins ever found Kailan to begin with. It was sheer luck for the Arch Chancellor that his letter would be picked up by a small gnome that Kailan would later run into in life. It was a miracle that Kailan befriended a witch at

[18]

just the most opportune time so that she could protect him from his attackers. What bothered Kailan the most was how the Arch Chancellor knew who he was in the first place. It almost seemed like everything that had happened was planned out.

                    *   *   *

He hopped of the raft and slung his bag over his shoulder. He looked up at the great wall that stood in front of him. He had arrived in the capital of Freltus. Harlem was a fairly large city, being one of the biggest in all of Arlbega. The main gate was guarded by two men, each of them carrying a large spear. As he neared the gate, he was stopped by two guards.

"Oy, where do you think you're going?" questioned one of the guards

"To the city," said Kailan. "I'm from Helforth, and I don't really know where I need to go."

"A tourist eh?" The man crossed his arms. "What business do you have in Harlem, or Freltus for that matter even?"

"I have a letter from the Arch Chancellor," said Kailan.

"Ha!" The man laughed in Kailan's face. "Did you hear that Garth?" he said as he looked back to the other guard. "Boy says he's got business with the Arch Chancellor." The other guard started to laugh.

"I do," replied Kailan as he pulled out the letter. The guard ripped it out of his hands and started reading it.

"Who are you exactly?"

"My name is Kailan Gallot," said the boy. The man continued to scan the letter until reaching a certain point. He instantly froze up and almost started shaking.

"Let him through Garth," said the guard. He handed the letter back to Kailan. "He's telling the truth." The guard named Garth moved out of Kailan's way and let him through the gates. "Best go up to Machesney Hall if I were you. You'll find the Arch Chancellor there."

Kailan had never before seen a place so crowded before. It appeared that he had stumbled upon the market district. It was quite loud, but Kailan didn't mind it too much. It reminded him of being in his uncle's barn. He had chickens, geese, ducks, cows, and many other different kinds of animals that made loud noises alike. He made his way to the top of the hill, where he found the large building. The area around Machesney Hall was even more deserted than the palace. People would be seen going in and out of the palace every now and then, but not like at Machesney Hall. The only people seen there were two guards that stood outside of the single door building. There was a well-kept garden in the front and a lavish walkway that circled the entire building. There were no guards by the doors, so Kailan stepped right through, unnoticed. As he walked down the hallway by himself, he noticed that the building was not well lit. The torches that hung on the walls gave the building a feeling that a dungeon would give off, rather than a place of government. There were tapestries and carvings in the walls as well. Statues stood along the hallway, portraying people that Kailan had no knowledge of. They didn't look anything like how Kailan had imagined kings would look like. They were frail old men, many of them holding papers instead of swords. There was a door at the end of the hallway. On the other side of it was the large, main room of Machesney Hall. This room was different from the first as it was lit up almost entirely by sunlight through the large windows. There was a large number of tables and chairs, some covered in books, charts and maps, while some were completely clean. There were many men in the room as well; many of them quite old, but there were some that seemed to be closer to Kailan's age, but not by much. They were so busy rummaging through the books and papers that they didn't even care about Kailan walking into the room. I wasn't until Kailan tapped one of them on the shoulder to get his attention. The man jumped as he turned around to inspect Kailan.

"How may I help you my dear boy?" questioned the old man.

"I came to speak to the Arch Chancellor," replied Kailan. The old man laughed at Kailan's words.

"Is the country in danger?" chuckled the little man.

"No, I have a letter from Orpeth Armenen," said Kailan.

"Jokes like that will get you into lots of trouble here," said the man as he turned back and continued reading over his papers.

"It's not a joke," replied Kailan. "Here, read it."

The old man's smile suddenly went straight. He ripped the letter from Kailan's hands and started reading it. "This looks real," said the man as his hands started shaking. "We'd better show this to Tanier, now shouldn't we."

He turned around and started running, hopping over chairs and tables in his way.

"Tanier, who's that?" Kailan asked as he tried to keep pace with the old man.

"Tanier Frost?" said the man, stopping dead in his tracks. "You dense boy, or have you just been living under a rock your whole life? Tanier Frost, Arch Chancellor of Arlbega."

"I thought Orpeth Armenen was the Arch Chancellor."

The old man stuck out his tongue, making raspberry noises. "He's been dead for at least eighteen years now."

Kailan stood motionless, his eyes wide as all thought escaped his mind. What was he going to do? Would Tanier Frost give him the same hospitality that Orpeth Armenen had planned? Beyond that, where were the other people on the list? It felt to him as though he was digging deeper into a mystery that might never be solved. According to the man, Kailan would have only have been a year old when Orpeth Armenen had died.

"This way," said the man, smiling. Kailan followed the man as he burst through a door and into an office. "This boy's got a letter here from Armenen," said the little man. The man sitting across the desk in the office looked up from his study at the little man.

"What are you talking about?" questioned the man. The little man grabbed Kailan by the sleeve of his shirt and pulled him into the room.

"This boy just showed me a letter that he received from Orpeth Armenen," said the little man. The other man's eyes widened. He grabbed the letter out of the little man's hands and started reading it.

"Who are you?" questioned the man as he started reading the letter.

"Sarl, but you've known me for years, sir," said the little man.

"Not you, idiot. I was talking about the boy."

"My name is Kailan," replied the boy.

"Kailan Gallot?" questioned the man.

"Yes." When the man reached the end, he nodded his head and looked up.

"I want Arkle in here now," said the man. In almost no time at all, a very old man with a long, white beard, walked into the room. He looked very frail and weak, but looked as though he loved working for the Arch Chancellor. He pulled a monocle out of his beard and held it up to his eye, his hands shaking. He scanned over the letter quickly and nodded his head when reaching the bottom.

"The document is real," said the old man. He placed the monocle back in his beard, turned around, and left the room.

[23]

Arkle had worked in Machesney Hall for over sixty years. By some chance, he was able to live long enough to work for three Arch Chancellors.

"Bring Bailan to me," said the man at the desk. In a matter of seconds, a young man, maybe a year or two older than Kailan walked into the room. "I want you to take this young boy and figure out what it is that he needs. Provide him with anything that we can offer." The boy nodded and stepped out of the room, followed by Kailan.

"Hello," said the boy.

"Hello," replied Kailan.

"My name is Bailan. Who might you be?" questioned the boy.

"My name is Kailan."

"Ha! Our names rhyme," laughed Bailan. He brought Kailan to a small, old door in a corner of the large room. Bailan opened the door, and on the other side was a dark, spiral staircase. Kailan didn't know what to expect at the bottom of the stairs. Bailan snapped his finger and a small flame appeared on his thumb. He then turned his hand over and the flame moved to the palm of his hand, growing slightly in the process. The staircase lit up and Kailan noticed how far down it actually went.

"There must be at least fifty steps," said Kailan.

"Fifty-seven actually," replied Bailan. "I counted every step on my third day here." As they neared the last steps, they came upon a door that looked almost the same as the one that they first entered. The one at the bottom of the stairs had a

[24]

strange emblem on it. Kailan reached into his pocket and pulled out the letter. The seal on the letter was the same design as the emblem on the door. A crowned gryphon, in its talons was a sword and axe. As they pushed the door open, they walked into the small room. It was filled with papers and books of all kinds.

"What is this room?" questioned Kailan. Bailan lit a candle in the middle of the room.

"This is the library of records and lore," replied Bailan. "Hopefully you will find what it is that you need in here." Kailan walked over to one of the books on a shelf and opened it up. In it were strange symbols that Kailan had never seen before.

"I was hoping to speak with the Arch Chancellor about this," said Kailan.

"What are you talking about?" Bailan questioned. Kailan handed the letter to Bailan.

"This letter was written by Arch Chancellor Orpeth Armenen," replied Kailan. "I thought that Arch Chancellor Tanier Frost might be able to help me with it."

"You already did speak to him," said Bailan.

"The man at the desk?"

"Yes, that's Tanier," said Bailan. "I know that he doesn't really seem like much, but he is quite powerful when it comes to politics." Kailan smiled and continued searching through the papers. "Who are these other people on the list?" questioned Bailan. Kailan stepped back from the shelves.

"I have no clue," replied Kailan. "All that I know about it is that my name is on it, and that it was written before I was born." Bailan put his hand to his chin and pondered for a second or two. Kailan pulled out another book and looked down at it. The language was neither in that of Lybidian, the common language of the world, nor the language that he had seen earlier in one of the other books. It was something that he understood though. Kailan's father was not born in Helforth as Kailan was. Instead, he made a pilgrimage with a group of settlers from Achland at a very young age. Because of this, Kailan's father was a native speaker of Feltsch, the language of Achland. Kailan spent the first few years of his life learning both Feltsch and Lybidian side by side. Kailan leaned over the book, slowly reading the words aloud in Feltsch. "SCHWARTZ ARKETSEN GRASCH NI ROCH."

"You know what that means in Lybidian, right?" questioned Bailan.

"The old order will be reborn," replied Kailan. Kailan closed the book and tossed in on the table. Bailan reached into the bookshelf and pulled out a number of papers. Each one was identical to the other, but each one was an original. He looked down at the letter in his hand and then at the papers.

"Kailan, come quick!" said Bailan. The papers were the same as the letter, just extra copies. It seemed as though either Orpeth Armenen needed additional forms just in case the messenger failed, or there were many messengers that he needed to send. Bailan and Kailan were a bit confused at this point. They continued to search for another full hour before Bailan finally decided that it was time to take a break. "I suggest that

[26]

you go and rest for a while," said Bailan. "I will speak to Tanier, and you can tour the city for a while. Your quarters will be fully prepared for you within an hour." The two boys stepped out of the room. As Bailan closed the door behind him, he quickly held out his hand and pulled the flame from the candle back to his hand and lit up the staircase again.

"Where did you learn magic?" asked Kailan.

"Picked up a few things here and there," Bailan replied. He showed Kailan to the main door of Machesney Hall and led him out into the front garden. "You should visit the market," said Bailan. "You might find something you'll like." Kailan smiled and walked away. When he reached the market, he found stands and vendors crowding the streets. People were arguing prices back and forth, while some were yelling just for the sheer fun of it. Kailan made his way straight to the weapons and armour. The first vendor that he found had very cheaply made weapons. Kailan realized the stressing of the metal at first glance. Most of the weapons that Kailan saw were poorly crafted, but cost almost as much as a decently made weapon. It wasn't until Kailan came across an unusual looking dagger. The pommel was shaped like the sun and had a yellow gem laid in it. The vendor, a thin Aradian man adorned with colourful cloths and shiny rings noticed Kailan looking at the dagger.

"I see that you have taken an interest in 'The Dagger of Inushka'," said the man with a thick accent.

"Dagger of Inushka?" questioned Kailan.

"Have you never heard the story of the great Inushka?"

questioned the man in shock. Kailan shook his head. "Well...,"
said the man, playing with his moustache, "I'll have to tell you.
Thousands of years ago, when Arad was part of the great dessert
country of Takash, there lived a very young man by the name of
Inushka, a foolish boy, but very wise for that matter as well. He
lived in a small town in Takash called Brakta." The man
emphasized on the rolling of his "R's" in the word "Brakta". "At
that time, there was a great war between Takash and their enemy
across the seas. Quite a pointless war, as neither of the two
countries had enough boats to move their armies from one land
to another. It is said that the gods became angry with the two
countries and spread darkness over the lands forever. Inushka
and his family suffered greatly as there was no sunlight for the
grass, and in turn no grass for their sheep. So, Inushka decided
to make a deal with the gods to have the curse of darkness lifted
off of Takash and their enemy. Inushka said to the gods that he
would sacrifice himself as part of the bargain. The gods realized
Inushka's bravery and decided to lift the curse without taking his
life. All of the gods except for one allowed him to live. The god
that ruled the darkness did not like this, and so instead took
Inushka's life and left a dagger in his place." The man picked up
the dagger and ran his bony finger along the hilt of the weapon.
"It is said to hold the power of a thousand suns as was Inushka's
wish," said the vendor. He handed the dagger to Kailan and took
a step back. It fit perfectly in Kailan's hand. The blade and
handle were in perfect balance of each other and the
craftsmanship was simply divine. Kailan looked into the rest of

[28]

the market and fiddled with the dagger in his hand. "Do you have a scabbard that…" When he turned around, the vendor and kiosk had disappeared. He looked down at the dagger in his hand and smiled, placing it under his belt to attach it on later.

"That was weird," said Kailan to himself. As he turned around, there were three men facing him. The men looked very threatening, even without the large clubs in their hands.

"Give us the money, boy," said one of them. "We'll beat the living daylights out of you if you don't."

"What money are you talking about?" questioned Kailan.

"That pouch on your belt is full of coins," replied another man. Kailan quickly whipped out his sword and held it in front of his face.

"A sword," said the shortest one. "That's against the law and that'll mean an extra hard beating." By this time, others had noticed what was going on. They backed away from the problem, but no one stepped in to try and resolve the problem. "Get him!"

"If you touch me, I'll make sure that you will never be able to touch anything again with your hands," said Kailan. The largest of the three decided to make the first move, swinging his club with one hand, and trying to grab the pouch with the other. Kailan stepped back and knocked the man to the ground by hitting him over the head with the pommel of his sword. He got back up and started swinging again. This time, there was no holding back. Kailan gave the man a chance, but he did not learn from the first time. Kailan gave a powerful kick to the face as he jumped through the air, knocking the man to the ground and unconscious. The other two men backed up slightly, even though they had some fear of Kailan, they hadn't seen enough to be too afraid to continue fighting. They ran at Kailan and before the even got near him, one was lying on top of the other with large cuts along their arms and legs. Suddenly, a trumpet could be heard from through the crowd. Many of the peasants backed out of the way to allow a brightly clothed man atop a horse through. Kailan took a step back and quickly wiped his sword off on one of the men on the ground. The man on the horse did not look much older than Kailan, but that could have been because he lived in the palace. With little work done in his life, he showed few signs of aging.

"What is this atrocity that I see here?" demanded the young man.

"These men attacked me," replied Kailan.

"Address your prince properly!" yelled the young man. Kailan was now speaking to the king of Freltus' son. He was even more arrogant than his father, but had no real power over anything. The king didn't have as many powers either seeing as it was the Arch Chancellor who controlled Arlbega.

"What are you talking about?" questioned Kailan.

"That sword at your side, where are the registration papers for it?" demanded the prince. Kailan pulled the badge that Bailan gave to him from his pocket and held it up in front of the prince. The prince grabbed the badge from Kailan's hand

and stared at it for a second.

"So Bailan has sent another one of his little thugs into the market to cause trouble," said the prince with a smile on his face. Stepping off his horse, he pulled his sword from its sheath.

"What are you doing?" questioned Kailan.

"I'm going to kill you," said the prince. He swung the sword at Kailan, only to have Kailan dodge the attack. "I've had enough of Bailan thinking that this is his city!" He took another swing at Kailan, but missed again.

"I don't want to have to fight you," said Kailan.

"That is not your choice," replied the prince. Suddenly, there was a gust of wind and Bailan appeared within the crowd of people. "What are you doing here?" snarled the prince. Bailan held up his hand a faced his open palm towards the prince.

"I've told you to stop drinking," said Bailan. He walked over to Kailan and placed his hand on Kailan's shoulder. As Kailan blinked, it felt as though he was being thrown around like a ragdoll for a split second. When he opened his eyes, he found himself back in Tanier Frost's office.

"How did you do that?" questioned Kailan.
Bailan laughed as he walked out of the room. "It's all magic," he said.

"Why is the prince such a jerk?" questioned Kailan.

"Who, Farol?" questioned Bailan. "He's a bit spoiled."

"Who's Farol?" asked Kailan.

"That's the prince's name," Bailan replied. "You don't have to listen to him though. You are under Tanier's power, not the king's. Watch out though, because they will never understand that." As the two young men walked down the hallway, they were met by Tanier.

"Kailan, come into my office," he said. "There is something that we need to discuss." Bailan followed behind as well, closing the door behind them. Tanier walked around to the other side of his desk and sat at the chair. Hunching over the desk, he spoke very clearly. "We have not yet figured out anything about the letter from Orpeth Armenen. In the meantime, while we are researching and trying to investigate, we've decided that it might be best for you to look for some of the people on the list."

"Sorry?" questioned Kailan. Tanier leaned back in his chair and looked up at Bailan, and then back to the other boy.

"Orpeth Armenen apparently went through a lot of trouble to send out these letters," said Tanier. "They are obviously of some great importance then. We need to figure out why he sent them out, as well as the mystery behind them. If you've made it this far on your own, you should be able to make it to Achland without any help."

"I'm starting to get the feeling that no one knows what's going on," said Kailan.

"That's the reason why we are sending you away," said Tanier. "We will provide you with everything you'll need. Because we know so little on this matter, we cannot spend any more expense on sending someone with you."

"Don't worry," replied Kailan. "I shouldn't have any

problems on the way."

By the next morning, Kailan was packed, packed up, and sent on another journey through Arlbega, with a horse instead this time. It wasn't long before he reached the end of the lush green pastures near Harlem, and came upon the dark, tall forests of Freltus. It was there that Kailan spent his first night of travel. Other than the howling of distant wolves in the middle of the night, constantly waking Kailan up, it was otherwise a good night's sleep. It was the second night that made Kailan worry. As the sun went down, soon after came the rain. It was a dark and cold night, with thunder crashing overhead, but that wasn't the problem though. In the distance, past many of the trees, Kailan would often see a small light. It was a lantern, bobbing back and forth, as someone walked from tree to tree. They didn't look like they were searching for anything, but were just walking through the forest. This wouldn't have seemed strange if it wasn't well past midnight. He continued to keep a watchful eye on the lantern until it disappeared into the distance.

As the sun rose the next morning, Kailan was already cleaning up his campsite. He couldn't find any sign of the mysterious lantern along his journey, but he didn't let it bother him that much. It was nearly a day and a half later before Kailan found the village of Schtein. As he followed the road into the small town, Kailan wasn't expecting to find himself in the territory of some of the largest people he had ever seen. The women were taller than Kailan, with one of the smallest being his size. The men had at least another foot of height on top of that. They weren't just tall either; they were strong too. Kailan was almost quivering at the mere sight of them. He walked up to the first house along the road and knocked on the large door. The door swung open, and standing over Kailan stood a very tall man. He said a few words in a strange language, confusing Kailan at first, but he recognised it very quickly. Kailan instantly began to think of how disappointed his father would have been if he had known that he didn't understand Feltsch. He quickly echoed the man's words in his mind, translating them quickly.

Kailan ignored the comment that the man made and proceeded to ask him a question. "I'm sorry sir," Kailan replied, in Feltsch. "I am looking for someone by the name of Thorstein Volfkin."

"Volfkin? Ya, they live on the second last farm," said the man in a deep voice.

"Thank you," said Kailan, quickly heading down the road. The man gave Kailan an odd look before closing the door. The boy led his horse through the streets, watching the villagers perform their everyday duties. They were pretty much the same jobs that Kailan and his father did at home, but the sheer size of the people made it seem so much more intense. After a few minutes, Kailan found the house that he was supposed to go to. It was much bigger than many of the others, which were already bigger than Kailan's home. He walked up to the door to find it already open, so he poked his head in and knocked on it.

"Oh, there's a little man at the door," said a tall, muscular woman. Kailan rolled his eyes.

[34]

"Hello," said Kailan. "I am looking for someone by the name of Thorstein Volfkin, and I was told that he lived here."

"Oh yes, but Thorstein is out at the moment," said the woman. "You can wait here until he comes back, or you could follow that path there until you find him."

Kailan looked into the distance at the treeline and saw the opening that the woman was pointing at. "I think that I can manage finding him," replied Kailan as he hopped off the front step.

"Just tie your horse up to the fence," said the woman, smiling.

Kailan followed the path into the forest. It wasn't an orderly path, but Kailan knew that it was there. It didn't take long before he found someone along the trail, but as he turned the corner along the path, Kailan came upon the stranger. Even sitting down, the man was taller than Kailan. With his back turned, Kailan began to inch closer to the man, ever cautious of his movements. Each placement of his foot was as careful as the last. "Excuse me," Kailan said hesitantly, remembering to speak in Feltsch. The tall man turned around as he stood up, forcing Kailan to jump back. The first thing that Kailan noticed about the giant was his long, orange beard. It was braided in two strands, reaching just past his collar.

"Hello little man," said the giant. Kailan raised one eyebrow.

"Why does everyone say that?" said Kailan, "You're just... well... huge!"

[35]

"That would depend on where you are standing," said the giant. "But yes, I am much taller than anyone else that I know. Now, what is it that you wanted to ask me?"

"Are you Thorstein?" questioned Kailan.

The giant, still smiling, replied, "I am indeed." Thorstein's size was considered a marvel in Arlbega, for he was not a giant at all. Achland had been known to be the home of very tall people, but none with the likes of Thorstein. As the tallest in his family, he reached his father's height by ten years of age, even though his father was a mighty seven and a half feet. Now that he was nineteen years of age, Thorstein would slowly stop growing, but he was already one of the tallest people in all of Arlbega. The only people that could match his height were the Northland Giants in Thoria; though, even they could not match Thorstein's muscle. One of his legs was about the same size as Kailan's whole body, being over six feet long and almost two feet wide, each. His arms were slightly smaller, but were still quite massive in size. Kailan could only begin to imagine Thorstein's abilities of his strength.

Without notice, Thorstein went silent for a second, taking his attention away from Kailan. He turned around and looked through the trees which were only a few feet taller than him. He held one of his fingers in front of his mouth, signalling Kailan to keep quiet. He pushed aside one of the trees slightly and created a place for Kailan to look through.

The four beasts walked along one of the other paths in the forest, hunting most likely. Thorstein slowly leaned to his

[36]

side, picking up a gigantic battle axe off the ground. The blade of the axe itself was almost as wide as Kailan was tall.

"Trolls!" Kailan yelled in fright. The thought of having Thorstein standing right beside him didn't reveal itself until the trolls started chasing Kailan.

As they broke through the trees, they looked up in terror as they came upon Thorstein. The giant man bent down and grabbed one of the creatures by the neck. He raised it in the air, and then threw it into two of the other ones. Behind the trolls, appeared a ginormous creature, almost twice their size.

"Ah," said Thorstein, "This ogre'll make for a bit of a challenge." The ogre was a very similar to the one that Kailan had fought before. He was pretty much just a larger version of the trolls, but bald, and had a much smaller nose.

Kailan quickly pulled out his sword and waved it in front of the trolls, pulling their attention from Thorstein. They were each about two feet taller than Kailan, but that didn't matter. Kailan's speed would make up for his lack of muscle against them. The only problem was that there were four trolls that he had to fight, seeing as they were not going to dare fight Thorstein. "I may need some help here, when you get a moment," said Kailan as he ran through the forest.

Thorstein looked at the giant mace in the ogre's hand. "I'm a bit busy at the moment," replied Thorstein.

Kailan jumped back after the first troll swung its arm. He brought his sword up, cutting the troll's forearm. Another swipe at the waist had the creature on all fours.

[37]

Thorstein looked back at Kailan while holding the ogre by the neck. "Just a bit longer."

Kailan stabbed his sword into the back of the troll's head. It only took a few more seconds for Kailan to fell another troll.

Thorstein lifted the ogre onto his chest, and threw it into the trees. Then, with his axe, he went after the ogre. After killing it, he turned around to find Kailan standing in front of the last troll. He took a few steps closer and grabbed the troll around the waist, launching it into the air behind him. There was a big chance that it wasn't going to survive from the impact of the landing or the force of the throw either.

Kailan wiped off his blade and walked towards Thorstein. "I didn't get to properly introduce myself earlier," said Kailan, forgetting to speak in Feltsch. He held out his hand to the taller young man. "My name is Kailan."

Thorstein grabbed Kailan's hand and most of his forearm and shook it. "It's nice to meet you," said Thorstein, in Lybidian.

Kailan was surprised the words that came out of his mouth were not tainted with an accent. "How did you learn to speak like that?" questioned Kailan.

"You mean Lybidian?"

"Perfect Lybidian," replied Kailan.

"I was taught at Algar University," replied Thorstein. The university was situated on an island just west of Achland in the Gardaign Ocean. It was a much respected school, one that taught almost everything that there was to know.

"How did you get into a university?" questioned Kailan.

"My mind is larger than my muscles," said Thorstein. "One of the professors was passing through my village one day and he found me. He was amazed by my size at first, but then asked me to come to the school to study."

The two boys began to walk back to the village. With the sun standing overhead, Kailan knew that midday was close. When they reached the village, Kailan was greeted back by Thorstein's mother. She ushered the two boys into the large house which was built to accommodate Thorstein's size.

"Is there anything that I can get you two?" questioned the woman.

"Milk please," said Thorstein.

"And you?" she looked over at Kailan.

"The same please," replied Kailan. Thorstein's mother quickly ran out of the house.

"So, what is it that you came to me for exactly," said Thorstein.

Kailan reached into his pocket and pulled out the letter. He handed it to Thorstein who started reading it immediately.

"What is this?" questioned Thorstein.

"I was given this letter a few days ago," replied Kailan. "It was given to me by a strange gnome."

Thorstein looked up at Kailan. "Why is my name on here?" questioned Thorstein.

"I was sent here by the Arch Chancellor in Harlem to find the people in the letter." Kailan held out his hand and pointed at a certain spot on the page. "My name is on here too," said Kailan. Both adolescents were just as confused as neither of them new anything about the letter.

Thorstein continued to scroll down the page before stopping suddenly. His eyes widened. "How could he? But that would mean…" Kailan knew what Thorstein was talking about.

"Arch Chancellor Armenen?" Kailan questioned.

Thorstein slowly nodded his head.

"The man that sent me to find you was the new Arch Chancellor's page," said Kailan. "He knew less than you and I about it."

"But he died almost twenty years ago," replied Thorstein.

"Me and the Arch Chancellor couldn't understand that either," said Kailan.

Thorstein's mother came back into the house with two bowls of milk in her hands. One of the bowls was small, the other quite big. She handed each of them to the boys.

"Thank you," said Kailan. He took a sip of the milk and quickly spat it out.

"Not like your cow's milk," laughed Thorstein. "This is dornbeast milk. The milk is as strong as the animal." He grabbed

[40]

the large bowl and guzzled it. He continued to laugh at Kailan for a little bit. "So, where are you going now?"

"I was told to keep going until I found someone that knew what I was looking for," said Kailan.

"Like who?"

"Everyone on the list, I guess," said Kailan. "My next stop is in Thoria."

"I'm coming with you then," said Thorstein.

"What?" said Kailan in shock. "The Arch Chancellor asked for my help alone. There is no need for you to come."

"I have the same amount of reason to look for answers as you do," replied Thorstein.

"But what about your family?" questioned Kailan.

"I am nineteen," said Thorstein. "When a boy becomes a man in northern Achland, he leaves his family and searches for a new one," stated Thorstein. "Anyways, you will need help getting out of Achland."

"Why would I need help?" asked Kailan. Thorstein giggled a bit.

"You'll never make it out alive. You have no experience of this area. It will take you a number of days to reach to borders of Achland in any direction. In this time, you will attract many types of creatures, none of them willing to help you in any sort of way. You might be able to live in Helforth by yourself, but the north is much more dangerous."

"Well then, you should start packing," said Kailan.

[41]

Thorstein seemed as if he was almost ready for Kailan, most of his necessities were already packed away in a bag when they reached his room. It didn't take long before Thorstein was fully packed and ready to leave the house. As he stepped outside, he walked over to his mother who was baking some bread with his younger sister by the large bread oven.

Kailan did not want to involve himself with the family affairs, so he tried to remain hidden. The mother walked over to the fields and called for Thorstein's father.

A strong, hardy man, Thorstein's father was. He was one of the head hunters in the village, and was treated with utmost respect by everyone. It wasn't long before all of Thorstein's family was standing around him. Thorstein explained to them what was happening. They exchanged their farewells and congratulated Thorstein now that he was leaving the village. It would be a big change for them. Thorstein was not something that you could miss very easily, visually or emotionally. He walked over to Kailan.

"We should get going soon," said Kailan. "Do you have a horse?"

"Do I have a horse?" Thorstein laughed. "I have a dornbeast!"

As they walked to the stables, Kailan realised why Thorstein would ride a dornbeast instead of a horse. A dornbeast was most comparable to a giant rhinoceros with fur all over it. A horse would not be able to lift Thorstein without stopping after very short intervals. The dornbeast, however, would be capable of taking Thorstein on a long journey without even breaking a sweat. The creature also suited Thorstein in Kailan's mind. He could imagine the large, horned beast charging into battle with no fear of what is ahead. Just like Thorstein, one brute force working with another.

"When a man from my village reaches the age of sixteen, he is sent with his father and a group of other men to capture a wild dornbeast. A domestic one does not give the power and speed that they want as warriors. For most people it takes about two or three tries, but I got it on the first try," said Thorstein happily. "We train them to be calm when we want them to." The tall boy jumped onto the creature and road it around the stables bareback for a short while to show Kailan what it was like. He then got off and tied some ropes to the dornbeast. He attached his bags to the ropes and hopped on. The size difference between Thorstein and his steed wasn't much. The creature stood at about ten feet tall and almost twenty feet long.

"We better get going then." Kailan hopped onto his horse and started walking away.

"Just a second, I forgot my axe." Thorstein pulled the dornbeast in the opposite direction and trotted towards the house, quickly returning with his battle axe in hand. The two young men started walking along one of the paths that led away from the village. The path was wide, but looked quite narrow when Thorstein and his dornbeast were walking it. Thorstein stuck his axe underneath his arm and started touching his beard.

"What are you doing?" said Kailan.

"I have to make sure that it is all braided," said Thorstein. "I don't want anything to get caught in it, plus, it keeps it from flying up in my face when I'm fighting."

Kailan nodded and looked away. He touched his chin and rubbed it slightly. He had always wanted some type of facial hair, but it was never really thick enough to grow a beard or a moustache.

The northern moors of Achland were not hard to traverse, just tiring for the horses. The constant up and down motion of walking over the hills would make even an experienced hiker feel weak after only a few minutes. Only after a day's travel would they reach the edge of a small forest that would cut their time considerably by cutting through it instead of going around. Kailan would have to be extremely careful in the thick wooded areas. He never knew what would be around the corner, unlike Thorstein who had a sixth sense for trouble, and a seventh for knowing how to deal with it. In the few hours that Kailan and Thorstein had known each other, Kailan had learned about most of Thorstein's life at the university.

"That wasn't much of a goodbye between you and your family," said Kailan.

"We Nordic Raiders know of what we must do at the age of eighteen before we learn anything else," said Thorstein. "It was just a matter of time before I was dent out by my parent's will. I was planning on leaving next week anyways."

[44]

Suddenly, Kailan's horse came to an abrupt halt. Thorstein had already stopped a few seconds before, peering through the forest. "What is it?" Kailan whispered.

"Goblins," he whispered back. "We need to get rid of them now so they don't kill us in our sleep," said Thorstein. Something concerning these goblins bothered Thorstein. He had dealt with goblins before, but these ones seemed different. They were all wearing matching armour, which was quite strange as goblins often wore light, leather armour so that they may move more freely. The only thing that he didn't really like about fighting goblins was that they only reached his knees. They could run right between his legs, which was a big problem. He slowly crept towards the trees, trying to stay completely silent.

Talking amongst each other, the goblins sat around a fire, eating whatever food that they had. The only warning that they received that they were about to be attacked was a light creaking in the forest. Almost instantly, two of the goblins were dead as the large tree came crashing down upon the campsite. Thorstein burst through the trees, swinging his axe around.

Before Kailan could even see the goblins, Thorstein had already killed another two. When Kailan burst through the trees, there was a few already waiting for him. It didn't take long before they were dead.

The rest started to run from Kailan and Thorstein. "Don't let them get away!" yelled Thorstein. "They'll track us down!"

[45]

Kailan chased after the small creatures. He threw his sword at one of them, with one motion, pulled it back out, spun in the air, and threw it at another. There were only two more goblins left to take care of. Kailan was after one, while Thorstein was chasing the other. Unexpected by Kailan, Thorstein grabbed a small tree out of the ground and swung it down at the goblin, swatting it like a fly into a much larger tree, splatting the creature. It didn't take much time for Kailan to catch up to the other goblin. He grabbed it by the hair and lifted it into the air. He tried to look into its eyes before it spat in his face and screeched.

"The Black Allegiance will rise!" screamed the goblin. Kailan threw the goblin down and thrust his sword into it.

"What is the Black Allegiance?" questioned Kailan.

"I can't remember anything from my studies," replied Thorstein. "But I do remember reading something in a book once about them. They are a group of mercenaries. Sometimes they are considered an actual army." The two young men hopped onto their horses and continued down the road. The next day was somewhat of a relief. It wasn't eve midday and they had already reached the edge of the forest. As they stood on the cliff that separated the forest from the hilly plains of Achland, Kailan let out a sigh. It was a new world to travel, a new world to discover. Every now and then, Kailan would be able to see a farm amongst the rocks, but there wasn't much. That day, Kailan and Thorstein had only visited one village, there; they bought some food, but not much. The next day was not much fun at all

[46]

for Kailan. It was another day, walking through the rocky plains of Achland, but this day, it rained. It wasn't till the fourth day that they reached a forest again. This one was much different from the other one where Thorstein came from. This new one was full of deciduous trees and hardwoods. Many different kinds of ferns and mosses grew along the forest floor. The trees in the forest here were huge though, some of them almost two hundred feet tall. They were covered in ivy and grape vines that neither strangled nor blocked them out, but made them even more beautiful. The actual colours that reached the ground from the sun were a mix a blues, greens, and purples. While in this forest, all of Kailan's thoughts were happy ones. He also seemed to be imagining about things more. In his head, he was creating his future, making himself king of Freltus, and reuniting all of Arlbega. His next thought consisted of him living in a small house on the top of a mountain somewhere. It seemed as though Kailan was being starved in Helforth. It was only here that his creativity and imagination were free. At home, they were caged up, while out in this forest, they could do whatever they wanted, whenever they wanted. As they strode along the path, Thorstein noticed something just off the road. It looked like a statue, lying on its side in the grass. Upon closer inspection, Thorstein noticed that even more statues littered the ground. Neither Kailan nor Thorstein knew exactly where they were within the forest. Behind a vale of ivy vines, there was a staircase. The two young men hopped off of their rides and cleared the vines away. Standing on one side of the staircase, was a statue of a naked

[47]

man, which later turned out to be an elf when they looked closer at the face. On the other side of the staircase, a statue used to stand. Possibly the exact same as the other one, but all that was left was the feet. As the two boys climbed the staircase, they both felt a sense of magic and mystery clouding their minds.

"What do you think it is?" questioned Kailan.

"I'm not exactly sure," replied Thorstein. "It might have been a shrine at some point, but it isn't any longer." At the top of the stairs, there was a large boulder, sitting directly in the centre of a large circle that made up the main shape of the platform. A tablet embedded within the stone was placed right after the last step. Thorstein knelt down and started reading the tablet.

"What is it?" questioned Kailan.

"It says 'You have been chosen'," said Thorstein. While at Argent University, Thorstein became almost fluent in a number of languages, Elven being one of them.

"Chosen?" questioned Kailan. He was confused by the whole statement.

"That's what it says," Thorstein replied. He walked past the tablet and up to the boulder. For him, it was a boulder, but for Kailan, it was huge. Thorstein examined the stone as not to make any stupid actions. The boulder could have been booby-trapped by either the elves, or someone hiding their treasure there. As he looked around it, Thorstein noticed that it was covering a hole. He pushed the boulder away and looked down the hole. Another staircase started at the hole. It was a decent sized hole, but Thorstein would have to crouch in order to go down the hole. As Kailan followed, they noticed that there was a short hallway at the bottom of the staircase. At the end of the hall were two, large doors. Thorstein shuffled forward and pushed them open. The doors opened to a little room, with light coming from the surface. In the middle of the room was an altar. On the altar was a small basin, filled with water. Thorstein crept closer to the Altar. An inscription ahead of the basin was carved into the stone altar.

"What does it say?" questioned Kailan. Thorstein picked up many languages while at the university, six to be exact. Thorstein tried to translate the words, but they were in a language that he knew nothing of.

"I don't know," he said. "I've never seen anything like this anywhere. Not even at the university." Kailan dipped his hand into the water and scooped some of it up to his mouth. "What does it taste like?" questioned Thorstein. The moment that the clear liquid touched his lips, all that Kailan could do was smile. He looked down at the basin and scooped another handful, allowing half of it to run through his fingers.

"You need to try this," said Kailan. Thorstein dunked one of his fingers in and licked his finger.

"That is an exceptional taste," said Thorstein. Neither of them knew what it was, but that it tasted great. Kailan pulled a small, glass bottle from his pocket, and filled it entirely with the strange liquid. Thorstein dunked his hand in this time, trying to get more of the sweet water.

"I think that we should go now," said Kailan.

"Why, what's the matter?"

"I don't know, but something about this place is telling me that we should not be here longer than we need to be," replied Kailan.

"I understand." They exited the room and walked down the tunnel, up the stairs, and down the other flight of steps. It wasn't long before they were on their journey again.

Kailan scrolled down the letter. "The person that we need to find next is Lena of Kril Haven," he called out.

"Where is that exactly?" Thorstein asked. Kailan quickly pulled out his map that Bailan gave him.

"It's right near the northern sea," replied Kailan.

"I haven't had fish in a while," said Thorstein, laughing a little.

They didn't come across anything too spectacular after coming across the elven ruins, but that night was different. As Kailan rolled from side to side on the ground, trying to find a comfortable spot to sleep, the forest was lit up with the most wonderful array of colours. Blue, purple, some bursts of green and yellow as well. The small bursts of light continued on for some time. He quickly sat upright trying to get a better look.

"Fairies, mainly," said Thorstein, startling Kailan in the process. "Some mushrooms tend to glow in these forests as well."

"How do they do it?" Kailan asked. Clearly Kailan had never really ventured out of his forest much.

"Generally magic, but some plants, when mixed together, can make glowing colours."

"Is that why the elves used to live here?" questioned Kailan. Thorstein, sitting across the fire from Kailan, picked up a stone and started sharpening his axe.

"The fairies live here because the elves used to," replied Thorstein. He paused for a few seconds before continuing. "There was once a fight between the fairies and the pixies. The elves ended up siding with the fairies, while the pixies were helped occasionally by the goblins of old."

"Goblins of old?"

"They used to be almost like dwarves in size and appearance," said Thorstein, "And were a lot like pixies and fairies, being mischievous and all, except much larger. They were often confused with gnomes to be honest, except that gnomes hid within the mountains and stayed to themselves. Goblins on the other hand, are very social creatures. Well, the goblins and the pixies ended up losing the argument as the goblins were slowly exiled from the forest folk. They now trusted more in technology, than nature. This was something that was frowned upon by the other creatures. The other forest folk kicked the goblins out of their 'group' and banished them from the forests. The goblins made no attempt to re-join their old friendship, but instead widened the gap. For a few thousand years, the elves have been sworn enemies of the goblins because of this. They were now dealing with dark magic and were making alliances with trolls, ogres, and orcs. Never in the eyes

[51]

of anyone had such an alliance been made. There is an old alliance of men, dwarves, elves, fairy folk, and elementals that still stands strong. They have been keeping their enemies at bay since the beginning." He turned his head quickly and let out a cough. "Back to your original question, because the pixies had no one to side with them, the fairies gained ownership of this forest." Kailan smiled and rolled over, closing his eyes.

"Thanks."

"A story always helps a restless sleeper," said Thorstein. Kailan had begun to realise that it was best for Thorstein to come along after all. It would take Kailan and Thorstein another three days to reach Lena. One day to reach Thoria, another to reach the northern regions, and a third to find the village.

As the night continued on, Kailan awoke to the sound of a bird in the distance, cawing in the lightly illuminated darkness. He turned to Thorstein, who was passed out and looked up at the stars. The fire in the middle of the camp was slowly dying away as Kailan hopped to his feet and began poking the coals with a stick. As he looked up from the fire, he saw something move about in the air.

"Who's there?" he called out. He waited for an answer, but none came. Thorstein was still fast asleep, wrapped up tightly in a blanket, his dornbeast lying next to him. As Kailan looked up, he noticed the leaves blowing through the air, landing behind the bushes. He made his way forward, keeping his actions vigilant. It wasn't until he came close to the bushes that the fear within him subsided, coming upon a familiar face. "I thought you had died," Kailan said, smiling as he ran forth through the bushes.

"Stop," she said, as Kailan tried wrapping his arms around the witch, only to find that his hands slipped right through. "I am dead," she replied.

Kailan stood looking down at his hands and then at the witch's face. "How are you doing this?"

"Magic," she replied. "I cannot live like I once did, as a physical being. On the other hand, I am free to venture this world as my spirit has not limits."

Kailan looked down at the ground as the short lived happiness within him slowly drifted away.

"Don't be sad, Kailan," the young woman said, smiling as she held one of her ghostly hands up to Kailan's cheek. "I will be by your side, guiding you." She slowly fell back, disappearing again into the leaves.

"Wait, you never told me your name!" cried Kailan as he watched the wind carry the leaves up into the sky again.

Out of the coldness of the night, there came a warm touch with the words whispered, "Aris."

*   *   *

The two boys left as early as they could the next morning. They ended up reaching the edge of the forest before noon even arrived. That night, Kailan realised that either his calculations were wrong, or that Thorstein and himself were going much faster than he had expected. The two boys reached the northern regions by that night, and made shelter within some of the large rocks that lay about. They spent the next day trekking through the rocky terrain, gaining little ground. In some places, the northern regions of Thoria resembled a giant quarry. No plant life; just stones and pebbles everywhere. Later that evening, Kailan and Thorstein reached a small village, not too far from Kril Haven. Thorstein was too big to fit in any of the buildings, so he ended up sleeping in an abandoned barn. Kailan decided to stay with Thorstein so that he didn't feel lonely, even though Thorstein didn't mind being alone. When they reached Kril Haven the next afternoon, the first thing that Kailan and Thorstein did was tie their steeds to some trees, just outside of the town. They made their way down the hill into the harbour village meeting an older woman along the way, asking if she knew where Lena lived. When she first looked at the two boys, her mouth slowly dropped. Something told Kailan that it wasn't because of Thorstein's height. Something seemed peculiar about the village. The two boys walked down to the docks and then around up by the side of the cliff. Almost all of the houses within Kril Haven looked the same. The walls were made of either wood or stone, while the roofs consisted of thatched straw. Kailan stepped up to the door that the woman had told them to go to, and knocked on it. It took a little while before someone came to the door, answering it. A tall, dark haired woman stood in the doorway. She looked like she was about the age of Kailan's mother, but the years had been kinder to this woman standing in the doorway, even though it was covered by makeup. She was wearing a long, red robe and black leather shoes, decorated with gem stones.

"Ah!" she jumped back a bit and slammed the door in front of the boys' faces.

"Are you as confused as I am?" questioned Kailan. Thorstein nodded.

"Deeply," replied Thorstein. Just as the boys were about to leave, the door opened again and the woman grabbed Kailan and Thorstein, and held onto them.

"I'm sorry about that," said the woman. She eyed up Thorstein amazed by his size. "I hope that I didn't frighten you." The two boys shook their heads. "Now, is there anything that I can help you with?"

"We were told that Lena Harkonen lives here," said Kailan. "We were wondering if we could speak to her." The woman smiled.

"I'll get her right away." Kailan and Thorstein quickly looked at each other as she left.

"Do the people here seem strange to you?" questioned Kailan, giggling to himself.

"They could all have been drinking last night." Kailan chuckled at Thorstein's reply. When he looked back at the doorway, the most beautiful girl that Kailan had ever seen before was standing in front of him. Her long, dark hair hung down past her shoulders. Her bright, green eyes seemed to reach into Kailan's soul. They were the kind of eyes that gave a welcoming feeling, even more so than Aris'. To Kailan, she was so beautiful that she created a smile so strong that it prevented Kailan from spitting out his words.

"I'm…. k-k-Kailan."

Thorstein quickly cut in the way to help Kailan not feel so much like an idiot. He scared Lena at first with his immense height, but she quickly warmed up to it. "This is Kailan, and my name is Thorstein."

"My name is Lena," said the girl in a soft, sweet voice. Kailan stepped back and let Thorstein continue talking, seeing as Kailan was not able to at the moment.

"It's very nice to meet you, Lena," said Thorstein. "Kailan has come from Freltus, looking for some answers that seem to pertain to all three of us. It seems that he came about to possess a very strange letter from the late Arch Chancellor, Orpeth Armenen. We are wondering if you know anything of this."

Lena stared at the two boys for a second, confused as she tilted her head, squinting her eyes. "Is this some weird joke?" questioned Lena.

"You might as well show her the letter, Kailan," said Thorstein.

The smaller boy nodded, stepping in front of Thorstein. Kailan fidgeted with the letter as he pulled it out of his pocket. As he handed it over to Lena, he accidentally dropped it on the ground. As Lena bent down to pick up the piece of paper, Kailan looked down Lena's shirt and stared at the cleavage of her breasts for a quick second. His hand quickly went for his forehead, slapping him backwards a foot or so. As Thorstein watched Kailan, he was about to start laughing out of sheer enjoyment of watching Kailan suffer.

"I'm sorry," said Kailan.

"Don't worry, I'm usually picking up after people."

Kailan hid his face behind Thorstein as he bit his finger. His apology was not geared to the fact that he had dropped the letter, but that he looked down her shirt, but Lena didn't even notice. This was good for Kailan, for he wasn't going to make a bad first impression. Thorstein began the chuckle.

"What's funny?" questioned Lena.

"Nothing," said Thorstein, seeming to laugh even more. Lena opened the letter and frowned.

"Can one of you help me read this," said Lena. "I only read Thorian Runes." Kailan dashed around Thorstein, his bravery finally reaching him.

"I can help you," said Kailan, smiling effortlessly.

THIS LETTER IS TO BE KEPT SECRET AND OUT OF SIGHT. ANY KNOWLEDGE OF THE WORDS ON THIS

PAGE COULD MEAN DEATH.

By the power entrusted in me by the six kingdoms and peoples of Arlbega, I, Arch Chancellor Orpeth Armenen, have requested that these children be brought to me: Thorstein Volfkin of Schtein in Achland, Lena Harkonen...

"Why is my name on there?" questioned Lena as she looked at the paper, almost taking it from Kailan's hands.

"We don't know why," Kailan replied.

"How could you not know?" Lena became confused and frustrated with the boys as the pitch of her voice and volume level both raised considerably. "You just said that you were sent by the Arch Chancellor, didn't you?"

"I was sent to find the people on this list until I found answers," Kailan replied, dropping his arm and the letter to his side. "I found Thorstein first, and he insisted on coming with me to find out more. Besides, the Arch Chancellor knows nothing of this letter."

"So it's a fake?" Lena asked.

"We don't believe it is."

"If the Arch Chancellor doesn't know anything of the letter that he wrote, then why would it be real?"

"Orpeth Armenen died many years ago," Thorstein stated.

Lena looked up at the tall man, biting her lip as she quieted.

"Don't worry, I didn't know that either," Kailan said,

[58]

with a smile on his face.

"Tanier Frost has been the Arch Chancellor for the past ten years with a temporary one in between the two," said Thorstein, taking a knee to better speak to Lena. "It almost seems like someone didn't want us to find these letters. I'm guess that is why neither you, nor I, ever received ours.

"I got mine from a gnome, who had actually found it on a dead man, and had been keeping it all these years," said Kailan.

Lena looked at the ground, thinking to herself as her eyes moved back and forth. "What does the rest of the letter say?"

Kailan raised his arm again and held the letter up, following along with his finger as Lena watched, unable to read the words herself.

Thorstein Volfkin of Schtein in Achland, Lena Harkonen of Kril Haven in Thoria, Kailan Gallot of Hapreth in Helforth, Guin Pelerin of Alandra in Arad, and Viktor Svetlenka of Dratana Letania. Bring these children to me immediately. They and their families are in immense danger. They will be given shelter and protection in Freltus.

"What danger are they talking about?" said Lena, looking up after the last word fell out of her mouth, her eyes widening.

"I was tracked down by goblins," said Kailan, smiling

[59]

proudly to himself. "I also got to fight off an ogre."

Thorstein chuckled as he turned to the side, away from Kailan's view.

"Well, I'm perfectly safe here," said Lena. "I'm sorry that I can't help you, but I just don't know anything about this." She slowly closed the door on the two boys as they looked at each other.

"Guess that we better head to our next stop," said Thorstein as he stood up.

Kailan nodded and turned with his newfound friend as they made their way back to the edge of town.

"I figured out why everyone was acting strange," said Thorstein, walking up the rocky path.

"Why?" Kailan questioned.

"Did something other than their actions seem strange to you?"

"Not really, no."

"There were no men in the village," Thorstein replied. "We were the only men here, and it seemed like none of them had seen any for a while."

"They must be out on the ships or something," Kailan replied, nearly slipping on one of the small stones. "Besides, it was probably your size that scared them."

"I guess you're right," chuckled Thorstein.

"Hey, I'll race you to the top," said Kailan, smiling like a child. Even though Thorstein's stride was much greater than Kailan's, the smaller boy was surprisingly fast compared to most people.

"Wait!" yelled Lena, running up the hill behind the two boys.

"You're coming now?" said Thorstein, turning around, noticing Kailan's giant grin.

"My mother suggests that I come with you," Lena replied as she caught up to the others. "I think that she just doesn't want me living with her anymore." Lena smirked as she walked ahead of the boys, facing away from the sun, the golden light shining up on her back. "So, where are we headed, anyways?"

Kailan made no sound as he stared at the girl's backside. He tilted his head to the side and smiled again, before being nudged by Thorstein. "Sorry?"

"Where are we going?" said Thorstein.

"I think that we need to go to Arad," said Kailan, reaching into his pocket, pulling out the letter. He looked down the page, stopping halfway. "Yes, we need to go to Arad next." He hurried up to his horse and untied it from the tree, jumping up and on top of the horse.

"Do you have a horse?" questioned Thorstein.

"No," replied Lena. "My family never really needed one. We generally stayed in the village most of the time."

"You can ride with me," said Kailan, patting his horse's back. As Lena hopped on, Kailan looked over at Thorstein and winked. The giant responded with a smile and a chuckle. As they left the village, Lena didn't want to look where they were going to, but what she was leaving behind. She seemed reluctant to leave, but as she was leaving, she expressed damp and cold emotions. There was something in the village that made her want to leave, but there were memories that she held onto dearly, holding onto her. Just as the village was out of their view, Lena hopped off the horse.

"This won't take a minute," she said, dashing for the tree line. Kailan hopped off of his horse and followed Lena towards the trees. She moved some of the branches and vines out of her way and made her way through the bushes. Kailan followed, even though he knew nothing of what to expect. A small stone ruin stood amongst the trees, covered in vines and leaning to one side slightly.

"How old is this place?" questioned Kailan.

"Much older than you think," replied Lena. She ran towards the small door and opened it. Kailan stood by the doorway and waited for Lena as she climbed up the ladder to the top of the small tower. When she returned, she had in hand: a bow, a quiver full of arrows, and a large glove.

"What is the glove for?" questioned Kailan.

"You'll see quite soon," replied Lena. They left the tower and made their ways back to Thorstein. When they reached him, Lena held her head up and blew a whistle into the air. The sound of it was very distinct, a sound that neither Kailan, nor Thorstein, had heard before. It was a high pitched, pulsating whistle that echoed throughout the air.

"What are you doing that for?" questioned Kailan

again.

"Patience," she said softly. Lena made sure not to offend Kailan with her words. Out in the distant sky, a white spec appeared from a distant tree line. As it neared, Kailan and Thorstein could make out that it was a bird. A large white eagle was soaring towards them. As Lena held up her hand with the large glove, the bird slowly started to descend from the air above. As it landed on Lena's falconer's glove, Kailan could see the beauty in the creature. It was as magnificent a creature as Lena was beautiful. The bird was covered in white, silver tipped feathers. The feet and beak looked as if they were made of pure gold. Its eyes were different though. So far, the bird was one of the most beautiful animals that anyone had ever seen before. The eyes were a strange colour though, unlike the brown colour that would be expected. They were a bright, reflective green instead, just like Lena's. Kailan stepped forward to touch the bird. Its wings went straight up and outwards, while giving Kailan a stare down.

"This is my friend, Kaela," said Lena. "It is probably best if you were not to touch her."

"Where did it come from?" asked Thorstein. Lena led one of her hands down the back of Kaela's neck.

"I just found her one day," said Lena. "I was walking through the forest and she just stopped in front of me. As I walked towards her, she didn't try to run away, but surprisingly came closer to me." Lena snapped her finger behind the bird's ear. Suddenly, the bird was flying again. "Well, we don't want

[63]

to dillydally," said Lena. As she walked back to the horse, Thorstein turned to Kailan.

"Dillydally?"

"I think it's a Thorian word for 'wasting time'," said Kailan. "Don't worry, in the end, you'll be a master of all Lybidian dialects." Thorstein smiled and turned to help Lena get on the horse. It wasn't long before the group was off again on their journey.

They spent their first night in a small town a few hours away from Kril Haven. Thorstein ended up having to sleep in a barn again, because the inns were still very small and there were no rooms that were big enough for him. While in town, they decided to buy some supplies and food for the journey ahead. The next day, they dealt with the exact same terrain; large, rocky plains that spread for miles and miles. When they rested for the second night, Kailan and Lena went to the inn so that they may find a room, with two beds of course.

As they entered the inn, Kailan went straight to the bartender to ask for a room. While Lena waited at his side, one of the drunks next to them leaned backwards and spanked Lena's backside. She quickly turned around and slapped him in the face, sending backwards, over the bar stool. Kailan lifted the man up by the collar of his shirt.

"If I catch you doing that again, you'll be screaming like a baby," said Kailan sternly. He threw the man to the ground and guided Lena away from the man. Three more men circled Kailan and Lena.

[64]

"Oy, you touch him again little fella and I'll beat you to a pulp," said one of the men.

"Listen to me carefully," said Kailan. He rested one of his hands on the pommel of his sword. "You don't know who you are dealing with, so just leave now." The three men laughed at Kailan and lifted their fists in front of them. In unison, they tried to jump Kailan, but at the same time, Kailan was dodging the attack. Before the three men had even finished their actions, Kailan was already out of the way with sword in hand. He swiftly gave a cut to all three of the men. The whole ordeal was over in about two seconds. When Lena looked, she saw that each of the three men had a cut along their foreheads. They weren't deep enough to cause serious damage, but Kailan made sure to draw blood and to cause them some pain. "Come, we'll find somewhere else to stay the night," said Kailan. He held her hand as he led her out of the inn and down the road.

"How did you do that?" she asked.

"I've always been very quick and agile," said Kailan. "From a very early age, I've been able to wield a sword better than anyone I know." Lena smiled as she looked at Kailan's face.

"Thank you," she said softly.

"I'm not going to let some idiot just do that to you," said Kailan. "By right, it was my duty and not much of a choice."

"Well, it was very honourable," Lena replied. Kailan looked over and smiled.

[65]

"Thanks." The two adolescents ended up sleeping in the barn with Thorstein that night. Kailan sat beside Thorstein at the small fire stove while Lena curled up in the one corner on the straw. "I want to be out of this town first thing in the morning," said Kailan with a scowl on his face.

"Problems at the inn?" chuckled Thorstein.

"Some idiot decided to grope Lena's butt," said Kailan.

"What did she do?"

"She slapped him, so I grabbed him and told him not to do it again or he'd be screaming," said Kailan. "Then, three of his friends decided to try to mess with me, so I left them with some scars."

"Now Kailan, we don't want to be making enemies as we go along," said Thorstein.

"I know, but they tried to attack us," said Kailan.

"I understand," said Thorstein. The two boys continued to talk about other things for a couple of minutes more before Kailan decided to go to bed. As he passed Lena, he noticed that the heat from the fire did not reach to where she was sleeping. He walked to his bag and pulled out a large tunic. On Kailan, the tunic fit with some extra room, but on Lena, it was like a blanket. He would have given her more, but he had nothing else to give her to stay warm. His bag was not full of clothes, but supplies for his journey instead. Kailan was always prepared for everything. There was something in his bag for almost any situation imaginable. It wasn't long before Kailan too, was fast asleep.

Lena tossed and turned as her nightmare got worse. Beads of sweat dripped down her forehead. She was breathing quite heavily when she jolted herself awake.

"Bad dream?" questioned Thorstein rhetorically. Lena looked up at her new friend, still gasping, then down at the tunic.

"What's this?" she asked.

"Oh, Kailan though that you were cold so he gave you the shirt to keep yourself warm." Thorstein had not yet gone to sleep yet since he had arrived at the barn. He just sat in front of the fireplace, thinking. It was something that he liked to do. Most people his age were busy having fun with friends and playing games, but Thorstein liked to think. He would sometimes take hikes away from his village and spend a few hours in the forests just thinking about life in general. "Why don't you come here by the fire and warm yourself up?"

"Just a moment," replied Lena. "I'm going to put on some warmer clothes." She dug into her bag and pulled out a light sweater. It was something that her grandmother had knitted for her before her death. She pulled out some other articles of clothing and walked behind one of the stable walls and started changing.

"We should all get some warmer clothes for when we go to Arad," said Thorstein. "Nights in the desert can get very cold." Lena smiled at Thorstein as she came out from behind the wall. As she walked towards the small bench by the fire, she gazed over at Kailan, asleep on the straw.

"Not much of a talker, is he?" questioned Lena.

"I don't follow," replied Thorstein.

"I can tell that he has feelings for me, but he isn't really saying anything," said Lena.

"Ah, I understand."

"I mean, he can sure care for a girl, defend her even, but I just don't know if he can talk to one properly," stated Lena.

"Don't worry, that'll change." Thorstein turned away and started poking the ashes with a stick. "Kailan just isn't fond of you at the moment," said Thorstein. "I'm sure that he will open up to you in a few days." Lena smiled and returned to her original spot in the straw.

"Goodnight Thorstein," she said softly as she dozed off.

"Goodnight." Thorstein wasn't just seen as a friend by the other two. He was seen as a big brother. Sometimes, Kailan and Lena would treat him as their superior as he was the wisest of the three. The words that came out of his mouth were full of purpose and soul. They were rarely squandered with swear words or slang. It wasn't long after that that Thorstein decided to go to sleep himself. He put out the fire and found a nice, big, open space of straw for him to curl up in. That night turned out to be quite peaceful. There were no roots sticking in anyone's backs, or rocks being used as a pillow. When Kailan awoke, he went straight to work by making breakfast. He pulled out some seasoned meat that he had bought the first day with Lena. He pulled out a pan from his bag and placed it over the coals of the fire to let it warm up before placing the meat on it. He had bought three pieces of meat, realising that his math would be perfect. He would be able to eat a whole piece of meat, while Lena would only be able to eat half. Thorstein would end up receiving what was left of it all. The other two companions awoke to the smell of the seasoned meat cooking over the fire. It was something nice that none of them were used to. Kailan hadn't had meat like that for almost a year, while Thorstein had it about once a month and Lena, only a few times in her life. When they were all packed and ready to go, the three friends decided to go into the village and buy a few things. As Kailan and Lena stepped into the town square, they knew that they were in trouble. The three thugs and the drunk all sat together at a table, each of them wearing a sword at their side. When the first one noticed Kailan, he stood up, made sure that it was Kailan, and hollered at the boy.

"I'm going to kick you're scrawny little ass!" screamed the man at the top of his lungs. His three friends turned around and stood up as well. It was then that Kailan noticed the insignia on their tunics. It was the same symbol that the goblins wore when Kailan and Thorstein first left Thorstein's village. The four men raced over to Kailan, pulling out their swords and screaming at the boy.

"I personally don't want to have to kill anyone today," said Kailan. Lena pulled out her bow and notched an arrow on the string.

"Stay back or I'll shoot," yelled Lena. The men laughed.

"Stupid lass!" said the drunk from the previous night.

"We run this town and we get what we want." He made a gesture to the other men about touching Lena.

"That's it!" Kailan sprang into action faster than he had ever before. The drunk fell to his knees, without making a sound, he looked up at Kailan just before his head rolled to the ground. "I warned you!" screamed Kailan. The other men looked at each other and decided that winning was highly possible. Another stepped forwards, getting close to Lena, so she shot him in the knee.

"I said stay back," said Lena. Thorstein looked around the building to see what all the commotion was about.

"Giant!" screamed the man with the wounded knee. Thorstein saw the insignia and decided to take action. He went for the two men that were capable of running first. He grabbed the two men by their legs and whipped them into the air as far as he could. The last man rolled onto his side, crying and panting. "Please, spare my life," begged the man. Thorstein slowly walked towards the thug.

"What should we do with him?" questioned Lena.

"Kill him," said Kailan. In Kailan's eyes, the four men had had their time to turn back. They had asked for this by not leaving Kailan and Lena alone.

"Let me speak to him," said Thorstein. He knelt down beside the man. "We will spare your life if you agree to tell us what the Black Allegiance's business is." The man sneered.

"This is pointless," said the man. "If I tell you, the Black Allegiance will send assassins after me."

[70]

"We can kill you right now," said Thorstein. "Your friends are already dead." The man looked into Thorstein's eyes.

"To spare me would be to leave me here," replied the man. "Telling you the information that you seek would be my death."

"You really fear the Black Allegiance more than a giant, standing right in front of you at this very moment, a young man that could make a thousand cuts to your body in less than a minute, or a young girl that has an arrow aimed right at your head," said Thorstein. The man slowly nodded. Thorstein looked up at Kailan and Lena. "Fine!" He stood up and turned away. Kailan and Lena looked at each other in confusion.

"What, are you just going to leave me here?" questioned the man. Thorstein walked back to the man and hit him in the head, knocking him unconscious.

"Kailan, stab him in the knee," said Thorstein. "We don't want him to tell others about us, and we certainly don't want him following us. Kailan looked up at Thorstein and then down at the man.

"I feel as though I shouldn't have pity for this man, but in fact, I do," said Kailan. Lena quickly turned away as Kailan thrust his sword into the man's leg. The man was in such shock already that he didn't wake up from his unconsciousness instantly.

"I hit him in the head to keep him from moving," said Thorstein. The three friends quickly decided that it was best not to go shopping in the town. They would have to wait until they reached the next town. As they continued their journey, Kailan and Lena decided to stay away from Thorstein for a little bit. There was something about him that seemed wrong.

"I don't feel that stabbing him was right," said Lena.

"Neither do I," said Kailan.

"It was for our own goods," said Thorstein, who was listening in.

"How was it for our own goods," replied Lena in a snarky tone. Thorstein came to a stop.

"You have never heard of the Black Allegiance have you, Lena." She shook her head. "Kailan and I have dealt with them before." Lena looked at Kailan and then back at Thorstein. "The first day that we spent on the road, outside of my village together, we ran into a troupe of goblins." He brought the dornbeast closer to Kailan and Lena. "Before we killed the last one, it let out a cry. 'The Black Allegiance will rise!' it screamed. Kailan didn't know anything of the Black Allegiance then, and I had only heard stories of them, not much of an expert." Lena leaned away from Thorstein, almost falling off the horse.

"Thorstein, can you stop please," said Kailan. "I'm pretty sure that she doesn't like that."

"I'm sorry, it's just that I feel that she should know about the Black Allegiance," said Thorstein. "They were originally an army that was created to destroy all life on the planet. They were defeated in a large battle thousands of years ago. Since then, the Black Allegiance is a name that has been

[72]

given to a mercenary group that claims to be part of the original. They have reached a few thousand members in the past, but now linger on a few hundred. These mercenaries, the experienced ones that is, are very skilled. I have heard stories of them going into a well-guarded fortress and having everyone in them slaughtered in half an hour." Thorstein clenched his fist hard. "These people are to be killed immediately. They would kill you before you have a second chance to kill them." He turned away and continued down the road. Before Lena and Kailan began to follow, Lena whispered into Kailan's ear.

"Thanks for the help," she said.

"You're welcome," he replied softly, looking back at Lena's face. Kailan's anger and confusion that he had gained towards Thorstein over his talk slowly died down as they neared their rest stop.

They ended up not being able to sleep in a village that night. The closest one was another few hours away. Thorstein decided to make everyone a nice little fort that would shield them from the cold. "I'm sorry if I offended you earlier," said Kailan as he walked over to Thorstein.

"No, I feel as though it was my fault for all of the tension," replied Thorstein. "I am the one who should be sorry. And if it would hurt, you could tell Lena that. I don't want to scare her any more than I already have." The two boys chuckled and Kailan was off collecting wood for the fire. Lena was taking a walk in the forest, looking for fruits or berries to eat. Kailan followed her into the forest and caught up to her.

[73]

"Lena," he yelled. She stopped and turned around to face Kailan.

"What is it?" she asked.

"Thorstein would like to say that he is sorry for the way he acted earlier," said Kailan. She took another step forward.

"Why didn't he come and tell me himself?"

"He didn't want to scare you again," said Kailan.

Lena giggled and turned away. She lent down beside a bush and started plucking off berries. "Tell him that I accept his apology." She made a bowl shape out of the bottom of her dress and placed the berries in it as she walked along. It wasn't until sunset that Lena finally returned from her little excursion. By this time, Kailan had a fire built with enough wood to last them the night, and the morning, and Thorstein had finished the temporary fort. The fire was perfectly positioned so that it would warm the whole fort. Lena was quickly talking to Thorstein again when she returned. It was a peaceful night. Thorstein ended up playing an old musical instrument called a kalaka on which he played an old Thorian lullaby. He didn't stay up too late either this day, for the next morning, they would be entering Arad. They needed to be well prepared for the mountains that surrounded Arad. In the rocks, there lived thieves, trolls, and hordes of goblins. Every now and then, someone would come across wild rock golems as well. They wouldn't be too hard for Thorstein to defeat, but for Kailan and Lena, they would make it very hard to get past. After the mountains, they would enter the deserts of Arad. There were five in total. The first two were

Agnok and Krelin. They were very dangerous places to live, as they both inhabited some of Arad's most feared creatures. Agnok was the home to the giant scorpion. With a pincer the size of Thorstein's fists, it wasn't something to be taken lightly. The biggest problem about them was that they could travel underground very easily. If someone wasn't paying attention, they might end up as scorpion food. In Krelin, the creature was not really a creature at all, but acted like one. Giant dust devils scattered the area. In legend, an evil wizard placed a curse on the desert, bringing the sand to life. The dust devils were almost the size of a normal tornado, but flung out stones and sand at high speeds. In the way that they acted like creatures was that they would chase after people. There weren't many a creature that could actually outrun the wind. The third desert was called Kekan. It didn't house the creatures that Krelin and Agnok did, but it was still quite harmful. It was the largest of all the deserts in Arad, but had no water. The only towns in Kekan had wells that were over fifty feet deep, but of those, there were few. The last two were called Grok and Gnok. They were considered the same by most people. Their landscape was constantly changing. No one ever wanted to live there because they might go to sleep one night on the top of a dune, and wake up in a lake the next morning. No one, not even the Wizards' Guild in Alandra knew how to stop the horrors that plague their lands. The next morning, the group finally reached the mountains of Arad. The first few minutes were a bit troublesome because the group needed to find a trail that would take them through the mountains first. They passed through the mountains along one of the roads, making sure not to go down any wrong paths. When they reached the desert, the group was surprised that nothing had interfered with their journey while traversing the mountain roads. It wasn't until they reached their final town before their long walk towards Alandra, that Kailan and his friends realised what they were getting into. No more water for the next few days. Everything that they needed, they had to bring with them. Thorstein, thankfully, was able to carry large sacs of water for both the people, and their rides. Even though they knew that it would lengthen the trip to Alandra, they decided to walk on foot, allowing the creatures to travel, without using up most of the water. They gathered food, water, and other provisions for the rest of the trip at the town. Since there were no trees for long distances, there would be no fire for the three companions. The decided to buy some warmer clothes for the cold desert nights that were ahead of them. By the time they were ready to leave the town, sunset was near. Thorstein stated that it was best for them to stay the night in the town and wait until the next morning to travel to Alandra. When they found a place to stay, Kailan sat down beside a fireplace and started plotting their journey.

"How long do you think it'll take?" questioned Lena.

"Only about three days," replied Kailan. "We'll reach Alandra by nightfall on the third day if I'm right." While Lena and Kailan were talking, Thorstein was sleeping in a larger building. He didn't mind sleeping away from Kailan and Lena. It actually gave him a time to think.

"What do you think the city will be like?" asked Lena. She had never really been away from her home of Kril Haven, and thus never really learned about the cultures of other countries.

"From what I've been told, it is a city with large buildings," said Kailan. "They don't take pride in beauty and art like our cities do, but are instead made using science. I once heard a story about a large stadium in Alandra that was built to perfection. The emperor can stand in one spot and everyone in the stadium can hear him, but if someone talks just a few feet away from him, they are not heard by the audience." Lena's eyes widened. Never had she heard of buildings with such precision as to do a job like projecting a voice. At first, she thought that it was magic, but later realised that it was because of the shape of the stadium. The next day, very early in the morning, Kailan and Lena were awake. They decided to leave early so that they would be able to make it through the rest of Agnok and Krelin bypassing the event of someone having to keep watch at night. The sun wasn't even up by the time they started leaving the town. It would be almost another twelve hours before they would arrive in Kekan. There first section of the day was slow, but still productive. By noon, Thorstein was starting to feel a bit hungry so he brought the group to a halt.

"Do any of you feel hungry?" he questioned. As Kailan turned around to look at Thorstein, he noticed something off in the distance. He held his hand over his eyes to block out the sun.

Thorstein turned around to see what Kailan was looking at.

"It looks like another rider," said Kailan. He pointed at the black spec on the edge of the horizon. This time, he pointed at the object so that Thorstein would see it as well. Lena gripped Kailan's arm.

"We should leave now," she said.

"Why? What's the matter?" Lena took a few steps forward and tried to look harder with less of the sun's glare.

"I don't think that that is a man," said Lena.

"What else could it be?" questioned Kailan. The two boy's jaws slowly dropped as they looked at each other.

"Get on the horse," said Thorstein sternly.

"Are you sure Lena?" questioned Kailan.

"My eyes have never failed me," she said as she hopped onto the horse. "It's been tracking us all morning," said Lena. "I noticed something earlier, but it didn't seem to be much of importance." Right when the group started walking away on their mounts, whatever was following them suddenly picked up pace. It wasn't long before the group realised that they were right about facing the first of Arad's challenges. They needed to figure out a way to get away from the giant scorpion without it knowing where they went, for fighting was completely out of the question. For Thorstein, the scorpion would be a bit of a challenge, but while fighting it, Kailan and Lena would also be in danger, having to watch for the swinging tail. The creature was nearing them at an alarming rate. It would only be about a minute before the creature was on them. Lena fired arrows back,

[78]

but they were deflected by its hard armour. "What do we do?" asked Lena in fear.

"Don't worry," said Kailan as he held out his hand to Lena. She grabbed onto it and squeezed hard.

"Go on ahead," said Thorstein. His dornbeast came to a quick stop as Kailan and Lena passed it on the horse.

"Don't be stupid!" yelled Kailan. He slowed down, but stayed clear of the scorpion. "Thorstein, we still have a chance to make it!" The horse was now moving around in circles. Kailan looked back at Lena. "Quickly, shoot at it." Lena shook her head.

"It's no use," she replied. "Its armour is too thick." By this time, Thorstein was already off the dornbeast with his axe in hand. The scorpion scanned over Thorstein, never seeing prey of such size before. The first move was made by the scorpion. It threw its tail forward, trying to jab Thorstein with the stinger. The boy dodged the attack and then went for a strike with his axe. This was blocked by a swing of the scorpion's claw. Kailan hopped off the horse and ran towards the scorpion. Kailan might've been able to last a certain amount of time against the scorpion because of his agility, but his attacks were not strong enough to do any real damage. He jumped into the air and tried to stab his sword into its back, but the attempt was useless. His sword could not pierce the armour. Without realising what had just happened, Kailan was thrown by the flailing tail that also acted as a mace. Thorstein took another hack at the creature, but didn't realise that its claws had harder armour than the rest of the body. He then took his axe and made a jabbing motion with it at the scorpion's mouth. It did not react to the attack, but Thorstein had done damage to the beast. Lena hurried over to Kailan and helped him up.

"Get out of here!" yelled Thorstein. He knew that Kailan's attempts at stabbing the beast would only put him in more harm. Kailan led Lena, the horse, and the dornbeast to the top of the sand dune so that they wouldn't be near the creature. When they reached the top, Kailan looked down and saw Thorstein being knocked around by the huge arachnid. The dornbeast let out a huff before charging down the mountain. Kailan chased after it, trying to stop it. A dornbeast could run more than twice the speed of a horse during a full charge. Running down a hill meant that Thorstein's dornbeast was nearly unstoppable. It flung the scorpion into the air, and started stomping on it when it hit the ground. What was left of the scorpion were bits of meat, and chunks of its armour which the dornbeast had crushed. Everything else was shoved down into the sand. Thorstein picked himself up and walked over to the dornbeast.

"Good boy," he said, petting the beast. Kailan and Lena held their mouths wide open. "What?" questioned Thorstein.

"You didn't think to get him to do that earlier?" said Kailan.

"I didn't really need his help earlier," replied Thorstein. "What, you seriously thought that I was going to lose?" Thorstein started laughing.

[80]

"This isn't funny!" yelled Kailan.

"It is a little bit," said Lena.

"Oh Kailan, please save me," said Thorstein in a feminine voice. Lena was now laughing a little more along with Thorstein.

"Oh shut up!" Thorstein was now rolling on the ground after Kailan's response to the laughter. The group grabbed a quick drink before continuing on their journey. For the rest of the day, Thorstein continued to make jokes. Some about Kailan, but most were about other things. When they finally got to rest, Thorstein was out like a light in an instant. As Lena curled up beside Kailan, she told him stories of her childhood. Making sure not wake up the sleeping giant; she kept it to a whisper.

"One day, when I was little," Lena said, "my older sister and I were picking flowers for my mother. I bumped into her and when I looked up, I saw that she was staring at the most magnificent creature that we had ever seen before." She rested her head on Kailan's shoulder. "A white unicorn was standing in front of us, just eating the grass. Its horn and hoofs were of a silvery colour that glistened when the sun hit it just right. It walked towards us and let my sister pet it. When I tried to touch it as well, it backed off." Lena looked down at the ground. "From that point on, I always thought of my sister as being the favoured one. Even my mother seemed to favour her, even after she died."

"Your sister died?" questioned Kailan. Lena nodded. "I'm sorry."

"She died about two years ago," replied Lena. "It was only a few days after her death that I met Kaela."

"The bird?" questioned Kailan.

"I named her after my sister," said Lena. Kailan thought that it was best to change the topic and start talking about something else. They continued to tell each other stories of their childhoods before drifting off to sleep. The night was cold, but it was quite refreshing compared to the hot days. The sky was clear, and the stars shone brightly. This was the only place that Kailan had ever been before where the whole sky could be seen at night. He was still awake, thinking about the next few days' journey. Suddenly, he was knocked out of his state of meditation by Lena's calls. He shuffled over to her and held one of his hands on her forehead.

"No!" she cried. Kailan noticed that her eyes were still closed.

"Lena!" suddenly, the young girl awoke and tears slowly started to drip from her eyes.

"Oh Kailan." she wrapped one of her arms around him, while using the other to wipe her tears.

"What happened?" questioned Kailan as he pulled her hair back and out of her face.

"I had a nightmare," she sobbed. "I dreamt the night that my sister died." Kailan tried to calm her down.

"Tell me what happened," he said.

"My sister and I were sleeping in our house when a group of men raided our village. Me and Kaela awoke to the screaming and hid, but she was captured by the men. I quickly grabbed my bow and quiver, and tracked the men down. I came upon their camp and started shooting at them." She stopped talking and took a few seconds to cry.

"You don't have to go on," said Kailan, but she decided to continue.

"I fought my way into a tent. I saw my sister tied up in the corner with blood dripping from her night gown and bruises on her face. I quickly ran to untie her, b-but one of the m-m-men was s-s-standing behind me." At this point, Lena was in physical pain because of her crying, but it wasn't very loud. "I shot the man, but there was another one near Kaela. He grabbed a knife and stabbed my sister. I had her dying in my arms. Her last words were 'I will always be there when you need me'. After that, she closed her eyes and died." Kailan wiped away Lena's tears and some of his own as well.

"Me and Thorstein will always be there to protect you," said Kailan. "No matter where you are." Lena looked up at Kailan, with the fear and sadness slowly clearing away from her eyes. When Lena drifted off to sleep, Kailan was now thinking of her and only her.

"Never let that promise down," said Thorstein. Kailan nodded and they both went back to sleep. The next day seemed very long. The blistering heat scorched from the sun and also from the sand. Most of the water had already been used up by noon. They were surprised when they went to sleep to see the city of Alandra in the distance. Another day and they would be drinking cool water. They reached the city by the late afternoon on the third day of travelling through Kekan. The city was on a giant landform called Ark Mesa. The group hiked up to the city and walked to the front gates. A small group of soldiers guarded the main gate. At the first site of Thorstein, the guards pulled out spears and tried to force him back. A second group of men ran towards the dornbeast. Kailan and Lena stepped back and readied their weapons.

"What is the meaning of this?" demanded Kailan.

"You are not allowed to enter this city!" yelled one of the guards.

"Why not?" questioned Lena.

"We have vowed to protect this city from all evil," replied the guard. Kailan slowly walked towards one of the guards and pushed the tip of his spear downwards.

"This man is nowhere near evil," said Kailan. The man pulled his spear away from Kailan's reach and then thrust it forward. Kailan dodged the attack by jumping to the side. He unbuckled his belt and sword, and handed it to Lena.

"Kailan, we aren't going to get into the city if you do this," said Thorstein.

"Stay back evil creature," said Kailan, mocking the guards as he charged forward. Thorstein shrugged his shoulders and sat on the ground. In a few seconds, Kailan had the entire group of guards lying on the ground. He pulled out the letter from the Arch Chancellor and held it in front of one of the guards' face. The man scanned over the piece of paper and then called over the other men who were still lying on the ground. As they rushed over, one of them grabbed a spear and held it up to Kailan.

"Don't attack him," said the guard that was holding the letter. "Let them through the gates!" he yelled. Kailan put his belt back on and walked with the other two and their rides up to the palace. All the way up the hill, people stared at Thorstein in fear. This was the first time when being that big had actually bothered him. When they reached the palace, another group of guards surrounded the group, but one of them actually decided to read the letter from Kailan. The guard then escorted Kailan, Thorstein, and Lena into the palace. The emperor of Arad was not a kind man. There was more blood on his hands than most kings found in war. The white walls of the palace held tapestries, drawn by artists whose style the three had never seen before. On the floor, a blue, purple, and green carpet of many different designs and shapes laid. There were also many pillars within the palace as well. A short man with a monocle and a shawl came running over to the three adolescents and the guard.

"Name?" demanded the little man. Kailan stepped forward.

"My name is Kailan, and we have come…"

"Last name?" demanded the man again.

"Gallot. Now, we have been…"

"I have no record of a Kailan Gallot making an appointment to speak with Emperor Silus Kain," said the man.

"Shut up and let me speak," said Kailan sternly. Rude

[85]

people like the little man made Kailan feel angry some times. "We were sent by the Arch Chancellor." He pulled out the letter and held it out in front of the man's face. The little man scanned over the letter quickly and looked back at Kailan.

"You are all placed under arrest," said the man as he tore up the letter. Before any of the guards were able to get near Kailan, his sword was out and the tip of it, pointing at the man's jugular.

"I suggest that you let us past," demanded Kailan. The man nodded and backed out of the way. As Kailan, Thorstein, and Lena, walked through the double doors, the emperor's head made a quick snap.

"What do we have here?" said the emperor. He wore not a regular crown, but what looked like a golden olive branch that did not touch his forehead. He was clothed in a purple garment that was accented with gold around the edges. His throne was made of marble and gold.

"We come on behalf of Arch Chancellor Orpeth Armenen," said Kailan. Emperor Kain looked at them oddly.

"Out of my sight," said the emperor.

"We have travelled way too long to turn back now," said Kailan.

"Leave!" he yelled.

"We have a letter from the Arch Chancellor," said Kailan, pulling another piece of paper out of his pocket. Lena looked back at the short man who was standing in the hallway and then at the shreds of paper on the ground. "I found extra copies when I was in Freltus," whispered Kailan to Thorstein. He handed the letter over to Silus Kain so that he could read it.

"Orpeth has been dead for almost twenty years," said Silus. "Why should I even read this?"

"Do you see the names on the page?" questioned Kailan.

"Yes, but what does that have to do with anything?" said Silus.

"Those names are our names," replied Kailan. "And none of us have been alive for that long."

"What?"

"This letter was written before we were born, sir," said Lena. "We need your help to find a young man named Guin Pelerin." The emperor smiled and laughed.

"Why should I give you help?" said Silus.

"I could go back to Harlem and speak with Tanier Frost," said Kailan. When Silus heard the Arch Chancellor's name, he froze in place. To begin with, Silus and Tanier were on the wrong side of friendship. Silus had done some things in the past that Tanier was very displeased about. Second of all, Tanier had the power to take away Silus's leadership and give it to whoever he pleased.

"Fine," said Silus. Kailan and his other two friends smiled. "On one exception though."

"What is it?" questioned Thorstein.

"You will fight tomorrow in the stadium," said Silus.

"Okay," replied Thorstein. Silus pointed at Kailan.

[87]

"You will fight against five men, and you…" he said as he shifted his finger toward Thorstein, "…will fight the same, but against lions." Lena's mouth dropped.

"This is stupid!" yelled Lena. "We can go back to Harlem right now and have this done our way." Silus laughed.

"You gave me your terms, so I gave you mine," said Silus. Kailan put his hand on Lena's shoulder and pulled her behind Thorstein.

"Don't worry," said Kailan. "I can have five men down in less than a minute. Besides, we aren't going to get his help if we don't do it."

"I'm more afraid about Thorstein fighting lions."

"Don't worry," replied Kailan. "He can take care of himself." Thorstein turned around to join the others' conversation.

"Are we going through with this?" questioned Thorstein.

"Are you up to it?" responded Kailan with another question. The tall boy nodded his head.

"We will fight tomorrow," said Kailan loud enough so that Silus could hear him.

"Good, you may sleep in the palace for the night and be guests of my halls." The next day was more of a trouble for Lena than anyone else. They were the only people that really cared for her anymore. If they died, she would feel lost. When Kailan was called into the stadium, he looked up at the crowds of people. It was only then that he started to feel nervous. He couldn't tell if the people were going to be cheering for him, or wanting him dead. When Silus appeared at his balcony, the crowds settled. He held out his hands in front of him.

"Citizens of Alandra," he called out as his voice was carried out into the stadium. "I bring you a gift today." He pointed to the gate that Kailan was standing behind. "From faraway lands, I bring you warriors. The first is a young man that has fought many a foe to reach Alandra from Harlem. The second is a warrior of the Nordic Raiders from Achland. This man is no mere warrior though; Twice the size of any man that you or I know." The gate in front of Kailan opened. "Let the games begin!" There was a loud cheer from the audience that shook Kailan. Lena placed her hand on Kailan's shoulder.

"Get it done with as quickly as you can," she said, flashing her eyes at the young man. Kailan nodded and walked out into the centre of the arena. Across the sand battlefield, there was another open gate. From it, out of the shadows, appeared five men. Each of them wore a helmet, leather boots and armour as well. In their hands, they either had a gladius, or a mace. The five men sized did not spare any time before charging at Kailan. His sword was out in the blink of an eye, readying for his first attack. Kailan started his attack by thinking. He thought of where to attack, how to attack, and when to attack. For some people, they would have loved for their aggressor to slow their movements so that everything could be done properly, but Kailan didn't want this. He loved the speed at which he moved. If he did something that he did not expect himself to be able to

[89]

do, a great rush of adrenaline would surge through his body. When the first gladiator attacked, Kailan went for a stabbing motion, keeping his legs bent, and his torso held forward. This would give him the ability to move backwards if he needed to. After the first strike, he then went for the man's leg. It was amazing to watch from the stands. The gladiator hadn't even stopped running before he was left on the ground. All that could be seen of Kailan's attacks was a silver blur. What was even more amazing was that Kailan never really had to wipe his sword of blood after a fight. His blade cut so quickly that the blood hadn't even been able to stain it yet. In the next two seconds, another three men were down. Silus rose from his seat.

"Stop!" he yelled. The emperor pointed at Kailan and stepped forward. "If I add another ten men to the battle, I'll give your request top priority." Kailan looked at the men lying on the ground. He thought to himself for a second or two. "Do we have a deal?" questioned Silus. Kailan looked up at the emperor.

"I accept your challenge!" The crowd cheered as ten more men entered the battlefield. It was not as Kailan expected though. The men were very heavily armed. They wore full plate armour, and wielded very large weapons. Kailan did the same as he did before though. He eyed them up and readied himself to attack. Each of them took a little longer than the other gladiators, but Kailan had them all on the ground in about a minute. He walked up to the emperor's wall. "I have won, and defeated your warriors!" Silus nodded and shooed Kailan away.

"I will keep to my promise," said Silus. Kailan walked

back to the gate and to Lena.

"See, that wasn't so hard." Kailan felt the sting of Lena's hand hitting his face.

"You said that you were going to get out of there as quickly as you could," she said, scowling at Kailan. He held his hand to his cheek.

"But now we will be out of here sooner," replied Kailan.

"You could have died," said Lena.

"But I didn't."

"Nobody knew that!" Thorstein walked up to Kailan before heading out into the arena. He pulled him away from Lena.

"Remember what I said about that promise the other day," said Thorstein. Kailan nodded and looked up at Thorstein's face. "Any promise that you make to her, you must keep." He backed away from Kailan and walked out into the open area.

"I'm sorry," said Kailan. Lena looked up at him and turned away. She walked to the other side of the tunnel and sat against the wall. A man came out of the darkness and walked up to the gate. He grabbed one of the boards that was leaning up against the wall and braced the gate with it. As Thorstein made his way into the light, and into the audience's view, the stadium was filled with a sense of awe. They had never seen someone of Thorstein's size before. As the first lion was released, it hid in the darkness, away from Thorstein. As the others came, they were not afraid of him anymore. Kailan, who was leaning up against the tunnel wall, slid down and hit something as he reached the bottom. He checked under himself to see what he had sat on. There was suddenly a look of fear on his face. At that same time, Thorstein realised what he had forgotten within the tunnel. He turned around to go back for his axe, but the gate was already closed and locked. The male lion walked up to Thorstein and roared, swinging its mane from side to side. Thorstein turned away from the gate and let in a large breath. The lion roared again, but this time, Thorstein roared back. Even the people in the stands were scared. All of the lions raced back to their gate and started clawing at it. Thorstein did nothing to stop them, but even decided to sit against his gate. Silus arose again and stepped forward.

"Fine then!" yelled Silus. "If you will not fight the lions, then I will pit you against a more suitable foe!" The gate for the lions opened up, and the lions dashed for safety. The gate to Thorstein's left opened up. There was complete silence amongst the arena. Thorstein, who was still leaning against the wall, noticed two, small, red lights coming from the tunnel. There was a loud thud. What Thorstein then realised was that Silus was completely mad. Within the tunnel was a stone golem. To Thorstein's surprise, and fear, it was almost as tall as he was. Thorstein stood up and walked into the middle of the circle. When Lena saw the golem, fear overtook her. She fainted at the sight of it and fell to her side.

"Run Thorstein!" screamed Kailan. A golem was one

of the most dangerous creatures. Even with a weapon, someone would have a hard time fighting one without dying. Even for Thorstein, a golem of that size could mean death. Kailan rushed out of the tunnel and up a flight of stairs. He had to find Silus' balcony to reason with him. Thorstein tried walking in a circle, to avoid the golem. Then, he remembered something that he learned while at Algar. His professor taught him that a golem was not very strong. Where its damage did come from though was from the momentum of its attacks, and the density of the rocks. This gave Thorstein an idea. All that he had to do was to outsmart the golem, and if best, keep behind it. From there, it could not attack Thorstein. Kailan ran down a hallway that had red cloth hanging from the walls and the ceiling. This must have been the route to Silus' balcony. Thorstein jumped on the back of the golem, forcing it to the ground. From there, he grabbed one of the arms, pulled it behind the creature's head and started bashing the collection of stones together. To his delight, the stones were not hard like they are in Achland, but much softer and brittle. Kailan leapt into the air, through the people, and held his sword at Silus' neck.

"Call the beast off!" demanded Kailan. A group of guards rushed over and hesitantly held their spears at Kailan.

Silus Kain looked up at the boy and smiled. "Why should I? Your friend seems to have beaten it."

Kailan quickly turned around and saw Thorstein, standing over what was left of the golem. One arm in Thorstein's hand, and the rest on the ground was mainly dust and pebbles. The sweat beaded down the faces of both the young men. "Now... I will have my men search for this person as soon as we get back to my palace." He smiled, rose up, and walked out of the balcony room. Kailan made his way back to the tunnel and found Lena still lying on the floor. He walked over to her and patted her face.

"Wake up," said Kailan. As the girl's eyes opened, she smiled for a second before remembering what happened before she fainted. The two adolescents ran to the gate and lifted off the board. As the crowds were cheering for Thorstein, Kailan and Lena helped him to the tunnel.

"Boy, am I tired," said Thorstein. Kailan looked up at his friend and both laughed.

"What are you laughing about?" said Lena. "He could've been killed." Thorstein laughed even more as he grabbed his two friends and held them close. When they returned to the palace, Silus was waiting for them.

"We already have him for you," said Silus as they walked through the main doors. The three companions looked at him with surprise.

"Where is he?" questioned Lena.

"He's in my throne room right now," replied Silus. "I already told him what you told me." When they reached the throne room, they saw a short, slightly chubby young man, sitting on a bench. On his face, he wore a pair of round spectacles.

"Are you Guin?" questioned Thorstein. The boy

jumped out of his seat and fell to the ground. Kailan laughed and helped the boy back on the bench.

"Don't worry, you're not the first person that he's scared like that," said Kailan.

"My name is Guin Pelerin," said the boy. "The emperor tells me that you need my services." Lena stepped forward.

"We were wondering if you would like to come with us," said Lena.

"Where are you going?" questioned Guin. Kailan pulled out the letter and showed it to Guin. He scanned the letter very quickly. "Why is my name on here?"

"How old are you Guin?" asked Kailan.

"Eighteen," replied the boy. Kailan nodded and pointed to the bottom of the letter.

"Notice here how it says that this letter was written by Arch Chancellor Orpeth Armenen?" questioned Kailan. Guin nodded his head and looked up.

"Wait a minute." Kailan smiled. "He died before I was born," said Guin.

"Before any of us," replied Lena. "This letter was written before any of us were born."

"We've come to figure out why," said Kailan.

"Are you sure it isn't a fake?" questioned Guin.

"It's not a fake. I've already been to Harlem and questioned Tanier Frost about the situation," said Kailan. Guin held one of his hands to his forehead. He let in a deep breath and then exhaled.

[95]

"I'll go with you, now that the Wizards' Guild is allowing me to leave," said Guin.

"What?"

"The Wizards' Guild won't allow any wizard to leave unless they have proven themselves," said Guin.

"You're a wizard?" questioned Thorstein. The boy replied with a nod. He held out his hand as a variety of lights swirled around his fingers. The other three adolescents looked at each other.

"When do you think that you'll be ready?" questioned Kailan. The boy laughed as he pulled a small pouch out of his pocket. He tossed the bag to Kailan, who untied the string and opened it up and looked inside. Filling the bag was an assortment of clothing, books, and other items. He looked up from the bag at Guin in confusion. Kailan pulled out one of the tiny shirts, which in a few seconds, changed to regular size.

"Where did you get this?" questioned Kailan.

"Everyone at the Wizards' Guild receives one when they reach the age of fifteen," replied Guin. The little bag meant that Guin would be able to spend less time worrying about his supplies and more time looking out for danger. It wasn't long before the group was ready to leave the city for their next companion. The group spent about fifteen minutes getting their supplies and mounts ready for the journey ahead. Silus gave Guin a horse as a gift to travel with his new friends. When they left the stables, Guin headed off in a different direction than the other three.

"Where are you going?" questioned Thorstein.

"To the Wizards' Guild," replied Guin.

"I thought you said that you had everything in that little bag there," said Kailan out of confusion.

"We can use a portal there that can take us to the edge of Arad," said Guin. The other companion's faces lit up with excitement. None of them had ever really done anything magical in their lives, and they would probably never get another chance like that. They made their way to the building that was situated just to the left of the Wizards' Guild. As they entered, they laid their eyes on a wondrous sight. A giant mirror stood in the middle of the room. The reflection from the mirror was a perfect image. There were no flaws, or imperfections within it. Guin stepped beside the mirror and tapped it lightly with a finger. The surface rippled and started to change colour. From the original silver, it became a filled with clouds and mists of green, blue, and bits of yellow. Guin placed his hand on the mirror. At first, it seemed to flow like fog, or even liquid at some times. When Guin touched it though, it was clear that it was a solid surface. He turned away from the rest of the group and uttered a few words, while keeping his eyes closed. "I've never gone this way, so just trust me and hope that the other end is still there." Guin stepped into the portal, disappearing into the fog. The three friends looked at each other. For about ten seconds, they stood motionless.

"Should we follow him?" questioned Thorstein. Kailan and Lena looked at each other. In their eyes, there were images of curiosity, fear, and a sense of adventure.

"Come on," said a voice from the portal. Guin poked his head back through and waved his hand, signalling the other three to follow. There was a quick flash, and Kailan stepped through to the other side. He opened his eyes and set them upon the East Aradian Mountains. The desert from that point towards the mountains didn't have as much sand, just dry dirt. There were some plants, but they were mainly shrubs.

"How was that?" questioned Guin as Thorstein and Lena passed through the portal.

"That was it?" said Kailan.

"What do you mean?"

"I was expecting a long tunnel that we had to walk through."

"Only wizards deal with that," replied Guin. "From there, they can find other routes to different places." Kailan turned around to look at the portal. To his surprise, there was no mirror. The portal opened in mid-air and suspended itself there. In only a few seconds after they walked through, the portal swirled in a clockwise direction, and shrunk until it vanished into thin air.

"Can you go anywhere?" questioned Lena.

"Only to the places that have been found by wizards," replied Guin.

"What do you mean?" said Lena.

"As I stated earlier, a wizard may travel within the portal. In there, they can find routes to exits. We can only transport to an exit that has been found." The group made their way to the mountains, where they found some familiar terrain. The coniferous trees and rocks everywhere that most of the group had grown up with was giving them a greeting from their desert travels. The mountains on this side of Arad were not as wide, but it did take the group about an hour or two to cross them. When they reached the other side, they came upon a gorge. It was about ten feet wide and almost twenty-five feet deep at most parts. When Kailan looked at his map, he noticed that the gorge would take them directly to Letania. By travelling it, they would be able to reach the town of Dratana within a period of five days instead of the originally intended seven. As they walked between the stone walls, Thorstein felt a sensation as though he was being trapped and squeezed. Even though the walls were almost as wide apart as Thorstein was tall, he still did not feel as though it was enough room for him.

"Does anyone else feel somewhat strange about this place?" questioned Thorstein.

"What do you mean?" replied Kailan.

"It doesn't feel like smart idea to travel this way."

"Don't worry; we're already almost halfway there," said Kailan. Thorstein looked behind himself, trying to ease his mind. Something was bothering him that the others felt strange about. Thorstein wasn't even really upset about being attacked by a giant scorpion, but being in a trench did? He continued to look back a number of times before something really started to bug him. Every now and then, when he would look back,

[99]

something could be seen scurrying behind one of the many boulders. After about the fourth time, Thorstein decided to grab a smaller rock and throw it at the boulder. When the stone collided with the larger one, Thorstein saw the man run out from behind. He was wearing armour and had a sword in his hand. The armour looked familiar to Thorstein though. Suddenly, his eyes widened and his jaw dropped. When Kailan turned to look at what Thorstein was doing, the giant grabbed Kailan and made sure that his words were heard.

"We're being followed by the Black Allegiance," said Thorstein. Kailan responded with an expression of deep fear. He turned around, trying to be as calm as he could.

"Lena, Guin, we need to get out of here as quickly as we can," said Kailan sternly. The other two looked around.

"What's the matter?" questioned Lena.

"Thorstein said that he saw a Black Allegiance member following us," replied Kailan. Guin, who was familiar with the history of Arlbega and the surrounding countries, knew what the Black Allegiance was. Before he could make a comment, a group of the soldiers started chasing after the group. This time though, they had arrows and were prepared for a fight. The gorge was wide enough for the horses and their riders to run through, but Thorstein would have to run on foot. Right when they started running, it was then that Thorstein realised their true problem. He heard a loud thud behind him. As he looked back, Thorstein noticed the giant chasing after them. It was almost one and a half times as tall as Thorstein, and had about the same muscularity.

"Hurry!" yelled Thorstein. Lena fired arrows backwards, hitting her targets in the head every time. Kailan looked back for a quick second to see how the others were doing and noticed Lena's impeccable aim.

"How are you doing that?" yelled Kailan as they dashed around corners and jumping over the rocks.

"I never miss," said Lena. The two thought of the ordeal as somewhat of a game. They weren't as afraid as Guin and Thorstein. Kailan quickly looked back at the new companion.

"Can you cast a spell on them?" said Kailan. Guin opened his eyes and nodded his head.

"I can create a wall of fire, but they would be able to just run through it," he replied.

"If that'll slow them down," said Kailan. Guin looked back and held out his hand. He muttered a few words and the next thing he knew; there was a wall of flames, blocking the Black Allegiance from advancing. He turned around and tried to keep his eyes open. Thorstein was falling behind and needed a way to catch up to the group. Kailan quickly pulled his map back out to check how far they needed to go until they reached the end of the gorge. All that they had to do was go about a hundred feet, make a complete right turn, then an extra two hundred feet and they would be at the end of the gorge. The only problem was that Kailan didn't know if it was a dead end, or if it did slope upwards to the surface. As Thorstein looked behind, he

[101]

noticed that the giant had charged through the fire, and was still on their tail.

"Guin!" yelled Thorstein. "Can you blast any of that rock down?" The small boy looked up at the top of the ridge and noticed some loose boulders. If he was to knock them down, he could injure the giant and stop it from chasing after them.

"I can try!" Guin held out his hand again. Without even saying anything, there was a bolt of purple light that shot from his hand and hit the boulders with might. As they fell, the giant backed off, but was hit in the head with one and knocked unconscious.

"Great job!" yelled Thorstein, who was now slowing down. He needed to catch his breath badly. From the right turn, it was a light jog for Thorstein until the end. To their delight, the gorge did slope up. This would be easier for them, and their steeds to travel. The chase was not over though. Before Thorstein turned the corner, he noticed that there were still three men chasing after them. They had run through the fire and were now continuing after the group. They didn't pose any threat, but they would be able to track the four companions. As Thorstein darted around the corner, he called out. "There's three more still after us!" yelled Thorstein. Kailan, Lena, and Guin were all at the end at that point and were making their way up the slope. When Thorstein's words reached Lena's ears, she quickly pulled out three arrows, notched them, and pulled back on the bow string. She took a split second to think and aim. When she fired the arrows, Kailan looked at her in disappointment.

"What are you doing, you can't even see them," said Kailan. When he looked back, he saw the three men fall out from behind the wall, each of them with an arrow in their head. Lena dropped her arm and turned to Kailan.

"As I said earlier, I never miss, not unless I mean to." Kailan was astonished by Lena's skill. Her three arrows had ricocheted off the stone wall, and then to the three men. There was much that Kailan still did not know about Lena. One day, shortly after her sister's death, while walking around with her pet eagle, Lena had found a small hut in the middle of a swamp. In the hut was an old elf. He told her stories of when he was younger, and that he used to be a great general. Lena became friends with the elf and he taught her how to wield her bow better than anyone else alive. It was only a week or two before Kailan and Thorstein arrived when the elf had disappeared. Lena took her daily walk into the swamp and noticed that the hut was gone. There was no trace of it ever being there, and nothing was left behind. Even the ashes of the campfire that stood outside were gone. Her life was shrouded in mystery and magic. There were so little that people knew of her life, and she knew almost just as little herself. Strange things would happen to her that wouldn't happen to other people. Thorstein slowly made it to the top of the gorge and lay down on the grass. From there, he rolled over and grabbed a water pouch from the dornbeast. It was empty in a matter of seconds.

"We need to find a place to rest for a while," said Thorstein. He lifted himself up and grabbed the reins of the

[103]

dornbeast. He started walking down the hillside and into the forest. Guin hopped off his horse and started walking next to Thorstein. When the group finally found a place to rest, they decided that it was time for them to make camp. "I'll get busy making the shelter," said Thorstein. "Kailan and Guin, you two collect some firewood and Lena; try to find us some food." All four went in their desired directions and started their duties. Lena placed a hand on Kailan's shoulder as he bent down to pick up a piece of wood.

"What?" he said as he stood up and turned to her. She ran her hand from his shoulder, down to his pocket, and pulled out the clear lens that he used for starting fires. "What are you doing with that?" said Kailan as he reached for the object. Lena pulled her hand back.

"You'll have to come and get it," said Lena. She turned around and started running. Kailan looked back at Guin and noticed that he had a large amount of firewood ready. He quickly dropped what was in his hands and chased after Lena. The grass travelled far into the forest and was not covered in fallen leaves or other debris, making it easier for the two teens to run. Kailan ended up chasing Lena to a large pond that was fed by a small waterfall that was about twenty feet above the water. The water was emerald green and clear enough that Kailan could see the stone floor below. Lena hid behind a large bush so that Kailan could not see her.

"Can I please have that back?" said Kailan.

"Come and get it," said Lena in a playful tone.

Suddenly, Kailan heard a splash and Lena's head popped up through the water. She raised the lens out of the water and waved it in the air. Kailan stepped closer to the edge of the pond and noticed the pile of clothes behind the bush and the lack of clothes on Lena as she swam through the water. It took a few double takes and another call by Lena before he started undressing himself. He jumped into the water and swam over to Lena. He reached for her hand with the lens in it, but she pulled back and placed her other hand under his chin, pulling him closer. Kailan lowered his head and rested his lips on hers. As they embraced each other, Kailan felt the love that they shared for one another. He envisioned their life together for a brief moment before their lips separated.

"Look out below!" yelled Thorstein as he and Guin jumped into the pool. Lena quickly dove downwards and swam to the edge of the pond. She collected her clothes and ran off. "What's the matter?" questioned Thorstein. Kailan looked at the giant and shook his head in disappointment. He swam to the edge and collected his clothes as well.

"What's his problem?" said Guin.

"I don't exactly know," replied Thorstein. He watched as Kailan walked away, back to the camp. All the while, Guin was splashing Thorstein with water. As the large boy turned to face the small wizard, a wave knocked the small boy almost out of the water. Thorstein laughed as he floated in place, almost started to sink as a result. Kailan sat beside Lena at the fire. She leaned over and rested her head on his shoulder. She pulled the piece of glass out of her pocket and held it out towards the sky. She leaned backwards and rested her back on the ground. Kailan followed her actions and stared up at the sky. Lena tried looking through the lens, but only saw a blur.

"Have you ever looked up at the clouds and wondered what is up there?" questioned Lena.

"Sometimes," replied Kailan. "I used to think that the clouds were actually castles that were made of marble and diamond." Lena smiled at Kailan's response.

"I like to think of it as a dream world," said Lena.

"What do you mean?"

"Everything there is peaceful. There are no urgencies or worries. Time stays still and we can live forever." The words that came out of Lena's mouth made Kailan feel warm inside. They struck something inside of his mind that made him want to hear more. It was about fifteen minutes until Thorstein and Guin returned. They found Kailan and Lena lying next to each other beside the fire. Kailan had his arm wrapped around Lena and they were both sound asleep.

"Now I understand," said Thorstein. As he sat down, he pulled out some dried meat that he had bought while in Alandra and shared it with Guin. The giant and his new wizard friend were bound to be good friends. Both the wizard and the giant had been taught at universities, and what one wasn't able to do, the other was most likely able to do. In the middle of the night, the group awoke to a disturbing scene. They had been tracked down by the surviving Black Allegiance members. Trying to hold Thorstein down was the giant that they had defeated at the gorge. There were sixteen men in total at the campsite. When Guin awoke, he didn't know what was happening until he saw the giant standing over Thorstein. Three men walked over to Kailan and Lena, and held their swords at the adolescents' necks. Guin hopped to his feet and clapped his hands together. There was a loud bang and a cloud of smoke filled the campsite. Most of the men ran out to catch some fresh air while a smaller group stayed within the cloud. The giant as well could not breathe, and therefore had to back away. When the smoke cleared, there were four men lying on the ground. Kailan was standing over them with Lena hiding behind. While the smoke filled the area, Thorstein went for his axe. They were now ready for a fight. Guin was busy trying to throw the attackers into trees with his magic, while Thorstein was occupied with the giant. He swung his axe in a circle over his head and brought it down on the giant's wooden club. He pulled the axe back and tried to make another hack at the giant's legs. This attack was blocked as well, but this time, his axe, and the club as well, were flung into one of the trees. Thorstein jumped at the giant, wrapping his arms around the chest and legs around the waist, bringing the giant to the ground. When he got up, there was a series of brutal swings with his fists. Kailan went for his sword and started fighting off the remaining attackers with Guin.

"No mercy this time!" yelled Thorstein. Guin already knew how dangerous the Black Allegiance was, and knew that they could spare no survivors for sake of their safety. Lena

[107]

ended up joining into the fight near the end, but ended up only getting two or three of them. Thorstein stood up from the mangled body of his attacker. The giants were a match for Thorstein's size, but not for his strength. The four friends came together in the centre of the camp, making sure that everyone was okay.

"I never realised that this is what we'd be doing all of the time," said Guin.

"Welcome to the real world," said Thorstein as he pulled his axe out of the tree. Kailan looked around at all the dead bodies.

"What do you think we should do with them?" he asked the rest of the group.

"We might as well leave them here," said Thorstein. "By the time we'd have all of them somewhere else, we probably wouldn't be able to go back to sleep."

"I'm not sleeping here with a whole bunch of dead bodies lying around," said Lena.

"We're going to move," replied Thorstein.

"Oh." Kailan let out a little giggle. Half an hour later, after packing up their supplies, the group found another suitable place to spend the night. They decided to sleep in the next morning so that they wouldn't be tired on their travels. When they did end up waking up, the group travelled until they reached a small town that lay just outside of the Veralias Forest. It was the largest forest in Arlbega, even larger than the one in Achland. It actually reminded Kailan and Thorstein of the forest that they went through on their way to Thoria. The trees weren't as tall, but they were just as plentiful, and the ferns and shrubs covered the forest floor. The strange thing about many of Letania's forests was that the forest floor had no leaves. The grass was a bright, healthy green colour that brightened up the forest floor. That evening, the group found a village to spend the night at. Thorstein ended up sleeping outside of the town because there were no barns for him to stay in.

During the third day of travel to Dratana, the group came upon a tower in the middle of the forest. Something about it made Guin and Thorstein feel a strange sense. Guin's talent of sensing magic attracted him to the tower, while Thorstein's crave for adventure and understanding caught him. Kailan tried to follow Guin and Thorstein into the tower, but Lena tried to hold him back.

"Don't go in there," said Lena. Kailan had an expression of confusion on his face.

"Why not?" questioned Kailan.

"I just don't like the looks of it," replied Lena. Kailan began to laugh.

"There's nothing the matter." He took a step back from Lena. "I'm going to see what is so special about it." He turned away and walked through the front door. Lena gave him a dirty look before storming away into the forest. She sat down on the hillside and started pulling at the grass. The spiral staircase in the tower went to the very top. When Guin, Thorstein, and Kailan reached the top, they came upon a purple sphere with dark swirls moving within. None of them knew what to make of it. Not even Guin had an idea of what it was. Hesitantly, he lightly tapped the object. Suddenly, a purple wave of smoke shot out of the sphere and dissipated as it left the tower. Lena pulled a clump of grass out of the ground and lifted some of the dirt with it. She noticed something in the hole that she made. A strange coloured tree root was in the ground. As Lena leaned closer, she noticed that the root started to move. Without having a chance to back away, the root grabbed onto her leg and started pulling her down the hill. She screamed in fear as she was dragged through the forest. When Kailan heard the screams, he immediately ran to help Lena. Before leaving the top, Guin opened his little bag, and scooped the ball into it. Kailan had a hard time running through the forest. The trees seemed to be much closer, almost as if they were trying to stop Kailan. It wasn't until he realised that it was better for Thorstein to lead that things became easier. They followed the screams, but more importantly, the trail left by Lena being dragged.

"Kailan!" she screamed. "Help!" Suddenly, the root stopped pulling her. She tried to pull it off her leg, but there was no need. The root released itself and slid away into the forest. She tried to run away, but it was then that she heard the creaking in the forest. She had left her bow with the horse. If she did have it, she would not be helpless against the attacking goblins. They were wild goblins. Creatures that neither dealt with humans, nor even their own kind as much. They were thought of as some of the worst because they didn't really care for anything. They were bloodthirsty monsters that infested the forests of the world. The only thing that they feared was an elf. They had never met Kailan before though. As he jumped into the crowd, they backed off and sneered at him. He stood in front of Lena and guarded her with sword in hand. Thorstein was behind a little bit, but was catching up quickly. As the creatures pounced, they were flung away by Kailan's sword. They did not fear his attacks, even though he knew what they were going to do before they actually did it. Swing after swing left the goblins dead on the ground. There didn't seem like an end to the carnage until Thorstein arrived and scared the rest away. Kailan turned and knelt beside Lena.

"Are you okay?"

"You arrived just in time," replied Lena.

"Remember my promise? I will always be there to protect you." Kailan leaned in and kissed Lena. This one was even more passionate than the one the day before. This one had meaning. It symbolised Kailan's love and his sacrifice for her. He wrapped one arm behind her back and lifted her up. They made their way back to the horses and met Guin halfway there.

"What happened?" questioned Guin.

"Goblins," said Thorstein.

"Goblins?" said Guin in fear. He had never seen the creatures in real life, but had read about them and seen sketches. Never had he seen the vicious creatures that they were. Thorstein remembered something when they got back to the horses and the tower.

"Kailan, do you remember how you didn't want me to come?" he said.

"Yes, why?" replied Kailan.

"You might have been able to live in the land of Helforth, but you could never survive Achland, Thoria, Arad, and Letania all by yourself," Thorstein stated.

Kailan smiled as he looked up at the giant. "You are right," he said. "I'm glad you ordered me to let you come." They spent the night in the middle of the forest again. There were no clearings nearby, nor had they seen any on their way since the tower. Kailan sat by the fire and plotted the group's course. He found out that it would only take them a day and a half to reach Dratana. They spent another whole day in the forest before reaching Dratana on the fifth day. It wasn't even a month yet, and they had found the fifth person on the list. It was a great help that they were able to skip a day or two's travel by using the portal at the Wizards' Guild. As they entered the village, their fears had come true. People were lying dead in the street with blood pooling from their bodies. Thorstein picked one of the corpses up and examined it. He noticed the two bite marks by the neck.

"Vampires," he said. The rest of the group stood back.

"Don't touch him then," said Kailan.

"This one has been killed, not changed to a vampire," replied Thorstein. "I'd say that he has been dead for a whole day now." He looked up and noticed that most of the buildings were either burnt or damaged slightly. They decided to go throughout the town, looking for supplies or other items. As they entered one building, they found a child lying on the floor. The strange thing though, was there was no blood. Lena knelt down and placed a hand on the child's back, trying to examine it. Suddenly, the child sprung up and wrapped its arms around Lena.

"Please don't let them get me!" the little boy cried.

"Don't worry, you're safe," said Lena as she shushed the child. "What happened here?"

"They took my mommy and daddy into the street and killed them," said the boy as he pointed out the door. "They took some of the people away as well." Kailan knelt down beside the boy.

"Do you know a boy name Viktor Svetlenka?" questioned Kailan.

The boy nodded his head. "They took him away to the castle," said the boy.

"Can you show us where this castle is?" questioned Kailan. The boy replied with a nod. As they exited the house, Thorstein looked down at the boy, but strangely, the boy made no attempt to look up at Thorstein, or even be shocked at his size. It was then that Thorstein realised what was actually going on. He kicked the boy away from Lena and into a nearby house, taking out one of the walls.

"What are you doing!" screamed Lena. She pointed an arrow at Thorstein. "Why did you do that?" Kailan pulled out his sword and held it up to Thorstein as well.

[113]

"Explain yourself, now!" he yelled. Thorstein pointed at the broken wall and the boy picking himself up from the rubble.

"You should have examined him properly," said Thorstein. He took a step towards the dornbeast, grabbed his axe, and threw it at the boy, knocking him to the ground.

"Stop it!" screamed Lena. Kailan was starting to realise what Thorstein was talking about. He pulled his sword away and placed it in its sheath. The boy lifted the axe up and off of himself, something that Kailan wasn't even strong enough to do. Thorstein walked up to the boy and grabbed him with both hands. He struggled as Thorstein squeezed tightly. Kailan placed his hand on Lena's bow and lowered it. "What are you doing? He's just a boy," she said, almost beginning to cry.

"The boy is a vampire," said Kailan.

"What?"

Thorstein walked over to Lena and held the boy in front of her. With two fingers, he tilted the boy's head to the side so that his neck was visible. There were two bite marks at the base of his neck. Lena took a step back in shock. Thorstein pulled the little vampire away and held him up to his face.

"Where is the castle!" demanded Thorstein.

The boy laughed before spitting in Thorstein's face.

Thorstein loosened his grip and slid his hand to the boy's hair. He wiped his face with his free hand and started spinning the boy around by his hair. He made sure not to do it too much, as the hair would snap, and the boy would run away

[114]

afterwards. "Where is the castle!" demanded Thorstein again.

The boy slowly stopped moving and decided to speak this time. "What do I get out of it?"

Thorstein whipped the boy into the ground below. "I won't kill you if you tell me now!" To the boy, Thorstein seemed very angry, but to the others, they knew that he was doing his job to protect the rest of the group. The boy was almost beginning to cry at this point. For a vampire, the pain would be significantly less, but the pain that Thorstein was dealing would have already have been enough to kill a regular human. Lena turned away and hid her head behind Kailan's shoulder. She couldn't bear to see a child cry, human or vampire.

"The castle is to the north," said the boy. "It is just outside of the mountains."

Thorstein smiled and nodded before he started spinning the boy again, this time, launching him into the air.

"You said that you were going to let him live," said Lena.

"He won't die from that," said Thorstein. "He might be in a lot of pain afterwards, but that is about it." The group got back on their horses and left the village.

About halfway to the castle, Guin started to ask questions. "How do you know that Viktor is alive?"

Thorstein twisted himself around. "Viktor is being used as bait, and they will ambush us there," replied Thorstein.

Guin's horse stopped immediately. "We're going to be

ambushed?"

"Don't worry," said Thorstein. "There used to be a vampire coven near my village until they started causing trouble." He turned away from Guin and looked forward. "I must've killed about twenty of them myself."

Guin gulped and started moving forward again. When the group arrived at the vampire's castle, they noticed that it was in a more shaded part of the forest. When they first entered the building through the main doors, Thorstein noticed something.

"I smell blood," he said. "The iron is what gives it the smell and flavour." The remaining three companions looked at Thorstein oddly. "War parties," he said, making the rest of the party fell less unsure about him. Guin created a light that lit the dark halls up. Immediately in front of the group was a large pool of blood. On the other side of the pool, were a group if vampires. When they noticed the four companions, they leapt over the pool and held each of the companions down except for Thorstein.

"What do you think we should do with them?" said one of the female vampires.

"We could seduce them, have our way, and then suck their blood," replied another. A look of fear entered Lena's eyes. It was something that they said that upset her.

"You can take the boys, but leave the girl to me," said a male vampire as he walked down the stairs. Something about him seemed strange. He was much more lavishly dressed than the others. His cape was larger, and had more detail in it. "The girl will make a fine wife for me."

"Thorstein!" cried Kailan. "Why aren't you helping?"

"I was just wondering why none of them saw me," replied Thorstein in a calm voice. The vampires turned around to see where the voice was coming from. Thorstein bent down and revealed himself from the shadows. As the vampires gazed upon the behemoth, they hissed and backed away from the other companions. Thorstein kicked one if the vampires into the wall and pushed his foot until blood started to squirt out. He then took his axe and cut off the head of another, but not without sending it flying into the pool of blood. The male vampire jumped on Thorstein's back and started clawing at his skin. The giant jumped up, threw his legs in front, and landed on the vampire. As the vampire tried to scurry out from underneath, Thorstein lifted his arm, and brought his elbow down on its back. The remaining vampires ran away into other parts of the building, for fear of being killed by Thorstein. "There are many other ways to kill a vampire besides a stake to the heart or cutting off its head," said Thorstein as he helped the others up. They heard screaming from the lower dungeon and decided to follow it. As they reached the bottom of the steps, they saw three people. Two were human, and one was a vampire. Sadly, the vampire was sucking the blood of one of the humans as the group entered. Lena quickly shot a few arrows into the vampire's heart, but it was too late. The human was already dead. The other human in the room was a young man. He shook his shoulder length hair away from his face and looked up at the five group members. He shook the chains, yelling for help.

[117]

"Get me out of here," he cried. "Help me before more come!" Thorstein walked over, grabbed the chains, and ripped them out of the wall. Before the boy could run away, Thorstein grabbed his head and checked for bite wounds.

"He's okay," said Thorstein.

"Do you know someone name Viktor Svetlenka?" questioned Kailan. The boy looked over at Kailan.

"Me!"

"We're glad that you survived," said Kailan with a smile on his face.

"Excuse me, but I suggest that we get out of here as quickly as possible," said Lena as she pointed to the staircase. The group ran back up the stairs, only to be confronted by a group of over twenty vampires. Everyone hid behind Thorstein for safety.

"Are you guys seriously expecting me to do all of the vampire killing today?" Thorstein shook his head in disappointment and swung with his axe. As Thorstein was fighting, Kailan and Lena were trying to get in on the action as well, but keeping themselves at a safe distance. Guin however, was busy looking through his small bag that he kept in his pocket. At some point, he pulled out the purple orb that they had found earlier in the week. He gripped it tightly with both hands and closed his eyes. There was another blast of purple smoke. He placed the sphere back into his bag and started running for the staircase to the top of the castle.

"Follow me!" Guin yelled.

"We need to get to the door!" said Kailan.

"Trust me!" When the group reached the staircase, a goblin appeared at the front door and started attacking one of the vampires. The group realised then realised what the orb did. It summoned forth goblins to attack. The only problem for the group of friends was that Guin didn't know how to keep the goblins from attacking them. When they reached the top of the staircase, the group entered a room and closed the door behind them. They tried to keep the door closed, but the vampires were very strong. Guin and Viktor crawled out through one of the windows, and jumped into a nearby tree.

"Run for it," said Thorstein.

"We're not leaving you behind!" said Kailan.

"Don't worry, I'll be perfectly fine." Kailan nodded his head and helped Lena out the window with him following after quite close. The four adolescents made for the horses and hopped upon them.

"We need to get away quickly," said Kailan.

"But what of Thorstein?" questioned Guin. Suddenly, there was a loud bang, and Thorstein burst through the wall with the window. The sunlight was allowed in and every vampire in the room was burned. The giant landed next to the dornbeast, not even a scratch on him.

"I think he'll be okay," replied Kailan, letting out a laugh as they started riding away. The group had now found their fifth companion and were now on the journey back to Harlem. The group explained everything to Viktor about the letter, and he agreed to join them. Viktor hopped off of Guin's horse when they reached Dratana. He walked into one of the houses and into the darkness. A few minutes later, Viktor returned with a bag full of clothes, and two daggers. He spun them in his hand before placing them in their sheaths that were opposite of each other on his belt. With a sigh of relief, Viktor hopped back onto Guin's horse and the group left the forsaken town.

"You don't seem too sad," said Thorstein. "You've lost your family and friends, but yet you seem neither sad, nor content."

Viktor looked up and replied, "My family died many years ago. Everyone that died from the vampires deserved to die. I have no friends."

Thorstein nodded and left it at that. "Where to now?" he asked Kailan.

The boy pulled out his map and dragged his finger along the paper. "Well... we could take a direct route through Arad, but that would mean about five days without any water," replied Kailan. "Instead, we could go around Arad and go through Thoria and Achland instead." Viktor leaned over and shook his head.

"I suggest that we take a boat," said Viktor. "There is a harbour about a day's travel north from here." He pointed at the map. "From there, we could be in Harlem in less than five days." Kailan smiled. It was the first time that anyone else had suggested a different and easier route to travel. The group left

Dratana and ended up at the port at about noon the next day. There was only one boat that was actually going to Harlem at the port. Thankfully for Kailan and his friends, the captain said that he would take them.

"My name is Captain Briggs," said the man. "I will be glad to be of service to the Arch Chancellor and his men." He wore a bandana around his head, with a tricorne on top, and had a large cutlass sword held to his waste by a cloth belt. When the boat left the dock, Kailan was becoming somewhat excited. He was happy to visit his side of Arlbega again, and to see Harlem for a second time. The boat ride for the first day was quite calm, until that night. The sky was completely dark, and then suddenly, a flash of lightning appeared. Kailan and the others went to the bottom of the ship and took cover there. Thorstein stayed on the deck to help the sailors with the ropes and sales. As the boat was tossed back and forth, Kailan hid in one of the corners of the room, trying to stay calm. He had never been on the sea before, and neither had any of the others. It was only till very late that night that the storm finally died down. The next morning, the group awoke to the sound of the waves gently splashing against the side of the boat. It felt strange for them to be on a boat. It was almost a full day to rest and get things in order. The group learned more about each other on the second day. What was nice for Kailan, Thorstein, and Lena, was that the boat only stayed about a mile or two off shore. From there, they could see their homelands quite clearly. The end of the second day was probably the biggest ordeal along the voyage. They boat

[121]

was passing Thoria, when suddenly, singing could be heard. The sailors and the five companions looked everywhere until one of the men saw a small island just off the side of the boat. On the island were three beautiful women. Each of them had voices that were just as beautiful as their appearances.

"Who goes there?" demanded Captain Briggs.

"Swim ashore and we will tell you!" said one of the women. Something strange happened just then. Kailan, Thorstein, Guin, and Viktor, all developed the urge to swim to the island. The sailors, even Captain Briggs as well, were caught in their trance.

"They're sirens!" screamed Lena at the top of her lungs. All three of the women on the rocks stared at Lena.

"A girl?" cried one of them. "You will die with the men as well." Lena quickly pulled out her bow and notched and arrow. She pointed it at one of the women and readied herself.

"Stop it!" yelled Lena. "I'm going to shoot."

"Wait a second, I know that voice," said the less dominant siren. "Harkon…" Lena fired the first arrow into the siren, sending her backwards and into the water. She fired two more arrows, killing the other women. When the echoes of the singing stopped, the men came back to reality.

"Where did they go?" questioned Kailan.

"They're dead," said Lena. "I shot the sirens with my bow."

"Sirens?" yelled Captain Briggs who overheard their conversation.

[122]

"The north sea is filled with them," said Lena.

"I've never run into sirens before," said Captain Briggs. "How close to death did we get?"

"Close," replied Lena. The next two days of travel were quite boring for the group. There was nothing for them to do on the boat, and most of them ended up feeling sea sick. When the boat arrived at Freltus, it travelled up the river to Harlem. When it arrived there, the five companions said farewell to the captain and entered the city. Kailan made it the group's top priority to visit Bailan first before anything else was done. As they entered Machesney Hall, Kailan came upon a familiar and almost heart-warming sight. The old men in the building were busy running around, searching for papers and other documents. One of the men noticed Kailan and his friends and recognised the boy.

"He's returned!" yelled the man. Just then, Bailan came walking out of Tanier's office and noticed the group of adolescents standing by the doorway. He rushed over and greeted Kailan.

"You've made it," said Bailan ecstatically. "Did you come across any troubles on your way?" The group let out a laugh. "I'll take that as a yes then."

"Everybody, this is Bailan," said Kailan.

Bailan didn't realise that Thorstein was alive at first and was shocked when he bent down to shake the apprentice's hand.

"My name is Thorstein," said the giant. After him was Lena.

[123]

"Hello, I'm Lena." She held out her hand to shake Bailan's hand, but instead, he bent down and kissed it.

"I'm Guin!" yelled the little man, waving his hand in the air.

"It's nice to meet you," replied Bailan as he shook the boy's hand. As he stepped in front of Viktor to shake his hand, Bailan noticed something odd. Viktor just looked around the room, not with amazement, but it seemed as though he was being bored by everything. Bailan held out his hand to Viktor.

"You must be Viktor," said Bailan. The other boy turned his head and faced Bailan.

"I am." He grabbed a hold of Bailan's hand and squeezed tightly. Bailan backed away from Viktor and situated himself in front of Kailan again.

"Well... Your room is still available, along with others for your friends as well," said Bailan. "If you would like to show your friends to their rooms, I would then ask you to meet me and Mr. Frost in his office." Kailan nodded and started walking towards the bedrooms. Kailan left his friends in their rooms and returned to the main room. From there, he made his way to the office. He knocked once.

"Who is it?" said Tanier.

"Kailan Gallot sir," replied the boy.

"Come in, come in," said Tanier excitedly. Kailan opened the door and sat across from the Arch Chancellor's desk. Bailan stood next to the Arch Chancellor, rummaging through a number of documents. "Bailan tells me that you had some troubles on your journeys." Kailan nodded.

"Yes sir," he replied.

"Please, don't call me sir. Right now, you might as well call me by my first name," replied the Arch Chancellor. "Now… what would those problems that you dealt with possibly be?"

"Well… first there were goblins in Achland. Then there were some drunks that we had to deal with in Thoria. It turned out that they were from the Black Allegiance…"

"Stop," said Tanier. He waved Bailan over. The boy lowered his head and listened to Tanier's instructions. He left the room in a hurry. "What do you know about the Black Allegiance?" questioned Tanier.

"Thorstein told me that they are a group of mercenaries that are very dangerous," replied Kailan.

"Your friend is partially right," replied the Arch Chancellor. Bailan returned with a large book and placed it in front of Kailan. He started flipping pages until he came to one that Kailan had seen before. "What does that say?"

"Well… it's written in Feltsch," said Kailan. "It says something about an alliance of evil beings."

"What would Black Allegiance be in Feltsch?" questioned Tanier.

"SCHWARTZ KUNGE," replied Kailan. The Arch Chancellor pointed back at the page in the book.

"SCHWARTZ ARKETSEN actually," replied Tanier. The book said almost the exact same thing.

"What does it say?" questioned Kailan.

[125]

"It tells of how there was once an evil that roamed the world. There was a very large battle thousands of years ago. The Black Allegiance was the name of the group of people that sided with the evil. Goblins, who were just becoming what they are now, lead the armies. They sided with trolls, ogres, vampires, ghouls, demons, and even men. The war raged on for years until the Black Allegiance was defeated. Since then, there have been other battles. Some say that the Black Allegiance still lives and fights for the evil, but others try not to think about it. The truth is what is scary though, being that every battle that had been fought by the Black Allegiance since the original battle has been in a certain place."

"Where's that?" questioned Kailan.

"There is an island in the Gardaign Ocean," replied Tanier.

"Why do they fight there?" asked Kailan.

"On the island is a tunnel that leads to the original source of the evil," said Tanier. It is what let out the evil in the first place. The surviving members of the Black Allegiance made it their duty to amass another army, waiting for their final battle."

"Why don't you just send some armies there and guard it?" questioned Kailan.

"When I found out about this information, that idea was my original thought. However, I have found out more information. I found out what happened to Orpeth Armenen."

"Wasn't he murdered?" questioned Kailan.

[126]

"No," replied Tanier. "He just disappeared. His death was faked, but it was quite obvious that he didn't really die. Orpeth was ready to make the ultimate army, to defeat the evil once and for all. Somehow, he looked into the future and saw you and your friends. He knew that you and the others were the most powerful warriors ever."

They cannot release the evil, but they can protect it."

"What is exactly that you are asking of me?" questioned Kailan.

"I am asking you and your friends to lead our armies against the evil," said Tanier.

"Are you serious?"

"The Black Allegiance found you many times, didn't they?" said Tanier. Kailan looked puzzled, but responded to find an answer.

"It seemed as though they were following us at one point."

"They know who you are Kailan. I'm sorry, but it is already too late," said Tanier. "You must end the evil so that you and your friends may live." Kailan looked down at his hands. He started fidgeting. The nervousness was now setting in. "There is something that I need you and your friends to do first though." Kailan looked up at the Arch Chancellor. "There are five artefacts that you must find. Each one will help you and your friends in battle." Kailan stood up, and walked out of the office. He had no expression on his face, and every limb on his body was stiff and rigid. He made it to his room and lay down on the

[127]

bed. He awoke later that night to the sound of footsteps. As he opened his eyes, he saw Lena tiptoeing towards the bed.

"What are you doing here?" questioned Kailan. It wasn't until Lena was standing in front of him that he noticed the tears. "Did you have another nightmare?" Lena nodded. "Come in then." Kailan pulled away the blanket and let Lena under. He wrapped his arms around her and kissed her neck gently. He looked forward and stared into the darkness. Taking a small journey was something easy to do, but leading the army of armies was much different. He was only eighteen. Such responsibilities should not be placed on a boy of that age. He did some thinking, but finally came to a conclusion. When he awoke the next morning, Lena was still there with him. He caressed her long hair and held her close to him. She turned over and stared into his eyes.

"I'm ready to fight along with you," said Lena.

"What?" questioned Kailan.

"You talk in your sleep," replied Lena. Kailan smiled at Lena and placed his hand on the side of her head and kissed her. When the group met up with Tanier Frost again, Kailan and the Arch Chancellor explained to the rest of the group what was happening. Thorstein thought of it as an adventure, Guin didn't really have a choice because he would have been forced to by the Wizards' Guild anyways, and Viktor had nowhere else to go. Tanier handed Kailan two maps that showed where they needed to go.

"The artefacts have magical properties," said Tanier.

"They will help you in the battle and along your journeys as well." The word "magic" put a smile on Guin's face as wells as a small one on Viktor's as well. Tanier decided to give the group a few days to tour the city and take a rest from all of the travelling that they had done. Tanier supplied the group with an extra two horses for Lena and Viktor to ride. When they were ready to leave, the group, along with Tanier and Bailan, left for the harbour. When they reached it, they found Captain Briggs' ship still in the port. Kailan informed Tanier about Captain Briggs' generosity from earlier, and he decided to grant the captain the opportunity of taking the friends to their destinations.

"It would be a great honour to help you personally," said Captain Briggs. "I just hope that my services will benefit your voyagers."

"We will pay you out of the royal treasury," said Tanier. "For a deed such as this on such a short notice, you rightly deserve it."

"What about my men?" questioned the captain.

"They will be paid twice the amount all together," replied Tanier. "That means a gold piece every two weeks."

"They won't need to work for me when this job is done," joked Captain Briggs. As the group left the port, they waved goodbye to the Arch Chancellor and Bailan. They were off to new lands that none of them had ever been to before. Captain Briggs was even unfamiliar with where they were travelling to. Only Thorstein and Guin had ever been taught of what they might encounter, but they only had vague ideas.

[129]

Before they left, Kailan wrote a letter to his father, explaining what had happened so far. Tanier said that he would send one of his messengers to take it back to Helforth. As the boat sailed away, the only person on the boat that wasn't nervous was the crew and Viktor. Kailan and the other friends felt almost sad to leave their home of Arlbega. They were now off on a new journey, one that would give certain meaning to their lives, and fulfil answers. Their destination was the great mountain continent of Karnok. From ocean to ocean, all that would be seen on the land were giant mountains. They were the home to dwarfs, mountainfolk, giants, and golems. On the other hand, they were also home to goblins, trolls, and ogres. Not to mention ghouls, ghosts, demons, and other creatures that lurked within the darkness. There, the group would find the first two items that the group was looking for. It took about two weeks for the group to finally reach Karnok. They came upon a small harbour in the town of Graile in Tarthis. The people there did not seem as though they mingled well with the mountainous area. Their town stopped about two miles from the first rock. It was one of the only spots on Karnok that wasn't covered in rock and stone.

"Me and the boys will stay with the ship until you return," said Captain Briggs.

"That may be a month or two away," replied Kailan.

"We will meet you at the harbour in Drailnott then," said Briggs. Drailnott was the capital of Tarthis. It was on the opposite side of the continent as Graile and was built at the edge of a very large forest. As the group journeyed through the mountains on the first day, they came upon the grand sight of the inner mountains. The roads through the mountains were shrouded in an eerie mist. Many of the trees seemed dead and lifeless. It was strange that the group did not see much moss either. It was quite hard for Kailan to understand the map that he had been given. He wasn't able to tell where he was going, or where he came from, just because the mist was so thick. When he looked down at the map, he noticed something strange. The mist had made the map a little damp, but that was a good thing. For some reason, the water revealed words near the group's places of interest. Only Guin and Thorstein knew the language that they were written in, but even they had problems trying to read the writing.

"This word means 'Titan'," said Guin.

"No it doesn't," replied Thorstein.

"See how the letter hooks just there?" Guin responded.

"Oh now I see." They then looked at the next word. "Sorcerer," cried out Thorstein.

"I don't get it," said Guin as he looked up at the others. Kailan took a step back.

"It makes perfect sense," said Kailan. "There are five locations that we must visit. Each of them has an artefact that we need to find." He pointed at the map and the word which was translated into "Sorcerer". "The artefact that lays there must be for Guin, the other one is for Thorstein."

"What about you, me, and Viktor?" questioned Lena. Kailan pulled out another map.

[131]

"These must be for us," said Kailan as he pointed down at the other locations. "Tanier said that these items would benefit us along our journey, and even more in the final battle." Guin leaned in and started translating the words.

"Archer, Champion, and Shadow," the young wizard said. Kailan gave the boy a puzzled look.

"What does it mean by champion?" questioned Kailan. "I haven't won anything."

"Champion could also mean hero," replied Guin. "Possibly leader even." A smile began to grow on Kailan's face.

"I have an idea," said Kailan as he backed away from the map. "I suggest that we split up into two groups. Viktor and Lena will go with Thorstein to the city of Grol, while I travel with Guin to Kelenath. We will be back on the boat in much less time. We'll meet in the city of Alabeth, right before finding Viktor's item."

"Are you sure that that is a wise decision?" questioned Thorstein.

"What is the matter with it?" replied Kailan.

"If we end up in a fight we will have a better chance of losing if we are split up," said Thorstein.

"I don't think that we will have any problems," said Kailan. "Besides, if we do run into anything that you don't think you can handle, you can always run." The group decided that it was best for them to wait until the next morning to separate. The friends found a spot to rest for the night and made camp. They had enough food on them to last them a number of days, so none of them decided to hunt, seeing as that wouldn't be a good idea in the thick fog. Kailan sat against one of the boulders, pulled out his sword, and started sharpening it. As he slid the rock along the blade, he looked up and saw Lena standing a few feet in front of him. She sat down beside Kailan and looked at him in a way that she never had before.

"Why are you sending me with Viktor and Thorstein?" she demanded.

"For two reasons," replied Kailan. "I don't trust Guin with a map, and I think that Thorstein and Viktor will need more help on their journey."

"Why not send Viktor with Guin, and you come with me and Thorstein?" questioned Lena.

"I don't trust Viktor with a map either," replied Kailan.

"He got us to the harbour in Letania," said Lena.

"We took one road to get there," replied Kailan. "It isn't that hard to follow one road."

"Is there no other way that this can work?" questioned Lena.

"We will be together again in about a week or two," said Kailan. "Don't worry. Nothing will happen to me or Guin." There was something about Lena that was starting to bother Kailan. He knew that she loved him and wanted to stay close, but he found that whenever she had a chance, she would be right with Kailan. She was never alone anymore, but almost always at Kailan's side. When the next morning came around, Kailan and Guin left the rest of the group first thing. They had travelled for another hour before Guin's stomach started rumbling. The trip to Kelenath was the shorter of the two. That was another reason why Kailan wanted to go with Guin instead of Thorstein and Viktor. The two boys could spend less time travelling, and more time learning about the item that they would find in Kelenath. As one of the original cities of magic, Kelenath was filled with wizards, mages, and other sorcerers that didn't use witchcraft. Guin would feel somewhat at home, but Kailan would be quite lost in the city. The city was said to be one of the first ever built on the planet. No one knows when it was built, or who built it. The first known settlers found it abandoned, but in perfect shape. The mysteries that surround the city cannot be answered, and never would in the future. People from afar would come to learn, practise, and even show off their magical skills. Every now and then however, witches, warlocks, and even dark wizards, would sneak into the city. Sometimes they would try to learn certain spells so that they could become stronger, while others might be there only to shop for ingredients or spell books for magic. There would be the odd time when one of these evildoers would actually cause harm to the city or its citizens. There was the occasional destruction of buildings, but the worst thing to ever happen to the city was when poisonous snakes were summoned from the darkness. One night, they slipped through the city unnoticed, biting people as they went along. It was only after a few hours of the whole ordeal that someone finally spotted the snakes and killed them. More than a hundred people were found dead the next morning. Since then, the city doubled their security and searches people's belongings as they enter and exit the city. From that point on, there have been no more events of that subject matter. Kailan and Guin were no longer blinded by the fog and mist. The sky became clear and the sun shone through brightly. It was then that they came upon the first of their many obstacles. They stepped off their horses and looked ahead. A large creature, unknown to both Kailan and Guin, stood over a dead body, eating what was left of the remains. It was the sight of the mutilated body that set Guin's stomach off. He quickly turned to the side and started vomiting. Kailan stepped forward as to prevent himself from smelling the barf. The strange creature turned towards the two companions after hearing the sounds of Guin's gagging. It was a large, hairy creature. It had two large, black, soulless eyes that were spaced very close together. The mouth of the beast was filled with many long, sharp pointed teeth that were covered in blood. The exact height of the creature was unknown, but it cleared Kailan's height by at least a head. It produced a low growl before letting out a mighty roar at the top of its lungs. Kailan's sword was already out at the first moment that he saw the creature, but it didn't seem as though it had seen Kailan's blade. It charged without hesitation and made a quick swipe for Kailan's face. What was strange about the creature is that it slightly resembled that of a human. The size of the legs and arms were completely proportional compared to the torso. As Kailan blocked the first attack, he backed off. It stepped closer and closer to Kailan and Guin. For each step that it took, Kailan took two to match it.

Every attack that the creature made was quickly blocked by Kailan. When Guin stopped vomiting, the creature was still standing in front of the two boys. Kailan hadn't made a single cut in the beast, but had only prevented it from attacking him. Something in the boy's mind was telling him not to kill the creature, not even to injure it. The beast stopped as it saw Guin inch closer. The darkness in the creature's eyes left and was filled with fear, rather than anger. It slowly backed away from Guin with its arms in front of it.

"I don't understand," said Kailan. Guin stepped out from behind Kailan and walked closer to the beast.

"I think that it's afraid of me," said Guin. He held out his hand and created a small fireball. It was then that Guin was sure of the beast's thoughts. It dashed away from the two boys, leaving the dead body behind.

"It's seen magic before," said Kailan. "As a matter of fact, it has seen wizards before."

"It must have bad experiences with magic," replied Guin. "Maybe it was a sorcerer's slave." Kailan walked towards the corpse. It was the body of a young man. He was around the same age as Kailan and Guin. On his shoulder, Kailan noticed an insignia on the man's shoulder. Four circles each placed at a corner of a square, all connected by one large circle.

"I've seen this before," said Guin. "I think that it is from a guard of the city of Kartol."

"Is it near?" questioned Kailan. "I left most of my food with the rest of the group."

[136]

"You don't want to go to Kartol," Guin responded. "Not a smart idea." Kailan looked away from the body and towards Guin.

"What's the matter with it?" questioned Kailan. Guin reached into his pocket, pulled out the magic bag, and from within it, he removed a book. The pages had indents in them starting at the beginning of the alphabet to the end. Guin ran his hand along the pages until he found the page that he was looking for, and opened the book. He handed the book off to Kailan, who began reading it. "I don't see what the problem is."

"Last line, fifth paragraph," said Guin. Kailan held his finger along the page and dragged it downwards.

"I understand now," said Kailan, closing the book. He handed it back to Guin, who placed it in the pouch. "We had better not mention our business while travelling through it then," said Kailan.

"We can't go through it," said Guin sternly. "We'll have to find a different way." Kailan shook his head as he brought out a very detailed map.

"There is no other way to get to Kelenath," said Kailan. He pointed at the map and held it in front of Guin's face. "We can't try to cross the mountains because of the horses. If we turn back to find a different trail, we would lose about three days' worth of travel.

"If we go through it, there will be no question about us being killed," replied Guin. "We have to find a different way."

"Can't we just go around the city when we get there?"

questioned Kailan.

"No, the city walls go from mountainside to mountainside," informed Guin. Kartol was filled with the vilest of men. It was a haven to outlaws, bandits, and robbers. For all Kailan and Guin knew, the Black Allegiance had men throughout the city. At some point, one of the boys made the suggestion that they should change their clothing to hide their identity. They were wanted by the Black Allegiance, and their appearances had become known. The two boys began to try on different types of clothing before they were happy with what they were wearing. Kailan hadn't changed much, but Guin had made a significant alteration. He went from looking like a wealthy scholar, to lowly beggar. When they reached the city, they each stepped off of their horses and grabbed the reins tightly. Their heads tilted upwards at the enormous gates that stood in front of them.

"Well, Guin," said Kailan. "Here we go."

*   *   *

Lena looked up at the morning sun and let out a long breath of air. Beside her was Kaela, busy pecking away at a mouse that she had caught. Lena placed her hand on the bird's head and started to pat its neck. The white eagle nestled closer to Lena and crawled under her arm. The girl looked down at the bird and gave another sigh of disappointment. "How am I supposed to do my job if he keeps running away," said Lena. Suddenly, the bird nipped one of Lena's fingers. She pulled it away and with the other hand, swatted at the bird. It took a few steps back and started screaming.

"What is it?" questioned Viktor as he walked over.

"I don't know," replied Lena. "One second I was petting her, the next she was trying to bite me and making those sounds. Viktor took a step towards the bird.

"I used to take care of some of the animals where I used to live," said Viktor. "I could try to calm her down."

"By all means," replied Lena. Viktor knelt down beside the bird and placed a hand on its head and closed his eyes. There was a quick flash of light and Viktor fell backwards, but the bird stopped making the sounds.

"Are you okay?" questioned Lena as she bent down to help Viktor up.

"I'm fine," said Viktor. "And so is your bird."

"What was that light?" questioned Lena.

"I picked up bits and pieces of magic throughout my life," said Viktor. "I tapped into her mind to see what was bothering her."

"You can do magic?" said Lena in astonishment. "What else can you do?" Viktor gave a large grin.

"Nothing too spectacular, but it is helpful every now and then," replied Viktor. Lena held out her hand to Viktor and pulled him up off the ground. The boy patted his pants, removing the dirt. As he looked up, Lena was looking directly into his eyes.

"How was your life before the vampires attacked your village?" questioned Lena. Viktor smiled again.

"My life was rather boring actually. My parents had died a few years before from a different vampire attack. I lived by myself, honing my skills as a hunter, perfecting my accuracy with my daggers." Thorstein walked over after clearing up the rest of the campsite.

"Are you two ready to leave now?" questioned Thorstein. Lena took a step back from Viktor and looked up at Thorstein.

"Yes... I'm ready," she said. The three adventurers made sure that they had everything that they needed and hopped on their mounts. Thorstein pulled out a map and gazed at it for a second before realising where they were positioned on it. He looked up and chose the road that best suited their direction. As the group ventured on, Thorstein began to realise how quiet the group was without Kailan and Guin. They were the two that talked the most. Kailan, knowing most about the journey than any of the other companions, always needed to go into great detail, and would remain talking for a decent amount of time. Guin, on the other hand, would talk about random things. Sometimes he would tell stories about his time at the Wizards' Guild in Alandra, while other times, talking about certain foods that he liked. The group had reached a small creek just after noon time. They stopped, and let their horses and the one dornbeast, sit for a while. Viktor sat beside his horse, spinning a dagger in the palm of his hand, never laying an eye on it. He didn't really seem to move, except for the slight movement of his fingers. He looked ahead and saw a small twig sticking just out of a tree branch about twelve feet off the ground. Behind the tree, about ten feet away, was the stump of a dead tree. In the blink of an eye, he had two more knives in his hand. Without any warning, the blades were flying in the air. Each of them cut an equal section of the twig and landed in the direct centre of the stump. The blades landed in a perfect position according to each other to create a triangle. Viktor walked over and grabbed the knives from the stump.

"If only there was a real challenge somewhere," said Viktor. As he turned away from the tree, he noticed a couple of ducks landing in the calm stream next to the horses. A smile appeared on his face and he held back his hand, ready to throw the blade.

"I wouldn't do that if I were you," said Thorstein, grabbing a hold of Viktor's arm.

"Why not?" questioned Viktor.

"Why would you?" replied Thorstein.

"I need to practice," said Viktor.

"Wouldn't it be smarter to go after something that wasn't alive?" questioned Thorstein.

"Moving targets present more of a challenge," said Viktor. Thorstein let go of the Viktor's arm, but by that time, the ducks had already swum downstream. Lena walked over to her horse, grabbed a hold of the reins, and hopped upon its back.

"Well, we should be off if we want to meet Kailan and Guin in Drailnott," said Lena. The two boys packed up their things and mounted their rides. The group continued to venture on the designated roads that were clearly marked. Anything that they were unsure about was ignored. When the three companions reached their first town in the day's travel, they decided that it was safest to rest there and spend the night at an inn, without having to worry about highwaymen, or other robbers. Thorstein left the other two, and decided to sleep under the stars, just a little ways outside of the town. By the time the campfire had gone out, Thorstein was fast asleep. A dream came to him. The giant was standing in the middle of an open field. There were mountains all around, but they would take almost an hour's walk to reach. It wasn't until a few minutes later that Thorstein realised that there was a tree quite close to him. It would provide shade, and possibly even food. When he reached it, Thorstein noticed that there were large fruits hanging off of it. He grabbed one, rubbed it on his shorts, and took a bite out of it. The rancid taste of the fruit caused Thorstein to involuntarily spit it out. He looked down at the fruit and noticed that it was changing colours.

"What is this?" he questioned. He reached his arm back and launched the fruit into the air. Suddenly, there was screaming behind him. A young girl grabbed Thorstein's arm and tried shaking it.

"Help!" she screamed at the top of her lungs. "Wake

[142]

up!" The dream faded into reality and Thorstein realised what was wrong. Parts of the town were ablaze. The little girl wrapped her arms around Thorstein's leg as he stood up.

"What is the matter?" asked Thorstein.

"Dragon!" cried the girl. Thorstein hurriedly walked the girl behind a pile of boulders.

"Wait here, you'll be safe." Thorstein picked up his axe and rushed into the town with the roaring flames towering over him.

*   *   *

A guard came to the gates and opened up one of the small entrance doors. "No trespassers!" yelled the guard, holding a spear at Kailan and Guin.

"We're not trespassers," replied Guin. "We're travellers."

"What business do you have here?" questioned the guard.

"Kartol is on our way to Kelenath," Guin replied. The guard quickly slammed the door in front of Kailan and Guin. The two boys looked at each other out of confusion. The large gate door started to swing open. "That was easier than I thought," said Guin. The two boys moved towards the opening. Suddenly, a group of armed guards ran out through the gates and

[143]

surrounded the two boys. Kailan went for his sword, but Guin waved him off. "We don't want to make enemies with the wrong people," said Guin. Kailan nodded and hopped off his horse.

"What is the reason for these guards?" asked Kailan. One of the men stepped forward and spoke up.

"For conspiracy to engage in dark magic, and the sabotage of Kelenath," said the man. Kailan and Guin jumped back in shock.

"There must be some misunderstanding," said Guin. "We are just travellers!" One of the guards hit Kailan over the head, knocking him out.

"You are a dark wizard," said one of the guards. "I can tell they come by here all the time." They grabbed Guin and Kailan, and brought them to the dungeon. When Kailan came to, he looked around and gazed upon the underground room. Almost everything in it was made out of stone. The cell bars were made out of a rusty metal however.

"Let me out!" yelled Kailan as he ran for the bars, shaking them violently. "We didn't do anything!"

"Oh shut up," said one of the guards, laughing at Kailan.

"It's not smart to anger me," said Kailan. The man stepped closer to Kailan and stared at his for a second. Then he spat in Kailan's face. The boy reached through the bars, trying to grab the guard, but Guin held him back. The guard left, laughing as he walked up and out of the dungeon.

"It's no use," said a voice from the dark corner of the

cell.

"Who's there?" demanded Kailan, cleaning his face. All that he could see was a faint shadow.

"You tell me your name," said the man in the corner.

"I asked you first," replied Kailan.

"That isn't the way things work around here," said the man. Guin stepped in front of Kailan and held out his hand. A small light came out from his hand and moved slowly towards the corner, lighting up the man's face. It was well worn. There were a few scars, but you could only really see them if you were searching for them. He had short, dark hair that swayed to the side, and a small, pointy beard protruding from his chin.

"My name's Kailan," said the boy.

"Glad to meet you Kailan," said the man. "My name is Craghoff Forten, but everyone calls me Crag."

"Why are you in here?" questioned Kailan.

"Same reason you are," replied Crag.

"We're not what they say we are," said Kailan.

"I already told you that it's no use," said Crag. "Nobody else really cares about why anyone else is in here. All that they care about is when they are going to get out, and when we get our meals."

"How do people get out of here?" questioned Kailan.

"Well…," thought Crag. "That's a good question. I don't think I've ever seen someone actually leave this place."

"How long have you been here?" questioned Guin.

"It's been almost a month," said Crag. The two boys

[145]

looked at each other and gulped.

"We can't stay here for more than day!" yelled Kailan.

"Be quiet," whispered Guin. "We don't want the guards to come back." A smile grew upon Crag's face.

"Don't worry boys," said Crag. "Me and the other men have been working on something and I think that tonight is an excellent day to make it work." Guin and Kailan leaned in.

"What do you mean?" whispered Guin curiously.

"A way out," said Crag.

The rest of the afternoon was spent explaining the plan to the two boys. There were some things that were self-explanatory, and others that weren't quite so. "There is a guard that goes up the stairs every night, after he's finished his jug of mead," said Crag. "When he leaves, one of the men will pry the cell door off, and sneak up after the guard. Most likely there will be a fight, so we will have to do this quickly."

"How will we get out of here?" questioned Kailan. "The town is filled with guards."

"Once I have my staff, there will be nothing to stop us," said Crag. They waited till nightfall, most of them slept until they were ready for the attack. Kailan and Guin watched as the guard slowly, stumbled up the stairs, nearly falling down at one point. The other prisoners were quick at their job. They sprang out of the dungeon, and attacked the guard from behind. One of them came back down the stairs and handed Crag his staff between the bars. The man held out the staff and a blue and purple glow appeared from it. Sounds of horns and trumpets resounded from outside the building.

"They're coming!" yelled Kailan. Crag's staff let out a bolt of lightning, which hit the wall of the dungeon, and obliterated it. The Crag and the two boys ran out of the dungeon, grabbed their things from the upper level and made for the stables. Every prisoner from every dungeon throughout the small city was running amok with guards chasing after them. The three friends hopped upon their horses and rode towards the city gates.

"Stand back!" said Crag. He held back his hands, and let a fierce ball off fire escape from his arms. It was bigger and more powerful than any of the ones that Guin had ever made before. The fireball crashed against the gate, bursting a hole through it. The two doors shuddered, and fell to the ground. Crag and the two boys fled the city, and had reached safety in a short time.

*   *   *

Thorstein gazed upon the giant beast as it strolled out from behind one of the burning homes. They looked at each other. It was going to be a battle between beast and man. Thorstein was a bit unfamiliar with dragons. One of his professors kept a small one as a pet when Thorstein was still in school. He studied them a lot, for fear of actually needing to fight one someday. The dragon quickly hid behind another

[147]

building, escaping Thorstein's sight. The dragon obviously had the upper hand at this point. Thorstein's vision was slightly blinded by the brightness of the fire, and the smoke that clouded the parts that were not ablaze. He quickly dashed through the town, trying to find the lizard again, but he couldn't find it. Suddenly, from behind him, Thorstein heard the terrible cry of a man in the dragon's clutches. As he turned, he came upon the dragon, trying to bite off the leg of a man that was still alive. The boy threw his axe at the dragon, hoping to stop it. The axe bounced off the creature, but knocked it backwards as well. A dragon's scales were some of the hardest known materials known to race. A suit of armour made from dragon scales was quite heavy, but offered protection from almost any weapon. The axe did little damage to the beast because of this Thorstein ran towards the dragon and pounced on it. He grabbed its neck, along with one of its wings. He was tossed around violently before being thrown off and into a building. Thorstein picked himself up from the ash and rubble, and grabbed his axe. This time, it was the dragon's turn to attack. It unleashed a burst of fire as it came closer. Thorstein tried blocking it with his axe, hiding the rest of his body behind a building. He then charged the creature, pulling his axe back and releasing it with immense power. The dragon was knocked into the air and landed on the street next to where it was originally standing. It arose to find Thorstein making another attempt at rushing it. The beast spun on its back, and tripped Thorstein with its tail. Both were on the ground at this point. The boy rolled over, grabbed the dragon by its mouth, and lifted it up. The dragon was now on its hind legs, trying to get out of Thorstein's grasp. The young man, however, knew something that the dragon did not expect him to know. Dragons are very similar to certain snakes in the fact that they can project fluids from their mouths. They have two glands in the top of their mouth. Each secretes a special fluid that is highly reactive to the other. This is what creates the fire that comes from the dragon's mouth. Like a snake, it spits the two liquids at its enemies. Thorstein knew that by blocking one of the liquids from releasing, the dragon would not be able to produce any fire. He quickly placed one of his fingers over the one hole, and started pulling apart the mandible from the top part of the skull. He could feel the dragon struggling as the pressure behind his finger become greater and greater. A small amount of the liquid leaked down into the throat of the dragon, and mixed with the other fluid. The dragon's mouth was now on fire, but Thorstein was in the most danger at this point. With all of his remaining strength, Thorstein pulled apart the two parts of the head. It squirmed for a very short moment before lying motionless. He picked up his axe and chopped off the head of the dragon. With one try, he pulled most of the flesh away from the skull.

"I never thought that I would get a trophy like this," said Thorstein with a smile on his face. As he looked around, the smile quickly became a frown. The town had been completely destroyed, and there was no sight of Lena or Viktor anywhere. Thorstein let out a long sigh, and walked back to the pile of rocks that the little girl had hidden behind earlier. He noticed that she was gone. Looking around frantically, he threw the dragon on the rocks and searched for the little girl. In a tree leaning over the rocks, the girl sat patiently. She jumped off one of the branches and swung her arms around Thorstein.

"Thank-you!" she cried. The girl turned towards the dragon's corpse and backed away.

"Don't worry," said Thorstein. "It's completely dead." Thorstein placed the dragon skull his shoulder again and walked with the little girl out of the town. He untied the dornbeast from a nearby tree, and placed the dragon's skull on it. He picked up the little girl, and held her in his arms.

The next day, Thorstein came across a group of survivors from the village. Among them were Lena and Viktor. "Are you two okay?" questioned Thorstein. The two friends nodded.

"We thought that we'd lost you," said Lena. Thorstein called the dornbeast over and showed his companions his new prize.

"You actually defeated it?" said Viktor. "I'm somewhat impressed."

"It's not that hard to fight a dragon," said Thorstein. "It's more honour than killing helpless ducks for fun as well." Viktor smiled through his teeth at Thorstein and turned away. Lena noticed the girl in Thorstein's arms and held her hand.

"What happened to her?" asked Lena with concern. Thorstein looked down at the little girl.

"She woke me up when the village was under attack,"

said Thorstein. "I couldn't find her parents near the village."
Lena pointed to the group of people near them.

"These are some of the survivors," said Lena. 'They said that any others would end up travelling to a nearby village just a few days away."

*　　　　　　*　　　　　　*

"So Kailan and Guin, where might you two be off to?" questioned Crag as they packed up their things the morning after the escape from Kartol.

"I'm pretty sure that we already explained that back in the jail cell," replied Kailan.

"We aren't surrounded by enemies right now, and you can trust me," said Crag. Kailan looked over at Guin, who was still unsure about following Crag the rest of the way to Kelenath.

"What I told you already is all that you need to know," said Kailan.

"What you have told me already is neither the truth, nor helpful for either of us," said Crag. Kailan glanced over at Guin quickly. The young wizard nodded his head and looked back at Crag.

"We were sent by Arch Chancellor Tanier Frost of Arlbega to retrieve an item from Kelenath," said Kailan, feeling as though he had been deprived of his security.

[151]

"Tanier Frost...," said Crag. "Now, I haven't heard that name in a long time?"

"I'm pretty sure that he's famous in these parts as well," said Kailan. "The leader of Arlbega is surely known by many." Crag snapped his fingers and pointed at Kailan.

"No, I know him personally," said Crag. "We both studied at the university in Kelenath." A smile appeared on Crag's face as he let out a sigh. "Tanier and I were great friends back in the day. We were the best in our classes, and neither of us ever got into any trouble. Well... that was because no one ever found out." He turned to Kailan and Guin again. "You see, Tanier and I were not just the smartest out of all the other students, but the most talented at being able to cast spells. It was only until our last year of school that a gap appeared between us. Tanier was into the politics, and I was more into wielding magic." Crag looked up at the sky and let out a long sigh. "We went our separate ways, and never really saw each other after that." It took a bit of time before Crag seemed to return to reality.

"Why are you here?" questioned Kailan.

"I already told you," said Crag. "I'm here for the same reason that you are." The two boys looked at each other and then back at Crag with confusion.

"What do you mean?" asked Guin.

"I'm pretty sure that you have already explained that for me," said Crag.

"What you have told us is neither the truth, nor will it

[152]

help either of us," replied Kailan. Crag smiled and pointed at Kailan.

"You learn quickly," said Crag. The group hopped upon their horses and started down the road. "I was captured because I walked around with a black staff."

"That seems a bit odd," replied Guin. "There isn't a crime against that."

"No, but people can be arrested for suspicion of dealing with black magic," replied Crag. "I guess that that is why you two were arrested as well." Crag's horse came to a sudden stop. The wizard hopped off of his horse, staring at the ground. Kailan and Guin turned back to see what was distracting the man.

"What is it?" questioned Kailan. Crag knelt down and cleared some of the leaves and sticks off of the road. Kailan then noticed the imprint in the dirt. "It's a footprint." The mysteries behind Crag only seemed to become stronger, even with the answers presenting themselves. The wizard placed his hand within the footprint, and muttered a few words as the impression instantly began to glow. Kailan and Guin both looked along the side of the road with amazement. Every footprint that was left within the dirt that was identical to the other lit up as well.

"Where'd you learn that trick?" questioned Guin.

"Gorgul's spell book," replied Crag. Guin's face changed from excitement and curiosity to fear. There was a good reason for that. Gorgul was an infamous wizard that would unleash scourges upon his enemies; wiping out numerous kingdoms in a matter of weeks.

"How did you come by it?" questioned Guin.

"After me and a group of other wizards killed Gorgul, I took his spell book and studied it," replied Crag. Guin let out a sigh of relief. He had fears that Crag was an apprentice of Gorgul.

"Didn't Gorgul die almost a hundred years ago though?" questioned Guin. Kailan stood out of the conversation. He knew nothing much of the stories of wizards and their legends.

"There were rumours of his death a long time ago, but all were wrong. We stumbled upon his home, and fought him to the death."

"Who were these other wizards that you went with?" questioned Guin.

"We were all taking classes at the university," said Crag. He held his hand to his head, trying to remember. "Tanier was one of them. There were three others; Dolci Garbote, Finn Clayse, and Bailan Nothos." Kailan's head made a quick turn.

"Bailan was there?" said Kailan. "The same Bailan Nothos that works as Tanier's page?"

"Yes…" replied Crag.

*   *   *

A young Crag walked up to the small door and opened

[154]

it, darkness filling the entire chamber. As he snapped his finger, he noticed two glowing eyes staring at him. He held out his hand, lighting up the room, right when it jumped out at him. Crag jumped backwards, swearing as he fell to the ground. Dolci and Finn stood behind Crag laughing.

"It seems as though Crag's been scared by the grounds keeper's ferret again," laughed Finn. The two boys stood just a little higher than Crag. Dolci stood at six feet even, while Finn stood at about six foot two. Finn had short brown hair, while Dolci had blond hair that went just below his ears. Dolci and Finn were best friends and had been since they first met each other at the university.

"Get lost," said Crag as he lifted himself up. "I was told to find the stupid ferret for the grounds keeper."

"You weren't told to piss it off," giggled Dolci. Crag gave a sarcastic smile before lighting a fire by Dolci's foot.

"Shit!" yelled Finn. He stepped back and held out his hand. Suddenly, a gush of water came from his palm, knocking Dolci to the ground and getting him soaked. "Sorry about that," said Finn as he helped Dolci back up. "I'm not quite used to these water spells yet." Dolci held his arm over Finn's head and wringed out his sleeve. Meanwhile, Crag was making his way back to the main hall of the university. As he stepped through the door, he found Tanier standing by one of the pillars with a book in his hands. As Crag neared Tanier, he noticed that the book was not a spell book, but a book about politics instead.

"Why are you reading that?" questioned Crag. Tanier

[155]

looked up from the book and closed it.

"Lately I've felt the urge to become a politician rather than a wizard," said Tanier. "I can make money and become quite powerful by being a politician." Crag laughed as he stepped backwards.

"Are you serious?" said Crag. "You won't get very far; the country is run by a king."

"I could go to Arlbega," replied Tanier. "Many years ago, their government slowly collapsed and it is now ruled by an Arch Chancellor."

"You seriously think that you are going to be chosen as Arch Chancellor?" laughed Crag.

"As a matter of fact, the last three Arch Chancellors have been random people that offered to take care of the job." A young boy rushed over to Crag and Tanier, grabbing both by the arm.

"Master Scholton wants to see both of you immediately," said the boy. Crag and Tanier followed the boy through the school corridors and hallways until they reached Master Scholton's office. Master Scholton met very few of the physical expectations of most newcomers. He was quite young to be the dean of a university. He was in his late-forties and his hair was only just starting to grey. He was also quite tall and muscular. Master Scholton showed Crag and Tanier to their chairs. It wasn't long before both Dolci and Finn were thrown into the room as well. They stood up, wiped themselves off, and each found a chair to sit on. It wasn't long before Bailan walked into the room as well.

"Well," said Master Scholton. "I believe that everyone is here right now, and we can get started." All five of the young men were quite confused. None of them even had a clue as to why they were there. "Each of you possesses a quality that the other professors and I have realised. Unfortunately, the university is no longer able to accommodate your education for the next five years." The five boys looked at each other with fear. "To make sure that your place in this school remains, the professors and I have agreed to send all five of you out on your own. We will provide you with supplies for you to live outside the grounds for at least a month, just until we can come up with enough funds to keep you here. We are giving you this chance first. If any of you shall not want to do this, your opportunity will be given to another student. You five were chosen first because you are the best at what you do." Bailan slowly raised his hand.

"What happens if we choose to stay?" questioned Bailan.

"You will remain here for the rest of the year, but after that, you will not be allowed to return."

"What happened to all of the money?" questioned Dolci. Master Scholton rubbed his forehead. "The money has been misplaced and there is not much that we can do about it."

"Sorry if I missed something, but you make it sound like there is going to be a lot of problems along the way," asked Tanier. Master Scholton sat on his chair behind his desk and leaned over it, with his arms holding him up.

"We chose you five because we have very little fear that you will fail," said Master Scholton.

"So you're saying that this is going to be a difficult journey," said Crag. Master Scholton nodded.

"Awesome!" yelled Finn. Both he and Dolci had very large smiles on their faces.

"That is the kind of behaviour that will get you into trouble young Finn Clayse," said Master Scholton. "You will need to be on your toes at all times." He leaned back in the chair and made sure to look all of the boys in the eyes. "What is it that you want?" The boys all looked at each other.

"Can we have a minute to talk it over?" questioned Tanier. Master Scholton nodded and left the room with the door closed behind him. The five boys huddled into a circle around each other.

"I'm in," said Finn proudly.

"Me too," added Dolci.

"I can't see why not," said Crag.

"I do have fears, but I'm going to do it anyways," said Tanier. The group of boys looked at Bailan.

"What the hell, I'm in!" he yelled. Master Scholton walked into the room immediately with the boy's bags already packed, waiting for them by the main entrance. The five boys stood up and left the room.

"We're leaving immediately?" questioned Bailan.

"We need you to leave as early as possible," said

Master Scholton.

"What's the hurry?" asked Finn. An unwanted expression appeared on Master Scholton's face.

"That is none of your concern at the moment," replied Master Scholton. The boys were herded towards the door, each of them with a bag and staff in their hands. They preferred not to wear their robes outside of the university grounds, so instead they wore their regular attire. A tunic, slacks, and a cloak was all that they really needed for clothes. The five boys began on their journey. They didn't know exactly where they were going, just that they were getting away and taking a break from the university. As they left the vicinity of the university, the five boys looked back at their home for the past eight years, and let out a sigh. Unlike Kailan and his friends, the five wizards had to venture on foot. They all stood in a perfect line in the open gateway.

"Well, this is it," said Crag.

"How about we all make a pledge," said Finn.

"What do you mean?" questioned Bailan.

With a big smile on his face, Finn responded. "None of us should die until we return!" Dolci and Crag both smacked Finn on the back of the head.

"That's a stupid idea you idiot," said Dolci. With their first step, the group realised what troubles were awaiting them in the future. They found themselves falling through a portal which had obviously been cast for them. The bright colours, as well as the shapes of the other portal passages, almost made a number of the boys feel sick. When they stopped falling and arrived at their destination, they regained their footing, picked themselves up, and brushed the dirt off themselves. As they looked up, their expressions changed drastically. They gasped as they looked at the landscape in front of them. Mountains as far as the eye could see. Above the mountains, dark clouds highlighted with shades of red. The five young wizards looked over the edge of the cliff that they were standing near. Fear shook all of them.

*　　　　　*　　　　　*

Thorstein knelt down beside Lena as she caressed the little girl's head. "How long has she been asleep?" asked Thorstein. Lena looked up with a smile.

"I didn't even notice that she had nodded off," whispered Lena. Ever since they had left the burning village behind, the little girl had treated Lena and Thorstein as caregivers. Never leaving their sight, the girl was always comfortably to have around as well. The three companions and the refugees were sitting around the fire, trying to create happy thoughts. Viktor sat opposite the fire to Thorstein and Lena. He didn't seem as though he wanted to be involved with the rest of the group, but rather hung back and just tossed his knives in the air to pass the time.

"I'm glad that you were on the list," said Lena to

Thorstein.

"What do you mean?" questioned Thorstein.

"You've been there for me and Kailan when we needed it since the beginning," said Lena. "We both think of you as a brother."

"Making people happy creates a feeling of happiness within you that cannot be achieved anywhere else," replied Thorstein.

"Does that make you selfish then?" questioned Lena.

"There is no such thing as being selfish I think," said Thorstein. "Every act is done for someone's gain. Not many people realise that however."

"It wasn't as deep as some of the other things that you say, but it made perfect sense," replied Lena. Thorstein smiled and walked away. He walked over to his dornbeast and lay down beside it. It wasn't until a short time later that he noticed that Viktor had been staring at Lena for some time. It wasn't a look that made Thorstein feel uneasy about Viktor, but there was something wrong.

As the blade landed back in Viktor's hand, he quickly pulled his wrist back and threw the blade past Lena's ear. She rolled over with the young girl protected under her. She looked up as the body fell just beside her. She let out a quick scream, waking the young girl up, before helping her to safety. There was a sudden commotion amongst the refugees. Some were screaming, some were wondering what happened. Thorstein and Viktor hurried over to the body. Viktor pulled out his throwing

[161]

knife and took a step back as the blood spurted out of the wound. Thorstein inspected the body and found what he had feared.

"How did you know that he was there?" questioned Thorstein. "It was pitch black."

"You couldn't see him?" asked Viktor. He smiled before turning back to the dead body lying in front of him. "The scout has been following us since we met up the day after the dragon went through the village."

"How do you know that?" interrogated Lena as she approached her two friends.

"I saw him not long after we found Thorstein," replied Viktor. "I thought that maybe he was just another villager for the past two days, but when I saw that smile on his face and the knife in his hand…"

"How does the Black Allegiance know where we are?" questioned Thorstein. "The last time that we dealt with them was back in Letania."

"Somehow they found us," said Lena. "We have to remain cautious as much as we can." One of the villagers walked up to the three adventurers and the body.

"What is it?" asked the man.

"We were being followed," said Viktor.

"By who?"

"All that you need to know is that we have this under control," replied Viktor. "We will stay awake and keep watch during the night." The group did just as Viktor had said. They took turns guarding the camp, with no sign of any trouble all

[162]

night. The eerie silence did give hint that the Black Allegiance was lurking somewhere still, watching them from afar. When dawn came upon the three companions and the villagers, they packed up their things and left. The sooner they could reach Grol, the better their lives would be. It was almost another full day of travelling before they reached the town that the villagers spoke of before. To the group's delight, most of the village had escaped the dragon. The girl's parents were waiting there too; for fear that their daughter had been killed. Many of the villagers thanked Thorstein and his friends for all that they did. They thanked Thorstein most of all for actually killing the dragon. For Thorstein, it was more of a prize than a duty. He could go back to his people and tell them the story of how he killed a dragon, and for proof, show them the clothing that he was hoping to make with its hide. The group rested for the night in the town and left early in the morning. They travelled for most of the day without stopping until long after noon. They had a quick dinner, but were off again until they were less than a day's travel from Grol.

*   *   *

Kailan, Guin, and Crag followed the set of tracks along the road until it broke off onto a path through the forest. "What are we tracking anyways?" questioned Guin.

[163]

"When I was taken prisoner, my assistant ran away," said Crag. "He's most likely killed a number of people by now."

"Why would he do that?" questioned Kailan.

"No real reason other than he's a Gnarlok," replied Crag. The two boys stood confused, looking at Crag. "Gnor Wildmen... you know, half man, half beast." The two boys still didn't know what Crag was talking about. "Don't worry, we're getting closer." The three men continued following the tracks until they came across the same creature that Kailan and Guin had scared away just before they were imprisoned. It's dark, bulbous eyes still seemed to dip into the boys' souls. Kailan unsheathed his sword and stood in front of Guin and Crag. He felt a hand on his shoulder, and then was pushed to the side. Crag stepped in front of the boys and walked over to the creature. "Dartann!" said Crag. He looked the creature in the eyes and snapped one of his fingers in front of its face. The creature took a step back and slowly curled up, leaning forward. Crag placed his hand on the creature's back.

"So this is your assistant?" questioned Guin.

"Assistant?" said a voice. "Is that what you called me?" Kailan and Guin backed away as the beast arose, revealing a much kinder face than before. The eyes were very much smaller, and the face was a man's.

"I want you two to meet my friend," said Crag. "This is Dartann."

"You ran away from us before," said Kailan.

"Your friend scared me," replied Dartann. "Crag asked

[164]

me to look out for other wizards and to steer clear of them."

"Why is that?" questioned Guin. He looked over at Crag.

"I'll tell you sometime later," answered Crag. "Right now, we need to continue on. This has already taken enough time out of our journey." The four men walked back to the road, and to their horses.

"Who's horse is Dartann going to ride?" questioned Guin. Crag laughed as he hopped upon his horse. He grabbed his staff and tapped Dartann lightly on the head. It was almost instantly that the beast-man changed into a horse. "How did you do that?" questioned Guin.

"I'm not going to tell you," replied Crag.

"You have to teach me, come on…" The men journeyed for the rest of the day, stopping twice for food and water. They went all the way until it was complete darkness and they could see no more. They set up a small camp, and rested for the night. Dartann told the other three about his time while Crag was locked up at the prison. He had killed two of the guards and made sure that none of the others came near him. It was somewhat strange for Kailan and Guin to be around Dartann. It wasn't the fact that he could be a civilised human or a wild beast, but rather the fact that he didn't wear much clothing, except for a loin cloth covering his groin. The hair that nearly fully covered his body was a light brown, almost orange colour. It was very thick, and only grew about a finger's length. That night, Kailan and Guin drifted off to sleep quite quickly. They

[165]

were comforted by the fact that they were quite close to their destination. They were almost two days away from reaching Kelenath. As the night grew darker, and Kailan's dreams become stronger within his mind, there was a commotion. Dartann was standing in front of Kailan and Guin, looking off into the forest. Crag was standing at the boys' heads with his staff in hand. Suddenly, a creature leapt from the bushes and brought Dartann to the ground. Kailan and Guin jumped to their feet and grabbed their weapons. Crag pointed his staff at the beast and hurled a ball of blue flame, knocking the creature off of Dartann. When Kailan and Guin looked at Dartann, they noticed that he had changed. His eyes were black again, and larger too. It was not Dartann that they worried about though. It was the werewolf that was standing almost twenty feet away from them. Dartann pounced on the werewolf and held it to the ground.

"We are very similar, you and I," said Dartann. "Listen to me… we are not enemies." The werewolf continued to struggle against Dartann, and eventually threw him off. Crag stepped closer to the werewolf and hit the tip of his staff against the beast's head, creating a flash of blue, and knocking the werewolf to the ground. Dartann again jumped on it, this time wrapping his arms around the werewolf's neck, slowly depriving it of air. "Stop," said Dartann. "You need to settle." Half a minute had gone bye before the werewolf lay motionless.

"Did you kill it?" questioned Kailan.

"I never kill another creature unless I must," replied

[166]

Dartann. The four men watched as the werewolf changed back into human form. A look of confusion appeared on the faces of Kailan and Guin. The werewolf had changed back into a young woman.

"I wasn't expecting that," said Kailan.

"Neither was I," added Crag. Dartann grabbed a blanket from Crag's equipment bag and laid it on the girl to cover her up.

*   *   *

It was a vision of hell for the five young men. The sky had been lit red because of the volcanoes and rivers of lava below. A layer of smoke hung just below the sky, but out of the boys' reach. Sharp, jagged rocks were everywhere, causing the wizards to worry about their footing.

"I don't think that this is the way," said Bailan. He took a step back, along with some of the other boys. Tanier pulled out the blank parchment that Master Scholton had given him just prior to their departure. As he looked upon it, he noticed that lines were faintly appearing. There was now a large, decorative arrow, pointing in the direction of the wasteland.

"The arrow is pointing in this direction, Bailan," said Tanier. Bailan walked in front of Tanier and grabbed the map. He turned the paper so that the arrow would point away from the

[167]

volcanoes, but to his shock and disappointment, the arrow turned and corrected itself.

"We'll just have to suck it up," said Dolci, taking the first step. The rest of the group followed, but with hesitance. For days, the group travelled through the land. They only slept where they knew they would not receive harm. If that meant travelling for an extra hour, then they would do so. They kept themselves hydrated and replenished by casting spells and creating small pools of water.

One day, Bailan felt the strange urge to constantly look behind himself. He felt as though something was watching the boys, following them. It wasn't until noontime that he realised why. The eight hairy legs and the many large, bulging, pitch black eyes made Bailan feel almost sick. He tried to yell, but his fear prevented him from doing so. All that came out was a high-pitched squeak. The creature pounced on Bailan, knocking him to the ground.

"Spiders!" yelled Finn, kicking the giant arachnid off of Bailan. The other three companions turned around to see not just one spider, but almost twenty of them. Without thinking, the boys started casting a variety of spells to kill the spiders. Wave after wave, the spiders continued to attack. They jumped on the boys, trying to pierce them with their stingers, their pincers clacking over the boys' faces. The whole ordeal lasted almost half an hour before Bailan finally had enough. He lifted his axe into the air and stabbed it into the ground. As the rock floor split apart, magma rushed to the surface. It covered too much room for the spiders to jump across, for the ones that dared, they were burned instantly. Five more days were spent travelling through the desolate terrain. On the third last day, the boys saw another set of mountains. It took the boys two days to reach the mountains, but when they did, they were overjoyed. On the other side of the mountains was a forest, full of green trees and many other types of plants. One after the other, they raced down the side of the mountain and threw themselves at the cool, damp ground. Tanier pulled out the blank map and saw that it was completely different than when they first arrived in the strange new place. Instead of an arrow showing them where to go, there were actual pictures of the land, as well as a picture of the boys and a castle. The castle was nowhere less than a day's travel from the boys' position, according to the map. They spent the afternoon in the forested area for fear of running into another wasteland later that night. The next morning, the boys decided to head towards the castle on the map. If it meant that it was a town, then the boys might be able to stock up on some provisions for their journey.

"Looks like it's about to rain," said Finn, pointing up at the dark clouds above. The closer to their destination they got, the darker the clouds grew. Dolci held out his hand, feeling for rain, but none dripped onto his palm. A strange and eerie feeling came over the boys. Bailan, the youngest of the group, knew that something was definitely wrong when they came upon the building. It was a large building with a very tall, central tower that looked as though one could see for miles and miles at the

[169]

top of it. The style of the actual building didn't look like anything that the boys were used to seeing in stone structures. The path went around the building brought the boys to a single door on one of the sides. Crag walked up to the door and knocked on it. After waiting for a few seconds with no reply, Crag knocked on the door again. After the second time, the boys agreed that the building had been abandoned and that no one was there. The five young men entered the large building. None of them knew who had once lived there, but they all had thoughts. The door suddenly slammed behind the last boy as he entered. All the torches within the building became lit as well. The boys made a circle, protecting themselves from all angles. There was someone else in the building, and they didn't seem too happy about the boys' presence.

*   *   *

As they entered the Dwarven city of Grol, the three companions looked at each other in amazement towards the city itself. Carved out of the mountains, Grol was a stronghold above all others. Out of all the places Thorstein had travelled to, Grol made him feel out of place the most. Since the city was only inhabited by dwarves, Thorstein felt even taller. Every dwarf that they passed stared at Thorstein because of his monstrous looking size. The group had only reached the second level when

[170]

they were suddenly surrounded by guards.

"Drop your weapons and surrender!" demanded one of the heavily armoured dwarves. Thorstein, even knowing that he would have no problem fighting the dwarves, threw his axe to the ground. Lena and Viktor quickly followed by placing their weapons on the ground.

"We are here by order of the Arch Chancellor of Arlbega," said Viktor. "By international laws, we must be provided diplomatic immunity." Thorstein looked down at Viktor and handed him the letter from Tanier. Viktor opened the letter and handed it to one of the dwarves.

"Do you seriously expect for…" The dwarf stopped speaking as he read the letter. The seal at the bottom of the letter was not the seal of the Arch Chancellor, but something much different. "Take these men, and the young lady, to the king at once!" demanded the dwarf. The guards lowered their weapons and assembled into a line. The three companions hopped back on their mounts and followed the guards up the road to the palace deep within the mountain. After passing through the large stone doors, there was a long, dark hallway. At the end of the hallway were even bigger doors. Beyond that was a very large throne room. The dwarf king was sitting at his large stone throne, propping his head up with his hand and elbow leaning on the arm of the big chair.

"What is it now, Trok?" questioned the king. The head of the royal guard stepped forward and knelt in front of the king.

"These travellers bring word from Arch Chancellor

[171]

Tanier Frost of Arlbega," said Trok.

"And let me guess… you want me to listen to what they have to say?" questioned the king. "I hardly believe that they are travellers judging by the weapons that they bring with them. Why would a giant be sent if there was no need for fighting?" The guard handed the letter from Tanier to the king.

"They have come about the Black Allegiance," said Trok. The king sat up straight and his eyes widened. He snatched the letter from Trok's hand and quickly began to read it. A large smile appeared on the king's face. He handed the letter back to Trok.

"You must travel to the top of the mountain," said the king. "When you reach the highest peak, you will find what you seek." The three young adults were shown out of the throne room and led back up to the surface.

"If you take the road to the east, you will eventually find a trail that will take you up the mountain," said Trok. "At some point you will find an old man that lives up there. He will help you find what you seek." For the first little bit of the trip, the group were able to ride their horses; but once the reached a certain point along the trail, the slope had become much too steep. As the group slowly ascended the mountain on foot, the air became much colder. Viktor pulled one of his blankets off of his horse and placed it on Lena's back. She smiled and looked back up the mountain.

"How did it ever happen, if you don't mind me asking?" questioned Lena.

"How did what happen?" replied Viktor.

"How did you lose your family and be taken prisoner?" Viktor's smile quickly disappeared. He looked down at the ground and began his story.

"I don't know much about what happened to my family. At my house in Dratana, we had a cellar with a heavy wooden door, just below the steps. The door was made like that so that me and my siblings wouldn't be able to lock each other in there when we were younger. About ten years ago, my mother sent me into the cellar to look for a jar of beets that we had harvested earlier in the year. She opened the cellar for me and sent me down into the dark, damp room. It took me a while to find the jar of beets. The next thing I knew, everything went dark and there was a loud bang behind me. The door had been shut and then locked. All that followed is too hard to describe in full detail. As the screaming and... laughing continued, I hid in one corner, feeling my way around. It took an hour of silence before I moved a budge. After almost two hours, I went for the jar of beets and started eating them. The juices ended up all over my hands and mouth. After I had eaten the entire jar of beets, I saw light again. The door to the cellar had been opened. Standing at the opening was a man with a scraggly grey beard. He yelled at me and grabbed me by the collar of my shirt, only after giving me a few hard hits to the face with his fist. I didn't know what was going on. He carried me out of the cellar like a rabid dog and threw me onto the main floor. As I looked up, I saw the grizzly remains of my parents, and my brothers and

[173]

sisters. The vampires did not just suck their blood; they actually started eating on my family's flesh. I was too scared for tears. A group of men rushed into my home and started kicking me. I did not realise why someone should be punished after doing no crime and seeing so much death. It was then that I remembered about the beet juice. As the men kicked me as hard as they could, I remembered the red stains on my hands and mouth. They thought that I had killed my family and cast me out into the street afterwards. It was then that someone recognized me. It was my friend Rina. She stepped in the way of the men and pleaded that they stop. I realised that her father was one of the men beating me. He stopped, but only to check my body for bite marks. He found none whatsoever. He made the other men stop, but did not help me. They left me at the outskirts of the village, barely alive. It wasn't until Rina came back for me that I felt life starting to return. She took care of me from then on. She made sure that I had enough food to eat and told me what was happening within the village over the next few weeks. They had cast me out. There was no evidence that showed I did it, but everyone had the same idea that I had something to do with it. One day, I found a small hole within a group of rocks I reached into the hole and pulled out two daggers. Attached to one of the daggers was a note. It said '*Take heed the one that is without honour and pride. These daggers will guide thee into the path of chosen desire.*' I did not understand what it meant at first, but then slowly realised it over time. It means that the daggers will show me my destiny. I brought the daggers to Rina and we cleaned the dirt off of them. I started to practise throwing the daggers. I wasn't very good at first, but after practising almost every hour of almost every day of the first year, I had become very good by the end of it. I was able to hit a housefly from twenty steps back after a year and a half." Viktor stopped and looked up at the sky. His feet didn't move either.

"Is something wrong?" questioned Lena.

"Then it happened," replied Viktor.

"What happened?"

"They came for me. The townspeople had found out about me still living a life within the forest. They didn't like that I was living in happiness with Rina occasionally there. They didn't like that I had become such an excellent hunter that I had become competition for the townsmen. They came after me. I ran away from them and tried to hide, but it wasn't good enough. They cornered me into a small cliff that was too high to climb up. I pleaded and begged that they stopped, but the continued to advance. One of them, Rina's father stepped forward in front of me. 'I used to think of you as a son,' he said. 'Then you became a monster, killed all of the wild animals in the forest, so that we can't hunt. You probably ate them while they were alive, just like you did your parents!' He pulled back his pitchfork and thrust it forward. I closed my eyes and heard a scream. There was no pain. I opened my eyes to see Rina standing in front of me with the pitchfork sticking out of her stomach. I grabbed her and held her back as she spoke her dying words. 'I believe you Viktor,' she said. She gave me a smile and then her eyes froze."

Lena held her hand to her mouth as a tear came down from her eye. Viktor looked back up at Lena. "It was then that they took me," he said. "The vampires rescued me from the townsfolk, but put me into the dungeon for food most likely."

"I didn't mean to…"

"Don't worry," said Viktor.

"I didn't want for you to continue if you didn't want to," said Lena. "I feel absolutely awful now."

"Don't," replied Viktor. "I haven't ever told that story before, but it does feel good to let someone other than me know my life." Thorstein, who had missed most of the story, was farther ahead of the other two.

"There is smoke coming from just over this next pass," said Thorstein. "That is most likely where the old man lives." They walked up to the small hut and knocked on the door. The door swung open and a gust of wind blew Viktor and Lena to the ground. Thorstein picked them up and peered into the building. There was nothing inside. The smoke stopped coming from the chimney above, but seemed to lower itself closer to the mountainside. Thorstein realised the point of the magic. There were wooden sticks that stuck about four feet out of the ground that lit up like torches when the smoke touched them. This showed the group another path up the mountain. They followed the torches until they were above the clouds. Once there, they found what looked like an open temple. There were no walls and the ceiling was supported by pillars that created a circle formation. In the exact centre of the pillars was an old man.

Thorstein stepped into the temple and stood before the old man. He didn't speak, but signalled Thorstein to kneel with hand gestures. The old man placed a hand on Thorstein's forehead. There was a sudden flash of light and Thorstein was knocked backwards, but felt nothing. As he picked himself up, he noticed that he was wearing a suit of black armour. The strange thing was that the armour seemed to meld with Thorstein's skin, replacing it. He didn't feel the armour's touch on his skin, and there was no single spot on Thorstein's body which was not covered in armour.

"This armour will protect you from any arrow, any sword, even the fire of a dragon," said the old man. "No matter what gets in your way, you will not have to stop for it." Thorstein smiled as he examined the armour. "Use it for the goodness of life," said the old man. "To remove it, simply wish it gone." Thorstein turned around to show Viktor and Lena. The craftsmanship was unlike anything Thorstein had ever seen before. As he turned around to thank the elderly man, he noticed that the temple and the man had disappeared. All that stood were a few rocks in its place.

*   *   *

As the next morning hit, the young woman rose up, quickly covering herself up with the blanket when she realised that she was nude underneath. Kailan, Crag, and Dartann were still asleep, but Guin had already been awake for almost an hour. The girl looked around and saw the three sleeping men just a few steps away. She had no recollection of the night before. She stood up and held the blanket as tightly as she could around her. She dashed into the forest, dodging trees and jumping over bushes. Suddenly she was knocked to the ground. On the ground in front of her, with his hand to his forehead, was Guin. He picked himself up and helped her up as well.

"Hello there," he said. The woman pushed Guin to the ground and continued running. As he picked himself up, he noticed that Kailan was now waking up. He noticed the empty spot of disturbed grass and then saw Guin.

"Where did she go?" question Kailan.

"She just ran off," replied Guin.

"I guess that she'll be fine, except that she isn't wearing any clothes," said Kailan. Within the next few minutes, Crag and Dartann had awoken and were now getting ready to leave again. After a quick breakfast, the group continued their journey towards Kelenath.

"I messed up on our time," said Crag.

"What do you mean?" replied Kailan.

"People only turn into werewolves at night," said Crag. "We encountered the girl quite early last night, and I'm guessing that she lives in Kelenath."

"What does that mean?" questioned Guin.

"We are mere hours from reaching Kelenath," stated

Dartann. "At the latest, we should reach Kelenath by this evening." The group of men continued their journey through the lands until they reached a town near Kelenath. It was much busier than Kailan would have expected. It would have made sense that more people would be buying and selling things within Kelenath itself. Dartann and Crag quickly moved off of the road and hid behind a large shrub. Kailan and Guin followed, but were only able to get a glimpse of the end of the spell. Crag had transformed Dartann into a human. Crag reached into his bag and pulled out some clothes, seeing as Dartann technically walked around naked the whole time, he would need them now with no fur to hide his unmentionables.

"You have to teach me how to do that," said Guin. Crag turned around and shook his head. After tying their horses up at the stables, the group walked into the middle of the town. They found a pub and sat down at one of the tables. Crag leaned over his shoulder and saw someone that he knew.

"Buy the boys a round," said Crag to Dartann. He stood up and walked over to another table and sat down with the patrons. Something seemed suspicious about the group that Crag was now sitting with. Guin realised the pile of staves when he first walked into the bar.

"Who are they?" questioned Guin. Dartann looked over at the table of men.

"They are just some of Crag's friends that he was planning on meeting here," replied Dartann.

"They are all wizards?" questioned Guin.

[179]

"Most of them are," replied Dartann. Guin thought nothing more of Crag and his friends while they were at the pub. After they finished their beers, Crag returned to the table.

"They are ready to advance at sunset," said Crag. Dartann replied with a nod.

"What do you mean?" questioned Kailan.

"My friends are coming with us to Kelenath," Crag answered. "They will meet us outside of the city this evening." After an hour or so more, they decided to leave the pub. Kailan and Guin went back to the stables and made sure that the horses were ready.

"What do you think is going on?" questioned Guin.

Kailan looked at the young wizard from across the horse and pondered for a second. "I don't have a single clue." The two boys brought the horses to the pub and waited for Crag and Dartann to exit. The four were off again, on their way to Kelenath. Kailan found it a bit strange that instead of taking the main road, Crag and Dartann took them along one of the side roads. It was along this side road that they met up with the other men. There were at least fifty of them in total, and most of them were wizards. They left their horses by a cart on the side of the road, and ventured on foot from there. They walked for another five minutes before stopping. Crag raised his hand and made a gesture, signalling everyone to get down on the ground. They hid behind the bushes that circled most of the city and waited.

Crag called out to one of the men. "Scholton and the others will be in that large building, three streets down on the left. Take your team and make sure that he doesn't escape." Crag turned towards another man and called out to him as well. "Subdue the guards at all costs. We must be able to get to Scholton and the other men with full strength or this will be all pointless."

"What's going on?" demanded Kailan.

"We are going to kill my old head master," replied Crag.

"You're going to kill him?" questioned Guin.

"He sent us to die!" yelled Crag.

*   *   *

The torches all went out at the exact same time, leaving the boys in complete darkness. There was a loud growling sound before one of the boys used his magic to start a fire in his hands to light up the room. The growling stopped, but the creature that made the sound was not absent at all. A giant dog stood over the boys, drooling copious amounts of saliva down on the wizards. It raised its upper lip and started to growl again. The teeth on the creature were about a foot long at the least. It was going to take some extra strength from the boys to get past the creature. As it went for its first attack, Bailan dodged the attack and hit the beast with his staff. The weapon almost broke against the dog's head, but it had had no effect. Crag held his staff up as it quickly

[181]

changed into a sword. Standing in front of the dog, he held the sword over his head, ready to jump out of the way and attack. Crag was the only one out of the five that knew how to fight with a sword properly. The beast seemed to know what a sword was and watched it carefully. The dog made its move, but didn't expect for Bailan to lash out with a ball of fire that almost instantly engulfed the creature completely. The attack was so hard on Bailan that it knocked him backwards. The giant wolf vanished before the fire could do any real damage. There was something much more powerful at work than what the boys expected. Suddenly, a loud voice could be heard throughout the building.

"Entering someone's home uninvited is not a wise decision," said the voice. "It has its price and now it should be paid for... in full!" There was a bright flash and the boys were knocked to the ground, blinded for a few seconds. When they regained their sight, the boys watched as an elderly man slowly walked down the tall staircase towards them. He wore a long robe that dragged a few feet behind him. His hair was silver and long. He lifted one of his bony fingers and pointed at Crag, who still had the sword in his hands. Before any of them could react, Crag was thrown backwards at the wall. The sword flew out of his hands and landed a few feet away. The old man looked at the other four and held his hand out in a cup with his fingers separated. The boys were lifted off the ground and were suspended in the air. Crag rolled over to his sword and quickly changed it back into the staff. He sent a fireball hurling at the old man, but the boys' attacker did not budge nor lose concentration. He simply held up his other hand and blocked the attack. The man turned his head towards Crag and laughed.

"Do you seriously expect to do damage to me boy?" said the man. He rose up off the stairs and hovered to the bottom floor.

"I didn't expect to do anything to you," said Crag, smiling. As the old man quickly turned around, he noticed a barrage of colours coming towards him. The boys were casting magic as fast as they could, trying to blind and distract the man while Crag snuck up behind. The man was thrown backwards after his force field had finally taken enough. Crag quickly jumped on the old man and held him down.

"Who are you?" demanded Crag. The old wizard started to mutter some words. Crag leaned in closer to listen. "What was that?" The man continued whispering, and after a few more words, Crag realised what he was saying. It was a long spell that Crag and the other boys knew about, but didn't know fully of how to cast it. Crag quickly placed his hand on the man's mouth, but it was already too late. The old wizard was starting to change. His skin slowly turned a greyish colour as his hair withered away. The boys looked at each other out of confusion.

"Did we kill him?" questioned Finn. Crag looked at the

[183]

motionless body with a look of fear in his eyes. A white, smoke-like figure arose out of the man's body. The five boys stood back in terror. The ghost's more intricate features slowly became visible and more detailed. As the boys slowly stepped away, it was Crag that had realised what was going on. The other four boys ran out of the building in fear as quickly as they could. The doors magically locked behind them, preventing them from getting back in. Crag was trapped inside and forced to deal with the ghost. He raised his sword and thrust it through the ghost. The ghost of the old man laughed.

"What did you expect to accomplish by doing that?" questioned the ghost with a smile on his face. Crag smiled and held his sword high in the air.

"It just further proved my points," replied Crag before stabbing the sword into the old man's corpse. The ghost yelled out in terror before disappearing into a cloud of smoke. For a few seconds, things were completely silent again. Crag was not even able to hear the sound of his friends kicking and banging on the door. Suddenly, there was a loud, menacing laugh that echoed throughout the walls of the building. Crag looked down at the dead body and noticed the ghost rising up from it. Crag took a step back, thinking that it was the same one as before, but it wasn't.

"Many kings and master wizards have fallen afoul to that illusion before," said the ghost. "You are the first one that has ever figured it out." The ghost was now smiling. "I believe that you are worthy of my spell book. Since I received it, after

[184]

waking from a dream, it has never been in anyone else's hands."
Crag was now smiling too at this point. He had just realised who
he had been fighting for the last few minutes. Gorgul's spell
book was considered the source of his power and the reason for
all of the destruction that he caused. Crag followed the ghost up
the stairs to the top of the tower, forgetting about his friends
outside. The top floor was one large room with the floor
bevelling towards the centre. At the lowest point in the centre of
the room, there was a stand with a very large book resting on it.
The ghost smiled and pointed at the book.

"Go to the book and read what it says," said the ghost.
Crag did just that. From the moment the first word left his lips,
Crag felt a sense of uneasiness, but he continued to read until the
end. Suddenly, the building was starting to shake.

"What is this?" questioned Crag.

"Stupid boy," said the ghost. "You just cast the spell
that will be the cause for your death." Stones and tiles began
falling from the walls and ceiling. Crag ran down the stairs, but
when he reached the main floor, he found that the door was still
locked. Crag was trapped with the building crumbling around
him. A hole appeared in the centre of the floor and started
sucking objects towards it. As the building crumbled more and
more into the growing hole, Crag could now feel himself being
pulled in as well. He grabbed onto the door handles and shook
them violently, and holding on for dear life as his legs were
raised into the air.

"Help!" yelled Crag. By this point, the building was

[185]

almost all destroyed. The young man tried to reach around to the side of the door, but the pull was too strong. Suddenly the ghost appeared again.

"Such will to live. So much knowledge and strength too," said the ghost with a frown on his face. "If only Master Scholton hadn't sent you to your death, even though he knew it from the beginning." An expression appeared on Crags face that was a mixture of fear and disgust. The ghost's frown quickly changed to a smile as Crag was carried away into oblivion.

*　　　　　*　　　　　*

It would be almost a week before the group would reach Lena's destination, a long journey over a number of mountains, and then through forest and swamp. There, they would find the elven city of Hileñar, another magical city, hidden deep within the forests and swamps. Thorstein chose not to wear the armour all of the time. It didn't hinder his movements or weigh him down, but it did make him feel strange. He was never able to relax with the armour on. It seemed to enhance his fighting abilities and make him more aware of his surroundings. Thorstein was always alert while wearing the armour, making him feel a bit edgy.

After the first few days of travelling, they finally reached open fields. It had been the first time in a week that the group would be able to open their eyes and just see green. It almost seemed like a dream. The colour of the grass was so rich, and the few trees that were in the fields were as full of leaves as they could get. The sun shone down brightly that day on the field. The group decided to take a break, sitting under one of the trees. Immediately next to the tree was a small pond where they collected more water from and bathed afterwards.

"I think that I could live here," said Lena. "I'd have a small house just over there." Lena pointed off in the distance. "Right next to my house would be a garden where I could grow anything. Whatever I felt like; roses and daffodils, an apple tree, and maybe even some nice vegetables."

Viktor and Thorstein chuckled under their breaths.

"This is no place to make a home," said Viktor. "You need a palace on a mountaintop where you can see for miles and miles."

"But how would you live?" questioned Lena. "You can't grow food very well on the top of a mountain."

"I'd have my servants make me food," replied Viktor. "I can't see me getting any less out of this journey."

"Servants?" laughed Thorstein. "A real man does the work himself. There is no real gratitude in having someone else do your work for you. The sense of pride and accomplishment when you build your own house with your bare hands, now that is what you really want." For the first time in a long time, a smile appeared on Viktor's face. Deep down, he felt a sense of happiness that he had not felt since his love, Rina, was alive.

[187]

"As for me," continued Thorstein. "My dream would be to live somewhere that I can live out the rest of my life in peace and happiness. Maybe I will find a nice woman and start a family of my own." Viktor's smile grew even more intense for a short while. Thorstein's words reminded Viktor of Rina, and the times that he spent with her. There was another hour of laughter and enjoyment between the three friends before they decided to head off on their journey again. Just over one of the grassy hills, the group came upon a small village on the outskirts of a forest that bordered the fields. They decided to head towards the village and gather a few supplies. As they entered the village, Thorstein felt quite strange. The people within the village stared at him upon first sight, but then quickly changed their expressions to that of joy and amazement. Children quickly ran up to the giant and his dornbeast cheering and wondering with amazement.

"And what might I be able to help you young travellers with on this fine day?" questioned a man as he approached the group.

"We are looking for some supplies and possibly even a place to spend the night," said Thorstein.

"Well young sir, my brother Andrew owns that store there" said the man. "As for a place to sleep, the only place that I think might work for a man of your size would be my barn."

"Thank you sir," replied Thorstein.

They first went to the barn to tie up their rides. Almost as soon as Thorstein had dismounted his dornbeast, the children of the village had swarmed around it. Curious and amazed, they stroked its fur and poked it here and there. All Lena could do was laugh at the dornbeast as she saw it look up towards Thorstein and almost whimper. The three friends were quickly met by a group of villagers.

"Tonight we will be starting our festivities," said the leader of the group. "Please, join us and tell us some of your tales." Never before had the group felt more welcomed on their journey.

"We'd love to," said Lena, quickly joining the crowd. "My name is Lena, this is Viktor, and this is Thorstein." Almost immediately, Thorstein and Viktor were out helping to set up the decorations and such for the party. Lena was quickly rushed into the kitchen, helping with preparing the large feast that would later take place. Something strange happened to the three friends after they crossed over from the mountains into the lush green pastures. Everything and everyone there seemed happy. As the sun slowly went down, the enjoyment was amplified even more. Almost immediately after they finished the large meal, the village began dancing and singing songs around a large fire pit in the middle. Even after a meal like that, they were still able to move freely without consequences. There was no stopping until the night had completely taken over. Thorstein, Viktor, and Lena, all went off to the barn, laughing and still half drunk.

Suddenly, Viktor awoke in the middle of the night. He pulled his legs in and sat upright. Looking around, he saw Thorstein and Lena, still fast asleep. There was a knock on the

[189]

open door of the barn, and a white figure swiftly ran away.

"Thorstein, Lena," said Viktor. Neither of them budged. He jumped up and ran to the barn door. Hiding behind one of the trees was a young woman with bright red hair, dressed in white. "Who's there?" Viktor stopped for a second and then took a step back after he finally got a good look at her face. She smiled at him before turning and running deeper into the forest. The full moon that night cast enough light the Viktor did not need the sun, or a torch to help him. He chased after her, but she always seemed to be going just as fast as he. They ran, from tree to tree, over bush and rock. As Viktor thought he had finally gained ground on her and was about to grab her, she jumped into a pond in the middle of the forest. Viktor waited for her, but she did not surface. He dove in after her, only to find that the pond was a mere puddle, only a few inches deep. "Rina!" he cried as he knelt in the puddle.

"She comes around almost every night, ya know," said a girl sitting next to a tree with her back rested on the trunk. Viktor looked up, with a tear in his eye. "There are others too. They don't talk, but they seem like really nice people."

"Why are you out here?" questioned Viktor as he picked himself up.

"I couldn't sleep, and besides, it is peaceful," replied the girl. "My name is Sophia.

"I'm Vi…"

"Viktor, I know," interrupted Sophia. "I don't quite know why they are here, but every time that I see one of them, I feel happy, but sad as well. Like a very happy memory that is surrounded by bad ones as well." Viktor wiped the mud off his pants and sat next to Sophia. "Who is Rina?" questioned Sophia. Viktor stared off into the night sky, eyes wide open.

"Rina was the woman that I was going to live the rest of my life with," replied Viktor. "She was the kindest, most loving woman to ever walk this world, not to mention the most beautiful." Both of them smiled as Viktor described Rina.

"What happened to her?"

"She was killed," replied Viktor as his smile disappeared. "In an attempt to protect me, she got in the way of my attacker, her own father. She died in my arms." A tear rolled down Sophia's cheek.

"I'm sorry," said Sophia. "I didn't mean to..."

"It's perfectly fine." Suddenly, screams came from the village. "What is that?"

"Not now!" cried Sophia. "Quickly, follow me!" She grabbed a hold of Viktor's hand and pulled him through the forest. In no time at all, they were back at the barn. Thorstein and Lena jumped to their feet and quickly grabbed their weapons.

"What's going on?" asked Thorstein.

"I don't know, I woke up when I heard the screams," said Lena.

"I was in the forest with..." Viktor stopped in the middle of his sentence to see Sophia pointing off towards the opposite window in the barn.

[191]

"An ogre," said Sophia.

"Well, Thorstein can deal with that," said Lena as she moved back to her bed.

"He's going to need our help, Lena," said Viktor, slowly stepping backwards. The giant club came crashing through the barn and smashed it to nothing but pieces. Thorstein picked himself up from the ground and looked up at the enormous ogre. Never before had Thorstein ever really had to look up to make eye contact, not since he was a child. The ogre was almost twice Thorstein's size, and more than enough muscle to match. Lena quickly scurried away, trying to gain some distance between her and the ogre before shooting. After her first shot, the beast quickly stared at her for a second or two, before letting out a roar that made everyone's ears ring. The ogre quickly charged at Lena, swinging his club. Thorstein went for his axe and threw it at the beast. It knocked the ogre to the ground, but left nothing than a minor bruise. The ogre turned and let out another roar at Thorstein. Before he could pick up his axe again, the ogre had charged him with full speed and hit him with its club, sending Thorstein flying through the air.

"Sophia," said Viktor, "I'm going to need you to run." As he looked next to him, the girl stood, staring in terror at the ogre that was now watching them. "Sophia!" She still made no movement whatsoever. Viktor picked the girl up and quickly threw her over his shoulder. Running as fast as he could with a twelve year old girl in his arms, Viktor evaded the ogre, and outran his charge. The ogre was back after Lena now. As it ran her down, she tripped over a rock and hit the ground hard. Would it not have been for Thorstein, she would probably have died then and there. He jumped through the air and wrapped his arms around the ogre's throat. He squeezed tightly, but the ogre fell backwards and landed on Thorstein, knocking the wind out of him. The beast stood up and grabbed Thorstein. With a smile on its face, the creature threw Thorstein into the forest. When he landed, Thorstein was unconscious. The villagers quickly surrounded the ogre, shooting arrows, using their shovels and pitch forks to try to penetrate the beast's tough skin. With one swing of its enormous club, the ogre had cleared away most of the villagers. A few lay dead, a few maimed and injured. Lena tried aiming for the beast's eyes, but every time she had a good shot, the ogre had a chance to make an attack that would kill her. She decided that it was best to find Thorstein as he was the only one strong enough to fight the creature. Lena ran into the forest, with the ogre following and clearing trees out of its way. When she found Thorstein, Lena patted his cheek a few times before he finally came to.

"What happened?" questioned Thorstein. He looked up past Lena and saw the ogre standing in front of him with the club raised above its head. Thorstein grabbed Lena and rolled to the side, dodging the attack. "Run!" he yelled at the top of his lungs. Suddenly, Thorstein remembered the armour that he had taken off. He quickly imagined himself wearing it. He was hit by the club again, but this time, Thorstein barely moved. Knowing that even with the armour, he wouldn't be able to actually stop the monster, Thorstein ran for his axe by the barn. When he was out of the forest, he found the remaining men ready with large ropes. Almost instantly, Thorstein had an idea to defeat the ogre. "Have a loop at the end of each of these ropes when I come back!" said Thorstein to the men. He picked up his axe and threw it again at the beast to taunt it and make it follow him. Once in the field, Thorstein realised that he had made a mistake with his plan. He wanted to take the ogre in a loop, bringing it back to the village, but the beast stood in the way, disallowing Thorstein from completing his plan. The ogre slowly moved towards Thorstein, dragging its club behind it. Suddenly, there was a roar, but not from the ogre. Thorstein's dornbeast charged the ogre from the side and sent it hurling through the air. It stood between Thorstein and the ogre, ready to fight. "Get out of here," yelled Thorstein. The dornbeast looked back and huffed. "Leave now!" The dornbeast had taken the ogre by surprise the first time, but going at it a second time could mean death. Thorstein chased the animal away, and went back for the ogre, who was picking itself up from the ground. It followed him back to the village where the villagers were waiting. Thorstein grabbed a hold one of the ropes with the other men and waited for the ogre to step in the loop. They pulled as hard as they could, sending the ogre to the ground. As it pulled itself up, Viktor quickly jumped out from behind one of the buildings with the other rope in hand. He threw the other loop over the ogre's head and pulled down, pinning it. Nobody else knew Viktor had the kind of strength it would have taken to do that.

With Viktor holding the rope at the head, and the villagers holding the rope at the feet, Thorstein quickly went for his axe and brought it down on the beast's neck, severing its head off.

It was now in the wee hours of the morning. The ogre hadn't done much damage to the village besides the barn, and a house or two, but there were numerous dead. For some strange reason, the villagers did not seem overly sad about their losses, but instead happy that the ogre was dead.

"We can finally go in peace!" cried out one of the men. The three friends were quickly ushered out of the town to find their steeds waiting for them, all packed up and ready to go off, deeper into the forest.

"We would like to help," said Lena.

"You have done all the help that we ever could have imagined," said one of the women. "It should be us who are helping you, but alas, we have much work to do."

The three friends gathered their things and headed for the edge of town. Some of the villagers had already rounded up the horses and dornbeast, and had them ready for the group. As the group was leaving town, Sophia yelled out.

"Wait, Viktor," she cried out.

"You two go on," said Viktor as he turned around, "I'll catch up." He slowly made his way towards Sophia.

"I have something for you," said Sophia, holding out her hand. Viktor leaned over the side of the horse to see what it was. As the young girl opened her hand, she revealed a small necklace, made of wooden and bone beads. Sophia placed it in his open hands. Upon inspection, Viktor realised that it was the same one that he had given Rina as a child. "She will be with you soon," said Sophia. Viktor quickly looked up, but there was no one there. Sophia had disappeared, along with the village as well. All that was left was the remnants of what looked like a village from decades before, but there were no buildings, no people. Ghosts cursed to walk the globe, until their demon was destroyed. Viktor quickly caught up to the rest of the group, but remained silent, keeping the necklace in his pocket.

*   *   *

"You are out of your mind, Crag!" yelled Kailan.

"If you don't want to help, then get out of my way," said Crag. Kailan quickly pulled out his sword and had it rested against Crag's throat before he could even blink. "You are fast, Kailan, that's for sure. Against a wizard though, I think not." As soon as Kailan could feel the magic pushing him away, he made his move, but it was too quick and powerful. Kailan was thrown back a number of feet, landing on his back. Guin quickly stood back and cast a fireball at Crag and Dartann, but it was cast off by Crag. He held out his staff as it changed into a sword. Slowly, he walked over to Kailan and tapped the ground beside the boy's head. "Get up!"

Kailan rolled over onto his side and picked himself up.

He held out his sword and pointed it at Crag. "You're not going to win," said Kailan. The two began in swordplay. With each strike and parry, Kailan could tell that Crag was no match for his speed. He slowly began to quicken his speed, making it gradually harder for Crag. This would at some point cause Crag to slip up and possibly miss a parry, or forget to block at all. Suddenly, that time came, but instead of attacking, Kailan found himself being thrown back again. "That's not fair!" cried Kailan as he lay on the ground.

"Life isn't fair boy!" said Crag. "I didn't deserve to be cast into oblivion, but it happened anyways!" With Dartann's attention being on Crag and Kailan, Guin made his move. He picked up a small tree branch that lay on the ground and swung it, hitting Dartann in the head. From there, Guin went straight for Crag's spell book which was lying on the ground by their belongings. Crag quickly turned around and pointed his sword at Guin, but the young wizard had already begun reading the pages from the book. As he held his hand up, a swirl of red light came from his palm. The swirl changed into a beam, and as it hit Crag, it cast him into the air. Suddenly, Guin looked down and found Dartann, grabbing at his ankle. Again, he read from the book. In an instant, Dartann changed. Not into a beast, nor a horse like he had before. This time, Dartann changed into a tiny mouse. Guin giggled, but then saw Crag coming back towards him. Guin recited the words from before and Crag was again cast into the air. This time, Crag was thrown into a tree, knocking him unconscious. As he lay motionless, Guin watched as Dartann quickly scurried to Crag, and nestled in one of his pockets. Suddenly, there was a blue light around everyone, and they began to feel immense pain.

"By order of the city of Kelenath, I place you under arrest," said a voice. Kailan and Guin rolled on the ground, clawing the dirt because of the pain. It felt like they were being crushed to death, but there was no end. Slowly, a man walked into the blue light and stood over Kailan and Guin. The blue light disappeared and the pain slowly went away. "You two aren't a part of this, are you?" questioned the man. Kailan rolled over on his back and looked up at the man. He wore a long green and brown robe, and had a large grey beard.

"No," said Guin, "We stopped them." The man knelt down beside Guin and picked up the spell book. He examined it for a few seconds before tucking it under his arm. "These two are going to the Council," said the man, pointing at Kailan and Guin. "Take the other one away." As Kailan and Guin turned around, they saw about ten men standing a few feet away.

"There are more," said Kailan. "This man wasn't alone."

"We've already caught the others," said one of the men.

The two boys were led through the back roads of the city before they ended up at large building. The man from before was still with them, keeping the book tightly against his side. Inside the building, they travelled up a long, spiralling stair case until they came upon two large doors.

"Stay here," said the man. He opened the doors slightly

[198]

and squeezed through. About a minute later, he came back, without the book. "Come in." Kailan and Guin walked through the doors and entered the pitch black room.

"I can't see anything," said Kailan.

"Stop talking!" said a booming voice. Before the two young men appeared seven, figures. The only light in the room came from them, lighting their faces.

"What business do you have in Kelenath?" questioned on of the Council members.

"We're here by order of Arch Chancellor Tanier Frost of Arlbega," said Kailan.

"Tanier Frost has no authority here!" yelled another member. "What business do you have in Kelenath?"

"Why were you found with this evil tome?" demanded another as he held up Crag's spell book.

"I took it from one of the wizards that were after Master Scholton," replied Guin.

"This is the spell book of Gorgul," said one of the Council members. "This is the book that gave a man the power to destroy kingdoms, and it was found in the possession of two young boys?"

"Listen, if you are not going to help us, then let us leave!" yelled Kailan.

"What business do you have in Kelenath?" demanded a member for a third time.

"Orpeth Armenen wanted us to find some objects," said Kailan. The Council members began talking amongst

[199]

themselves.

"Orpeth Armenen has been dead for almost twenty years," said one of the Council members.

"Just show them the letter," said Guin. So Kailan pulled one of the letters from his pocket and handed it to one of the Council members. As they read it, they began discussing again.

"Who is this Thorstein Volfkin?" demanded one of the Council members.

"We split up into two groups to find these items," said Kailan. "Thorstein, Lena, and Viktor all went in one direction, while we came to Kelenath." The Council members continued talking until one of them opened Gorgul's spell book.

"They're telling the truth," said the Council member. Everything went silent and the others looked at him.

"What are you talking about?" demanded the others. He passed the book on, and as it went from person to person, their expressions were all the same after reading the words.

"What happened?" questioned Guin. The book was closed and handed back to the man that led the boys to the Council.

"Have you ever heard the story of Gorgul's spell book?" questioned one of the Council members. Kailan shook his head.

"I've heard bits and pieces," replied Guin.

"Gorgul's spell book was actually made over a thousand years ago," said the Council member. "There used to be a great page by the name of Aroculus. As soon as he could read, he began studying spells. As a page, he did not use magic, but instead memorized thousands of spells and their uses. Before his death, Aroculus pleaded with another wizard to bind his soul to a book. He would become immortal, but would be forever stuck in the tome. That is how the spell book was created. No matter what page you flip to, the book will tell you what spell you need, depending on your desire. The book's first few owners used it for good, and only that. Before Gorgul, there was a wizard named Falzar. He started off as a good man, but when he became the new owner of the spell book, he was slowly corrupted by his power. After murdering his family in a spat of blind rage, he realised that the book was not what he needed. He read what was on the page of the book and it disappeared. This is how it came to be in Gorgul's possession."

"The book has told us that you are telling the truth," said another Council member.

"It is yours to keep."

"Do not let it fall into the wrong hands." Without any warning, the Council members disappeared and the only light in the room was coming from the open doors. The boys were escorted out, and onto the main floor. The man held out the book and handed it to Guin. They made their way back to the horses just outside of the city. Now with Guin's item found, the boys set out in search of Kailan's.

*   *   *

The group of three made their way deeper into the elven territory. The further they went, the more magnificent the land became. The lush, thick forests of the elven kingdom grew trees as tall as the sky, with hanging vines that seemed to go on forever. The flowers and shrubs that covered the forest floor left nothing to bore the senses. The sheer colour and beauty, as well as the soothing, uplifting aroma, made this place a paradise. It didn't seem long before the group had reached the entrance into the city. The road came to a sudden stop with vines hanging in front of them. Two, very wide trees, stood at each side of the road, with steps spiralling up to a wooden platform at about ten feet up, then again at twenty.

"We are going to need you to stop," said a mysterious voice. The group members came to a halt and looked around, but couldn't see who was speaking to them.

"Who's there?" questioned Viktor.

"Place your weapons on the ground," said the voice.

"Only when you show yourself!" yelled Thorstein.

"We have twenty arrows aimed at your heads," said the voice. "I suggest that you listen to me." Thorstein quickly made his armour appear.

"Shoot!" yelled the voice. Instantly, twenty arrows flew through the sky towards the three friends. The arrows had no effect on Thorstein, but Viktor and Lena needed to perform some tricky maneuvering to dodge the arrows. Viktor was able to block most of them with his knives, while dodging the rest. Lena, on the other hand had a bit harder of a time. Having one arrow skim her arm and leave a large cut along it. Other than that, she had dodged every attack. Thorstein noticed Lena's cut and quickly stood in front of her with Viktor at their side. Lena held up her bow with an arrow notched on the string and pointed it into the forest.

"That was a warning shot!" said the voice. "We won't let you live after this."

"Can you see any of them?" questioned Thorstein. Viktor shook his head.

"They're too deep in the forest," responded Viktor.

"I can," said Lena, poking her arrow through the small space between Thorstein's arm and side. The arrow flew towards one of the trees and banked off the railing of the first platform. An elf appeared from the other side of the tree with an arrow sticking out of his armour.

"That was a warning shot!" yelled Lena. "Now let us through." The elf smiled and slowly walked down the steps to the forest floor.

"Even though your marksmanship is quite extraordinary, I still cannot allow you to pass," said the elf. Viktor slowly made his way towards the elf. Staring directly into the elf's eyes, Viktor spoke.

"Let us enter the city," said Viktor. For a second or two, neither the elf, nor Viktor, made a sound or moved. When the elf did finally move, he rubbed his eyes and turned his head

[203]

away from Viktor.

"I will take you to the palace," said the elf. "My name is Gelob, now you must tell us your names."

"I am Viktor Svetlenka."

"My name is Thorstein of the clan Volfkin," said the giant looking down on the elf.

"We don't usually have travellers coming through here, especially none of your size," said Gelob. "And what about you, what is your name?"

Lena picked herself up, holding her cut as the blood slowly dripped through her fingers. "My name is Lena Harkonen."

"I am sorry that we had to shoot you, but we had no choice," said Gelob, walking closer to Lena. "Let me look at that wound." Lena held out her arm in front of her, and pulled her hand away, clenching from the pain. Gelob inspected the wound quickly before pulling a small glass vial from his pocket. "This should do the trick." He poured a drop of the clear liquid inside, onto Lena's cut. The liquid began to fizz and slowly spread over the rest of her wound. Gelob grabbed the corner of his shirt and wiped off the liquid, to reveal that the cut had scabbed over. "It should be all healed by tomorrow."

"What is that?" questioned Lena.

"Just a simple remedy," replied Gelob. "Now, if everything is in order, we should make our way to the palace and speak to the king." The three companions mounted up and made their way up to the palace. As the group passed between the two trees and through the vines, they came upon the wondrous beauty of the elven city. The white buildings reached to just under the forest canopy. Moss and ivy covered the sides of some of the buildings, while the city floor and pathways were made of flagstone and bright green grass. Streams naturally ran through the city, with the structures built around them. Tiny waterfalls at every drop in elevation gave a little extra magic to the already wondrous city of Hileñar.

"What was that back there?" questioned Thorstein, whispering to Viktor next to him.

"Just a little magic that I learned along the way," replied Viktor.

"I didn't know that you knew magic," said Thorstein, curiously.

With a smile on his face, Viktor spoke. "After my parents died, I had to learn how to take care of myself," said Viktor. "I found that the easiest way was to learn magic. Sure, it may not be as grand as a wizard, but when used properly, these little tricks of mine can do powerful things." Thorstein smiled, then nodded and continued on. As the group came upon the palace, they were surrounded by guards.

"Where are you taking these people, Gelob," questioned on of the guards, stepping out of formation.

"They wish to speak to the king," said Gelob.

"Gelob, what is wrong?" said the guard.

"Nothing is wrong Artilas," replied Gelob. "They wish to speak to the king, so I am taking them to see him."

"Gelob, in all of the many years that I have known you, you have never let someone see the king without being arrested and restrained first," said the guard. Thorstein looked to his side and saw Viktor clench his fist tightly and begin to sweat. He took a deep breath in and then let it out.

"They have some important information," said Gelob. The guard walked up to Gelob and inspected him. He placed a hand on Gelob's forehead, and looked into his eyes.

"You tell the truth," said the guard.

"Of course I do," replied Gelob with a strange look on his face.

"Very well then, you may pass," said the guard. Thorstein watched as Viktor quickly relaxed and loosened his hands. The guard stepped out of Gelob's way and allowed the group to enter the palace. The palace was unlike anything that they had ever seen before. Thorstein had heard of high elves and their great buildings of gold, silver, and marble, but Hileñar was a wood elf city. They thrive off nature, but also let it go as it pleases. The main room in the palace was one, large, circular throne room. At the far side, opposite of the doors was the throne. A tree that had seemed to grow perfectly into the shape of a throne, complete with a back and armrests. In the centre of the throne room was a very tall, silver birch tree. There was no roof above the throne room. This was so that the sunlight could shine in and light up the large room. The floors of the palace were made of moss and tiny purple flowers speckled the ground every so often.

[206]

"Gelob my dear boy!" yelled a voice from one of the walkways that spiralled up the inside walls of the throne room.

"Uncle!" Gelob yelled out. An elf, wearing a purple and gold coloured robe waved from above, and made his way down to the floor level. Gelob walked up to the man as he made it down the last few steps, kneeling before him when they met each other.

"Get up," said the man. "I've told you numerous times to stop treating me like some kind of high elf king." Thorstein turned to Viktor and glared.

"You used magic on the king's nephew?" whispered Thorstein.

"How was I supposed to know that he was the king's nephew?" replied Viktor. "If you had a better idea of getting into the city, why didn't you say anything?" The two young men continued to bicker back and forth for a little bit before Lena stepped in.

"I suggest that you both shut up immediately!" said Lena sternly, with a bit of a scowl on her face. The king patted Gelob on the shoulder and then noticed Thorstein. He stepped forward and eyed Thorstein up with an enormous smile, about to burst with joy.

"What do we have here?" questioned the king.

"My name is Thorstein Volfkin, your majesty," said the boy.

"He speaks too!" The king clapped his hands and pranced around in circles. The three friends looked at each other

[207]

oddly, as if the king was crazy. "Let me guess, thirteen feet?"

"Closer to fourteen feet tall, actually," replied Thorstein.

"Well, I was close," laughed the king. "It's a good thing we didn't bet on it. I'd be out of some money." The king then jumped to the side and pointed at Lena. "Wow!" The king slowly inspected Lena. "Now aren't you a beauty."

Lena smiled. "Thank you sir."

"Can I hold it?" asked the king.

"Hold what, sorry?" questioned Lena.

"Your bow, I've never seen one before as magnificent and beautiful."

"Oh," said Lena. Viktor burst out laughing. Lena instantly gave him a dirty look, but then both the king and Thorstein started chuckling. Gelob continued to stay to the side, arms crossed and silent.

"And what is your name my dear?" questioned the king.

"My name is Lena Harkonen," she stated. He smiled and then took another look at Lena's bow.

"Where did you get your bow from?" questioned the king. Lena pulled the bow from over her head and held it in front of her.

"I had an old elf mentor me on the ways of elven archery," said Lena. She eyed up her bow and ran her fingers along the art engraved into the wood. "His name was Drast." The king's face lit up with excitement.

[208]

"I knew Drast actually," said the king. "He was a friend of mine for many years before he just disappeared one day."

"He did the same to me," said Lena.

"If Drast trained you, then you must be an amazing archer," said the king. "Whether he disappeared or not, he would still have taught you skills that even some of my soldiers can't perform." Lena smiled and gripped her bow tightly before putting back over her shoulder. The king took a step to the right and stared at Viktor for a second of two. He looked at the daggers by Viktor's side. "How good are you with those daggers?" questioned the king. Viktor smiled and pulled the daggers out, spinning them in his palms.

"Words cannot describe," replied Viktor. The king laughed and placed a hand on Viktor's shoulder.

"You are all going to have to show us your talents tomorrow," said the king. "My name is Grakken, and this is my nephew Gelob. I think that you've already met though." The king turned around and held his hands up towards the back of the palace. "For as long as you wish, you are guests here at the palace," said the king. "If there is anything that you need, do not hesitate to ask." King Grakken and Gelob showed the three companions to their rooms for the night. This was one of the first times in a long time that the group had felt relaxed while sleeping in a city. There was no rush for them to leave, nor was there day very busy before it. That night, as Lena slept in her room, she dreamt. In the dream, she was in the forest near her home, and it was dark. Mist passed through the tree trunks,

[209]

blinding most of Lena's vision. Out of the corner of her eyes, she could see a light in the distance. Slowly making her way from tree to tree, Lena quickly discovered what the source of the light was. Men were standing in front of her with weapons of all kinds and torches to light their way. Lena stood back, but bumped into something, causing her to fall to the ground. As she looked up, she saw Kaela, her sister, standing over her. She was wearing a white robe and had a golden band holding her long brown hair tied behind her back.

"Kaela!" Lena cried out. "What are you doing here?"

"You need to leave here," said Kaela.

"Come with me," said Lena. "I know where we can hide."

"I am safe, Lena," replied Kaela. "You must get yourself to safety. You don't need to worry about me anymore." Kaela's robe began to glow as she walked towards the crowd of angry men. "I love you Lena; always remember that."

"I won't lose you again," cried Lena, reaching out to her sister. Kaela walked into the crowd as if they didn't even notice her. Suddenly, Kailan and the others came to Lena's rescue and began to fight off the violent men.

"We need to leave now," said Kailan.

"No, I won't leave Kaela!" cried Lena. She watched as the white glow of her sister faded away behind the horde of men. "Kaela!" Lena awoke crying, and covered with sweat. She gasped for air and held her chest as the pain slowly went away. Lena wiped the tears from her eyes and rolled over to her side.

"Why do these things happen?"

         *   *   *

Guin walked over to the camp fire and placed a few more logs on it. He sat down next to it and pulled out his new tome, running his fingers over the engraved leather covered. The designs on the front of the book consisted of gold and silver inlays. He placed his index finger underneath the metal latch and flipped it up. It wasn`t the first time that Guin had inspected the book, but it was the first time that he didn`t feel rushed. He let the cover and the first few pages flop to one side. On the page were only a few words written; "I will help you when you need me". He flipped to the next page, but there was nothing on the next page.

"I'm hungry, teach me how to make food," said Guin in a joking manner. He waited for the book to reveal more words, but it remained blank.

"That fire better not be out!" yelled Kailan, laughing as he made his way to the camp, holding a line with two fish strung on it.

"Don't worry," said Guin. "I actually can't think of a way that could happen with me around." Kailan placed the fish on a rock and pulled out the small knife that he had in his pocket. He placed the knife between the gill and head of one of

[211]

the fish and proceeded to cut the head off. "I wonder Viktor, Thorstein, and Lena are doing," said Guin. "What do you think Thorstein's item is?"

"I have no clue," said Kailan, as he gutted the fish. "I just hope that nothing bad has happened to them."

"Why do you say that?" questioned Guin. Kailan cut off the tail and spread the fish open before looking up at Guin and letting out a large sigh.

"I've just been having these feelings every now and then," replied Kailan, twirling the knife in his hands. "Take last night for example."

"What happened last night?"

"I had a dream where you, me, Thorstein, and Viktor, were all running in the same direction through a forest. I didn't know what was going on, but I knew that something was wrong." Kailan picked up the other fish and began to prepare it as well. "For some reason, Bailan appeared and told us that we needed to protect Lena. We asked where she was, but there was no response. Bailan just smiled and disappeared. We continued running in the same direction until we came upon a group of men, carrying torches and other weapons. They attacked as, but we made our way through; there was something they were after. We quickly found Lena, but she seemed distraught about something. I can't remember what it was. As I took her hand and pulled her away, the dream ended." Kailan placed the two fish upon a large rock in the middle of the campfire. He then wiped his hands on the grass and washed them with some water from his canteen.

"So you're more afraid of Lena's safety," said Guin.

"Well, yes, but I still care about the others as well."

"They'll be fine, don't worry about it. Anyways,
Thorstein is humongous, Lena is an expert marksman, and
Viktor is…" Guin scratched his chin. "Well actually, I have no
clue what Viktor's talents are." Kailan laughed while flipping
the fish over on the rock with a stick.

"Don't worry," said Kailan, laughing. "I don't have a
clue either."

The two boys were now at the bottom of Mount Belok.
It was not as high as most of the other mountains in the region,
but it was the home of many dragons. Mount Belok was riddled
with caves, providing perfect protection for the great beasts. The
main problem, for Kailan and Guin, was that neither of them had
ever heard of the mountain. They had no clue as to what was
going to happen atop the mountain top. Kailan's special item
however, was at the top of the mountain, so they had no choice
but to scale it. One of the amazing things about the geology of
the mountain was that the rocks have transformed over the years
and eroded to create a natural pathway up the mountain. This
would make it much easier for the boys to walk up the mountain
because they could use their horses instead of having to actually
climb. As they slowly made their way up the mountain, Kailan
began to feel anxious.

"What do you think I'll end up getting?" questioned
Kailan.

[213]

"I don't know," replied Guin. "Maybe a nice chalice or something."

"Seriously?" laughed Kailan. "It will probably be something like a shield, or a magic staff."

"Magic staff?" questioned Guin. "More like a magic chalice."

"Will you shut up," said Kailan, giggling.

"Well, hopefully it will be better than this crummy book," said Guin, pulling the tome out of its pouch. Just then, the book sprung open to a page with words on it.

"I'm not a crummy book," said the tome. Startled, Guin threw the book to the ground.

"What is it?" questioned Kailan.

"The book just spoke to me," said Guin.

"What do you mean?"

"You didn't hear it talk?"

"It talked?" said Kailan, curiously. Guin hopped off his horse and picked the book back up.

"You know, it isn't very nice to just throw literature around on the ground," said the book as the same words appeared on the page.

"There, it did it again!" yelled Guin.

"I think you're delusional," said Kailan. "I can't hear a thing."

"I am not an 'IT'," said the book. "My name is Aroculus."

"How can you not hear it, Kailan?" said Guin. "It's as

[214]

clear as day."

"Now if you let me be, I was resting," said the book, in a snooty way.

"Books don't rest," Guin replied.

"My name is Aroculus," the book stated for a second time. "Please call me that."

"Why are you talking through my book?" questioned Guin.

"How bad is your memory, boy?" questioned Aroculus.

"What's that supposed to mean?"

Kailan stood back and began to giggle. "I'm travelling with a lunatic," he whispered under his breath.

"The council members of Kelenath spoke to you about Gorgul's spell book," stated Aroculus.

"Oh, so you're the soul of the page that is inside of it?" replied Guin.

"Exactly!" responded Aroculus. "Now if you let me be, I was thinking." Guin nodded and put the book back into the pouch that hung at his side. He hopped back on his horse and looked over at Kailan.

"Are you two done now?" questioned Kailan.

"I must be the only one able to hear him," said Guin. That way only I can it.

"Not 'IT'," yelled Aroculus.

"Sorry."

The two boys continued walking up the side of the mountain until they reached their first cave. Guin snapped his

[215]

fingers, lighting a fire in his hand and went into the cave first. The dark, wet walls of the cave gave a mouldy smell to the area, causing Guin to cover his nose. It wasn't long before Guin found the end of the cave. It was a dead end with nothing but a small pool of water on the floor. As the boys turned around, Kailan noticed something strange.

"What is it?" questioned Guin. Kailan held out his hand in front of Guin's mouth.

"I can't see the opening of the cave," whispered Kailan.

"You guys are going to need my help with this one," said Aroculus.

"What?" questioned Guin, pulling the book out of the pouch.

"Get to the very back of the cave and don't say a word." Guin nodded and did just as Aroculus said. Kailan, out of instinct, followed along with Guin and did the same. "Open me, hold your hand out, and read the words." Guin opened the book and held out his hands. As soon as he began reading the first word in the book, Guin and Kailan could feel the air become cooler. The water on the walls flowed down and into the small pool of water, making it much bigger. As Soon as Guin had finished, the water burst out of the pool and shot towards the entrance of the cave. "Run!" yelled Aroculus. "Kailan and Guin bolted out of the cave on their horses past the dragon. The beast reared and let out a few bursts of fire before landing its front feet and turning around. "Guin turned around, and began casting spurts of water at the dragon's mouth, trying to douse the

[216]

flames. All that it did, however, was annoy the dragon even more. "Guin!" yelled out Aroculus. "Use the next spell!" Guin opened the book and read out the words on the page. Suddenly, another dragon seemed to appear in front of the two boys. This dragon wasn't real though. It was made of smoke and fire, but to the actual dragon, it looked very real. It reared up, and flew up, blowing bursts of fire at the fake dragon before heading back towards the cave.

"How come you've never shown spells like that before?" questioned Guin.

"I've never needed to," replied Aroculus.

"You could teach us a spell so that we could make our way up to the top of the mountain much quicker," said Guin.

"Ah, but what experience would you gain?" questioned Aroculus. "You might have an easy way up the mountain, but you would not learn anything from it."

"Will you please stop talking," said Kailan. "It's really getting creepy."

"Sorry, Kailan," said Guin, placing the book back into his bag. The boys continued up the mountain, keeping one eye behind them for the dragon. After an hour, they had neared the top and the mountain had begun to level out. The boys searched from cave to cave and found nothing until they came around a corner and stumbled upon a frightening view. Kailan signalled Guin to stop before backing up himself, very slowly.

"What is it?" questioned Guin.

"Dragons," replied Kailan.

[217]

"We already took care of one," said Guin. "How hard would it be to deal with a few more?"

"Take a look," said Kailan. Guin poked his head around the corner of the rocks to see the dragons. Hundreds of scaly beasts were around the bend.

"How do we get around?" questioned Guin.

"You don't," said Aroculus in a muffled voice.

"We are not going straight through them," said Guin.

"There is no way around," replied Aroculus. Kailan quickly interjected.

"What is he saying?" questioned Kailan.

"He says that there isn't a way around and that we have to go this way," replied Guin.

"There is no way around. All that you need to do is walk straight through," said Aroculus. "The dragons will not attack you"

"How do you know that?" questioned Guin.

"Just trust me!" Guin nodded and hopped off his horse.

"What are you doing?" questioned Kailan.

"I'm walking through them," said Guin. As made his way around the corner, the dragons noticed him and began to roar and hiss at him. Guin slowly moved forward, very cautiously.

"Let Kailan lead!" yelled Aroculus. At that instant, one of the larger dragons flew up and landed in front of Guin, shaking the ground and knocking him over. It let out a monstrous roar before Kailan jumped between Guin and the beast, with his sword pointed up at it. The dragon brought its head down and sneered at Kailan. The boy was full of terror and fear, but he did not show even a hint within his eyes.

"Get back!" yelled Kailan. The beast took a step back and let out a burst of fire into the air above. Guin quickly picked himself up and ran behind the rocks again. "Does the book have any spells for this?"

"No, he must learn to face the dragon and be brave!" said Aroculus.

"He said that you should stand your ground," replied Guin.

"I hate that book!" yelled Kailan.

"I'm not fond of you either," replied Aroculus, unheard by Kailan. The dragon waved its tail back and forth before pulling its head back and lunging at Kailan. The boy jumped to the side, striking the dragon with his sword, but with no reward. The dragon's scales were too hard for Kailan's sword to penetrate, especially with his level of strength. "No matter what happens, he mustn't back down! He has to remain dominant in this fight."

"Kailan!" yelled Guin. "Don't let him think he's winning!" Kailan nodded and took a step to the side. Stepping left over right, Kailan made his way closer to the edge of the mountainside. He slowly knelt and picked up a stone in his fist and clenched it tightly. First, he threw the stone to the opposite side of the road in front of the dragon's face. Secondly, he threw his sword in the same direction before running to the nearest

[219]

side of the dragon and jumping on its neck. The dragon's eyes stayed on the sword and attacked it instead of Kailan, engulfing the blade in flames for a number of seconds. Kailan held on for dear life, pulling the dagger that he had bought at the marketplace in Harlem. Grabbing onto the dragon's scales, Kailan pried the knife underneath, and thrust it into the soft flesh underneath. The beast reared into the air, throwing Kailan from its back.

"Are you ok?" yelled Guin. Kailan slowly picked himself up off the ground and readied himself for another attack. The beast, instead of attacking Kailan, brought its wings up, then down with immense force, shooting itself into the air. Slowly, it made its way out of sight and into the clouds. Kailan looked at Guin with an expression of confusion on his face.

"Is that it?" questioned Kailan.

"He won't be bothering us again," said Aroculus. Guin smiled and walked up to Kailan.

"I think that it's ok to go ahead," said Guin. Kailan walked over to his sword and tried to pick it up, but it was too hot.

"Guin, can you cast some water on it?" questioned Kailan. The young wizard walked over to Kailan and clapped his hands together, letting out a shower of water from his hands. Kailan tried picking up the sword again, but it was still too hot, so he dropped it. As the blade hit the ground, it shattered in two. The two boys stared at the broken sword for a second before anything was said. "Well that just sucks!" yelled Kailan. "What am I supposed to do now?"

"It must have been from the constant heating and cooling," said Guin. "Don't worry, we'll find you a new sword soon. We can get your old one fixed later." They picked up the two shards and placed them in one of the saddlebags. Now that the dragons were out of the way, the two boys could see that the road was much wider at this point, as it finally came to an end. Road went straight into the mountainside with a small opening, just big enough for the boys on foot, and their horses. Kailan looked at Guin.

"Should we go in?" questioned Kailan. Guin snapped his finger, creating a small ball of fire in his hand.

"I think you should let me lead this one," said Guin jokingly. As the two boys stepped into the hole in the rocks, they stared upwards in awe.

"I don't think that we'll need your fire," said Kailan. The boys had stumbled upon a temple within the mountain. The walls of the room were lined with pools of a burning liquid that lit up the entire area. At the far end of the temple was a staircase which went just above Kailan's head. At the top of the stairs, there was an altar, with an old man sitting behind it on an oaken chair. His hair thinning, but very long, as well as a beard that reached to the floor.

"Ah, Kailan!" said the old man with excitement. "You've made it finally." Kailan stared at the man for a quick second with a look of confusion.

"How do you know my name?" questioned Kailan.

[221]

"That's not relevant at the moment," said the old man. "Now, come up here." Kailan slowly, and cautiously, made his way up the steps to the altar. Lying across the top of the altar was a red velvet cloth, with a beautiful, ornate sword resting on it. The hilt and pommel were shaped to resemble fire. There was also a bright red ruby inlaid into the pommel, and the blade had a red tinge to it. "Pick it up my boy," said the man. Kailan slowly grabbed a hold of the handle and lifted up the sword. He held it in front of his face before seeing a quick spark. He jerked his head back out of surprise, just missing the flames that were now shooting from the blade.

"Why is the sword on fire?" questioned Kailan, with his eyes fixed on the blade. There was no answer.

"Kailan, I think he's gone," said Guin, standing at the bottom of the steps. Kailan looked over to see that the old man had disappeared from view.

"Where did he go?" questioned Kailan. "I still want to know how he knows who I am."

"I guess we'll never know," replied Guin. The flames in Kailan's sword quickly died away.

"I think that we should get going," said Aroculus from Guin's book bag.

"Who said that?" said Kailan, confused.

"Can you hear me?" said Aroculus.

"Of course I can," replied Kailan. Guin smiled and stared at the sword for a second.

"I think that it's because you now have your sword that

[222]

you can hear Aroculus," said Guin.

"Great!" yelled Kailan. "Now I'm crazy too!" Kailan made his way down the steps, quickly learning how to ignite the flames with his sword by thought. The boys made their way through opening in the stone wall again and to the outside. As they reached the other side of the wall, they found themselves in a bit more trouble than before. This time, there were a number of dragons in the boys' way. As they turned around to flee back into the temple, they found that the hole had disappeared and sealed itself behind them.

"What do we do Aroculus?" questioned Kailan.

"If Guin uses magic now, then all of the dragons will attack," replied Aroculus. The beasts hissed at the boys, roaring and some of them even snapping their jaws together. Kailan raised his new sword in front of him and pointed at the dragons, before engulfing it in flames.

"I'm pretty sure that dragon's don't really mind fire that much," said Guin, hiding behind Kailan, keeping the horses still. As the first dragon unleashed a blast of flames, the two boys closed their eyes and cringed, thinking of the end. Kailan felt strange. There was no pain, no burning sensation or stinging. Maybe death is not painful. Maybe it happened so quick that Kailan had already passed on. As he opened his eyes, he found himself still standing in front of the dragons. They let out another burst of fire, but this time, Kailan kept his eyes open. As the fire neared the boys, it was sucked into the flaming sword and made it glow brighter. Kailan smiled and pointed the sword

[223]

at the dragons again. He slowly walked towards them, making sure not to take any physical attacks. He raised the sword straight into the air and unleashed a ball of fire straight into the air. The dragons backed off immediately and moved off the road.

*   *   *

The three friends suited up after a quick morning meal and made their way, with Gelob and King Grakken, to the far side of the city. On this side of the city, the foliage seemed to be much more lush and closer spaced.

"Where do you think they're taking us?" questioned Lena.

"I don't know exactly, but I think it'll be fun," replied Thorstein.

"We're on our way to the bat trench," said Gelob.

"Bat trench?" questioned Viktor. "What is a bat trench?"

"A trench with bats," replied Gelob. "It isn't that hard to figure out." When the group arrived at the hole, they found a stone staircase leading to the bottom. From the top, all that they could see was blackness. There was only a small amount of light that actually reached the bottom of the ditch. All that the trench was, was a giant crack within the ground, the perfect place for these bats to live. The walls of the hole were just far enough that Thorstein was able to walk without feeling squished.

"Why are we here?" questioned Thorstein. "I don't understand how this helps us on our journey."

"You are here to prove yourselves," replied Gelob.

"Wait, you have us out here fighting bats?" asked Viktor.

"That's just cruel!" said Lena in anger.

"You won't think that when you see the bats," replied Gelob.

"What do you mean?" questioned Thorstein.

"These are not the same types of bats that you have where you come from," Gelob informed them. "These bats stand at knee height, have a wingspan as wide as I am tall. They eat meat, and they are always hungry."

"They shouldn't be too hard to fight," said Viktor.

"They are almost impossible to see down here," replied Gelob. "Their fur is almost the same colour of black as the darkness they call home."

"When do we get to see these bats?" questioned Lena, looking around.

"Right now!" yelled Gelob, throwing a small stone into the abyss. At first, they couldn't see a thing, but they could sure hear the bats. The squeals and shrieks of the bats echoed in their ears, as loud as trumpets. Gelob quickly ran behind the group and up the stairs.

"Where are you going?" demanded Thorstein.

[225]

"I'm not stupid enough to fight the bats down here," said Gelob. Suddenly, the sky went black with bats and the three companions were in total and absolute darkness. The sounds of the bats grew louder, and then it began. As the bats flew by, they knocked into the companions. Lena pulled out her bow and started shooting. Her eyesight was so well trained that she could see well enough in the dark to still fight. Thorstein on the other hand, crouched against the wall of the trench until his eyes adjusted. They tried to make their way back up the steps, but there were too many bats. Thorstein began swinging his axe wildly.

"Thorstein, watch what you're doing," said Lena.

"I'm sorry, I can't see a thing still," said Thorstein. The bats had now realised that they were not alone, and had now begun to attack the companions. Lena reached behind her head to pull another arrow from her quiver, but she had run out. She ran over to Thorstein, who was shielding himself with his armour and hid behind him. Suddenly, the bats started falling out of the air. As Lena looked up, she noticed elves surrounding the top of the hole, shooting arrows downwards.

"Don't worry!" yelled Gelob from up top. "You were never in any real danger!" As soon as the bats were gone, the elves made their way down the steps.

"You bastard!" yelled Lena, pushing Gelob to the ground. "Why would you do that?" The elf picked himself up and patted the dirt off his clothes.

"We had to be sure that you were who we thought you

[226]

were," said Gelob. "Your aim is remarkable. Within a few seconds, you had killed almost twenty bats, with only seventeen arrows I might add."

"Well, maybe if I had some more arrows, I'd have killed more," replied Lena.

"And for that reason exactly, the king has something special for you," said Gelob. "Follow me."

"Wait," said Thorstein. "Where's Viktor?"

"I'm over here," said a voice, stepping out of the darkness. Thorstein eyed up Viktor and then himself and Lena.

"You are completely unscathed," Thorstein pointed out. "Me and Lena are covered in cuts and scratches." Viktor smiled.

"They didn't seem to want to touch me," he replied. The three companions and the group of elves made their way back into the main part of the city, coming upon a small, white stone building. The wooden door on the front was old and worn with holes in it. As Gelob pushed the door open, the three friends found the king standing inside.

"Ah, good," said King Grakken. "You passed the test." The inside of the building was dark, and smelled of mould and dirt. "This is where Drast used to live." Lena's eyes widened.

"He lived here?" she questioned. "This is just a simple shack. I thought that you said he was a great general."

"Oh, he was. He chose not to live in a more luxurious house though," responded the king. "We have not touched it since he left, but we know that he left a present for the one most in need of it." In the far corner of the small room, there was a

[227]

wooden chest on the floor. It too was old and worn. The latch on the box had rusted to the point where Lena could break it off with one hand.

"How long has he been gone?" questioned Lena.

"Almost two decades ago," said Gelob. "Just walked into the palace one day and said that he was leaving. He mentioned the gift here and then just vanished into thin air." Lena slowly opened the chest to reveal a quiver.

"It's so pretty," said Lena with a smile on her face. The quiver was made of red leather, with golden rivets and clasps on the belt. It was full of arrows as well.

"That quiver there is an amazing thing," said King Grakken. "It never empties of arrows." Lena slung it over her head and shoulder.

"Thank you so much!" said Lena, hugging both King Grakken and Gelob. "This is a beautiful gift." Thorstein pulled out his map and stared at it for a few seconds.

"Excuse me, but do you by chance know how to get to the city of Alabeth from here?" questioned Thorstein from outside the door as he was too big to go inside. "We are supposed to meet some friends there."

"Alabeth?" questioned King Grakken, scratching his head. Gelob leaned in to his uncle.

"I think he means Farfol," said Gelob to King Grakken.

"Oh, Farfol!" The king had a smile on his face. "Sorry, but we have different names for some of these cities." The king stepped out of the small building and looked both ways after exiting the door. "If you continue down this road, it should take you maybe a day at the most to reach Farfol." Thorstein smiled and rolled the map up.

"Thank you very much," said Thorstein.

"Actually," said the king. "If you leave now, you should be able to reach it by sundown."

"We'll leave immediately," said Viktor, hurrying out of the house. The group made their way back to their quarters and collected their things. Thorstein then remembered the water that he and Kailan had collected in the beginning of their journey in the elven ruins. He described the ruins to the king as they were leaving. The king smiled and whispered the secret of the ruins to Thorstein. Thorstein smiled and held onto the wineskin of water tightly.

"Don't tell anyone it's secret though," said King Grakken.

In less time than it had taken for them to enter the city, the three companions were gone and on their way to the city of Alabeth.

*   *   *

Kailan waved the new sword around in the air, lighting it on fire, and then quickly extinguishing the flames. He never realised it before, but his new sword fit his old scabbard perfectly.

"I find it a bit odd that my sword broke immediately before we came upon this one," said Kailan. "I think that that old man had something to do with it."

"I wouldn't worry about it too much there, Kailan," said Aroculus. "You have a much better weapon now."

"I just find that this journey is like a big mystery and nobody knows what is going on. Every single time we go somewhere, the person in charge has no idea what is happening. Take Tanier for example," said Kailan. "When I first went to Harlem, he knew nothing about the letter. It seems like the only person that knew what's going on is Orpeth Armenen, and he's dead!"

"I guess that does dig deeper into a mystery," said Guin, scratching his head. "Hopefully Tanier will know more by the time we reach Harlem again."

"Hopefully," replied Kailan. As the boys ventured down the road, they came upon a sign. On it was the word "ALABETH". The two boys smiled intensely. Guin bolted forward on his horse and galloped down the road.

"Come, Kailan!" yelled Guin. "It's only a little ways down the road!" Kailan quickly chased after the other boy, digging his heels into the horse's side. The two boys raced down the road until they could see the buildings ahead. The ground quickly changed from a dirt road to stone bricks. Alabeth was only a city because of the amount of trade that it did. It was the centre of trade for most of the continent, and because of this, it was also the centre for crime. The boys would have to watch themselves very carefully in Alabeth. It wasn't long before they were already in trouble. As the two boys were tying up the horses at the stables, a young boy came by and quickly grabbed Guin's book bag from his saddle.

"Get back here with that!" yelled Guin. The boy took one look inside the bag and then looked back at Guin.

"It's mine now," said the boy, sticking his tongue out before turning in the opposite direction and running away. He was quickly knocked to the ground by Kailan, standing in his way.

"I think that you need to give that back to my friend," said Kailan.

"I think you should mind your own business," said a deep voice from behind Kailan. As he turned around, he found himself looking into the chest of a very large man. He looked up to face the man, who was pushing almost right against Kailan. The boy smirked and stepped to the side.

"You should listen to my friend," said the boy. The man one of his fists in the other hand and cracked his knuckles. Kailan looked down and removed his sword and scabbard from his side, and threw it on the ground.

"If you would like to fight, then by all means, we shall fight," said Kailan with a smile on his face.

"Don't do anything stupid, Kailan," said Guin. Kailan turned around to look at Guin.

"Don't worry," said Kailan, looking to his side. "This'll

[231]

be over in a second." In all of Kailan's cockiness, he did not notice the gargantuan fist flying towards him. He was thrown a few feet back and hit the ground hard. He rolled over on his stomach gasping for air.

"That'll teach him to mess with us!" cheered the little boy. He picked the book bag up off the ground and walked over to the large man. "Let's sell these and see what we can get for them."

"I don't think so," said Kailan, picking himself up off the ground. "Just had the wind knocked out of me, that's all." He wiped himself off and placed his hands in front for a fighting stance. As the large man made his first attack, Kailan moved to the side, dodging it, and countering with a punch to the armpit. The man was knocked back a bit and snarled. He rolled his shoulder and rubbed his armpit.

"I'm going to kick your ass!" yelled the man. As he lunged forward, something grabbed his collar and pulled him back.

"If you kick his ass, I'm going to kick yours," said a familiar voice. The large man turned around, only to find himself doing the same thing that Kailan had done a few seconds before. Thorstein stood over the man with a smile on his face. "Now, if you could give my friends back their things."

"Thorstein!" yelled Guin in excitement. The little boy quickly ran over to Guin and placed the book bag in his hands before running off into the city. The large man almost did the same, but a bit more cautiously.

"How's that for an entrance?" laughed Thorstein. Kailan and Guin hurried over to Thorstein and gave the giant a hug.

"Kailan?" said Lena. The boy stepped to the side of Thorstein, his eyes as wide as possible, and his smile just as large. Kailan ran up to Lena, picking her up off the ground and holding her tightly.

"I missed you so much," said Kailan.

"You did not," said Lena jokingly.

"Do I look like I'm lying?" questioned Kailan. Lena smiled and rested her lips on his. She closed her eyes, and upon opening them, released.

"What is that?" said Lena.

"What is what?" replied Kailan.

"Are you crying?" questioned Lena.

"No," said Kailan, wiping a single tears from his eye.

"The great champion, Kailan of Arlbega, cries for the love of a girl!" yelled Lena.

"I could just drop you," said Kailan, smiling.

"You wouldn't dare." Kailan loosened his grip slightly and then tightened again so that Lena would slide down a few inches. The two of them smiled at each other for what seemed like minutes before Viktor came up from behind and patted Kailan on the back.

"Hey, Viktor!" yelled Kailan. He slowly lowered Lena to the ground with one arm and wrapped his free arm around Viktor.

[233]

"Anyone up for a few drinks tonight?" questioned Viktor with a mischievous grin on his face. The group of friends all laughed. They showed off their new items to each other and told stories of their adventures. Thorstein walked over to the dornbeast and grabbed his dragon skull. Kailan looked at it in amazement.

"You actually killed one?" questioned Kailan. Thorstein filled up with pride, nodding his head.

"Ripped the head in two with my own hands," laughed Thorstein.

"Kailan almost had one the other day," said Guin.

"Oh really?" said Viktor doubtingly.

"Stabbed the bugger right behind the neck before he decided to fly away," said Kailan. "I'd say that he was about twice the size of yours actually." Thorstein patted Kailan on the back, knocking him forward and forcing Kailan to stumble.

"I would've loved to have fought one like that," said Thorstein.

"Damn beast broke my sword, but my item turned out to be a new one," said Kailan.

"Can I see it?" questioned Viktor. Kailan picked his sword up off the ground, forgetting to reattach it after the fight, and handed it to Viktor. The boy grabbed onto the sheath and slowly pulled the sword out, admiring the craftsmanship. As the blade was fully retracted from the scabbard, there was a flash, and the handle itself went on fire this time. Viktor dropped the sword to the ground and held his hand underneath his arm.

"Are you ok?" quickly asked Thorstein." Viktor pulled out his hand and inspected it.

"Just singed the hairs, that's all," replied Viktor. The flames on the handle quickly went away.

"I've never had that happen before," said Kailan. He knelt down and cautiously picked up the sword by the handle. The flames did not shoot out this time at the handle. This time, Kailan took a step back, and held the sword into the air, igniting the flames.

"It must have some sort of defence mechanism so that only you can use it," said Guin.

"Only I can use mine," said Thorstein.

"What is yours?" questioned Guin. Thorstein smiled and quickly summoned his armour. Guin fell backwards in amazement. "You can armour yourself as quickly as I can blink?" Thorstein nodded and smiled.

"It also heightens my senses and awareness," said the giant. "I can tell when a mouse is creeping up behind me in the dark." Guin quickly pulled out his magic tome.

"Everyone, meet Aroculus," said Guin, showing the book around.

"I don't get it," said Viktor. "It's just a book."

"You should probably explain to them what I am first," said Aroculus.

"Did the book just speak?" questioned Viktor, taking a step back.

"I did indeed," replied Aroculus.

[235]

"Wait a second," said Kailan. "How can you hear him?"

"Well can't you hear him?" asked Viktor.

"Well I can hear him, but you shouldn't be able to yet," said Kailan. Viktor raised an eyebrow.

"Why's that?"

"Because I had to find my sword before I could hear him speak."

"It must be because Viktor knows some spells," Thorstein piped up. Guin's attention quickly changed from the book over to Viktor.

"You know spells?" questioned Guin.

"Where did you learn these spells?" interrogated Aroculus. Viktor backed up as Guin stepped in closer.

"I picked them up here and there," replied Viktor. "Is that a problem?" Guin backed off immediately.

"Not a problem at all," said Guin. "We were just curious."

"Well actually, I think…" said Aroculus before Guin closed the book shut.

"Leave it alone Aroculus," said Guin. The boys began to laugh. By the time Kailan and Guin had reached the city, it was already late in the afternoon. As the sun slowly set, the group decided to find a nice place to sleep as a whole party again. They found an empty barn on the outskirts of town and made it into a nice place to sleep for the night. Thorstein gathered as much loose straw as he could and laid it out around the floor, leaving a larger pile for himself. He pulled a blanket from his saddle for the dornbeast, who was resting inside as well as the horses, and placed it over the straw. In the middle of the barn, the farmer had a small forge made for crafting horse shoes and fixing tools. The companions decided to use this as a fire place that night, as the seasons were beginning to change, and the temperature was much colder. While Guin, Viktor, and Thorstein were sitting around the forge, having a few drinks, Kailan and Lena were outside taking a walk.

"Nothing like a walk by moonlight; now is there?" said Kailan. Lena smiled and held his hand.

"Tell me why you didn't want me to come with you?" questioned Lena.

"Sorry?"

"Why you sent me with Thorstein and Viktor instead of coming with you."

"Because our trips would have taken much more time," replied Kailan. If we were trying to find my sword and your quiver as well, we would be taking almost twice the time that it took us to go the way we did."

"I guess that makes sense," said Lena. "But what if something were to happen to me?"

"That is why I sent Viktor with you instead of bringing him with us. That way, if at any time, you needed help, one of them would be there for you." Lena smiled and wrapped her arms around Kailan.

"Thank you," said Lena, smiling and occasionally

looking up at Kailan.

"That's what friends do," said Kailan. "We look out for each other." As they made their way back to the barn, Lena turned to Kailan and gave him a peck on the cheek.

"Next time, if we split up again, I'd prefer to stay with you," said Lena, smiling. "Seeing Thorstein go swimming naked was a bit too much for me." The two of them burst out laughing, nearly waking the other companions. They walked into the barn, closing the door behind them. Kailan laid out the blanket for him and Lena and the quickly fell asleep. Kailan laid next to her with his arm wrapped around her. The night was not as cold as anticipated, nor was it very dark. The moon light up everything enough that one would be able to see where they were going, even in the forest. At some point in the middle of the night, Kailan awoke. He couldn't figure out why he woke up, but he wasn't able to go back to sleep. So instead of just lying there, Kailan got up and decided to go for another walk. When he stood up, he noticed something very strange. The man-door was wide open. He looked around and noticed that all of the other companions were still fast asleep. Cautiously, Kailan went to inspect it, but not before grabbing his sword and belt. He poked his head out the door and saw someone quickly run around the corner of the barn.

"Who's there?" he called out. There was no answer. Kailan stepped out of the barn and slowly made his way to that corner, with his back to the wall. He turned the corner, but to his surprise, no one was there. As he turned back, he saw, out of the

[238]

corner of his eye, someone in white, run into the forest next to the barn. Kailan decided that it was best to see what they were up to and chase them on foot. For all he knew, it could be a spy for the Black Allegiance. The moon was very bright, but Kailan still felt that he needed more light. He pulled out his sword and lit it on fire, but just enough so that it would glow and not burn down the forest. The deeper he ran into the forest, the more Kailan felt as though he shouldn't have left the barn. As he was running, Kailan slipped on a wet log and began rolling down a hill, launching his sword into the air, landing out of reach. He tumbled most of the way down the hill before coming to a complete stop. As he stood up, Kailan found himself dizzy and disoriented. He walked over to his sword, which was still glowing enough for him to find it, and placed it into his scabbard. The moon gave enough light in the forest that Kailan could see the person perfectly now. It was a young woman, maybe a few years older than Kailan, sitting next to a tree. She was wearing a white gown, and seemed almost to glow. She was wearing a golden band around her dark hair.

"Who are you?" questioned Kailan. The woman looked up and smiled.

"I am a friend," she replied. As she stood up and walked closer, Kailan noticed something strange about the woman. Something about her face seemed familiar.

"What were you doing near the barn?"

"I have something to tell you," said the woman. "It's about Lena."

"Why?" questioned Kailan. "What happened?" He quickly turned around, trying to run back up the hill.

"She's fine at the moment," replied the woman. "Don't worry." She was now standing directly in front of Kailan, and it was then that he realised who she was. "No matter what happens, she loves you, and you must always be there to protect her. Remember that, Kailan." The woman then proceeded to punch Kailan in the face, waking him up. As he opened his eyes, Kailan found himself still lying next to Lena, her pet eagle standing beside him, staring at him.

"Are you two going to wake up?" said Guin, kicking at Kailan's feet.

"I'm too tired to get up," said Kailan. Guin kicked again, but this time, Kailan kicked back, knocking Guin's feet out from under him, landing him on Kailan and Lena. "Now you've done it," laughed Kailan. He quickly rolled onto his stomach and held Guin down. Lena quickly moved to the side, getting out of the way of the wrestling duo. It wasn't long before Viktor jumped on the two boys and started horsing around as well. Lena walked up to Thorstein and sat next to him on a bail of straw.

"Just like a bunch of children," huffed Lena. Thorstein pulled an apple out of his bag and handed it to Lena.

"Oh come now," said Thorstein. "If I was there size, I'd be messing around with them too." Lena looked up at Thorstein, showing him the expression on her face that she was not impressed. The giant laughed and picked up a bale of straw with one hand. "Watch this," said Thorstein with a smile on his face. He threw it at the three boys who were rolling around on the ground, knocking Guin, who had been struggling to gain dominance the whole time, back onto the ground. The three boys stared at the bale of straw, and then at Thorstein.

"Get him!" yelled Viktor. The three smaller boys quickly charged at Thorstein, knocking him over on his back.

"He's got my leg!" yelled Guin in a panic.

"Go for the shins!" yelled Kailan. Viktor and Kailan wrapped themselves around Thorstein's legs, trying to hold him down. The giant had Guin by the one leg and lifted him into the air, standing up. Kailan looked at Viktor in shock. "Well this isn't working." Thorstein lifted the leg with Viktor on it and began to shake him off, throwing him into a pile of straw.

"You will never defeat me!" yelled Thorstein, beating his chest. Viktor made his way to the second level of the barn without Thorstein noticing and jumped on his back.

"Feel the wrath of the mighty Viktor!" The boy then began to rub his knuckles into Thorstein's head, bringing him back down to the ground.

"I'm going to take a walk," said Lena. The boys continued to wrestle, not hearing Lena. "I said, I'm going to take a walk!"

"We'll be here when you get back," replied Kailan. Lena grabbed her bow and quiver, and made for the door.

"Come, Kaela," said Lena. The bird flew up and perched on Lena's quiver. The sun shone very brightly that

[241]

morning, making for a nice, warm walk. The dew twinkled on the grass beneath her feet. The trees near Alabeth had just started to change colours for the season, making for an amazing view. Lena decided to take her walk within the city instead of just walking along the treeline. As she walked past the merchants, Lena found many exotic items. She saw some foods that she had never heard of before. Even some of the animals that were being sold were unknown to her. There was one that looked like a goat, but with a much longer neck, and it had tusks coming from its mouth instead of horns. There was another animal that looked like a giant beetle, but was covered in a thick coat of fur. As Lena observed the animals, the merchant came up to her and stood next to her. He was a short man, wearing a long, colourful robe.

"Have you decided what you like?" questioned the man. Lena turned her head and smiled.

"I'm just browsing," said Lena. "Thank you though." The man nodded.

"I see you have a very nice bird there," said the man. Lena smiled.

"Thank you."

"How much do you want for her?" Lena's smile quickly vanished.

"She's not for sale."

"You have a white eagle with green eyes." The man pulled a small sack of coins from his pocket. "That is a very rare thing."

"Listen," said Lena. "I'm never selling this bird."

"Suit yourself." Lena walked away and continued to go through the market. It wasn't long before she was stopped again. This time, it was an old woman, adorned in numerous bracelets, necklaces and pendants, rings, and colourful clothing.

"Young girl, I can read your future," said the woman. Lena smiled and shook her head. "It's free of charge." Lena looked up at Kaela.

"Should we go in?" questioned Lena. The bird seemed to nod, and Lena turned again to the woman. "What have I got to lose?"

The old woman smiled. "Come in to my tent then." Lena followed the woman into a small, but wondrously colourful tent. "Sit, my dear." There was a small table, with two, old chairs sitting across from one another. Lena sat down and the elderly lady sat opposite. "My name is Madame Ita."

"Nice to meet you," said Lena. "My name is Lena."

"Now, Lena let us begin." Madame Ita held out her hands, palms up. She closed her eyes. "Give me your hands."

Lena placed her hands in Madame Ita's palms and smiled. "What do you see?"

"You are on a long journey, from many lands away," said Madame Ita. "You travel with four companions. One of them…" Madame Ita stopped for a quick second.

"What is it?" questioned Lena.

"My vision is a bit clouded at the moment, but it is coming." The woman made a few strange faces before opening her eyes. "I know what your intentions are for the boy."

"Pardon?" questioned Lena.

"I think that you know what I am talking about," said Madame Ita. "You only do this because of your mother."

Lena stood up, knocking her chair over. "I'm leaving!" she exclaimed, walking out the door.

"You will not be forgiven for it!" yelled Madame Ita. "Death shall find you!"

As Lena made her way through the tent opening, Kailan stood in her way. The girl took one look at his face and then burst out crying, pushing past him and running into the crowd.

"Lena!" yelled Kailan. He turned to face Madame Ita. "What did you do to her?"

"I read her destiny," replied Madame Ita. "And you should not follow such a girl." Kailan turned around, running into the crowd in search of Lena, but she was gone. Out of anger, he kicked out one of the poles holding the tent up, making it collapse.

*   *   *

As Lena ran through the city, she couldn't stop thinking of what Madame Ita said. How could she have known? Would she tell Kailan? She finally came to a stop, hiding in an alley. She continued to weep for another few minutes.

"I should never have gone in there," Lena said allowed to herself. "I promised myself that no one would ever find out." She pulled her bow and quiver off her shoulder so that her back would rest more easily against the wall of the building. "Why do these things happen to me?" She wiped the tears from her eyes to see a man standing at the entrance of the alley.

"What's a pretty girl like you doing around here?" said the man as he walked closer to her.

"I'm sorry, but I need some time alone," said Lena, turning away. The man continued to advance towards her.

"You should never be alone," said the man.

"Please, just leave me alone." The man was so close now that he was able to grab Lena's arm. "Let me go!" yelled Lena. The menacing grin on the man's face made Lena realise what was actually happening. She punched him once in the jaw.

"Feisty," said the man, rubbing his chin. He then grabbed Lena with his other arm, ripping her shirt.

"Help!" she screamed out. Lena continued to kick and punch as much as she could, but the man was too strong. He threw her to the ground, knocking her head against the stone wall. The man then began to unbuckle his pants.

"Time for a little fun," the man laughed. He knelt down at Lena's feet, and leaned over her. She tried to wriggle away, but the man grabbed her wrists and held her down. "Stop squirming, ya little bitch!" Lena cried out as the man pulled her pants down and ran his hand up her leg. As the alleyway quickly became dark, Lena closed her eyes and cringed. There was a

[245]

fraction of a second where Lena could only think of her sister, and how she was raped and murdered. It wasn't until the man was thrown off that she realised it was over.

"Lena!" yelled Kailan. "Get out of here!" Lena, dazed, quickly rolled onto her side, pulling up her pants, and ran out of the alley, into Viktor and Guin. "I'm going to kill you!" screamed Kailan at the top of his lungs. With each hit, Kailan grew more and more angry. He did not care about the pain that was beginning to grow in his hands. All that he could think of was what the man was about to do to Lena. He would never be able to live with himself. In a sense, Kailan was not just saving Lena, but himself as well. When he finally emerged from the alley, Kailan was covered in sweat, his knuckles bruised, and bleeding.

*   *   *

It wasn't until later that night that Lena actually began to speak again. Kailan was sitting against the outside wall of the barn, holding his bandaged hands together.

"Do they hurt?" questioned Lena.

"Very much," replied Kailan. "He didn't hurt you did he?"

"I hit my head, but that was about it," said Lena. She began to cry again, this time hugging Kailan. "I'm sorry,

[246]

Kailan."

"Sorry for what? You did nothing wrong."

"I need to go home," said Lena. Kailan felt like his stomach was being ripped out of his gut.

"What do you mean?"

"I'm going to put you in harm's way, I just know it."

"Don't say that," said Kailan.

"It's true though."

"No it's not!"

"Yes it is, and you know it!" cried Lena. There was a short silence between the two for a brief moment.

"I had a dream last night," said Kailan. "I think I saw your sister."

Lena's eyes lit up. "What?"

"She looked almost exactly like you," said Kailan. "The same bright green eyes that you have, the same long brunette hair." Lena began to smile. "She was wearing a white dress and I think that she was wearing a gold crown on her head."

"What did she say?" questioned Lena. Kailan looked down and hesitated for a moment. "Please tell me."

"She told me that you love me no matter what," said Kailan. "And that I always need to be there for you. I intend to do just that." Lena smiled and held Kailan tightly, kissing him passionately. The pain in Kailan's stomach quickly went away.

"That's all that I needed to hear," said Lena. She rubbed her eyes, and stood up.

The next day, the group left Alabeth and continued

their journey. They were now bound for the underground city of Ultar. There, they would find Viktor's item and complete their quest on the continent of Karnok. From Ultar, it was only a two days travel until they would meet up with Captain Briggs in the city of Drailnott. It was a long first day for the group. The terrain after Alabeth quickly changed from forest and plains, to much more rocky terrain. It made it very hard for the horses and the dornbeast. Because of this, the group members had to dismount and walk most of the way. It didn't seem very promising either. The group had prepared themselves very well physically for the journey ahead, but they were not ready mentally. As far as they could see, the only things visible were rocks until the edge of the horizon. It wasn't until the end of the first day that the group finally cleared the rocky terrain, but they weren't doing any better. What the map had neglected to tell them was that Ultar was in one of the largest deserts in the world. Thankfully for the group, their journey would have them go through a narrow section of the desert, but even then, it would still take them a number of days. They decided to camp in the desert for the night, but still keeping the rocks in view. It was a cold night, and they could start to feel the effects of autumn beginning to set in. Guin had to make a fire for the five companions to huddle around that night. The one upside to the desert was that for as far as they could see, there were stars.

"Anyone know any scary stories?" questioned Kailan.

"They forbid us from telling stories like that at the Wizards' Guild," said Guin.

"I never liked scary stories," said Thorstein. "Never found them to be fun.

"Lena?" questioned Kailan She shook her head. "What about you, Viktor?"

"Do you really want me to tell you my life story?" The group laughed.

"Well, does anyone have anything to do?" questioned Kailan.

Thorstein pulled out his Kalaka and began to play the Thorian lullaby that he had played in previous times. The notes fluttered like the wings of butterflies, dancing in their ears.

"You know?" said Lena. "I really like this song. There is something about it that reminds me of home."

"I really like it to," said Guin. "Puts me to sleep very quickly." The next day, the group headed out early, and continued on their journey through the desert. Even during the beginning of autumn, the desert was still relatively hot and dry. As the sun beat down harder throughout the day, the group members had to dismount their rides so that they could let their clothes dry from the sweat. At one point, they even decided to make shelters my sticking their weapons into the ground to hold up blankets for shade. They tried as much as they could to keep the horses and dornbeast cool, even by partially burying them in the sand. It wasn't until the third day that things really started to get hard for the group though. As they were travelling, Lena noticed something strange.

"I see footprints," said Lena. The group all stood

together at the top of the dune, looking for the footprints, but because Lena had such good eyesight, she could see them from much farther than any of the others. When they finally reached them, Guin laughed.

"Looks like someone else is here in the desert," said Guin. Thorstein shook his head.

"Those are our footprints," said Kailan.

"What do you mean? They can't be."

"Unless someone else is walking with a giant," said Kailan, pointing at the supersized footprint beside the others.

"Great!" said Kailan sarcastically. "We're lost in the middle of the desert."

"I'll just get Kaela to find the way for us," said Lena. The bird quickly flew into the air, climbing higher and higher. "She'll come back and tell us the way when she finds it."

"How long do you think that'll be," said Kailan.

"It most likely could take her from a few hours, to a day to return," replied Lena.

"Doesn't Aroculus have any spells that we can use?" Kailan asked Guin. The boy pulled the book out of his bag and opened it.

"I think he's sleeping," said Guin.

"He doesn't sleep, he's a book," said Kailan.

"Well, he's not talking," said Guin.

Kailan threw up his arms and sat on the ground. "I guess we're waiting for Kaela to get back," said Kailan. The group made up their shelters again, and covered the animals in the sand. The sun slowly began to become more intense. It wasn't long before most of the group had fallen asleep underneath the shade. About an hour later, Kailan awoke from his slumber, dehydrated, and his mouth completely dried out. He went over to his pack and pulled out his wineskin. The water in it was hot, but he didn't care, as long as he had some water. When he turned around, Kailan saw something that did not make him happy.

"Where's Viktor?" said Kailan, looking around for the other boy. He searched in a full circle before realising that Viktor had indeed left the camp. "Everyone, wakeup!" yelled Kailan.

The other group members slowly, but surely, awoke to Kailan's call and stood up.

"What's the matter?" questioned Thorstein.

"Viktor's gone!" said Kailan. The other's frantically looked around before coming upon the same conclusion that Kailan had. They called out his name, but there came no reply. It wasn't long before the group found a set of footprints, leading away from the camp. They began to follow them, but even as they reached the top of one of the dunes, the sight did not seem promising. There was still no sign of Viktor, only his footprints.

"Do you think he's been kidnapped?" worried Lena.

Kailan shook his head. "There's one set of footprints. Unless they carried him, he most likely wandered off." Kailan quickly turned around and made his way to the bottom of the dune and to the camp. "Guin, we'll need you to watch the camp, just in case anything happens."

The wizard nodded. "Don't worry, I've got it covered."

"First we get lost, and then this idiot has to run away," said Kailan, huffing as he walked back up the hill. Kailan, Lena and Thorstein began following the footprints. It was very strange with them because every now and then, they would take an immediate sharp turn. The sun was beginning to mess with their minds. They would see mirages, and visions of home, but they knew that they were just that, and continued on searching. The group found themselves searching for almost two hours before they finally found another sign of Viktor.

"I think I see him!" yelled out Lena with her keen eyes.

Laying in the sand, unconscious, was Viktor. As the three friends ran up to him, they pulled out all of the water they had. Thorstein knelt down beside Viktor and flipped him on his back.

"Are you okay?" questioned Thorstein. The boy made no sound. Thorstein pulled the cork out of his wineskin and held Viktor's mouth open at the same time, pouring some of the water in. The boy began choking on the water and coughing. He rolled on his side, coughing up sand and water. Thorstein lightly patted Viktor's back. He poured the rest of his water over Viktor's head and back, hoping to cool him down. He could hear Viktor mumble something, but couldn't make it out.

"What are you trying to say?" questioned Thorstein.

"Rina," whispered Viktor. Kailan and Lena knelt down beside the other two.

[252]

"Why did you leave?" demanded Kailan, scorching in the sun.

"Rina wanted me to follow her," said Viktor.

"Who is Rina?" questioned Kailan.

Lena put her hand on Kailan's chest and pulled him back. "Let's just give him some time," said Lena. "He's obviously suffering from the heat."

"And we aren't?" said Kailan, angrily. He noticed the look on Lena's face. It was the face that meant that she knew where he was coming from, but that he still had to fight his urges to be angry. "I guess you're right." The group slowly made their way back to the shelter. Thorstein carried Viktor in his arms, keeping him out of the sun and in his shadow. Viktor, somewhat conscious now, continued to mumble words throughout the trip back, but the only think that anyone could understand was Rina's name. When they finally made it back to the camp, the sun had almost set. By this point, Viktor had regained most of his strength and was able to walk. Guin had a fire going, using his magic and some more water for them. While the group was gone, Aroculus had taught Guin a spell that consisted of digging a hole into the ground and sucking water from the sand underneath. As Thorstein put Viktor down, he quickly made his way over to the water, which was in a metal bowl, scooping it up with his hands to his mouth.

"Why did you do that?" demanded Kailan a second time. He was clearly angry and annoyed by Viktor's actions. "We had to spend most of the damn day looking for you because you decided to run off into the middle of the desert. Kailan was now standing directly behind Viktor, who just turned and smiled.

"I just…" said Viktor, slurping up more water. "I just followed Rina."

Kailan yelled out in anger and pulled Viktor away from the water, throwing him to the ground. "I've had enough of you and this stupid desert! I've had enough of your stupid Rina!" Guin quickly stood up, the other two staring in awe. Viktor quickly jumped to his feet, and threw himself at Kailan. Viktor was much stronger than Kailan had ever expected. With each punch, it felt like Kailan was being pelted with rocks for fists.

"Don't you ever say anything about Rina!" cried Viktor, with tears rolling down his cheek. Kailan quickly broke free and wrapped his arm around Viktor's neck, and his other arm beneath Viktor's arm. He held him down, unable to move before they were both suddenly elevated in the air.

"You two need to stop and think about what you are doing," said Guin, holding his open hand out. "This is no way to treat each other!" He closed his hand and pulled away, dropping the boys to the ground. The boys picked themselves up, and walked in separate directions. Viktor walked up to the top of one of the dunes and lay there, staring up, into the sky as the stars slowly appeared. Kailan on the other hand, made his way over to Lena, who was resting underneath the shelter.

Lena turned to Kailan and slapped him across the face. "You are really something, aren't you," said Lena, getting up and walking away with a scowl on her face. Kailan sat underneath the shelter for a few seconds, trying to piece things together quickly before chasing after her.

"What was that for?" questioned Kailan as they walked into the desert. She ignored him. "Lena stop!" The girl turned around, hitting Kailan in the chest.

"You should feel ashamed for yourself," said Lena.

"For what?" said Kailan. "For getting angry because he made us waste hours in the desert searching for him?"

"Do you want to know who Rina was?" said Lena with tears in her eyes. "Rina was Viktor's love."

"If he loved her so much, then why did he leave her and come with us?" questioned Kailan.

"She's dead!" cried Lena. "She died in his arms just a few days before we came to find him!"

"How was I supposed to know," said Kailan. "He doesn't say anything to begin with."

"Well when he does, maybe you should listen," said Lena. "You'd be surprised to hear the stuff that he has to say." Lena turned around and began to walk away, back to the camp. Kailan stood there, thinking to himself.

"I'm sorry, Lena!" said Kailan.

"I'm not the one you should be saying sorry to," said Lena without turning around. Kailan slumped to the ground, falling backwards. He lay there for a number of minutes, gazing up at the stars.

"What would happen if Lena died?" he thought to

himself. "Would I act the same way as Viktor?" The boy tossed around thoughts in his head for a couple of minutes before standing up and returning to camp. As he returned to camp, Kailan walked past the fire and up the dune to Viktor. "Listen bud, I'm sorry for what I said earlier," said Kailan. He sat down beside Viktor and looked up at the sky. The other boy made no sound, nor any motion, recognizing Kailan's presence. "Lena told me all about Rina." Viktor quickly turned his head and stared at Kailan with anger in his eyes. "I'm sorry about what I said. Had I known what had happened, I never would have said those things." The anger in Viktor's eyes slowly drifted away. "If that happened to Lena, I'd probably kill someone if they said something ill about her too." Kailan turned to Viktor and held out his hand. "What do you say, forgive and forget?" Viktor looked at the outstretched hand and grabbed onto it.

"Forgive and forget," said Viktor.

*   *   *

As the sun rose, Kaela was just returning from her flight from Ultar. She jumped on Lena a number of times, bouncing around, trying to wake her up.

"She's back!" yelled Guin with a smile on his face. The group members quickly jumped to their feet, packing their things up. They waited a bit, letting the bird rest before heading back

[256]

out to the city of Ultar. As the sun began to set that night, the group came upon a light, not too far in the distance. It was the entrance to the city of Ultar. None of the friends had ever really heard much of the city of Ultar, except for the fact that it was underground. There were no gates at the entrance, just a tunnel, leading under the sand. Oil lamps lit up the tunnel entrance. The tunnel was very long. It took the five companions almost twenty minutes to finally reach the city. As the group made their way into city, they came upon the beauty that was Ultar. It was a giant hole in the ground, with buildings carved into the sides. The ceiling was a large stone dome, spanning from one side of the city to the other. As far as they could see down, there were buildings. The city was not just lit up by lamps as the entrance, but was instead lighted by mushrooms that grew along the sides of the city. They glowed blue and white, lighting up the entire city, from the deepest point below, to the stone ceiling above. There was one road in the city, spiralling down, and circling inwards as it went down.

"First time in Ultar?" Guin looked down to his side and noticed the little, pale man standing next to him.

"How could you tell?" said Guin.

"Well, first of all, I've never seen anyone over six feet here before," said the man. Guin glanced over at Thorstein and giggled. "Second, you look amazed."

"Well, you are right," said Guin. "This is the first time that any of us have been here before."

The little man smiled and held out his hand to Guin.

[257]

"The name's Belario Shaveets." Guin shook the man's hand and stood back, introducing him to the group. "You'll be needing a guide through the city then."

"I think that we should be able to do without," replied Kailan.

"I highly suggest that you take my help," said Belario. "It's very easy to get lost in the city."

"Isn't it just this main road?" questioned Lena.

The little man shook his head. "There are tunnels that reach out from the main part of the city," said Belario. "That's where most of the stuff is."

"Stuff?" pondered Kailan.

"You know, stuff. Things to buy, homes… stuff." Belario held his hands behind his back and walked around the group. "Many people have gone missing going through those tunnels. They take one wrong turn, and before they know it, they never see the surface again." Kailan turned around to Thorstein, who leaned over and listened in.

"What do you think?" questioned Kailan.

"I think it'll be beneficial," said Thorstein. "We should be able to trust him."

Kailan turned to Belario. "Glad to have you on board, Belario," said Kailan. As the group slowly made their way down the street, Belario began to tell of the history of Ultar.

"The city was founded over two hundred years ago," said Belario. "Before that, it was originally a giant ant nest."

"An ant nest?" said Lena, with shivers down her spine.

[258]

"The giant ants went extinct not too long before that, I'm guessing," said Belario. "They were once one of the fiercest creatures in the land, but then reduced to nothing."

"How did they all die?" questioned Viktor.

"Nobody knows. They most likely ran out of food." Belario took the group all throughout the city. He brought them through many of the secret passages and tunnels that only he and a few others knew about. As the slowly made their way down through the city, it became darker and darker as the lamps were used less and less. They finally reached a point where there were no more lamps, and the city was only being lit by the mushrooms on the walls. "So what are you guys actually doing here in Ultar," said Belario. Kailan and Thorstein looked at each other, unsure of Belario.

"We're on a quest," said Guin quickly. Kailan and Thorstein glared at Guin for a quick second.

"A quest?" said Belario, scratching his scruffy, little goatee. "Let me guess. You are here from Arlbega?" Kailan and Thorstein looked at each other in shock.

"How did you know that?" questioned Thorstein.

"Some men came by a few days ago," said Belario. "Said they were from some sort of dark group." He held his hand to his head. "Nah, can't remember the name."

"Black Allegiance?" said Viktor in excitement.

"That's it!" yelled Belario, pointing at Viktor. "They said they were looking for five children. Said you guys killed a bunch of people over in Alabeth." Kailan stood, furious, clenching his fists.

"What did you say to them?" worried Lena.

"I told them that you were on your way to the town of Verii," said Belario with a smile on his face. Guin began to laugh, almost unable to control himself.

"What are you so cheery?" questioned Viktor. Guin pulled out the map and showed the group's position to Viktor.

"Do you see that?" said Guin. "Verii is at least a week's journey south through the desert."

"Wow," said Kailan. "Thank you very much for that."

"Oh, don't worry about it," replied Belario. "I didn't believe their story anyway." Kailan smiled for a brief moment. "So why are you guys in Ultar exactly?"

"We're looking for an item," said Viktor.

"What kind of item?" questioned Belario.

"We don't know yet," replied Viktor. "We've been chosen and sent here from Arlbega to find a number of items."

"Did you look in the shops?" questioned Belario. "They've got some nice trinkets there."

"The item would most likely be in a shrine of some sort," said Kailan. Belario's eyes widened.

"I know exactly what you mean," said Belario. "Follow me!" The small man quickly turned around and began running down the road. The group followed after him, keeping pace. It wasn't long before the group could no longer see most of the city as they were that far down in the hole. The group members slowly began to feel the pressure growing greater and greater. In the darkness, they came upon a hole in the wall.

"We're going in there?" said Lena. Guin snapped his fingers into fire and held it in front of the hole.

"I don't think I'll be able to fit," said Thorstein.

"You two stay behind then," said Viktor, with excitement in his voice. Belario crept inside the hole and looked around. At first, he could not see anything, but then he grabbed Guin's hand and held it in front of his eyes. It revealed a long tunnel that curved out of a slight distance. Kailan, Guin, Viktor, and their guide, Belario, climbed into the tunnel and made their way through. The walls and ceiling of the tunnel progressively became smaller until they had to crawl on all fours to make it through. They crawled for a number of minutes until finally reaching the end of the tunnel. It opened up into a very large room, covered in stone tiles. There were torches on the side walls that lit up as the boys entered the room. Guin closed his hand, extinguishing the fire in his palm. There was a central path in the middle of the room with pools of water on either side of the path. The torches on the wall lit up most of the room, making the water seem to almost glow. On the other side of the room, there was another hole. As the group neared it, Belario stepped forward and stood in front of Kailan and Guin.

"Only Viktor may enter," said Belario. "He was chosen for this." Viktor smiled and quickly hopped into the hole. Belario stepped to the side and stood behind Kailan and Guin.

"What do you think he'll get?" said Guin, trying to look down the tunnel.

"I don't know," said Kailan. "Whatever it is though, I don't think that it could be as cool as a flaming sword." Guin smiled and leaned against the wall. It was a number of minutes before Viktor returned. Something seemed strange though. Viktor's eyes were wide, and they stayed wide for some time. His face was much paler as well. Kailan proceeded to wave his hand in front of Viktor's face, who quickly snapped out of his trance.

"What did you get," said Guin with a huge smile on his face, jumping to his feet. Viktor's look of bewilderment quickly changed into a smile, even though he was still staring in the same spot on the ground. He held out his hands forward, in front of Kailan and Guin, palms open. Two daggers shot from beneath his sleeves, but he caught them in his hands before they went too far.

"You have a sword that lights up," said Viktor, chuckling. "I have poison daggers."

"What do you mean poison," said Kailan.

"Even the smallest of cuts can cause death within a minute," said Viktor. Suddenly, Viktor made the strangest face.

"What is it?" questioned Kailan.

"Where'd Belario run off to?" said Viktor. Kailan and Guin quickly turned around to find that Belario was no longer in the room with them.

"Why do the people always disappear after we find the items?" said Guin.

"Who disappears?" said Viktor.

"When Guin received his spell book, the men that we were talking to disappeared when we turned around," clarified Kailan. "The man disappeared, along with the entire shrine, for my sword."

"Oh," said Viktor. "I spoke to someone though on the other side of the tunnel, and he disappeared as well."

"That's weird," said Guin.

"What is?" questioned Kailan.

"Belario must've been more than a guide," said Guin. "I didn't expect him to be in on this whole thing." The three boys walked back over to the tunnel back to the city and climbed into the hole. Guin at the front, with his hand and fire stretched out, Viktor in the middle, and Kailan holding out his sword for extra light. The trip back didn't seem to take as long as the way into the tunnel, but it was still just as dark, and cold as the first time they went through. Upon coming out the other side, the three boys noticed that Lena and Thorstein were no longer at the tunnel entrance.

"They must've gone back to the city to look for food," said Guin.

"Do you ever stop talking about food?" said Kailan, laughing.

"I can't help that I'm always hungry," argued Guin. The three boys made their way back up to the city. They were half way when Viktor stopped dead in his tracks and began to stare at the ground.

"What is it?" said Kailan, looking back. Viktor made no

[263]

sound. Instead, he knelt down, inspecting the ground.

"Do you see something?" said Kailan. Viktor launched two daggers from his wrist, into his hands.

"This isn't good," said Viktor. He stood up and began to walk up the road, constantly inspecting it.

"What do you see?" questioned Kailan.

"Thorstein and Lena are not in the city looking for food," said Viktor. "They've been dragged away."

"What?" yelled Guin.

"These tracks suggest that something large was dragged," said Viktor. "They weren't there when we came down here, and the only thing large enough to do this would be Thorstein." Kailan pulled out his sword, igniting it in flames.

"Guin," said a muffled Aroculus. "Do you remember when you two and Crag first had to find Dartann?"

"Yes, but what does…" Guin paused for a second, thinking. "The footprints!"

"Use the spell!" said Aroculus. Guin uttered the words that he had heard before, watching as the footprints in the dirt floor began to glow a mustard colour. Viktor was indeed correct. There were marks in the ground from something very large being pulled up the road. The boys followed the glowing footprints up the road until they reached the city again. The trail quickly went behind a building and trailed off into one of the back tunnels. It wasn't long before the boys found Lena and Thorstein, unconscious on the ground, surrounded by a number of men. To the boys' surprise, one of the men was Belario. The short man slowly walked over to the three boys and stood between them and the other men.

"We knew you'd show up," said Belario.

"You little bastard!" yelled Guin, trying to take a swing at Belario.

"I wouldn't do that," said Belario with a smile on his face. "You see, we have your friends at our mercy. Guin looked at his two friends lying on the ground and noticed the knives against their necks.

"What do you want?" said Kailan, ready to throttle Belario, but managing to keep himself calm.

"We want those daggers that Viktor just found," said Belario. "As well as your sword, and Guin's book there as well."

"Never!" yelled Aroculus. Guin lightly hit the book. Viktor stepped to the side, away from his two friends.

"You want the daggers?" said Viktor.

"Yes," said Belario. "They could fetch us quite the pretty penny."

A smile appeared on Viktor's face. It was sinister though. A look that none of the others had even seen on him. "Then have them!" Viktor launched the knives from his wrists, throwing them at the men with the knives first, then at the others behind. Each time he threw a knife, another slid out from under his sleeve. Kailan pulled out his sword, charging into battle, but there was no point. Viktor had taken down all nine of the men in a matter of seconds. He then walked over to Belario, who was hunched over on the ground, waiting for the knives to stop

[265]

flying.

"Get up!" yelled Viktor, kicking at Belario.

"Please don't hurt me," Belario whimpered. He slowly brought himself to his knees and tried to grab a hold of Viktor. "I'll do anything." Kailan and Guin rushed over to Thorstein and Lena, untying them and trying to wake them up.

"Hold out your hand," said Viktor. Belario did as the boy asked, and held out his hand, palm wide open. Viktor again, made the same sinister grin that he had made before, and took one of his daggers and placed the point in Belario's hand ever so softly. He held it upright, slowly turning it. "I thought that we could be friends," said Viktor. "Instead, you decided to betray us." Viktor slowly pressed down harder and harder on the blade. "You sicken me." As Viktor spoke those last few words, he had breached the skin, and drawn the tiniest drop of blood from Belario's hand. He pulled the knife away, and then threw it at the wall. "Get out of my sight." Belario hopped to his feet and ran out of the tunnel, into the main street.

Thorstein lifted his head, unknowing of what had just happened. He slowly lifted himself up and brought himself to his feet. Lena came to as well, but had Kailan hold her up. Kailan and Guin explained as to what had just happened. They decided that it was best for them to leave the city and spend the night in the desert. It would be much safer out in the desert, and they would be much more familiar out there. As they exited the tunnel, Viktor stopped and stared at a crowd of people for a second.

[266]

"Are you coming Viktor?" said Kailan.

"Right behind you," replied Viktor, smiling. Viktor turned away, following after the group. As the crowd spread apart, Belario's dead body became visible.

*   *   *

In the two days following their time in Ultar, from desert terrain to forest, the other group members never once asked what ever happened to Belario if Viktor had set him free. Many of them had had enough of the greed and destruction that they had run into on their journey. That people would rape, sell, or even kill people just for pleasure or out of greed. Human lives meant nothing according to many of the inhabitants of the world anymore. They were seen as currency, as toys, as garbage. It was better that the five companions did not dwell on things like that. Through all that they had been, there was very little that actually pleased them in this sense.

Thorstein pulled out the map, looking at it carefully. "We're only another day's travel from Drailnott, boys and girls," said Thorstein.

"Girls?" questioned Lena. "There's only one girl." Thorstein laughed.

"What are you talking about?" said Thorstein. "Guin's been acting like a girl since we left Alandra." Four of the friends laughed, except for Guin.

"Who has the long hair here?" replied Guin.

"He does have you there, Thorstein," said Kailan, chuckling.

"Well, what about Viktor?" Thorstein argued

"I don't have hair that long," said Viktor.

"I'm also the only one here with the ability to grow facial hair it seems as well," said Thorstein, grinning.

"What are you talking about," said Guin. "I've got facial hair." The boy rubbed his chin until he found a small hair and held on to it. "See, this is a hair," said Guin.

"An invisible one," said Viktor, inspecting it very closely.

The group waited till after sunset to set up camp for the night. They found a small clearing within the forest. They made a fire in the middle of the clearing, and everyone slept around it in a circle. It wasn't long before all of the group members had fallen asleep. As the moon shone on the five companions, Guin awoke to the sound of a crow, cawing in the trees behind him. He turned on his side and covered his ears with the blanket, trying to block out the sound of the bird, but the sound only grew louder. This went on for a few minutes before Guin jumped to his feet and decided to take a walk.

"Stupid birds," muttered Guin. He held out his hand, and started a fire in his hand. "What I'd give for a nice warm bed again." Walking through the trees, Guin couldn't help, but wonder as to why the birds were making so much noise in the

[268]

first place. He looked around, but saw nothing of interest. Suddenly, the feeling hit him. "Gotta go pee!" yelled Guin, almost waking the others. He ran deeper into the forest and pulled down his pants partially. Halfway through, Guin heard something behind him. Twigs snapping, leaves rustling. He turned his head and came face to face with a man dressed in black.

*   *   *

When Guin awoke, he found the other four companions tied up and gagged. They were all grouped together on one side of the fire, which was now even bigger than before, on the other side of the fire stood their captors. Five men, two Northland giants, as well as a number of goblins that danced around, poking at the five companions.

"Thought that you could trick us?" said one of the men, standing in front of the group. "Thought that you could just slip away, unseen, and without anyone noticing a giant and four children travelling through the desert." It was with one word, Kailan knew who their captors were. "You won't last very long," said the man, walking closer to the group members.

"Stop," said one of the other men. He hurried over to the five companions, and knelt down beside Viktor, grabbing his hair ad lifting his head up. He was a very pale man, dressed in a cloak with his hood down. As he sniffed Viktor's scent, he smiled, showing Viktor what he was. "There's something strange about this one," said the man.

Viktor quickly spat out the cloth in his mouth and yelled out, "Bastard!"

The man smiled again and then shoved Viktor's face into the dirt. "You should not talk to your elders that way."

Thorstein quickly remembered his armour, but it made no use. He quickly had it appear on him, but it did not help him escape from his binds. Even with all of his muscle, the ropes were too strong, and too many.

This ignited a spark in Kailan's mind. He stared at his sword, lying across from them on the other side of the fire. Within a few seconds, the blade was fully engulfed, quickly growing larger and larger with flames. It was now larger than the fire, but soon after, it stopped growing.

"No matter what you do, you cannot escape," said the first man. He kicked Kailan in the side, knowing that he owned the sword. "Now tell us about the forces of Arlbega!" He grabbed the gag out of Kailan's mouth and ripped it out.

"You and the rest of your Black Allegiance will die!" yelled out Kailan. He then began to light his sword on and off, creating flashes of light. One of the goblins quickly ran over to Kailan and smacked him across the face.

"You won't be saying anything much longer," said the goblin in a raspy voice. "This is just the search party." The captors chuckled for a moment. Suddenly, one of the men cried

[270]

out, and dropped to the ground.

"Get them!" yelled a voice from the forest. A number of men quickly ran through the forest, attacking the Black Allegiance members. The five companions held their heads down, as not to get hurt by any of the attackers. It wasn't long before the Black Allegiance members were dead, or scared off. Kailan looked up and saw Captain Briggs standing in front of him. "Looks like you're having a bit of trouble," laughed Captain Briggs.

"Right in the nick of time," said Kailan, laughing as one of the men cut the ropes binding his hands.

"You guys are about a week late," said Captain Briggs. "We decided to post men outside of the city to wait for you. When we saw the flashes of light, we ran towards them immediately."

"Wait… how close are we to Drailnott?" questioned Guin.

"We ran here in about two minutes," said Captain Briggs.

"And we thought that we were supposed to be at least a day away," said Guin.

"Who can't read maps, Kailan?" said Lena, with a sarcastic look on her face.

The group made their way into Drailnott and slept there for the night. Under the careful watch of Captain Briggs' crew, the five companions were safe from the Black Allegiance for the rest of the night. The next day, the group packed their things and set sail for Arlbega. For the first two days, the seas were rough. There were a number of times when Guin and Kailan had to lean over the side of the boat out of sickness. It was two weeks later that the group members finally reached Harlem. They were ecstatic when the man yelled out, "Harlem, dead ahead!" Guin and Thorstein were leaning so far over the side of the boat that the others were surprised they didn't fall in, or at least swim to shore.

As they pulled into the port, Captain Briggs called out, "Willy! Tell the Arch Chancellor that we've returned!" One of the sailors jumped off the ship and onto the pier, running up to Machesney Hall as fast as he could. The five companions quickly began unloading their things off of the ship. It was almost questionable whether it was Thorstein, or his dornbeast that was more excited to be on solid ground again. Within a few minutes of unloading the ship, Bailan appeared at the foot of the pier.

"And how are we on this fine, sunny day," said Bailan with a smile on his face. Kailan ran up to Bailan and gave him a hug.

"Oh, we're great. A little sick, but otherwise great," replied Kailan.

"Good, good. I have much to talk to you about since you were last here," said Bailan. He turned away from Kailan and looked up at the ship. "Captain Briggs!"

"Yes me boy?" said Captain Briggs, chuckling.

"I need to speak to my friends. Will you be ok without

[272]

them?"

"Oh, me and my men have things covered." Captain Briggs smiled, and then began yelling more at his men in a joking fashion. The five companions quickly led their horses, and the dornbeast off the ship, and then made their way up to the stables and Machesney Hall. Upon reaching it, Bailan decided to give them a quick tour of some changes. They now had their own separate wing of the building. There were five bedrooms surrounding one central lounge area at the rear of the building. Thorstein's bedroom was made especially large. His doorway was twice the height and width of a normal door, meaning that Thorstein wouldn't have to bend down to enter rooms anymore. The last time that he was at Machesney Hall, to accommodate Thorstein's size; they put two king-sized beds beside each other. This time, they had a whole new bed made for Thorstein. They had extra supports in it to support his weight, and it was made to be extra soft as well. As he lay on his back, Thorstein almost instantly fell asleep. Guin had to smack him a few times to get Thorstein to move again. In the middle of the lounge area, there were potted plants everywhere. In the centre of the room, was a short table, with a couch on each side for sitting on. At the one end of the table, there was a very large wing chair for Thorstein. Bailan called the group members to the table and had them sit around it. He pulled up a wooden chair on the end opposite to Thorstein and sat down.

"Where's Tanier?" questioned Guin.

"Tanier left a number of weeks ago to the same place

[273]

where you were," said Bailan. "We received word that an old friend of his, who we thought was dead, is being held captive in Kelenath."

"Crag?" question Guin. "Ya, we're the ones who got him into jail."

"That was also in the message," said Bailan, laughing. "I'm in charge of Arlbega until Tanier returns."

"Have you heard anything new about the Black Allegiance?" questioned Kailan, leaning over the table.

"Not much more. Very insignificant details that don't even affect you," said Bailan. "I would like to tell you more, but my hands are a bit full at the moment. Since before Tanier left, I've been more in charge of running things, while Tanier has been looking after you and items concerning the Black Allegiance."

"So, are you saying that we have free time?" questioned Guin. The whole room instantly went silent. The five group members leaned in to hear Bailan's answer.

"I guess so." All five of the young adults jumped into the air with excitement. They had suddenly become children, exploding with laughter and joy. For the first time in a couple of months, the group members had a chance to go off and do their own things.

"How much time do we have?" asked Guin.

"I would say at least a couple of days," replied Bailan. Within the next few minutes, all of the companions had left Machesney Hall, and were out, running through the city. Bailan smacked his hand to his forehead, shaking his head.

*   *   *

The five companions each met together later on that evening back at Machesney Hall. They had forgotten how tired they were from being on the sea for over a week. As soon as they got back, Thorstein went back to his room and fell asleep, flat on his bed. Guin and Viktor made their ways to bed not long after. Soon, the only two left were Kailan and Lena. They curled up on the one couch, watching the magic fireplace on the one wall of the room.

"How was your day?" questioned Lena, wrapping her arm around Kailan.

"I had fun," replied Kailan. "What about you?"

"I just can't wait for tomorrow." The two of them smiled, until Lena pulled Kailan in tighter.

"Is something wrong?"

"Oh, quite the opposite," said Lena. She leaned in and kissed Kailan on the cheek, trying to get his attention. He slowly turned his head from the fireplace and stared into Lena's eyes, smiling.

"What is it?" he said slowly. Lena leaned to the other side of the couch and grabbed the pillow and swung at Kailan with it.

"You're dead," said Lena, sticking her tongue out. Before she knew it, Kailan had the other pillow already coming down on her head, knocking her off the couch and onto the ground. She hit with a thud and didn't move for a second or two.

"Are you alright?" said Kailan, rushing to her side as he knelt down. Lena kicked Kailan's feet out from under him, sending him toppling to the ground next to her. He reached out with one hand, trying to grab her arm, but she rolled to the side and escaped. Kailan picked himself up on all fours and then began to charge Lena. She ran into her bedroom with Kailan chasing directly behind. Lena then jumped onto her bed, holding onto the corner post. When she looked over the side of the bed, there was no sign of Kailan. As she looked around, from one side of the bed to the other, Lena could no longer find Kailan.

"Kailan," said Lena, in confusion. "Where'd you go?" There was no response. She lied down on her stomach and looked over the one side of the bed. Just then, Kailan slid out from underneath the bed and grabbed onto Lena's arms, pulling her over. He then rolled under the bed, bringing her with him. He threw his arms around her, holding her tightly, and kissed her on the lips roughly. "What are you doing?" questioned Lena.

"Kailan chuckled before responding. "I'm trying to get in touch with my inner child."

"Really?" said Lena. "You are going to act childish in a moment like this?"

Kailan's smile changed to a look of confusion. "Have you never noticed how children always seem to have some of the best answers?" Lena nodded. "There is always something to learn from children." Lena smiled and gave Kailan a peck on the cheek.

"Well then, if you are going to act like a child, then I guess that it is time for you to go to bed," said Lena.

"You have got to be kidding me," said Kailan, rolling out from under the bed. Lena followed quickly after, pulling herself out on her back.

"I never said your bed," said Lena with a seductive smile. Kailan blushed, and then burst out laughing.

"I'm not sleeping with Guin," said Kailan. Lena's smile disappeared quickly.

"I'm not talking about Guin, silly," said Lena.

"Thorstein smells," Kailan joked again. Lena stood up and walked over to the door, closing it behind her. She slowly walked over to the bed and helped Kailan up. She sat him on the bed, and took a spot next to him. Lena then began unbuttoning the top few buttons on her shirt. She gently reached for the collar of her blouse and began to pull down on it, revealing her shoulder. Kailan was confused at first and was oblivious to what was going on. In his mind, he was still joking around as a child. Lena began to unbutton her shirt a bit more. She pulled the collar down on the other side as well. It was then that Kailan realised what was going on. Just before Lena pulled her shirt down all the way, Kailan jumped to his feet and turned away.

"What is the matter?" said Lena.

"I'm sorry," said Kailan. "I'll leave you to change." He

[277]

began to head for the door, but Lena grabbed his hand again and sat him back down.

"I want you here," said Lena. She pulled down her blouse all of the way, revealing her breasts. Kailan looked for a second, then quickly snapped his head forward and closed his eyes. "Am I not beautiful, Kailan?" questioned Lena.

"No, you are very beautiful," said Kailan.

"How beautiful?"

"The most beautiful creature in the entire world," responded Kailan. Lena smiled and gently pulled Kailan's hand up and placed it on one of her breasts. The boy's eyes widened immensely. "Nope!" he said as he jumped to his feet and ran out of the room. His heart was beating faster than it ever had before. He leaned up against the wall in the lounge and began breathing heavily. Lena quickly rushed out, wearing a robe and walked up to Kailan.

"What's the matter?" questioned Lena.

"I'm… j-j-j-just…" Kailan could barely spit out his words.

"I'm sorry," said Lena. She crept slowly towards Kailan and held onto his arm. He jumped slightly at her touch, but then calmed quickly. "I thought that you were ready." Kailan looked down at Lena and wiped the sweat from his forehead.

"I am ready," said Kailan. "I love you with all my heart, but I'm just nervous." Lena smiled and placed her hand on Kailan's shoulder. She pulled him down, closer to her, and kissed him on the cheek.

"Good night, Kailan," said Lena before walking back into her room. As Kailan turned around and took a deep breath, he saw Viktor sitting on the couch with his back to Kailan. He walked over to the couches and sat on the other one.

"Didn't work out too well, now did it?" said Viktor, chuckling. Kailan glared at the other boy.

"Shut up." Kailan got back up and went straight to bed.

*   *   *

Bailan had a special breakfast prepared for the five group members. Fresh fruit, smoked meats, and some of the finest breads and biscuits in the city. The five friends were actually quite amazed as to how much work Bailan put into making their stay the best possible. After the meal, the five friends decided to make their way throughout the city. Lena and Kailan made their way through the marketplace, while Thorstein and Guin made their way towards the libraries. Viktor instead left the main part of the city and made his way to the ocean shore, spending most of his day either fishing or sightseeing. While in the library, Thorstein and Guin decided to look deeper into the mystery surrounding the Black Allegiance. The Black Allegiance did not start out as just that. It was a time shortly after the dispute between the elves and the old goblins, then referred to as kobolds, that the history of the Black Allegiance had begun. The main kobold kingdom within Kartol declared war against the dwarves of Rolandt, a kingdom south of Kartol. The kobolds were not alone in this fight though. There were groups of humans that came to the aide of the kobolds. The humans, being twice the size and strength, helped to defend the kobolds. Eventually, they ended up interbreeding, resulting in a new race called hobgoblins. These hobgoblins were much bigger than the kobolds, being almost the same height as the humans. Hobgoblins were feared very much in the beginning. As the kobolds and their alliances slowly turned to evil, they began to change as to what everyone is accustomed with now. Dark skinned creatures with long, pointy ears, and protruding noses. The hobgoblins at first almost looked the same as the elves, but as they changed too, they became very noticeable. Their facial features were very similar to the new goblins, but their bodies still resembled that of men. Their skin was much paler than the goblins and almost resembled that of humans. The behaviour of the hobgoblins was definitely taken from the goblin side. They hungered for blood, and became fierce warriors. Being as strong as men, but with the same abilities as the goblins, they were considered unbeatable by some. It wasn't long before the goblins and hobgoblins attacked Qatrak, the capital city of Rolandt, and home to the dwarf king. They were defeated by the dwarves, and when their armies returned to their cities, they found that the elves and humans had destroyed almost everything. The remaining soldiers of the goblin armies hid within the barren wastelands south of Rolandt. It was here that they encountered their new allies of ogres and trolls. With their new alliance, they began to search for more allies. Within the next few decades, they also made pacts with some of the great vampire kingdoms, the giants of Kartol and Greer, the dark elves of Mortlok, and many other beasts. Then one day, on the island of Trekta in the middle of the Gardaign Ocean, a rock, fell from the sky and opened a hole within the ground. Out of the hole emerged a young woman. Her name was Terilla, a sorceress born from pure evil. The men from the nearby village instantly became entranced by her beauty. With just the faintest smile, she seduced the men and took control over them. To cause utter chaos and bloodshed, she sent the men into the village, killing every last woman and child. When they returned, she sent them again, across the seas to find the new alliance that the goblins had created. Separate from the main alliance of the goblins, Terilla created a new alliance called the Black Allegiance. The king of the goblins did not approve of this, and was so murdered in his sleep. There were few that did not join Terilla, and these were left alone at peace. They remained a safe haven for those that chose to leave with Terilla. She amassed her armies together on the island of Trekta. As soon as the forces of Arlbega, Takash, and Kartol found out about this, they immediately sent out armies to fight against the Black Allegiance. It was a champion from Arlbega who slew Terilla. He cut off her head and threw it back into the hole that she crawled out of. Her body was burned and paraded about. The remaining forces of the Black Allegiance dispersed throughout the lands, hiding from

[281]

their enemies. They would wait, with the world oblivious to them, until Arlbega, Takash, and Kartol forgot. Thorstein and Guin had chills that ran down their spines when they read more about the Black Allegiance.

*   *   *

Kailan and Lena walked through the busy marketplace, admiring the variety of items being sold. Every now and then, Lena would make Kailan stop and watch as she tried on jewellery or clothing. It was a while before Kailan found a vendor with wares that he was interested in. A table was set out with a red cloth spread out on top, with an assortment of knives lying on top.

"What is it with you and knives?" questioned Lena. Kailan was too entranced by some of the knives to pay any attention. "Kailan!" she said ever louder.

"Sorry," said Kailan. "There is something about them. Maybe it is the intricacy, the detail and decoration that just… mesmerises me." Lena smiled and grabbed onto Kailan's hand, pulling him away from the knives with little effort.

"So you're amazed by knives, and not me, is that it?" questioned Lena.

"What? No!" replied Kailan. He placed his hands gently on her cheek and jaw, and leaned in, touching forehead to forehead. "You are just the same as the day that I met you. If not, even more beautiful." Lena smiled and batted her eyes.

"Thank you," replied Lena before turning around and running off into the crowd ahead.

"Now where are you off to?" Kailan asked.

Lena looked back, with a smile from cheek to cheek. "I'm going to look for a present for you!"

Kailan threw his arms in the air and brought them back down to his sides. He looked at the vendor with the knives and spoke, "What can you do?" The man chuckled before turning away to load more knives onto the table. Kailan then slowly made his way down the road in the same direction as Lena, not noticing an old "friend" sneaking up behind.

"I have no clue what you are doing back here," said a somewhat familiar voice from behind Kailan. Kailan turned around to face the young man who had fought with him the last time he was in the marketplace. Prince Farol walked out from the crowd. This time, the peasants did not bow down as they did the last time. Farol was wearing a cloak, hiding his identity until he pulled off the hood. It took a couple of seconds before people noticed, but once they did, they dropped to the ground. Everyone except for Kailan had taken a knee.

"Get down," said the shopkeeper behind Kailan. "Don't you know your prince?"

Kailan smiled. "He's not my prince."

The prince walked forward, placing one hand on the pommel of his sword. "I think that you should listen to this

[283]

man," said Farol. "He sounds like he has at least some brains."

"Farol, if I wanted to hear your voice, I'd listen to the pigs," said Kailan.

"How dare you!" yelled Farol. "And you will address me as Prince Farol!"

"Farol, we've already talked about this with Bailan and Tanier," said Kailan. "You have no power over me."

"Disrespecting little…" Prince Farol pulled out his sword and charged at Kailan, who in turn, quickly drew his sword as well and blocked the attack.

"I'm warning you Farol," said Kailan. The prince began to laugh, pulling his sword back and slowly walking in a circle around Kailan.

"You know that I can have you jailed just for not getting down on your knees," said Farol. "And now you decide to attack me with a sword?"

"I don't apply to the first law, and you attacked me, not the other way around!"

"Kailan, what's going on?" questioned Lena, slowly making her way up through the clearing of people.

"Kneel before your future king!" yelled Farol. Lena quickly dropped to the ground.

"We don't have to bow for him," Kailan stated. "He's just a jerk!"

"It seems that your woman has more brains than you do," said Farol. "Then again, that wouldn't have to be much." Kailan quickly swung his sword, knocking Farol's sword out of his hands. He held his own with the tip of the blade at the prince's neck.

"Don't ever make degrading comments to me or her ever again!"

"Kailan, leave him alone," said Lena, slowly making her way through the crowd.

"He needs to learn that no one here cares for the way he treats them," said Kailan, pulling the sword away gradually from Farol's neck. He turned around to face Lena and stepped towards her. There was something strange about the look on her face though. Her eyes were wide, and filled with fear. Kailan ducked to the side and spun around bringing up his sword as it began to glow red hot, and stopped Farol's attack. The flames on the sword began to grow ever larger.

"Kailan, just take his sword and we can leave," said Lena.

Kailan looked at Lena and nodded before he kicked Farol in the gut, knocking him backwards. Then, he swung his sword in an arc, knocking the prince's sword out of his hand again and to the ground. Kailan stepped towards the young man who was now on the ground, and held out his sword against Farol's neck again. This time, the blade was red hot.

"Kailan, don't do it," said Lena. Kailan let out a breath before cooling down his sword and pulling it away.

"Have you noticed how none of your subjects are coming to your aid?" questioned Kailan. Farol lifted his head and looked around slowly, examining the citizens of Harlem.

They watched, but did not do anything other than that. "They do not respect you. They only bow because it is the law." Kailan squatted in front of Farol and looked straight into his eyes. "They would rather that you die, that way they wouldn't have to deal with you ever again." Farol's face began to fill with the colour red as he began to succumb to his anger. Kailan stood back up and turned around, not expecting Farol to jump straight up and tackle Kailan from behind. They tussled on the ground for a few seconds before Kailan gained the upper hand and held his hand at Farol's throat, kneeling over him. He held the prince on the ground for a second or two, watching as he quickly ran out of breath.

"Kailan!" Lena cried out. "Let him go!" With one quick motion, Kailan punched the prince in the face, knocking him out. The couple said nothing to each other as they hurried back to Machesney Hall. When they reached it, Kailan went straight to his room and sat down on his bed. His fingers began to tingle and pulse as he stared at them. He began to think of how he could have ended Farol's life right then and there. How he could have continued to choke the life from the prince of Harlem, with no one doing a thing to stop him. Lena quickly burst into the room with tears in her eyes.

"What is wrong with you?" demanded Lena hitting Kailan once in the arm.

"He came after me," said Kailan, trying to justify his actions. "I protected myself!" Lena paced between the bed and the door a number of times.

"You nearly killed him."

"I didn't," replied Kailan. "I probably would've been doing this country a favour though." Lena extended her arm, and with an open palm, brought it against Kailan's face with force, knocking him over on his side. She then stormed out of the room, slamming the door behind her.

*   *   *

It wasn't until later that night that Kailan finally emerged from his room. He saw Guin, Viktor, and Lena all standing in the lounge area.

"Kailan!" yelled Guin. "We're going to the pub, are you coming?" Kailan looked over at Lena, but he did not show her the same usual expression that he often gave her. It was definitely not the look shared between two loves.

"Ya, I'll come," replied Kailan, hurrying over. Suddenly, Bailan burst into the lounge area and blocked Kailan's way.

"You need to come with me, now," said Bailan, sternly. Kailan looked back at his three friends.

"Don't wait for me," said Kailan. "I'll catch up." He followed Bailan out of the lounge area and down the hallway to Tanier's office. Kailan walked in and was seated in front of Tanier's desk, but Bailan did not sit at it. Instead, he closed the door behind Kailan and locked it. When the boy realised what had happened, he quickly sprang to his feet and began pulling on the door knob, trying to open the door. "Let me out!" he yelled at the top of his lungs. His cries for help were worthless though, for Bailan had sealed the room, making Kailan's voice unheard. He continued to hit and kick the door, trying to break it, but nothing worked. After a number of minutes, Kailan had given up at trying to escape. He sat down in the chair and waited. Almost an hour had passed before the door swung open, with a familiar face standing in the doorway. "Tanier!" yelled Kailan, jumping from his seat. "Bailan locked me in here."

"Sit down!" yelled Tanier, slamming the door behind him. Kailan quickly planted himself in the chair and observed Tanier as he made his way around the room to the other side of his desk and sat down at the large chair behind it.

"When did you return?" questioned Kailan, with a smile that seemed unsure as if it should be on his face. Tanier stared at Kailan, menacingly for a moment before handing him one of the papers in his hand. It was a letter, filling almost the entire page.

"Do you know what this is?" questioned Tanier. Kailan quickly skimmed over the first few lines.

"It looks like it's from the King of Freltus," Kailan replied.

"It's a warrant for your arrest!" yelled Tanier. He rubbed his chin, stretching his jaw open at the same time.

"What for?" demanded Kailan, knowing full well what

[288]

it was for.

"Never should I have to come back from a trip and return to the news that someone under my direct authority has just beaten the king's son, and left him in the street!"

"He attacked me!" yelled Kailan, grabbing the arms of the chair ever tighter out of frustration. "Besides, both you and Bailan said that we didn't have to bow down to him!"

"So instead of bowing down, you... you hold a knife up to his throat?"

"He attacked us first!" yelled Kailan. "What was I supposed to do, just let him kill me?"

"No, but you don't go and try to suffocate the damn boy!" Tanier sat back in his chair, catching his breath. He paused for a brief moment before continuing again. "Do you know how hard and how long I've been trying to create proper relations with Arlbega's kingdoms?"

"More than I can imagine," said Kailan, rolling his eyes.

"You're damn right! Ever since Arlbega broke up into separate kingdoms, it has been the main goal of the Arch Chancellor to resolve the issues and bring the country together again. We spend all of this time, trying to please the kingdoms, keeping peace between all of them, slowly working our way back to governing them, and then some kid comes along and ruins that!"

"We'd be better off without them anyways," said Kailan. Tanier wiped the sweat from his forehead.

[289]

"I might be able to fix some of this problem while you are away," said Tanier. Kailan looked at the man funny, cocking his head to the side.

"What do you mean?"

"I can probably have the charges dismissed," replied Tanier.

"No... you said something. You said 'while you are away'," said Kailan. Tanier looked up at the boy, placing his hands on the desk.

"You and the rest are being shipped out tomorrow," said Tanier. Instantly, the pink drained from Kailan's face and only white was left. "You are being sent away to train."

"What are you talking about!" yelled Kailan, throwing his arms to his sides. "We just returned from Karnok, and now you are sending all of us back?"

"No."

Kailan sat back in his chair, taking in a deep breath.

"Not all of you."

Kailan's eyes snapped back to Tanier. "What do you mean by that?"

"You each fight differently," said Tanier. "So you are all being sent to different places."

"You're splitting us up?" questioned Kailan. "You can't do that!"

"I'm tired of arguing with you Kailan," said Tanier. "Tell the others to pack. You are all leaving in the morning." Kailan stood up and turned towards the door, reaching for the handle. "Oh, and leave your sword here."

*   *   *

The man slowly poured the green liquid into the drink, dissolving quickly and unnoticeable. He picked up the platter of drinks and stepped away from the bar, slowly and cautiously making his way through the crowded pub. The patrons, bumping into him as he walked by, but he made sure not to spill. Finally reaching the table, he removed the mugs from the wooden platter and placed them on the table before disappearing into the crowd.

"I don't think that you know how vital wizards are to Arlbega," said Guin, drunkenly slurring his words.

"I don't think that you realise how stupid it all sounds," replied Viktor, who too, was almost too drunk to have a reasonable conversation.

"Where'd this beer come from?" said Guin sarcastically, smiling and staring at the three mugs. Viktor quickly grabbed the mug and started downing the clear amber liquid within.

"You should probably slow down with those," said Lena, laughing. "What is that, your fourth? Besides, you guzzled the last two without a single breath in between." Viktor stopped drinking for a quick second and looked up at Lena. As he

[291]

brought the drink away from his lips, he took in a deep breath, so as for Lena to hear him, mocking her, but only to bring the drink right back up, emptying the mug of the ale.

"I bet that neither of you can drink as much as me," said Viktor.

"Is that a challenge?" said Guin, quickly gulping down the beer.

Lena looked at the two boys and leaned away from the table in disgust. "You know, you two should really look for some girls," said Lena. "Maybe you'll start acting like gentlemen instead of a bunch of boys." She picked up the full beer mug and slowly began to sip at it.

"Now why would I need to find a nice girl when I've got all the wenches I need at the mercy of my coin purse?" laughed Guin. Lena quickly realised that what she said might offend Viktor, and quickly put her beer down, and her hand to her mouth. As she looked at him though, she noticed that he was not paying attention, and was instead gazing around the pub, eyes wide and lost.

"Are you alright?" said Lena, watching as Viktor's mind floated away. "Viktor?" The boy continued to drift away."

"Hey, stupid!" yelled Guin, nudging Viktor's arm. The boy snapped around to face Guin, rubbing at his eyes.

"Are you alright?" asked Lena.

"Ya, I'm alright," replied Viktor. He continued to rub his eyes, for his vision was blurry.

"If you'll excuse me," said Guin, standing up. "But

[292]

there is a lady over there dying to meet me." With a crooked smile on his face, Guin stumbled away from the table and through the crowd. Viktor watched as the young man walked away, but as he turned his head back, something stopped him.

"Rina?" said Viktor at the sight of his late love.

"Yes Viktor," said Rina, sitting across from him. Viktor began to cry at the site of Lena, throwing his arms around her and holding tightly.

"Are you real?" He asked. "I mean, are you alive?" There was a brief silence as Viktor slowly pulled himself away from Rina.

"Only for a short time," said Rina, "only for tonight." She placed a hand on Viktor's shoulder and leaned over the table. "I want to spend every moment of it with you." Viktor wiped the tears from his eyes as he took a hold of Rina's hand and followed her through the crowds and back to Machesney Hall.

*   *   *

Lena suddenly felt ill for a quick second, holding her stomach. She thought that it was the alcohol starting to come back up. The feeling quickly went away though, and when it did, Lena felt perfectly fine. As she looked up, she found Kailan sitting across from her at the table, with a look of sadness on his face.

"Listen," said Kailan. "I know that you probably don't want to talk to me after what happened today…"

"This is neither the place, nor the time for this discussion," said Lena, looking away from Kailan out of protest. The boy jumped over the corner of the table and made his way around to Lena's side, kneeling in front of her.

"I know that what I did was wrong," said Kailan. "I am sorry." Lena turned her head again, looking away from the boy. He brought one leg up and raised himself, placing a hand gently on her arm.

"Please," said Kailan. "I want to make it up to you. I'll do anything." Lena turned her head and looked in Kailan's eyes.

"There is only one thing that I desire right now," said Lena, with a devilish grin on her face. Kailan slowly reached for her hand as he led her out of the pub.

*   *   *

As the boy made his way through the crowds of people, he already knew that something was wrong. Passing from person to person, he could not find his friends. It was a couple of minutes before he was stopped by a large man, standing at the bar.

"Oy," said the man loudly. "Is this your friend, here?"

The boy looked at the drunk standing next to the man, as a small smile made its way between his cheeks.

"Yes," said the boy. "What has he done now?"

"He keeps talking as if there's someone next to 'em," said the man. "He was groping the air about a minute ago."

"Guin, are you alright?" said the boy.

"Kailan!" said Guin, almost falling off his stool.

"I guess not." Kailan quickly threw an arm under Guin's shoulder and propped him up. "Where are the others?" questioned Kailan. Guin looked up at his sober friend and smiled.

"They're over…" He pointed in one direction through the crowds of people, but continued to move it back and forth. "I'm too drunk to answer that question." He slumped over and closed his eyes.

"You've got to be kidding me," said Kailan, rolling his eyes.

"Over there!" yelled Guin, jolting upright. Kailan pulled Guin through the crowd, but there was no reward waiting for him when he reached the table. Both Lena and Viktor were gone.

"They must've gone back to Machesney Hall," said Kailan. He again pulled Guin through the crowds of people, on his shoulder. It wasn't long before Kailan and Guin reached Machesney Hall. As they entered the building, they made their way straight to the lounge area of their wing of the building. Kailan sat Guin down on one of the couches, making sure that he wouldn't fall forward and onto the table in front. After making sure that Guin was not going to move, seeing as he was too drunk to stay out of trouble, Kailan headed towards Lena's room. He heard talking from outside as he neared the door. When he reached it, he knocked. The only reply that he received was a cry for help from Lena. Kailan kicked in the door to see Lena and Viktor on top of the bed. Viktor was on top of Lena, holding her down by the wrists.

"Get off me!" cried Lena. Her head turned to look at Kailan, who stood frozen and in shock. "Help, Kailan!" It was at that exact moment that Viktor came to his senses as well. He turned to Kailan and was about to say something, but it was too late. The boy charged at the bed, ripping Viktor off of Lena and throwing him against the wall.

"You bastard!" he yelled out in anger, giving a kick to Viktor's chest. As Viktor slowly fell to the ground, Kailan went in for more, but Lena grabbed his arm, holding him back. He was about to pull away, but a spark within him lit up. He began to realise that his anger was beginning to grow ever stronger, and that he was never able to deal with it. It was because of this that Lena began to distance herself from Kailan. It all started when he stopped the man from raping Lena in Alabeth. It was then that the fire arose within Kailan. Because of his love for Lena, Kailan nearly killed a man, but when she would ask him to stop fighting, he would ignore her. As he turned and looked into Lena's eyes, a tear rolled down his cheek.

"I'm sorry," said Kailan.

"Me too," replied Lena.

Suddenly, Kailan found himself with an arm around his neck, being pulled to the ground. Lena shrieked as Viktor ripped Kailan away from her and threw him to the ground.

"I hate you!" screamed Viktor, kneeling on Kailan's chest and throat. The boy struggled for a bit, gasping for air.

"Let him go, Viktor!" cried Lena, trying to pull Viktor off. He tried swatting her away, but she continued to hold on. Kailan brought up his free hand and punched Viktor in his crotch. The boy instantly fell over to his side, holding his stomach and lower regions. Kailan rolled over on his side and began breathing deeply and heavily. Lena rushed around to his front and placed a hand on his shoulder.

"Are you alright?" said Lena, fear emanating from her. Kailan nodded as he slowly picked himself up and hunched over on all fours. It was then that Viktor came after him for another attack and elbowed Kailan in the ribs. "Stop, Viktor!" Kailan spun around and kicked Viktor into the wall. As the two boys picked themselves up, Viktor quickly went for one of his poison knives, as Kailan picked up the wooden chair that was beside the bed.

"If you cut me, I'm going to bring you down with me," said Kailan.

"Stop fighting!" screamed Lena at the top of her lungs. Just as the two boys charged each other, the door swung open and Tanier stood in the doorway, freezing everything in place. He quietly stepped into the room and looked at the two boys' faces. They looked as though they were snarling beasts. Their mouths were wide open, gums and teeth showing. Their eyebrows were raised far into their foreheads, and their nostrils flared open. Lena, on the other hand, was curled up in the corner, crying. Her face was soaked with tears, but warm to the touch as Tanier kneeled down next to her and wiped the tears from her eyes.

"I'm starting to think that this was a bad idea," said Tanier.

"Don't lose faith in them," said Bailan rounding the corner and entering the room. "They will learn how to cooperate with each other."

"I hope that you're right," said Tanier, looking up at Bailan. "Remember that the fate of this world relies on your decisions."

"Fear not, Tanier," said Bailan as he walked over to the two boys and inspected them. "It has been said to me many times that humans are weak. Some creatures are fast and some are strong, some have claws and some have wings. Humans have nothing of these great powers, but what they do have, is much more powerful. What you do not realise is that when humans were created, they were given the gifts of great emotion, passion, and will. No matter what, they will persevere and achieve their goals. Until they realise how to use these powers, they are weak, but once they capture that essence, they become great beings." Bailan looked away from the boys and sat beside Lena in the corner, placing a hand on her cheek. "That is why

I'm here, Tanier. That is why all of us are here." Tanier smiled and nodded.

"I guess that faith is one of these powers," said Tanier. Bailan smiled and jumped to his feet.

"Now you're getting the hang of things," said Bailan as he walked back to the door.

"Is it time to get started?" said Tanier.

"I'm thinking so," replied Bailan. Tanier stood up and walked in between the two boys, taking in a deep breath before starting time again. The two boys moved slightly towards each other before being thrown back against the opposite walls. Tanier the proceeded to lift the boys off their feet and held up by their necks. They both began to struggle as Tanier looked down at the ground with an expression of disappointment on his face.

"What is wrong with you two?" questioned Tanier, in a calm voice. "I could've sworn that both of you had grown up." He dropped the boys to the ground and turned his attention to Lena. "Bailan, please take her out." Bailan nodded and walked over to Lena, wrapping an arm around her, shielding her from the two boys and bringing her out of the room. Tanier walked over to the door and closed it behind Bailan and Lena, standing still for a moment afterwards.

"He…"

"I don't want to hear it, Kailan!" yelled Tanier. "First you get into a fight with Farol, and then you pick fights with your friends!"

"He's not my friend!" yelled Kailan. "If I could have it

my way…" Kailan clenched his fist, watching as the blood and sweat dripped down his arm. "I'd… I'd…"

"You'd what?" questioned Tanier.

"I don't know!" cried Kailan, pulling his fist away and slamming it on the ground. Tears rolled down his cheek as he began to weep in his hand. "I'm sorry."

"Sorry?" questioned Tanier.

"You wanted me to change," said Kailan. "My friends wanted me to change, Lena wanted me to change!" Kailan took in a deep breath. "I want to change," he whispered away. "But I couldn't! I couldn't change for anyone!"

"You have no idea what happened," said Viktor.

"I saw you on top of Lena, holding her down. That is all the reason I needed!"

"Both of you stop!" yelled Tanier. "Obviously I cannot speak to both of you at the same time, so I'll separate you two." The Arch Chancellor walked over to the door and opened it. "Kailan, go to your room and I will meet you there in a little while." Kailan lifted himself up, wiping the tears from his eyes. He slowly limped out of the room and closed the door behind him gently. As he made his way back to his room, he could hear Tanier continue to yell. When he reached his room, Kailan slammed the door shut behind him and threw himself on his bed. Letting out a yell, Kailan began to cry into his pillow.

"I can't take any more of this!" yelled Kailan. He then rolled over on his side and curled up into a ball. "I'm not the same person that I used to be," Kailan said to himself. "I've changed. I never let my anger control me like this before." He then rolled onto his back and took in a large breath. Suddenly, there was a knock on his door, but Kailan ignored it, trying to pretend that he was asleep so that Tanier would not bother him until the morning. There was a second set of knocks before the door slowly opened.

"Don't worry, Kailan," said Bailan. Kailan turned his head and watched as Bailan walked into the room and sat down on the chair in the corner. "Lena told me everything that happened."

"What do you mean?"

"While they were at the pub, someone drugged them," replied Bailan.

"They were drugged?" questioned Kailan, propping himself up against the headboard.

"Lena thought that Viktor was you, and Viktor thought that Lena was Rina," said Bailan. "Lena realised what was going on immediately before you showed up, and she panicked at first, but realised what had happened."

"So they weren't trying to have sex?" said Kailan.

"Well… thankfully the drugs wore off right before they were about to," replied Bailan.

"Tanier is going to kill me," said Kailan holding his hands to his forehead.

"Lena also told me that you backed off when she asked you to, but Viktor attacked you afterwards."

"I shouldn't have fought him in the first place though,"

[301]

said Kailan.

Bailan sighed and walked over to Kailan, sitting next to him on the bed. "Kailan, let me tell you something. For as long as I can remember, I've seen humans fighting. They've fought over some of the stupidest things."

Kailan turned away, looking down at his covers, keeping eye contact away from Bailan.

"But then again, I've seen men fight for some of the noblest things imaginable. In all of my life, I've seen many kings fight and die for what they thought was right. When asked why, they justified it, but never made any sense. When asked why you fought the prince, you told us that he began the fight. When asked why you fought Viktor just now, you tell me that you should never have fought him. Let me tell you this though. Peace has never been achieved without a little violence."

Kailan slowly lifted his head as he looked up at Bailan. "Are you saying that it is okay to fight?" asked Kailan.

"I'm saying that no matter how silly your ideas might seem to another, if deep down, something you care about is threatened, you must protect it. If someone challenges you, it doesn't mean that you are wrong; it just means that they think differently than you. In you and through you, you are right. If you decide that it was the wrong thing to do, then it was the wrong thing to do. Until then, you are always right in your mind. I do not believe that you were wrong, and therefore, in my mind, you were right by your actions."

Kailan smiled. "So you're saying that what I did was

right?"

"I'm asking you a question," replied Bailan. "Do you feel like you did the right thing or the wrong thing?"

Kailan looked down at his feet again, thinking. "I can't really say."

"Now you are beginning to think properly," said Bailan. "It is not our duty to know the difference between right and wrong. It is our duty to act upon our instincts. We will never truly know what is right and what is wrong."

"I'm very confused right now," said Kailan with a smile on his face.

"Don't worry Kailan, you will live a rich, full life," said Bailan as he stood up and walked towards the door.

"You're just saying that," said Kailan.

"One day you will know the truth behind what I say," said Bailan, exiting the room.

*   *   *

As the five companions made their way with their belongings into the lounge, they were met by Tanier and Bailan.

"As you all know as of last night, each of you will be sent off to a different destination to train," said Tanier, pulling out a map and laying it flat on the table in the middle of the room. "I suggest that after this meeting, you all say your

[303]

goodbyes, as you won't be seeing each other for at least a couple of months." The five companions looked around at each other quickly before paying attention again to the map. "Thorstein, you will go to the city of Traknok on the island of Greer, north of your Algar University. You will need to dress warmly as it is almost always winter there. Viktor, you are being sent to the Assassins' Guild of Vestille, in northern Takash, just south of Arad. It is an assassins' guild, and we hope that you learn well there. Lena and Guin, you two are going back to Kartol. Lena, you will stay with the elves in Hileñar. Guin, you will go to Kelenath where you will study at the same university that me and Bailan spent our childhoods at." Tanier peered at the edge of the map and noticed something strange. "Last, but not least, Kailan, you will be heading to the country of Korchetska on the other side of Letania. I can't show you where it is on this map, but I will show you later on another." The five companions looked at each other, and then again at Tanier.

"We're leaving immediately, aren't we?" said Guin.

Tanier nodded. "There is a ship waiting for both you and Lena at the docks, as well as one for Thorstein. Viktor, you have a carriage waiting to take you to Takash." There was a brief silence before Kailan spoke up.

"What about me?" questioned Kailan.

"Oh you have no need to worry," said Tanier. The five friends quickly said their goodbyes, but there was still a very strong tension between Viktor and Kailan. They tried their hardest not to look at each other throughout the whole ordeal. As the remaining four waved Viktor off in the carriage, Kailan felt as though a weight had been lifted from his chest. He no longer needed to worry about Viktor until he returned. Kailan followed the other three members of the group down to the harbour and helped them load their items onto the boats. Kailan made sure to load Lena's things first so that he could have some time to quickly talk with her before she left. He then pulled her aside and hid with her behind one of the large crates on the pier.

"You know that I'm still angry at you," said Lena.

Kailan nodded and looked down at the ground. "I know, and I am sorry for everything. I regret every action."

"I'm angry at you, but I still love you," said Lena, smiling.

Kailan looked up and into Lena's eyes and smiled as well.

"You were there to protect me though, and for that I cannot remain angry," said Lena. She wrapped her arms around Kailan and pecked him on the cheek. "I will miss you every day." Lena stepped away from Kailan and boarded the ship. As the boarding ramp was kicked away, the ship quickly began moving away. "Kailan!" yelled Lena as she reached into her pocket. "I almost forgot!" She quickly threw something into the air to Kailan. He jumped up, catching it and held it in front of his face. It was a leather necklace with a bird shaped pendant. "It's a phoenix!" Kailan smiled as the boat left the docks and slowly made its way towards the horizon.

"Don't worry," said Thorstein, standing behind Kailan.

[305]

"She'll be perfectly fine."

Kailan turned around and smiled, throwing his arms around one of Thorstein's legs. "I'm going to miss you, big guy," said Kailan. Thorstein chuckled before taking a knee next to Kailan.

"We'll all make it back, safe and sound, said Thorstein. A couple of months isn't that long of a time anyways. You've already been gone from home for almost a year if you think about it."

"Ya, I guess you're right." Kailan stepped back from his best friend and watched as Thorstein made the ship wobble at first as he stepped aboard. In what seemed like no time at all, Kailan was now the only one left. He slowly made his way back to Machesney Hall, heading straight for Tanier's office. Upon reaching it, he let out a big sigh and sat at the chair in front of Tanier's desk.

"Feels a bit strange to be the only one around, doesn't it?" said Tanier, busy filling out paperwork. Kailan nodded his head and looked around the room.

"So how am I going to get to Korchetska?" questioned Kailan.

"Gather your things and return to my office," replied Tanier. Kailan jumped to his feet and quickly made his way back to his room where his things were waiting for him. When he returned with all of his equipment, Kailan dropped his bag to the ground, making a loud thud sound. Tanier looked up and smiled. He pulled away from the desk and pulled Kailan's sword out from under the desk. As Tanier stood up, and Kailan's sight was set upon the sword, the boy smiled. "While in the city of Tolnsk, you will meet a man named Oran Gerbetski. I want you to give him your sword and have him look at it. You won't be needing it for at least the first week that you are there anyways." Kailan nodded and took hold of the sword, attaching it to his belt and letting it hang at his side.

"How am I getting there?" questioned Kailan. Tanier smiled as he slowly held his hands wide apart.

As he quickly brought them together, he yelled out, "KARABOUCHE!" Tanier was again alone in his office, left with nothing but a pile of papers on his desk.

*   *   *

As Kailan opened his eyes, he was standing in the middle centre of a city square. All of the people around him were shocked by his sudden appearance there, some of them even being knocked to the ground.

"Ah, Kailan!" said a man as he hurried over to the boy. When he spoke, his accent was very similar to Viktor's, except much thicker. His hair was grey, and Kailan couldn't tell if he was short because of how much he slouched or because of his actual height.

"Are you Oran?" questioned Kailan.

"Yes, yes," said the man as he took Kailan's bag in one hand and slung it over his shoulder. He then put the other hand on Kailan's back and guided him through the city.

"Are you messing around in that magic business again, Oran?" yelled one of the men that was knocked to the ground.

"Oh, go back to farming turnips," said Oran. He hurried the boy into a building and lit a candle on one of the tables. Kailan undid his scabbard and placed the sword on the table.

"I was told to give my sword to you," said Kailan.

"Ah, yes," said w, picking up the sword. "Tanier told me about this in the letter."

"He sent you a letter?"

"Yep, told me to meet you in the square on this day, at this time," replied Oran. "Also said that Geamille will be here shortly."

"Geamille?" questioned Kailan.

"Tanier didn't tell you?" said Oran.

"No, Tanier pretty much told me to give my sword to you, and then he teleported me here."

"Not much of a talker is he?" said Oran, laughing. "Not funny?" Kailan was neither smiling, nor frowning, but continued to have a confused look upon his face. "Anyways, Geamille is the man that you will be training with for the next two months. He's a master swordsman extraordinaire." A slight smile appeared on Kailan's face before it was wiped clean when there was a knock at the door. "That'll be him now." Oran hobbled over to the door and opened it. "Geamille!"

"Is Kailan here yet?" questioned the man. As he stepped in, Kailan quickly eyed the man up and down. He was a bit taller than Kailan, with short, light brown hair and a goatee, wearing a light brown leather trench coat. In one of his hands, he carried a green cane that glimmered in the light. Kailan walked over to the man and shook his other hand.

"You must be Geamille," said Kailan.

"Nice to meet you Kailan," said Geamille before turning again to Oran. "I thank you again for helping us in situations like this, Oran."

"Oh, but always a pleasure," laughed Oran.

"Grab your things Kailan, we have a carriage outside waiting to take us to my estate," said Geamille. Kailan picked up his bag and walked out of the small building, up to the coach. He began to load his items on the back of the carriage, making sure as to not scratch the delicate wood artwork.

It was about an hour later that Kailan arrived at his new temporary home. Kailan never realised it before, but the leaves on all of the trees were already changing colour in Korchetska. The colour orange filled the sky like an eternal fire. The sweet smell of autumn filled his nostrils. For miles, all that Kailan could see were pumpkins, squash, corn, and other assorted vegetables. There was almost no green left in Korchetska, as it had all left for the winter, hiding beneath the fallen leaves. As Kailan stepped out of the carriage, he took in a deep breath, filling his lungs with the fresh air. As he gazed upon the immense, but beautiful house, he felt a sense of happiness that he had never felt before. Maybe it was because he was used to moving from place to place. Seeing as he never really had much of a chance to spend time at Machesney Hall, he might find Geamille's home to be a bit more welcoming after the first few days. As Kailan rounded the carriage and reached for one of his bags on the back, he was stopped by Geamille.

"Don't worry about your things," said Geamille. He turned and waved his hand to someone in the house before turning back to face Kailan. "My servants will get that for you."

"Servants?" questioned Kailan. Suddenly, a tall, skinny man hurried out of the front door of the house and ran down the steps.

"Take Master Kailan's belongings and bring them to his room, please Winthrow," said Geamille. The man nodded, and then proceeded to pull Kailan's bags off of the back of the carriage. "You must be hungry," said Geamille, smiling at Kailan.

"Yes, slightly," replied Kailan.

"Winthrow, please inform the cooks that Kailan will also be joining us for lunch." The man in the suit nodded and hurried with Kailan's bags into the house. "Come Kailan." Geamille began by showing Kailan around the grounds first, before taking Kailan inside to see the house. The perimeter of the house was filled with gardens; roses being the main flora of choice. They crept up the walls like fingers outstretched, blocking most of the white wall from the sun. On the four main walls of the house were large windows, creating little need for candles or lamps within the home. Just outside of the rear of the house, Geamille had a much larger garden, along with a small barn beside the garden. As they neared the barn, Geamille spoke up. "Did Tanier explain to you about the training process?"

"No," replied Kailan. "Actually, he never really explained anything at all." Geamille smiled as he and Kailan entered the barn. Geamille lifted his cane and held it up in the air, pulling off the top and revealing a sword.

"You are going to have to learn the hard way," said Geamille. He lunged at Kailan with the sword, but the boy quickly dodged the attack.

"What are you doing?" yelled Kailan.

"You need to defend yourself," replied Geamille, smirking. Kailan patted his side, only to remember that he gave his sword to Oran.

"I'm unarmed!" said Kailan.

"You will not always have your weapon on you when danger strikes. You must be prepared for anything." Kailan quickly searched around and found a shovel handle lying underneath some straw. He grabbed it and brought it upwards, but only to be blocked by Geamille. He spun around, trying to fight Geamille on the other side, but he was just as quick as Kailan. With each attack that Kailan made, Geamille was faster, and only blocked the attack before Kailan could get close.

"You're fast," said Kailan.

"The fastest," replied Geamille. "That's why I'm teaching you." Without even a hint or notion of what he was

[311]

about to do, Geamille swung his sword in a circle, knocking the wooden stick out of Kailan's hand. As the boy quickly looked for something else to fight with, Geamille made his way closer with his blade and held it at Kailan's throat. The boy quickly gave up without a struggle, making sure not to be cut by the sword. "You will learn soon," said Geamille. "You have two months of training ahead of you. In that time I can teach you almost anything." He pulled away the knife and placed it back into the cane sheath. "Now, let's eat."

*   *   *

Upon arriving at the island of Greer, Thorstein instantly knew that the next two months would be very hard to get used to. Thorstein never realised it before, but the island of Greer was also one of the northern dwarven kingdoms. The boat was greeted by a number of the small people, many of them specifically there for Thorstein. The first dwarf to welcome Thorstein to the new land was different than any dwarf that Thorstein had seen before. He did not seem stocky, or having stubby arms and legs. Instead, the short man was rather skinny, clean shaven, and somewhat taller than most dwarves.

"You must be Thorstein," said the little man, hurrying up to the giant's side. He held out his hand to shake Thorstein's. "My name is Yolltz."

[312]

"That doesn't sound very dwarfish," said Thorstein, confused while shaking the small man's hand.

"It's Feltsch actually," replied Yolltz. "My mother was an elf from the borders of Achland and Thoria."

"You don't look like a full dwarf," said Thorstein.

"I get that a lot," replied Yolltz. "I'm a bit of an outcast, but hey. How many other dwarves can run as fast as I can?"

"There's always a positive to things like that," replied Thorstein. Yolltz smiled before calling over a horse-drawn wagon.

"You may put your belongings on here," said Yolltz, smiling as he turned away and hopped onto the wagon. He picked up the brown leather reins and proceeded with a clicking noise, making the pony move forward. Thorstein's dornbeast was already off of the ship and waiting for the giant by one of the large wooden crates. He quickly mounted the woolly rhinoceros and began following Yolltz down the road. They moved at an easy pace, making sure that nothing would fall off the side of the wagon. Most of the area between the docks and the capital city was very hilly, with rocks cast about. It reminded Thorstein of the plains of Achland. As the wind blew over the small cliffs, through the emerald grass, Thorstein took in a deep breath of relief. His chest expanded and his lungs filled up with the crisp, flavourful breeze of air. He began to then think of the letter and what it would give to him and the others. Were they being trained so that they would be able to protect Arlbega from

[313]

the Black Allegiance, or was it all just an idea concocted by an old man? Thorstein quickly began to doubt Orpeth Armenen's plans for the group. It didn't seem right to him that Tanier, Bailan, and the many others, were so dedicated to this ordeal, even though they knew little to nothing of what was going on. Orpeth Armenen had spent a number of years gathering all of this information, and they still know nothing, or at least chose not to reveal any of it.

Upon arriving at the city, Thorstein stretched his head back so far, straining his neck as to see the colossal mountain ahead. There were two giant stone pillars carved out of the side of the mountain. Between the two pillars, there was a large opening into the city. It was a well-known fact that most dwarven cities were situated beneath the ground. It is said that when the dwarves first walked the planet, the only thing they did was dig. Because of their diminutive stature, they were easy prey for some of the larger predators. It didn't matter how stronger they were, because eventually it became time to run, and they weren't ready for that. So, to protect themselves even more, they began to craft tools and dig beneath the surface. Thorstein studied much about the dwarves while at Algar University, but even then, he still knew very little of them. Thorstein followed closely behind the wagon as they entered the city, even as everyone stared at him. Sure, Thorstein was already a giant, but compared to the dwarves of Greer, Torstein seemed almost twice that size. The children that run amok throughout the streets looked up at Thorstein the same way as he had to the mountain.

[314]

Standing in the exact centre of the city was a large stone statue of one of the ancient dwarf kings. Rows of torches lit up most of the city. Other parts of the city were lit up by some of the remaining light from the giant forges. Yolltz brought Thorstein to a large building on the opposite side of as the main entrance.

"We have prepared this home for you," said Yolltz as he made his way down from the wagon. "Tanier Frost informed us of your size, so we crafted a building that would suit you perfectly. Thorstein was quite amazed as to how much work was put into making sure that the house was the right size. The door was slightly taller than he, and the steps leading up to it were spaced apart perfectly for him. Inside, there was a large table that Thorstein was actually able to sit on a chair at, instead of having to kneel or sit cross-legged. "There is a stable next to the house for your... creature," Yolltz stated.

"It's called a dornbeast," replied Thorstein. "Don't worry, my friends had never seen one either before."

Yolltz smiled as he unloaded the last of Thorstein's belongings. "If you would like, I can give you a quick tour of the city now, or I can show you it in the morning before we begin your training."

"I think that the morning might be best. I'm quite tired at the moment and would love to get some rest," said Thorstein.

"As you wish," replied Yolltz. "You have a fully stocked kitchen on your first left, your bedroom is the second door, and on the right is the living room and bathroom. I will leave you now and meet you hear first thing in the morning."

[315]

"Thank you very much, Yolltz," said Thorstein, eagerly leading the dornbeast into the stable. It was quite a strange feeling that Thorstein had. Never in his life had something actually met his size, except for clothing. Even the new wing at Machesney Hall was built for the smaller group members. The only thing that fit Thorstein there was his bed. At this new home, Thorstein felt a sense of deep belonging that he had never felt before. He made his way into the living room first and lay back in his large wing chair. He stretched out his legs and propped his feet on the ottoman in front. There was a fireplace beside him, with a collection of books on either side. Thorstein was almost scared to leave.

*   *   *

Kailan ran as fast as he could through the fields. He could not see his pursuer, but knew that he was close behind. There was a tree and in front of him which he quickly chose to hide behind. He panted heavily, trying to regain his breath, but trying to remain silent as well. He did not want to be caught. The longer he waited within those bushes, the more his pride swelled up. He had chosen a great hiding spot; he had not been found yet. It was almost ten minutes before Kailan noticed the horse appear over one of the distant hills. He made sure not to make a sound, but smiled as he had fooled the one chasing after him. It was almost another minute before Kailan realised that something was wrong. As his eyes came into focus upon the horse, he noticed that it was not moving, but grazing, and there was no rider. Suddenly, a great amount of fear brought itself upon Kailan. Where was the rider? Kailan slowly lifted himself up as to get a better view before feeling the cold tap of the sword on his shoulder.

"Damn!" cried Kailan out loud. He turned around, but there was no one there, confusing the boy even more. "Ok, where are you?"

"Above you," said Geamille. The spry man leapt from the tree and landed beside Kailan with a smile on his face.

"How long were you up there?" questioned Kailan.

"I reached this tree about two minutes before you did," replied Geamille. He whistled for his horse and smiled.

"How did you know that I'd be here?" asked Kailan inquisitively.

"Well, first of all, this *is* my land, and I do know the best hiding spots. Secondly, this is a horrible hiding spot and I know after years of training that someone like you would go straight for a tree."

"What's wrong with a tree?" said Kailan.

"It is too obvious of a spot for hiding," replied Geamille. "Almost anyone would think to hide there. You need to be creative when it comes to hiding. The best hiding spot would have been beneath that ledge over there." Geamille pointed off in the distance, near where the horse was standing

[317]

earlier. "You could have ducked underneath there and waited till I passed over on the horse. Then, you would make your way over the ledge and run out of sight. Geamille called for his horse and the two of them made their way back to the house.

Upon returning to the house, Kailan and Geamille were met by Winthrow. "Excuse me sire, but we received word while you were out that you are needed immediately, to meet with the city council," said Winthrow.

"This is what I expect it to be about, am I correct?" questioned Geamille.

The servant nodded without hesitation. "I believe so," replied Winthrow. "Your carriage is waiting for you around the front of the house." The tall man looked at Kailan and stepped to the side to get a better view of him. "Shall I put the boy to work while you are gone?"

"This might actually be a great learning experience for him," replied Geamille. "He will learn much of how I help to run the city." Kailan smiled upon hearing these words. It was the first real break that he had received after first arriving at Geamille's estate a few days prior. "Tell the driver that we will be ready within the next few minutes." Winthrow nodded and made his way back towards the other side of the house. Geamille then turned to Kailan and exhaled as though he was trying to keep most of the air in. "I suggest that you find something nice to wear. The city council consists of some of the most prestigious men in the state."

"You sound almost as though you don't want to go,"

said Kailan, taking a step back.

"To be honest, I have no real desire to go, but it is my duty," replied Geamille.

"Why don't you want to go?" questioned Kailan. "I would love having that much power."

"There is no real power in running Tolnsk," said Geamille, responding to Kailan's second comment. "There are fourteen other men there, and all they do is argue. Other than my two friends within the council, everyone there knows nothing of what is actually going on."

"Do they help you?" asked Kailan.

"Who?"

"Your friends."

"No, they are too afraid to speak. Not because they might be beaten, but because they fear being outspoken and pushed aside." Geamille hurried over to the stable, leaving Kailan to go to the house.

The boy made his way up to his room and began rummaging through his clothes. Many of them seemed to either be dirty or tattered. He didn't think it was suitable to wear the suit that Geamille had tailored for him. He found one of his old shirts though, and decided that it wasn't as dirty as the rest, or as worn. He removed his clothes quickly, first with the pants, and then the shirt. There was a brief pause as Kailan stared into the abyss. Something was bothering him, ticking within his mind. For some reason, at that instance, Lena passed through his head. It was a slow thought, staying there for a short-lived time.

Kailan sat down on the bed and pressed his fist deep into the cushion.

"I don't know whether to still chase after her or to forget," Kailan muttered to himself. He took in a deep breath, and then began exhaling slowly as to almost not make a sound. He leaned over the bed and grasped onto the clean shirt. He pulled it over his head and tied it up. When he reached the carriage, Geamille was already waiting for him.

"What took you so long?" questioned the man.

"Just a hard time finding the proper shirt," replied Kailan.

"Ah," Geamille said with a smile on his face. He opened the door to the carriage and motioned Kailan in. The carriage quickly left the estate and made its way to Tolnsk.

*   *   *

The city of Traknok was beautiful in the morning. There was little light that made its way into the city, but the morning sun shone directly through the two pillars at the entrance. The entire underground room was filled with immense warmth from that light. Thorstein rolled over onto his side after having the best sleep in years. A small book was sitting on the stone nightstand next to his bed. The book was written in dwarven runes which Thorstein could not decipher. While at

Algar, Thorstein learned how to speak some elvish, and numerous human languages, but that was the most of it. His thumb covered most of the page as he pulled it back. There were a number of books that he was given access to that were much bigger, but this one in particular fascinated Thorstein. Suddenly there was a knock at the door. Thorstein hurried out of bed, putting his pants on quickly. Upon opening the door, he found Yolltz standing in the doorway.

"Good day," said Yolltz. "Are you ready to meet our king finally?"

"I just woke up," replied Thorstein. "I haven't had a chance to eat yet."

"Don't worry about that," said Yolltz. "The king's servants will prepare you a glorious breakfast. Have you ever had bacon before?"

Thorstein ran back into his room and began throwing on clothes. When he emerged, from the door, Yolltz led him along the streets towards a long road with pillars all along the side. Thorstein had spent a number of days within the city, studying about the dwarven culture. Most of his time, Thorstein spent within his temporary home, reading over books and listening to stories from Yolltz's life. As they walked up the large stone steps towards the throne room, Thorstein began to feel a sense of nervousness. The training that he had received so far was not much of training at all. This was the first time since being back at home that Thorstein would really be worked. For him, even most of the fighting he did was effortless and didn't force him to think either. He had no clue as to what would be in store for him as he entered through the doorway in front of him. It seemed strange for Thorstein as there were no guards anywhere. This was the first time that he had come upon royalty and not run into any guards on the way. A man stood in front of Thorstein, with arms spread.

"My dear Thorstein," said the king. "We are so glad to welcome you to our city of Traknok!" Thorstein smiled, not because of the man's kind words, but because of the likeness that they shared. The man's appearance was almost exactly that of Thorstein's, other than the size difference, but even then, that wasn't far off. This man stood much taller than any of the other dwarves, even towering over Yolltz, who was already almost the height of a human. His hair was the same light-red that Thorstein had, and his beard was almost kept in the same fashion, except for the fact that the man allowed his to grow over his lips. "How has your stay been? We tried to do our best."

Thorstein inched back slightly, and lowered himself a bit. "Everything has been wonderful," replied Thorstein. "Thank you."

"No thanks needed," said the man. "We just hope to make sure that you have an excellent stay while you are here."

"I'm sorry, but I have no idea who you are exactly," said Thorstein.

Yolltz stepped back and let out a quiet gasp. The two dwarves looked at each other in shock. "This is the king," said Yolltz as he pulled down on Thorstein.

[322]

The giant took a step back and quickly dropped to one knee. "I'm sorry sire, but I didn't mean to disrespect you."

The king's look of astonishment quickly changed to a smile, and then a laugh. "Get up, Thorstein," said the king. "Don't worry about bowing. As well, it was just a little joke that Yolltz and I like to play with our guests." The king walked stepped closer and grabbed onto Thorstein's hand, shaking it. "My name is Archus." After the king released his grip, Thorstein rose to his feet. "We will begin your training today with some simple exercises."

Thorstein lifted the heavy log over his head, hauling it onto his shoulders. The soldiers watched on as the behemoth raised the two thousand pound tree into the air.

"Run Thorstein!" yelled Archus. "I want you to not be able to walk when we are done tonight!"

Thorstein took one step, buckling under the weight of the log, but quickly regaining his hold. With each step after that, Thorstein felt himself gaining pace. Within seconds, Thorstein was at an easy jog, covering great distances in no time.

"I want to hear you roar!" cried Archus.

Thorstein let out a grunt, but it failed to get past even his ears.

"I said roar, dammit!"

"Ah!" shouted Thorstein. By this time, Thorstein was running, but he was quickly losing strength. He could feel it in both his legs and his arms.

"Throw the log!" yelled Archus.

[323]

As Thorstein slung the log into one of his arms, he could feel how weak he was, but he didn't want to be weak, so he pushed himself. He threw the log into the air, crying out as he did so. Before the log hit the ground, Thorstein had already made friends with the earth. He hit the soil, tearing up most of the terrain.

"I don't see him moving," said Yolltz to the king.

"We should probably make sure that he did not hurt himself too badly," replied Archus. The two tall dwarves made their way over to Thorstein, who remained motionless until they arrived.

"Are you ok?" questioned Yolltz. All that he received as a reply was an almost inaudible moan. "I'm sorry, I didn't hear that."

Thorstein quickly rolled onto his back, showing a number of small cuts to his face. He held out a single hand to the king and raised his thumb into the air. "What's next?"

*   *   *

Lena awoke that morning, with a magnificent view out of her window. The morning sun shone through the tree tops, glistening as it hit the dew drops on each emerald leaf. The colourful birds outside her window sang familiar tunes, giving life to the sounds of the forest. There was a knock at the door, releasing Lena from her sense of utter peace.

"Are you decent my lady?" questioned Gelob, putting his ear up to the door.

"Yes Gelob," replied Lena pulling the covers over her clothed body. Gelob slowly opened the door, stepping in without making a sound.

"The king has sent for you, requiring your assistance," said Gelob. "He would like for you to meet him in his office as soon as possible."

"Thank you, Gelob," said Lena with a smile on her face. The elf exited the room, closing the door behind him until it clicked. Lena sat upright in her bed, revealing the white gown that the elves had made for her when she returned to Hileñar. She let out a bit of a sigh before turning her legs to the side of the bed and hopping off. She walked over to the mirror against the wall and dipped her hands into the water bowl, splashing her face with the cool liquid. The towel beside the bowl was soft to the touch of her fingers, and even more caring to her cheeks. Lena then began to stare into the mirror, feeling as though she was leaving her physical body. It was a number of minutes before Lena began to dress herself. As she pulled on the white gown, she imagined Kailan's hand, caressing her shoulder, pulling the white fabric down to her arm. Goosebumps slithered up her arms and back, causing Lena to shake for a moment. This was followed by a brief imagination of Viktor, pulling the other strap down. Lena snapped to and shook her head frantically from side to side, trying to release herself from the thoughts. As she stood naked at the foot of her bed, Lena pondered as to what she was going to wear. She decided to wear her usual clothes, but instead left her belt, quiver, and falcon glove behind. The door slowly creaked open as Lena poked her head out and began making her way down the hallway. Upon reaching the footbridge in the centre of the palace, Lena felt a sense of uneasiness coursing through her body. Suddenly, at either end of the walkway were armed soldiers, but none of them looked as though they were from the elven army. The armour they wore was dark and tattered. The armour of the elven army was white with a gold trim, and always kept in pristine condition. The soldiers began to charge towards Lena, so she reached for her bow. She then realised her problem. She had left her bow and the other weapons in her room. There was no reason for her to bring them with her through the palace to meet with thee king. As they neared her, Lena made the quick decision to charge at one of the soldiers, jumping up and kicking his shoulder. He went down instantly, but Lena was still surrounded by about five other soldiers. She tried to punch one of them, but her hand was grabbed out of the air and pulled behind her back. The soldiers lifted Lena into the air, restraining her. She struggled, shaking back and forth, but it did no use. There was no question as to where they were bringer her. Lena could tell that they were bringing her to the king's study.

"What is the meaning of this?" Lena yelled, trying to break her arm free. As they opened the door to the study, they found the king, sitting quietly at his desk.

"Bit of a shame," said the king with a slit frown on his face. The soldiers placed Lena on the ground gently, but blocking the door.

"They've taken over the castle!" yelled Lena.

"Don't worry, my child," said the king.

"What are you talking about?" questioned Lena.

"It was only a test," replied the king. "I wanted to see how well you would be able to fight off your enemies without any weapons.

"You set this all up?" asked Lena as she sat down in the chair in front of the king's desk.

"I did indeed," replied King Grakken.

"You were in no real danger," said Gelob, pulling off the worn helmet to reveal his smirking face.

"That wasn't very funny," said Lena as she looked up at Gelob.

"It wasn't meant to be," replied the elf. "It was meant to put you into a state of fear so that you would react with instinct rather than rational thinking."

"How well did I do on this test?" questioned Lena.

"Well, to be honest, you technically failed," said Gelob. "The whole purpose of it was for you to not be captured. Sure, you defeated one of our soldiers, but you were captured none the less." Gelob walked up beside his uncle and placed the helmet on the desk. "We will train you to be able to fight, and to flee if needed. Your body will be strengthened, your skin toughened. We will teach you how to fight without any weapons; we will teach you how to break free from your attackers."

"Drast may have taught you how to shoot an arrow, but we will teach you more," said Grakken. "You will be able to beat some of our best warriors when you are done." Lena's faint grimace slowly went away as it changed into a smile.

About an hour later, Lena was fighting Gelob just outside of the city barracks. They did not wear any protective equipment whatsoever, not even on their faces. Lena had a short sword and a small buckler, while Gelob attacked with a wooden staff. For the first few minutes, with every attack Lena made, Gelob had a perfect counterattack. Every time she thrust the sword at him, Gelob parried it with ease. Every time she tried to bring it down upon his head, Gelob blocked. There were a number of times when Gelob decided to attack instead of defending, throwing Lena into confusion.

"You need to relax," said Gelob. "Let's try this slower."

Lena nodded before making another move. She gracefully brought her sword to the side, bringing it in with no sudden movements. Gelob gently blocked the sword, using no strength to deflect it. With that, Lena saw her chance. She spun to the side, still moving slowly, and struck Gelob in the side with the small shield.

"Better," said Gelob, smiling. "Let's try that again." It took a while before Lena understood that the purpose of the exercise was not to make quick attacks, but to make sure that her attacks were precise, and planned.

*   *   *

The only sound that could be heard within the dark tunnels was the sounds of distant mice. Viktor could not hear the footsteps, let alone the voices, of his fellow trainees. He wore nothing but a tattered cloth covering his loins. It was so dark within the tunnels that Viktor couldn't even see his hands in front of his face. The ground was damp, giving off a musty smell that he associated with death. It reminded him of when his mother locked him in the cellar. All that he could think about were the voices of the villagers.

"Murderer!" they screamed.

"You little monster!" cried one of the women.

"We should kill it right now!" yelled one of the men leading the group.

It never dawned on Viktor to think of Rina; his one true saviour. Never once within the darkness of the tunnels did Viktor think to imagine her voice, even though it was the only thing that could comfort him. At this point, Viktor wasn't sure if the two red eyes in the distance were real, or just imagination.

[329]

They taunted him, filling him with fear, anxiety, and more so, anger. They danced back and forth within the darkness, but never seemed to come any closer. To Viktor, the eyes were a symbol of pure evil. They were the madness within the caves personified.

"Get away!" Viktor growled.

The eye's snapped their attention to Viktor, squinting as if they were trying to focus in the dark. Slowly they seemed to move towards him, ever cautious. Viktor could have sworn he saw a set of teeth, smiling at him, but he knew that it could only be his mind, playing tricks on him.

"Stay back!"

The creature, whatever it was, stopped and cocked it's head to the side. At this point, Viktor could not see a smile, but he knew that there was one beneath the darkness. For the first time since being locked in the tunnels, Viktor heard something that he knew was real. The terrifying laugh deafened his ears and forced him to take a few steps back. He closed his eyes and continued to imagine the voices, but this time, there was a different voice.

"Kill it!" the voice cried. "Kill it before it kills you!" It was a strange voice; one that Viktor had never heard before. For some reason, it seemed like this was the only sane voice within his mind. He quickly searched the ground for the largest rock that he could find. "This is the beast that killed your family!" Viktor looked up from the ground to find the eyes directly in front of him; with a stench, so unbearable, being breathed on him. "Kill it." Viktor stepped back. "Kill it!" Even though he couldn't see it, Viktor looked down at the rock, and paused. "KILL IT!"

The beast hissed at Viktor as he brought the stone up and to its head. With one hit, he knocked it on its side, but he knew that he had to finish it off. He stood over the invisible creature and continued hammering the stone into its skull.

"Die!" Viktor cried at the top of his lungs. With each strike, Viktor could feel the power growing within him. There was something about this anger that Viktor had never felt before. It didn't make him want to cry afterwards. Instead, it actually made him feel good. The voice inside his head was like a drug, giving him a surge of adrenaline.

It was a few days later when Viktor was finally released from the tunnels. When he was brought out, they found him covered from head to toe with blood. Within the tunnels, the men discovered the remains of young man. He was only distinguished by the greyish colour of his skin, as his body was too mangled to tell. The trainers decided to keep the findings secret from their superiors. It had turned out that a dark elf had infiltrated the tunnels and was tasked with killing Viktor, but by some strange miracle, he killed it instead. Dark elves were stronger warriors than their day dwelling cousins, even considered stronger than most men. It was surprising that a mere boy could kill one with his bare hands.

They men were given a few days to rest before classes started again. The next task for the young assassins was to create suitable poisons. They were each given a small pouch, along with a small knife to scour the land for the most suitable ingredients. It didn't seem to take Viktor very long to find his items. The young men were given a full day to look for what they needed, but Viktor returned within the hour.

"He can't be done already," said one of the men.

"Don't worry, he's crazy," said another. "Probably has a bag full of sand."

"Did you hear what he did in the tunnels?" said the first man.

"It sounds like a total lie to me," said the second boy. As he turned back, he found Viktor standing directly in front of him.

Viktor reached into his pouch and pulled out a live scorpion by the tail. "You know, it's not nice to talk about people behind their backs," said Viktor. He held the tail up to the boy's face, who stood almost motionless except for a slight quiver. He stroked the boy's cheek with the tail. "Don't worry, I won't hurt you," Viktor then looked up from the scorpion to the man, "You on the other hand." He raised the scorpion so that one of the claws rested on the man's cheekbone. The small creature opened its pincer and clamped it down on the man's face. He made no movement from the pain, except for the same slight shaking that he did before. "Good boy," said Viktor, ripping the tail from the scorpion.

Guin knew that if he fought back, he would most likely be removed from the university. On the other hand, he could swear that Aroculus was encouraging him to fight.

"I thought you were supposed to be a better man than this," said Guin.

"I said I was a great page, not a great person," replied Aroculus. The tall boy took another swing at Guin, knocking him to the ground.

"I've had enough!" yelled Guin. He snapped his fingers and lit up a ring of fire around the other boy, whose name happened to be Garth.

The boy stepped back, but then began to laugh. "You seriously think that's going to stop me?" He swept he hands to the side, clearing the fire away. "You'll need to be a bit more imaginative than that.

"I could always give you a spell that would turn him into a frog, but I think that might be a bit too cliché," said Aroculus, giggling.

"That's not funny," said Guin, thinking to himself of another spell.

"There is one that you could try," said Aroculus. "It would probably get you into a lot of trouble if they found out, but then again, he won't bug you anymore. Garth took another swing at Guin, sending him into the air. Upon landing, he looked

[333]

up and threw his book to the side.

"HEPHESHES!" yelled Guin. Garth was suddenly thrown back, and slowly began sinking into the earth.

"Pull me out!" yelled Garth. Two of the other boys quickly ran over to Garth and helped pull him back onto the surface. "Listen here, you little shit; I will ruin you."

"Try ANGKALA," suggested Aroculus.

Guin called out, "ANGKALA," holding his hands in front of him. There was a dark green light that emitted from his palms, but did nothing until he pointed his hands towards each other. It was then that the dark green light seemed to come together to form a ball of the same colour, with swirls of black. The more power he forced into the ball, the bigger it grew. Guin stopped when the orb was about the size of his chest and threw it at Garth, who quickly stopped it just before it reached him.

"What is this supposed to do?" said Garth, laughing. Suddenly, one of Guin's classmates, a young girl named Tateena, ran over to Garth and punched him square in the face, forcing him off his feet. She was between the levitating orb and Garth, standing over the boy.

"Get her out of there!" yelled Aroculus.

"Why?"

"Just do it!"

Guin hurried over and tackled Tateena to the ground, clearing her from the orb as it pulled Garth into it. As he turned over and looked, Guin watched as Garth screamed and was dragged into the orb. "I killed him," said Guin, standing motionless out of fear. Suddenly everyone around Guin, Tateena, and the orb, took three steps back before turning in the opposite direction and running.

"He's not dead," replied Aroculus. "He's just trapped."

"You mean within the orb?"

"Exactly!" Aroculus said with confidence.

Guin knelt down to his book to find a pair of feet standing next to it. He looked up to find one of the older wizards standing over it.

"You're in a great deal of trouble there boy," said the man with a scowl on his face. The wrinkles on his face wouldn't pose a threat to most people, but Guin took it as a sign of wisdom, and that meant strength at the university. Guin quickly found himself being hauled off into the building. Tateena stood confused next to the orb, while the old man had Aroculus under an arm.

"Two hours it took us to find a counter spell!" yelled one of the Kelenath Council members.

Guin found himself in the same room that he had been when they first gave him the spell book. He was again under scrutiny, and facing the powerful judgement of the Wizards' Council.

"Under normal circumstances, we must cast you out, and ban you from taking any more classes," said the lead Council member.

Guin looked at the ground, somewhat shameful of his actions, but mainly to hide the look on his face. Never before had Guin been involved in trouble before. He always abided by the rules. If an ethical issue arose, Guin tried to stay out of it to avoid any problems.

"These aren't normal circumstances though," said the Council member. "We have requests set out by Tanier Frost, and we must fulfil them."

A small grin began to grow on Guin's face as he slowly looked up. The single tear that ran from his eye had disappeared, and was no more.

"However, even though Tanier Frost was a great student at this university, and still is a great wizard, that does not give you full immunity."

"We have confiscated your spell book until we believe that it is time for you to have it back," said a Council member.

"But it's mine!" yelled Guin. "You even said so when you gave it to me!"

"It may be your book, but you are not capable to handle it yet," said the lead Council member. "You will get it back at the end of your time here."

Again, just as before, Guin was suddenly left alone in the room. The only light that shone in was from the doorway leading into it. Guin slowly made his way over to the door with his shoulders almost as low as they could go. Without making even a sound, Guin walked past Tateena, staring at his own feet.

"What happened?" questioned Tateena. "If it was because of me, I'm sorry." Guin walked through the courtyard until he reached another door, slamming it shut behind him.

[336]

*   *   *

Lena picked up the small stone and threw it into the air.
Within the split second that she had until it came back down,
Lena timed and aimed for where she was going to hit. She
brought the wooden rod up and smacked the stone out of the air,
sending it flying into the trees.

"Good," said Gelob. "We will try this now while
running."

Lena looked at him strangely, turning her head to the
side. "What is that supposed to teach me?"

"In battle, do you ever find yourself standing still?"
Gelob said with a smirk. "You are always moving, never
stopping. One motion denotes the next, and so on." Gelob knelt
down and picked up a handful of stones. As he stood back up, he
laughed to himself. The first stone was no problem for Lena to
deflect, but after that they seemed to get much harder to hit.
Gelob was no longer lobbing the rocks in the air, but throwing
them directly at Lena.

"Can we slow down?" said Lena, missing a stone by
the tip of her earlobe.

"Your enemy will never slow down, they will never
take breaks," replied Gelob as he advanced even faster. When he
emptied his hand of stones, Gelob reached down and grabbed

[337]

more. This time, he aimed the stones at Lena's weak spots; areas that he knew she would have problems protecting. "Faster."

"I can't," said Lena.

"Faster! Gelob yelled. He was whipping the stones so fast at Lena that she could barely keep up. She missed one, striking her in the stomach. "I'm not going to stop."

"Please!" Lena whined. "This isn't fun."

"War is never fun," replied Gelob. "It goes until someone is dead, or has lost the will to live." Lena turned, and darted in the opposite direction of Gelob. He continued to pursue the girl, throwing stone after stone. Every now and then, Lena would look back to deflect a shot, even after being hit by a number of them. Gelob reached down again and picked up a number of stones.

It was then that Lena realised his weakness. Every soldier has a weakness of some sort. Gelob's was his short supply of ammunition. Every time he ran out of stones, he would have to bend down, leaving him defenceless.

"That's not part of the exercise though," Lena thought to herself. However, if Gelob wanted to fight, Lena would give him a fight. She deflected a number of the stones, taking a direct hit to her forehead. She looked back with a gash on her head to find Gelob picking up stones again. This time, Lena threw the stick at Gelob's knees, knocking him over onto his seat. As he looked up, all that he could see was Lena's foot flying towards him. She held him in place with her foot, and grabbed both of his arms, pulling on them and pressing her foot down on his chest. "I've won!" cheered Lena.

"That's not fair though," replied Gelob.

"War isn't fair," replied Lena. "If it was, no one would ever win."

Gelob smiled and loosened his arms. "I guess you have won." Lena let go and removed her foot from his rib cage. She jumped up, throwing her arms into the air, laughing. "Don't get too excited," said Gelob. "We still have much more training to complete before the day is done."

As the two walked back to the palace, Lena stopped and stared at two birds sitting on a tree, nestled up two each other. "I wonder what the others are doing," said Lena, smiling.

"Others?"

"My friends," replied Lena. "I wonder if they are having as much fun."

"I guess that in some ways, it might be considered fun for them, but it might also be very hard work," replied the elf. "If I had any guess, Thorstein is doing as much physical work as possible. Guin on the other hand is probably sitting in a classroom for hours on end, studying spells."

As before, Lena had quick thoughts of both Kailan and Viktor. For some reason, even how much she still loved Kailan, Viktor was always present in her mind. She didn't know why, but it constantly confused her, even keeping her up at nights.

"Lena, run," said Gelob.

The girl quickly snapped out of her daze and watched as the bushes across the small clearing began to rustle. "What is it?" questioned Lena.

Gelob reached for his sword, but realised that both him and Lena were without weapons. The bushes began to rustle violently as two ugly men stepped out to the side. The elf spit to the side, speaking as he wiped his mouth. "Hobgoblins." With their weapons out, the creatures laughed as they slowly advanced.

*　　　　　*　　　　　*

Kailan and Geamille arrived back at the manor in little under an hour. Geamille hurriedly made his way up to the house, throwing his cane to the floor out of anger as he stepped inside.

"Is there something that I should be aware of?" questioned Winthrow, looking at Kailan.

"The council meeting didn't go very well," replied Kailan.

"I suggest that you stay clear of him for the rest of the night," said Winthrow. "He tends to stay like this for a while. Don't be surprised if he isn't in the mood for working with you tomorrow morning."

Kailan nodded and slowly made his way up to the house with Winthrow directly behind. They watched as Geamille walked out of the lobby and into his study.

"I can't believe it!" yelled Geamille. "They'll ruin this

city before the winter even comes."

"You'd better hurry up to your room," whispered Winthrow. Kailan turned and was beginning to move when he heard Geamille's voice.

"Kailan, what went wrong in there?" questioned Geamille. "I don't remember saying anything wrong. My plan was fool proof, but then again it wasn't idiot proof."

Kailan made his way over to the doorway. "You made a very good argument," the boy replied. "I just think that they weren't going to listen to you anyways."

Geamille walked over to his desk and slammed his fist down hard. The sound rang throughout the house, leaving Kailan and Winthrow in shock. Geamille stepped around to his chair and leaned back with his hands on his forehead. "How does your friend Tanier do it?"

"Sorry?" questioned Kailan.

"Tanier Frost," said Geamille. "How does he run the entire country?"

"Well, he doesn't to be honest," Kailan stated. "Arlbega is in almost worse shape than the city."

"Don't lie to me Kailan," said Geamille. "I'm not in the mood." Winthrow quickly made his way into the room, placing himself in front of Kailan.

"I'll take the boy up to his room after fixing him up some dinner," said Winthrow.

"I'm not lying though," said Kailan, pushing out from behind the tall man. "Tanier Frost is losing more and more

[341]

control every day. The kings have almost turned Arlbega into separate kingdoms again. The king of Freltus is using all of his power to try and have Tanier removed from command of Arlbega."

Geamille slowly looked at Kailan with a look of realisation. It was in that moment that Kailan himself had a revelation; it was all clear to him now. He never once saw Tanier dealing with the kings, so he took his actions for granted, never thinking of how angry it actually made him. It wasn't until watching, first hand, Geamille arguing with the rest of the city council. No matter what he said, they wouldn't listen. No matter how much sense he made, they wouldn't listen. Kailan had realised that it was his anger that was his weakness. It was Geamille's and it was also Tanier's. Not once did any of them ask for help; they simply became angrier. Kailan never asked for Lena's help while dealing with Prince Farol. Tanier never asked for Bailan with help, unless he had a side job. Geamille's friends were already too scared of the other council members, so he had no help.

The next morning, Kailan found a strange box at the foot of his bed. He opened the box slowly to find the box lined with red velvet and an object rolled up in a fine black cloth. The weight of the object was heavy, but familiar. As he unravelled it, Kailan quickly realised that it was his old sword, fixed and polished to perfection. It was in the original sheath that Kailan had swapped out. He quickly put his clothes on and ran out of the room and down the hallway to Geamille's room. He burst through the door, only to find the room empty. As he looked outside, he saw Geamille standing by the stables, waiting for him. Kailan ran almost faster than he ever had before. Upon reaching the stables, he quickly ran to Geamille and threw his arms around him.

"Thank you!" yelled Kailan.

"Tanier told me that you had broken it, so I had it fixed," said Geamille. "As well…" He pulled another sword from behind his back and handed it to Kailan. This one was a little less familiar, but Kailan still recognised it quickly. It was the flaming sword that Tanier had confiscated from him. "Last night I realised that you have earned this back. You only have a few weeks left here, and I think that you had better start to train with your own weapons."

"Do you think that you can beat me with both swords?" said Kailan with a smirk on his face.

"I don't ever expect you to use two swords at the same time," replied Geamille. "It will take years of practise for you to master that. Keep the old one safe, as a reminder of hard work."

Kailan smiled and wrapped the sword back into the black cloth. He placed it on the ground and then faced Geamille again, with the fire sword drawn and ready. "Should we duel then?"

Geamille pulled his sword from the cane sheath and bent his knees slightly as he stepped back. He sliced to the side with his sword, only to find Kailan's blocking it. The smile on the boy's face was either from his amazement, or sheer cockiness. It seemed like cockiness to Geamille at first, but not after Kailan had Geamille knocked on the ground within the next two seconds. Kailan reached down and held out a hand to his teacher.

"You're doing well," said Geamille. "It is nearly time for me to step aside and have you study your sword instead."

"What do you mean; study the sword?" Kailan asked as he pulled Geamille up, off the ground.

"Your sword has magical properties," replied Geamille.

Kailan stood back as his sword turned bright red. "I know how to control it."

"You may know how to control the sword, but the sword can also control you," Geamille stated.

"What do you mean?" questioned Kailan.

"Tanier explained to me briefly about the weapons. These five weapons don't just burst into flames, or make the earth shake. They amplify feelings within us. Tanier said that he didn't know what they were exactly, but he read it from the old Arch Chancellor's notes."

"You mean anger, don't you?" said Kailan, staring at the sword intently.

"Possibly." Geamille nodded, finding himself staring at the sword as well.

"No, I know for sure," said Kailan. "Whenever I hold this sword, my anger becomes great, and almost uncontrollable."

"Then we need to figure out how to control your anger when you are in this state," said Geamille. "If we let it control

[344]

you, you may do something that you will end up regretting."

Kailan, for that split second, began to think of Lena. If he ever wanted to be with her, he would have to change his ways.

It was later that night that Kailan decided to step away from the mansion, taking a quick walk by the moonlight. The stars twinkled high above him, cascading across the sky, lighting the tips of the hills behind the house. He pulled his coat in close to him as the wind howled, nearly sweeping him off his feet. Out of the corner of his eye, Kailan saw a familiar view rise into the night sky. Slowly blocking out the sky as they flew by, the leaves fluttered in the wind, rustling like the papers in Tanier's office. Just like before, Kailan felt the warm touch of the air against his skin.

"Aris!" he called out, smiling.

The beauty stepped out from her veil of leaves, walking up to Kailan as she placed a hand on his shoulder.

"I've missed you," Kailan slurred out as he tried wrapping his arms around the witch, only to find that his hands slipped right through her like smoke. "I forgot."

"Don't worry," said Aris, smiling softly at the boy.

"So much has happened since we last talked," said Kailan, bouncing around like a small child.

"And what would that be?"

"Well, first of all, I have this amazing sword that lights on fire," Kailan said, pulling the sword out of its sheath. He engulfed it in flames for only a few seconds before putting it out.

"I've met some new friends as well. Thorstein, he's a giant, Guin is a wizard, but a bit of a funny guy, Viktor is quite strange, and then there's Lena." Suddenly, Kailan went frozen.

Aris watched as the boy went stiff for a second, staring with eyes open, biting his lower lip. "Kailan, there is no need to hide your feelings for her from me." Aris lowered herself to the ground, lying on her back against the dark green grass. "I might as well tell you a story."

Kailan crouched beside Aris, sitting cross-legged.

"Before Duskerlin was the place that it is now, it was a beautiful little town, just on the edge of the river. People were able to travel from miles away, but no one ever did. We were peaceful people, living peaceful lives." Aris reached up, placing her hands behind her head. "I was a young girl at the time, maybe about fifteen years old. My mother and I were both witches, but we lived harmoniously with the other people of Duskerlin. We were the healers of the town, curing sickness, and treating broken bones most of the time."

Kailan began to feel the warm air slowly disappear as the bitter cold nipped at his nose.

"One day, a strange man came to town. He told stories of witches that would murder children, eating them alive. We knew of such witches, but we were nothing like them. At first, the townspeople dismissed the stories as just that; mere stories. After a couple of weeks though, they began to believe him, banishing me and my mother to the forest. Then one day, I was gathering berries by the river when I noticed the smell of smoke.

[346]

The large clouds filled the sky, but I couldn't figure out why there would be such a large fire. The river was right beside the town, so there was never a real chance of a house fire. As I neared closer, I began to hear the muffled screams. At first, I didn't want to go near the village, but something compelled me to go further. Before I reached the square, the shrieking stopped." Aris turned on her side as she began to weep heavily. "I watched as my mother was burned alive, the townspeople watching in a circle. Filled with rage, I ran into the town with a large branch and hit one of the men on the head. As the others turned to face me, my eyes turned red like fire as I slowly floated into the air. My mother was tortured before she died, and so I made sure that they would endure the same. I burned some of them, ripping the limbs off of others. With my magic, I tried to keep them alive as long as possible, making sure that they would endure the most amount of pain." She looked back up into the sky as she wiped the tears from her face, staring into the starry abyss above her. "No one besides me set foot in the town for a couple years, until a young man arrived. I was sitting by the river when he handed me some flowers, saying that I was the most beautiful woman that he had ever met. We immediately became friends, spending weeks together, living in the empty houses. He spent hours, running through the forest, often returning to the house covered in mud."

Kailan leaned back, staring up into the sky, but not before noticing the grin on Aris' face.

"His name was Wittor, and he was the light of my life.

[347]

He made me feel true happiness again after years of loneliness and despair. He was my first and only true love, but our love didn't last long." Aris let out a long sigh, pausing her story for a short moment. "He told me that he needed to leave for Freltus to deliver a message for the Arch Chancellor, but would be back within a couple of weeks. I was sad to see him go, but I reluctantly waited for his return. As the days turned into weeks, the weeks into months, and the months into years, I waited, slowly withering away." She turned on her side again, this time facing Kailan. "Twenty years later, when you walked into the town, I almost swore that it was him, but no. My heart was broken, and the pieces scattered about at an early age. There is no need to hide your feelings of her from me." She placed a hand on Kailan's forehead, running her fingers through his hair. The boy could almost feel it too, but to him it still felt too much like wind. "Your kiss was the only thing that I needed to help me rest." Without Kailan even noticing it, Aris slowly drifted away, her leaves making their way up into the sky.

He reached out, plucking one of the leaves from the air, holding it in his hand, examining it. To his eyes, it was just a leaf, but to his heart, it was part of a soul.

*   *   *

Guin sat at the table, eating his meal with the rest of his

fellow classmates.

"I do have to congratulate you on that spell," said a boy sitting across the table.

Guin looked up to see the boy smiling. "It didn't do me any good," replied Guin, stirring his soup back and forth with the wooden spoon.

"I wouldn't say so," replied the boy. "You gained everyone's respect." Guin looked up from his bowl of soup again. "You've even gotten the attention of some of the girls." The boy nodded to a group of girls at another table, who were staring at Guin. As he looked over at them, they giggled and turned around.

"What do you want, Darol?"

"Me? I want nothing," said Darol. "Well, if you put it that way. I'll tell you where to find your book if you introduce me to one of your lovely friends over there." Guin looked back at the table of girls.

"No," he replied.

"What do you mean, no?" questioned Darol. "You conjured a spell that took the elder wizards hours to undo. You could pretty much have any girl that you want. You could even have Dailanna over there." Guin looked turned to look completely behind him to see one of the most beautiful girls at the academy.

"No."

"What?"

"I prefer adventurous girls," replied Guin. "Not

someone who is going to sit with their nose pressed into books for the rest of their life. I've fought men, killed beasts, gone up against dragons. I want to be with a girl who will be there, standing beside me instead of cowering behind me."

"D-d-dragons?" said Darol, stuttering.

"Just tell me where to find my book."

"You are even greater than I thought," said Darol. "Fine; there are tunnels underneath the Council room that lead to a room. Apparently that is where they keep their confiscated items. It is guarded though, so be careful."

"Thank you," replied Guin, grinning slightly. He stood up and walked away from the table over to the group of girls. Darol could not hear what they were saying, but when Guin walked away, the girls smiled at Darol.

Guin decided to go searching for his book later in the night. At that time, he predicted that most of the guards would be gone, but it would also be easier for him to slip unnoticed in the dark. It took a couple of minutes before Guin found the way into the tunnels. There was a small door within the Council room, hidden by the darkness. On the other side of the door was a set of stairs. Guin could only see the first two steps without a light in his hand as it was so dark. This posed as a problem, seeing as even a small flame in his hand would draw someone's attention. So instead, Guin felt around as he made his way down the steps, sitting at the last step until his eyes adjusted to the darkness. The stone walls were damp and cold, but the air was somewhat warm. For the first little while, Guin followed the

[350]

tunnel in a straight line, finding no turns what so ever. It wasn't until a few minutes later that he came upon another tunnel. There were now two ways in front of him that he could go.

"Great," whispered Guin, sarcastically. He peered down each direction to try and see if there was anything promising about one of the halls, but to his disappointment, they were both exactly the same. He stood there for a minute, tapping his foot and contemplating which way he should take. "Why didn't I think of that before?" said Guin, smacking himself in the forehead. He placed his hand on the floor and whispered the same words that both he and Crag had before. Suddenly, there were bright yellow footprints that appeared on the floor. As the glowing started to get farther and farther away, Guin cancelled the spell. "Left it is then," said Guin with a smile as he rounded the corner. From now on, for some reason, the tunnel never stayed in a straight line. There was corner after corner of darkness. A few minutes had passed before Guin realised how close he was to the end. There were noises coming from down the hall. In a way, it was good, because it meant that Guin was close; however, it also meant that someone was in the room, possibly guarding the book. Guin quickly slowed his actions, making sure as to not make a sound as he crept around the corner. The stone walls echoed every breath and footstep throughout the dark corridors. There was a cold breeze on his back. Every hair on his neck stood on end, causing shivers to dance through his entire body. He slid down the side of the hallway, hugging the wall tightly. When he reached the next corner, he felt the same breeze again. This time was slightly different, however. It was stronger than and not as cold as the first. Guin could have almost sworn that he had heard the sound of the rushing air, but he ignored it. The office room was almost in sight as Guin could now see a faint glow, emanating from the flickering candles within. Just as Guin was about to make his way around the corner, he felt the breeze on his neck again. As he turned around, he came face to face with a ghost-like face. He let out a short shriek as he fell backwards to the floor, remembering to keep quiet by placing a hand over his mouth. The face slowly came out of the darkness, laughing, but without a sound.

"Tateena!" whispered Guin, angrily. "Don't do that." He picked himself up off the floor and patted the dirt from his pants. "You shouldn't be here anyways."

Tateena stopped laughing, but continued to give Guin a mischievous smirk. "Well neither should you," she replied. Guin turned around and poked his head back around the corner, watching the light dance around. "Besides, I thought you said that you like adventurous girls."

Guin quickly tensed up as his cheeks blushed faintly, but out of Tateena's view. "You weren't supposed to hear that," said Guin as Tateena moved her head to his side to look around the corner also.

"So, we're going after your book? Turning into a bit of a rebel now, are we?"

"*We're* not going anywhere," replied Guin. "*I'm* going

[352]

to get it back. You are going to go back to your bedroom so that you don't get into trouble.

"I could just tell someone what you're up to."

Guin turned to his side and looked into Tateena's eyes as she smiled. They were filled with a sense of danger, but it was her smile that said that she was thrilled to be there. "Stay out of sight, and don't make a sound." Guin began grinning as he made his final push towards the office. He held his breath as he hugged the wall, making no noise at all. Slowly shifting his head around the corner, Guin made sure as to not be seen. He felt Tateena poke her head beside him again.

"Is that it?" she whispered softly. In the centre of the small room was a table with an assortment of items on it, but more specifically, the resting spot of Guin's magic tome.

"Yes it is," replied Guin. On the other side of the table was a man, sitting beside a number of candles whilst reading a book. "Don't make a noise." Guin held up his hand, closing the book from outside the room, and causing it to slowly rise and float towards him. There was a sense of adrenaline coursing through him, but most of all a feeling of relief. He was only a matter of feet from his book.

"Oh no!" said Tateena as she held her hand straight out. Suddenly, the book flew even faster, hitting Guin in the face, and sending him backwards to the ground.

"What was that for?" demanded Guin. When he looked up at Tateena, the only thing he saw in her face was that of fear. The man was now standing in front of his chair, staring at the

[353]

two intruders in the hallway.

"Guin!" yelled Aroculus. "Think of your bedroom!"

"What?"

"KARABOUCHE!" yelled Aroculus.

"KARABOUCHE?" Guin and Tateena suddenly found themselves within Guin's bedroom. They stumbled for a brief moment, but quickly gained their footings.

"What was that?" questioned Tateena.

"I think I just learned how to teleport," replied Guin as he looked around the room.

*   *   *

As he sat in the dark dungeon, with only a small light from above and the torches around the room to give him light, Thorstein sat as the tiny children beat him with sticks. There was nothing that he could do; nothing that he was allowed to do. He was locked up, with chains and shackles, wearing nothing but a cloth around his waist.

"This isn't working very well," said Thorstein. "They aren't hitting me hard enough."

"Well, then I guess that we'll just start pelting you with rocks," said Archus, smiling.

"That doesn't really seem fair," said Thorstein. As the first stone hit him, Thorstein instantly began to feel annoyed.

"I'm not sure if this is a good idea," said Thorstein, taking a stone to the face. The children continued to pelt stones at Thorstein, increasing his anger, whilst Archus watched on in amazement. For nearly two minutes, Thorstein sat, taking a barrage of rocks of various sizes.

"Children, you need to leave," said Archus. As the children hurried out of the room, he knelt down to the ground and picked up a large rock. He tossed it in the air, switching his view from the rock to Thorstein, and back again. "You know, Thorstein, its little things, just like this stone, that can cause big events." Archus pulled his arm back and whipped the stone at Thorstein's chin.

"Hey!" yelled Thorstein. "Knock it off!"

"Why should I?" said Archus, chucking another stone.

"Dammit Archus!" Thorstein could feel the anger swelling up in him. It was the pain from these stones that were really bothering Thorstein.

"I don't think that I should stop," said Archus, smiling. He grabbed one of the sticks from the pile against the wall and started breaking them against Thorstein's back. "How does that feel Thorstein?"

"I swear Archus, when I get out of here, I'm going to wring your neck!"

"Oh really?" said Archus. "How are you going to do that?"

"I don't care if you are the damn king of this country, I will still punch you!"

[355]

Archus quickly began smashing two sticks at a time, even as Thorstein flinched and tried to move from the attacks. He made his way to the other side of the giant and looked into his face. "You know why you can't get me?" Thorstein blew the sweat matted hair out of his face. "It's because you are too stupid to figure out how to break free.

"Ah!" cried Thorstein at the top of his lungs, ripping the chains from the walls with his hands. He reached for Archus, but he slid just out of grasp and hid in the small corridor. "Get back here, you coward!" Thorstein picked up the pile of sticks and snapped all of them at once. Out of anger, he began punching the walls, chipping away large amounts of stone. As he bashed against the stone, he knocked one of his shackles off. As it hit the ground, Thorstein quickly gained an idea. He now tried, with all of his effort to remove the rest of the shackles. It was a few minutes later, as his anger was slowly subsiding, that he finally had the last one off. Suddenly, his suit of armour appeared, and Thorstein began bashing the stone wall, digging into it like dirt. It wasn't until almost ten minutes later that Thorstein's anger had left him. He fell to the ground, wheezing as he rested his back against the stone wall. There was suddenly a sound of slow clapping coming from the tunnel.

"You did well," said Archus as he emerged from the tunnel. "I think that it's time to take a break for today, but tomorrow, we have one final test."

Thorstein woke up the next morning, still feeling some pains from the day before. He quickly threw on some clothes and left his house.

"Thorstein!" yelled Yolltz, running up to him. "The king needs your help!" Thorstein stopped dead in his tracks

"What do you mean?" questioned Thorstein.

"We're under attack!"

Thorstein spun around and sprinted for his dornbeast, ripping the gate off its stable. He grabbed his axe, and hopped on the creature's back, riding up the road to the entrance of the city. There were a number of thoughts that coursed through Thorstein's mind. The first being that it was a trap, trying to get Thorstein to have an outburst so that he could try to channel his anger. It wasn't until he heard the screams and yelling outside that he knew it was not a test. The attackers were out of view, but as Thorstein watched from just inside, he could see dwarves being tossed across the snowy fields. Thorstein charged out, only to find a site that he had never seen before. There was a legion of giants, advancing on the city. There must have been at least twenty of them by Thorstein's count. He quickly rushed into battle, with his armour appearing shielding him from any attacks. The dornbeast charged one giant, goring the huge man with its horn. Thorstein quickly jumped off and swung his axe in front of him, cutting a large hole in one of the other giants, spilling blood and guts onto the snow below.

"Thorstein!" yelled Archus. "Split them down the middle!"

Thorstein turned to the king and nodded before mounting the dornbeast again. The thought of anger never once

[357]

came to mind, but Thorstein could feel the strength that he had from the day before. He made his way back towards the entrance before charging again, creating a break between the legion of giants. The dwarves would not have had much of a chance if not for their long axes and pikes that they used. Archus, however, fought much differently than the other dwarves. Because of his tall stature, he was able to get closer. Instead of wield one large axe like Thorstein, Archus chose two smaller axes that were still rather large compared to the once that the smaller dwarves were using. Archus charged into one of the groups of giants, swinging his axes about wildly. As he ran up to one, his soldiers distracted it, while their king ran up behind, jumping with his axe landing partway up the titan's back. He quickly pulled himself up and hacked away at the creature with his other axe. Thorstein, on the other hand, was all by himself. He didn't have as many dwarves supporting him, but they were there none the less.

"Go for the big one!" yelled one of the giants. Thorstein tried to run away on the dornbeast, but he knew that he would be blocked in eventually. He slid off the back, and made his way over to one of the giants. As it swung its club at him, Thorstein dodged without even making an effort. He raised his axe and brought it back down between the giant's shoulder and neck, killing it instantly. As he turned around, there were about five other giants already waiting for him. Thorstein smiled as he quickly worked himself into a frenzy.

He let out a battle cry, shouting at the top of his lungs. With no time at all, Thorstein threw his axe in a spinning motion at the giants, chopping into one, and slicing deep into a second. While it was still in the air, Thorstein was making his next move as he darted for his enemy, jumping in to the air with his hands out. He grabbed onto two of the giants' necks and began throwing them around like rag dolls. The third that was left tried to attack from behind, but Thorstein saw it coming and kicked it in the ribs, almost certainly breaking most of them. It fell to the ground as Thorstein hopped to his feet and grabbed one of the giants on the ground by the ankles, spinning it into the air, and sending it flying. He picked up his axe and walked back over to the other two that were left, crawling on the ground. One swing with his axe on either giant was all that was needed to split them both in two. A number of the other giants were now cautious of Thorstein and backed off after seeing what he had done. It wasn't until the giants began to group back together again that they tried to go after Thorstein again. The seven that were left all grouped together and charged at Thorstein, head on, leaving no room for escape or fancy manoeuvres. Thorstein would have to run in, fighting them on their terms. The dornbeast ran up, taking out two from behind, leaving only one dead. The other quickly picked himself up and regrouped. Archus quickly made his way over and took another giant down from the end of the line. At this point, they realised that they were no match for Thorstein and the dwarves, but it was already too late. Thorstein broke through the line, sending two of the giants flying backwards, and stomping a third into the ground, leaving the skull shattered. The two on the sides tried to close in, but with a single, clean swing

[359]

of his axe, Thorstein had made quick work of them. The two that he had knocked over were quickly finished off by the dwarves.

"You did very well," said Archus, smiling as he tried to catch his breath. He patted Thorstein on the back, standing on his toes to reach.

There was no grand farewell for Thorstein, no parade, no feast. He packed his things and made his way for the boat. It was possibly the last time that Thorstein would see the island of Greer, but something told him, deep down, that he'd be asked to come back. Archus stood at the boat dock, waiting for the tall, young man as he arrived.

"Thorstein, we can't thank you enough for everything," said Archus. "You defeated a horde of giants almost single handed, saving countless numbers of my dwarven brethren."

"There are no thanks needed," replied Thorstein. "It was my final training, and I passed." He stepped onto the boat with the dornbeast lugging his few items over his shoulder.

"Could you give us a bit of a push off?" said the captain, jokingly.

Thorstein didn't take it as a joke and walked up to the dock, pushing away from it.

*   *   *

There was a large, open field, spreading out upon the

horizon, and over the hills. The sun shone brilliantly, but still quite softly. In the centre of the green pastures, there was a single tree, old, but full of the dark green leaves. They twinkled against the sun like stars in the night sky, giving contrast to the light sky above. Viktor rested his head on a tuft of tall grass that grew just next to the tree's trunk. Every cloud above seemed to have a life of its own, changing shape every so often. Softly, he let out a breath, making sure not to disturb himself from the pure bliss.

"Paradise!" he yelled to himself, placing his hands behind his head. In the distance, Viktor could see someone slowly coming closer. At first, they made no sound, but as they progressed closer, he could start to hear the words. It was constantly a whisper until suddenly he heard the yell.

"Viktor!" yelled his teacher, swatting at him with a stick, awaking the boy from his slumber. "Pay attention, dammit!" Viktor stood upright, leering at his instructor. "I'm pretty sure that the Arch Chancellor doesn't want you to be wasting all of his money by sleeping." The other young men quickly turned their attention to Viktor, some of them gasping slightly.

"Do you mean the Arch Chancellor of Arlbega?" questioned one of the men.

"The exact same," the teacher replied.

"Spoiled and crazy," said one of the men. Viktor snapped towards the man, throwing a small stone at the man, cutting into his skin. "You bastard!"

[361]

"Settle down, Fileur!" yelled the teacher. The young men stared at each other, with looks of malicious intent. The one had pure anger on his face, but Viktor had something different. It wasn't anger, but more of a mix of happiness and confidence, causing a strange, hidden fear to emerge within the other man. It wasn't until the lesson was over, and the men were done with their exercise that Viktor's plan came into effect. Throwing the stone at the man was just the start of the retaliation. He greatly expected the other man, Fileur, to wait for him after the lesson, asking for a number of his friends to stay.

"Now, Viktor, we can't have people not pay for their crimes," said Fileur, placing an opened hand in front of Viktor. The dark haired boy slowly lifted his head to reveal the same smile that he had shown before. Fileur's friends quickly surrounded Viktor. There were six of them in total, and a number of them were quite large compared to Viktor, making him one of the shortest people there, and the youngest.

Viktor's face quickly changed from the eerie smile to a more cautious face as sense of reason made itself a home within his mind. "I suggest that you remove yourself from my way," said Viktor.

"What, you think you can take all of us?" said Fileur, grinning.

"It will be easy," replied Viktor.

"Well, I guess he's cocky too," said Fileur, laughing with the rest of the men.

With one prepared move, Viktor brought his elbow

[362]

back, jabbing it into the gut of the man directly behind him, then bringing it forward and up to meet Fileur's chin, launching him into the air. He did the same motion again, but to the side this time. Within a single second, Viktor had taken out four of the six men. The other two were knocked to the ground with a single swift, spinning kick. Fileur quickly picked himself and charge at Viktor, which was one of the worst ideas possible. Viktor picked up the young man, using his own momentum against him, and threw him far over the heads of the other men. They continued on for another minute until none of them could move anymore; none of them except for Viktor. He slowly made his way back to the building, checking on the men as he walked by. He inspected them, not to make sure that they were well, but to make sure that they weren't going to get up any time soon.

It was only a few minutes later that Viktor found himself at the mercy of the guild leaders. Three of them stood in front of Viktor, enraged by his actions.

"No matter how amazed we are with your fighting abilities," said one of the men, "we still can't allow any of this. You are forthwith banned from the Assassins' Guild!"

"Tanier Frost has a carriage to take you back, and it will be waiting outside."

"Do you have anything to say in your defence?" said the third man.

Viktor looked down at his hands, picking the dirt from underneath his fingernails. Placing his fingertip in his mouth, he grazed the underneath of his nail atop one of his canine teeth.

"Not a word," said Viktor, smiling as he lowered his hands to his waist.

*   *   *

Kailan stood next to Geamille at the podium, staring onwards, past the fourteen council members. "You must vote with me on this," said Geamille, pounding his fist down on the stand. "We can do it your way, and have no supplies to last us through the winter, or we can ration properly."

The men in the room quickly began yelling back and forth, some of them even laughing at Geamille.

"That is a horrible idea," said one of the men. "I will not live like a dog this winter."

"You're ideas are hopeless, Geamille!" yelled another.

Without hesitation, Kailan lashed out. "Shut up!" There was infinite silence within the room. "You people sicken me! You sit here, listen to each other, and argue constantly. None of you can damn well agree on anything. Geamille is one of the only ones here with brains, and the only one with the heart to say what is right."

One of the council members scooted his chair backwards, and proceeded to stand up.

"Where are you going?" demanded Kailan.

"I'm not listening to anymore of this hogwash," said

the man as he slowly made his way for the door.

Kailan unsheathed his sword, pointing at the man. "Sit down!" There was uproar again as the men yelled back and forth, but like before, Kailan quickly commanded silence. His sword burst into flames, pinning the men in their seats. "Listen!" yelled Kailan. "You are all too stupid, too selfish, to give up your luxuries for a few months. Oh, yes, a nice smoked pig might sound nice in the winter, but not the next spring, when the people who sold it to you in the first place have starved to death!" The men stared around for a second; half of them listening, the other half wondering to do about Kailan and his sword, which had died out by that point. "Live is not worth living if you aren't going to sacrifice something here and there!" Kailan slowly placed his sword back into its sheath, observing the men as they talked back and forth.

"Even though you are not a member of this council, you have opened our eyes to see the importance of Geamille's notion," said one of the older men with white hair.

"I say that we put it to a vote immediately," said one of the other men. "All in favour of Geamille's proposal?"

Kailan watched as a number of hands lifted into the air; some moving slower than others. He gave a number of the more stubborn members a quick glare, before they too raised their hands.

"Eleven to four," said the man. "We will continue with Geamille's plan until it fails, or we find something better."

As Kailan and Geamille exited the room, the young

[365]

man was patted on the back by his teacher. "You know, Kailan? Never in all my years have I seen someone rule this council like you did today."

"I have a feeling that I'm going to be in trouble with the law soon," replied Kailan, laughing.

"Don't worry; I think you'd make a fine politician." The two laughed as they walked over to Oran Gerbetski's house. They knocked on the door, waiting for the older man to answer.

As he opened the door, he held out his arms wide, embracing Geamille. "And, how did it go?" Oran asked.

Geamille smiled and patted Kailan on the back again. "The boy here should become a politician; maybe give Tanier Frost a run for his money." The three laughed as Kailan followed Geamille into the house.

"Can I get you two, anything?" questioned Oran. "A tea, perhaps?"

"Nothing for me," said Kailan, waving his hand.

"I'll have a tea, thank you," replied Geamille. The two sat at the small table as Oran quickly hobbled over to the other room.

"Are you happy to go back, mister Kailan?" Oran said from the other room.

"I'll be glad to see my friends again, but I will definitely miss Korchetska," replied Kailan. It wasn't very long before they heard a ruckus outside of the building.

"That must be Mr. Frost," Oran chuckled, walking in with Geamille's tea. The door quickly swung open, with Tanier standing in the way.

"We must leave immediately," said Tanier.

Kailan looked up at the Arch Chancellor with a confused expression upon his face. "Is something wrong?"

"They're assembling their forces," replied Tanier.

Kailan's look of confusion quickly changed into complete and definite fear. "What have you heard?"

"They have already retaken the island of Trekta," Tanier stated. Geamille and Oran stood back, listening in on the conversation, trying to piece together as much as they could.

Kailan turned to his two friends that he had been with for the past two months. "I'm sorry, but I have to make things short," said Kailan.

"Leave quickly!" Geamille replied, concerned. Kailan nodded and picked up his bag from the floor, as he followed Tanier out into the street, he stopped in the doorway and turned around.

"Thank you." As Kailan turned around, all that Geamille and Oran saw was the boy dissipate into nothing as both him and Tanier were transported back to Machesney Hall.

*　　　　　*　　　　　*

Gelob sprinted through the forest, with Lena right behind him. "Faster Lena!" yelled Gelob. "They are catching up!"

"I can't run much longer!" said Lena, panting as she ran.

"We must!" cried Gelob. As the elf continued, dashing from tree to tree, he would constantly look back, to make sure that Lena was still behind him, never gaining too much distance. It wasn't until she tripped that he actually stopped.

"Wait!" screamed Lena. She tried to pick herself up, but her foot was caught in the roots.

"Farnok!" yelled Gelob, screaming into the air. He quickly turned around and slid beside Lena, grabbing onto her ankle and pulling her out, but not with enough time. It was then that the hobgoblins were standing over them, smiling their menacing grins.

"What'll you have?" said one of the hobgoblins.

"I think I'll…"

Suddenly, Kaela swooped down, digging her talons into the back of the man's head before flying into the air again. He fell to the ground in pain, covering the hole with his hand.

"Stupid bird!" yelled the hobgoblin. There was nothing more that passed out of the man's lips after the arrow pierced his gullet. Lena and Gelob quickly looked over to see a rescue party of five other elves, hurrying over. The other hobgoblin didn't even get three steps away before he was killed as well. The elves rushed over, helping Lena and Gelob to their feet.

"Your eagle came and found us just in the nick of time," said one of the elves. The bird swooped in, landing next to Lena. It rubbed its head against her leg, nuzzling from side to side. Lena bent down and grabbed the bird, holding it in her arms as she stood up.

"Thank you, Kaela," said Lena, smiling. She then turned to Gelob. "Thank you as well."

"I'm just doing my duty," replied Gelob.

Lena, Gelob, and the other elves quickly made their way back to Hileñar, keeping a watchful eye for other creatures of evil. Upon reaching the city, they were quickly welcomed by King Grakken. This was the first time that Grakken had not been there with his arms wide open for Lena. Something seemed strange to her; especially after seeing Bailan step out from behind the king.

"My lord!" yelled one of the elves, racing ahead. "They were attacked by two hobgoblins."

"Yes, it isn't safe anymore," replied Grakken. "Come, Gelob and Lena. We must speak immediately."

"Bailan!" cheered Lena as she ran ahead of the rest of the group. She placed her bird on the ground and embraced the seemingly young man. "How have you been?"

"Personally, I have been very well," Bailan replied. "On the other hand though, I need to bring you back to Freltus immediately."

"Already?" said Lena, pouting. "Can I at least grab my things?"

"They're already waiting for you at Machesney Hall," replied Bailan.

"I'm sorry, Miss Lena, but we won't be seeing each other for a while," said Grakken.

"Close your eyes," said Bailan. The wizard placed a hand on Lena's shoulder, disappearing with her and Kaela.

Before even reopening her eyes, Lena could feel the change in place. The air was warmer, and smelled less fresh. She found herself standing in her room at Machesney Hall, standing next to Bailan and Kaela. "What happened?" said Lena, looking around in amazement.

"The others are waiting for you in the lounge area," Bailan said. "We will tell you more, later."

Lena rushed out of the room and down the hall, running towards her friends. Kailan stood, opening his arms, but was confused when she ran to Thorstein first, who proceeded to pick her up like a child and raise her into the air. "I've missed you guys, so much!" yelled Lena. Thorstein put her down, and then she embraced both Viktor and Kailan, respectively. For a brief second, she looked to Kailan's side, and then around the others. "Where is Guin?" questioned Lena.

"He will be with us shortly," said Tanier, walking over to the couch and laying back. "He's just finishing up a few things at the university."

"Finishing up?" said a familiar voice to Kailan. "From what I hear, the boy is causing quite a commotion."

*   *   *

Guin closed his notebook, smiling up at his teacher as he walked forward and placed it on his desk. "Listen here, Pelerin," said the man with a scowl on his face. "Just because we can't figure out how to pin anything on you, doesn't mean that you'll get away with it in the end."

"Well, you should have a fun time trying to figure out how I did it." The boy walked out of the room, throwing his hands into the air before running down the hall and cheering. At the Wizards' Guild in Alandra, Guin spent nearly his entire time studying book upon book. To him, this was pure joy; the pursuit of knowledge. For some reason, along his journeys, Guin changed inside. He was no longer amazed by the effects of chemicals when added to each other, or how spells worked in theory. Guin was now fascinated by the outside world. He no longer liked to stay inside, being cooped up with many other students. Guin began practising with Aroculus the same way that Kailan would practise with Geamille. For Guin, everything in live seemed much brighter and livelier than before. When he reached his room, Guin found Tateena, standing just by the doorway, leaning against the wall.

"Leaving?" questioned Tateena.

"I am indeed," replied Guin, walking right past her with the biggest smirk on his face.

"But you haven't even finished your training!" Tateena

whined. "You can't go!"

"I'm the top student in the entire university," replied Guin. "I don't think that training here much more will help me." Guin picked up a pile of books and placed them into the large bag on his bed. "Can you pass me that large one there?" Tateena just stared at Guin, arms crossed, no movement whatsoever. "I guess not then." He grabbed the book, and just like the others, placed it in the bag.

"What do you want me to tell the others?"

"Who?"

"Your friends," replied Tateena.

"I don't have any friends here," laughed Guin.

"What are you talking about?" said Tateena. "Everyone in the school respects you, they worship you."

"They don't worship me," Guin responded. "They fear me. They saw what I did to Garth, and they fear that I will do the same to them." He walked over to his closet, pulling numerous clothes from their hooks.

"So you are telling me that you never made a single friend while you were here?"

Guin tied the strings on his bag together and hauled it over his shoulder. "Nope."

Tateena turned around, weeping as she ran out of the room. Guin quickly ran after her, dropping his bag to the ground. He placed his hands on her shoulders, stopping her, and then walking around to face her. He pulled her hands from her face, wiping the tears from her eyes.

[372]

"Listen here," said Guin. "There's something that I need you to do." She nodded, with a small smile on her face. "At the sound of the final chime of the bell tonight, I want you to place your hand on the floor in my room and say these words." Guin leaned in and whispered the magic words into Tateena's ear. "You will have five minutes." Guin walked away, picking up his bag and lifting it again over his shoulder. Within an instant, Guin was gone, vanishing without a trace.

Tateena turned away, and slowly began walking back to her room

"Can't believe I almost forgot this," said Guin, quickly rushing up to Tateena. He grabbed her like he did before, this time spinning her around to face her. He embraced her softly, tenderly pressing his lips against hers. Tateena's body immediately emptied itself of all the sadness, and filled itself with pure joy instead. She kept her eyes closed, saving the moment in her mind forever, but suddenly, just like before, Guin was gone again.

As the final chime sounded, Tateena placed her hand on the floor of Guin's bedroom. She uttered the same words that Guin had said numerous times before. Instantly, there was a bright yellow glow coming from the floor as the boy's footprints lit up. Tateena smiled, making her feel as if Guin was still in the room with her. She slowly began following the footprints out of the room and down the hallway. As she followed, she quickened her pace, as her walk turned into a jog, and then into a run. It wasn't long before the footsteps led her outside of the building,

[373]

and away from it. It was by a large tree, a bit of a distance away from the university buildings that Tateena found the end of the trail of footprints. Nailed to the tree was a note.

> *Dear Tateena,*
> *I hope that this letter brings warm comfort to you as I have already left for Freltus. I'm sorry that I could not have stayed longer, but I am needed urgently. Fear not though, for I will return sooner, rather than late. For now though, I have set up a little show that I think you might enjoy. If you turn around and wait for it, you will see a sight unlike any other.*
> *Yours truly,*
> *Guin*

Tateena turned around and stared at the university for a number of seconds, waiting for Guin's gift. She waited and waited, but nothing happened. The young sorceress began to feel the same as she did when Guin first left. She felt almost like something was taken from her, even though there was never anything there before. Tateena ripped the letter from the tree and held it in front of her as if to rip it. It was then that her vision suddenly lit up. The entire university had light, shooting out from every window, door, and crack that made its way through the walls of the buildings. For nearly ten seconds, there was blinding light, but at Tateena's distance away, she was at perfect distance to not be fazed by the intense brightness. As it cleared, and the night returned to its usual darkness, all that Tateena could hear from within the university were the angry curses of

[374]

the elders, and the older students. As Tateena walked back, she gave that same mischievous smile that made Guin fall in love with her in the first place.

*   *   *

Kailan, Tanier, Bailan, and Crag, all stood around the table, with a map of the island of Trekta laid out on top.

"We received word just this morning that Trekta is not completely taken yet, as opposed to what we had thought earlier," Tanier stated. "They do, however, have most of the island covered." Tanier placed his finger on the eastern part of the map, showing a large building. "This is the Castle of Vulk. They will be using it as a stronghold, keeping some of their archers in the towers."

"What about this area over here?" questioned Kailan as he pointed to the small town, north of the castle.

"We still control most of this land, including the shores next to it," stated Bailan. "This is where most of our boats will dock. If we can defeat them here, then we will have won the war. There are hundreds of them on the island, but we have reports that tens of thousands are on their way."

Kailan and Crag both slumped backwards as they came to the realisation of what was about to happen.

"Sire, we have visitors!" yelled Arkle, still shaking as

[375]

he made his way to the side of the room.

"Tanier!" said a voice that Kailan had never heard before. Five men walked into the room, ordained in armour that was more ornate than practical.

"Who are you?" said Crag, inspecting the first of the five men.

"I happen to be the king of this land!"

Crag raised his lower lip over his upper and nodded, backing away as he stepped beside Kailan. "Does everyone here act like they have a stick up there rear?" Crag whispered to Kailan. The two of them giggled as the king glared at them for a second.

"Where's Silus?" questioned Tanier, looking about the five men.

"Silus was not able to make it today," said King Graen, of Helforth. "He will be here tomorrow."

"Sounds like Silus to me," said Bailan, chuckling.

"Kailan, Crag, these are five out of the six kings of Arlbega," said Tanier, holding out his hand. "You are quite familiar with King Partril's son, Farol."

"This is the little brat that I nearly killed my son?"

"This is the man that you will take orders from while in my presence," replied Tanier. "He will be leading our armies, with the aid of four more."

"Can we just get this over with?" said one of the kings to King Graen.

"Get what over with?" questioned Crag.

[376]

The doors quickly swung open as Silus Kain burst into the room, covered in cuts and bruises. "Run! It's a trick!" The five kings quickly pulled out their swords, attacking the Arch Chancellor and his friends. King Partril went straight for Kailan, swinging his sword violently, and without purpose. It almost made Kailan laugh deep inside, seeing the same worthless technique passed down from the king to his son. Kailan didn't even need to take any time to focus on his attack, as King Partril was not protecting himself whatsoever. Kailan quickly sliced the man's head off, kicking his body over as it slowly slumped to the ground. When he turned he found that Crag and Tanier had taken care of most of them, but Bailan on the other hand was not in a particularly good predicament. The king of Thoria had his sword at Bailan's throat, backing up slowly through the large room.

"Tanier, do something," said Bailan.

"I'll kill him!" shrieked the king.

"Tanier!"

"Come on, Bailan," laughed Tanier. "We can't fight every battle for you."

"I don't think this is a good idea," said Crag. "He might actually be in trouble."

"No, he can do it."

"Tanier, I've told you numerous times; I can't get involved!" yelled Bailan.

"Shut up!" said the king, cutting Bailan's neck slightly.

"You idiot!" Suddenly, the king dropped to the floor,

dead. Bailan walked past Tanier and ignored the smirk on his face, storming out of the room.

"What was that?" questioned Crag. "I've never seen that kind of magic before."

"Don't worry about it," said Tanier. "You most likely never will again."

One of the scholars in the large room caught Silus as he stumbled, nearly falling to the floor. He carried him over to the group of three, and sat Silus down in a chair.

"What happened to you?" questioned Tanier, wiping some of the blood from Silus' face with a cloth.

The emperor had trouble spitting out the first word, but after that he had no problem. "They beat me, and tortured me," said Silus. "They were planning on killing all of you, and siding with the Black Allegiance."

"They were going to do what?" gasped Kailan.

"They had made plans that they would be spared, along with their belongings. They would be allowed to continue governing their kingdoms, but forever as allies of the Black Allegiance."

"Let me guess," replied Tanier. "You said no."

"Exactly," said Silus. "No matter how much we disagree, I would still rather follow you than one of them."

"Kailan, I want you and the others to meet me in the lounge in two hours," said Tanier, wiping the sweat from his brow. "We need to clean this mess up."

Thorstein patted Guin on the back. "Good boy," he laughed. "We were almost thinking that you would never find a nice girl."

"What about you!" argued Guin. "You don't have a girl at home!"

"I'm married to my work," replied Thorstein. "Hard work fills the void in my life."

"That's a load of…"

"Everyone, Tanier wants us to meet him here in two hours," said Kailan as he entered the lounge.

"Why?" questioned Lena.

"Well, you just missed the sparring match that me and the king of Freltus had," Kailan replied.

"Did you get into a fight again?" said Lena, jumping to her feet.

"Well, it was more like the kings were committing treason against the country and wanted to kill us."

"Are you okay?" worried Lena as she rushed up to Kailan, inspecting him.

"The king was even worse of a swordsman than his son," replied Kailan.

"Did you kill him?" questioned Viktor.

"I didn't really have much of a choice," said Kailan,

[379]

watching the tiny smirk, creep its way upon Viktor's face.

It was over two hours later that Kailan had gotten worried, and decided to look for Tanier when he didn't show up. As he neared his office, Kailan could hear yelling coming from inside. He held his ear up to the door, listening in.

"You know that I'm not allowed to intervene directly with any of this!" yelled Bailan.

"Yes," Tanier replied.

"Then why did you make me kill him? If it was someone else; someone not important, then sure, I could have killed them, but not someone that is in the big picture!"

"I'm sorry, Bailan. I wanted to see some more of your abilities," replied Tanier. "My curiosity overpowered me."

"Tanier, I have tried to teach you numerous times, curiosity can be a dangerous thing. Men die in the pursuit of knowledge. There are some things that people should not know, no matter how important they seem."

"So I still cannot convince you to help us in the battle," said Tanier stepping away.

"Even though this problem was started by *him*, *I* will not be the one to end it. I will not fight him here. This place is too full of life." Tanier nodded and walked towards the door, opening it and finding Kailan on the other side.

"How long have you been there?" demanded Tanier.

As the boy stepped back out of shock, Bailan spoke up. "He's been there the entire time."

"And you're all right with this?" questioned Tanier.

Bailan turned to Tanier and stared at him. Kailan watched as they made no sound, but somehow, he knew that they were communicating. "As you wish." Tanier closed the door behind him, placing a hand on Kailan's shoulder. "Let's go, shall we?"

The two of them walked down the halls until they reached the lounge area. Kailan sat down on the couch beside Lena, staring up at Tanier.

"As some of you already know, the Black Allegiance has infiltrated our ranks," Tanier stated. "Lena was attacked by hobgoblins, just before Bailan arrived to take her back, Viktor was being stalked by a dark elf during his testing, and Thorstein ran into a problem with some giants."

"How many were there?" questioned Guin.

"Sorry?"

"How many giants?"

"There were nearly twenty," replied Thorstein smiling.

"Shut up, both of you," Tanier snapped. "I'm pretty sure that Kailan has already told you what happened earlier. We can no longer afford to wait. We have to strike at them now before anything goes wrong."

"Wait, what's happening?" questioned Guin.

"We're heading off to war in two days," said Tanier, hanging his head. "Do whatever you need to do now, because you might not be able to do it later." Tanier turned around and began walking down the hallway, leaving the five young adults quiet and without words.

Later that night, as the other three slept, Kailan and

Lena were sitting outside, staring up at the full moon.

"It really makes you wonder," said Lena, plucking a tuft of grass and blowing it into the air.

"Wonder about what?" Kailan replied.

"If we're going to survive or not."

Kailan propped himself up. "What kind of talk is that?" Kailan retorted. "Of course we'll survive. Why do you think Tanier had us do all of this training?"

"What about that look he gave us?" said Lena. "He obviously doesn't have any real hope for us, or himself."

"That's not what he's upset about," said Kailan.

"What is he upset about?"

"I don't know exactly," said Kailan. "It seemed strange to me, but it doesn't concern us anyways."

Lena held out her hand and grabbed onto Kailan's softly. She played with his fingers, scratching the inside of them.

"Is something wrong?" questioned Kailan.

"No. Why?"

"You haven't touched me like that, or even at all, since before the night that me and Viktor fought."

"We haven't seen each other for two months," said Lena.

"I'm talking about the other times. We didn't say a word to each other after the event. You barely saw me as a friend since we've been back."

"Well that isn't my fault," argued Lena. "I needed some time to think and get my mind straight."

[382]

"I see," said Kailan, taking a hold of Lena's hand. He turned on his side using his free hand to pull Lena in closer, turning her onto her side as well. He pressed his forehead against hers; staring into her bright, green eyes. In this moment, Kailan seemed to be lost within them, trapped by Lena's beauty. "I've learned to control myself."

Lena gave him a strange look. "What do you mean?"

"It was my sword that would cause me to become angry," Kailan replied. "I have learned to control its power."

Lena let out a beam of happiness, as she looked down from Kailan's face. "That isn't enough though."

"I know," said Kailan. "I'm getting better every day though." He placed his hand on her sleeve, caressing her arm, up and down.

Lena looked up, with a twinkle in her eyes as she leaned closer, embracing Kailan and caressing his lips with hers, closing her eyes again. The short stubble that he gained over the past few days gently rubbed against her upper lip, but caused no discomfort. Her hand gently hovered over to his cheek, bringing it up and brushing the hair from his face.

"I think I'm ready," whispered Kailan, smiling. Lena opened her eyes and pulled back slightly, revealing a smile that she had kept hidden for so long. She rolled over, pushing herself off the ground and running towards the doorway.

She looked back to find Kailan, just staring in awe. "Well, are you coming?" Kailan chased after her, following into the lounge area. They quickly made their way into Kailan's

[383]

room, closing the door, softly, behind them. Lena jumped on the bed and quickly hid underneath the covers. Kailan on the other hand, stood next to it as he undid the laces on his shirt, hastily untying them. He then continued by sitting on the edge of the bed, kicking off his shoes, and slowly pulling his pants down from his waist. He stopped for a brief second, taking in the full feeling of the moment. It was something that he had never felt before, and possibly something that he would never feel again. Kailan wiped the sweat from his forehead, smiling as he slid in next to Lena.

*   *   *

When Kailan opened his eyes, he saw thousands of men, unloading ships of numerous sizes. He turned around and found the other four companions standing with him, showing just as much awe as him. Kaela quickly leapt from Lena's hand, flying high into the sky.

"Welcome to the island of Trekta," said Tanier.

"Is there anything else that you need?" questioned Bailan from the back of the group.

Tanier looked at the sky, and then back at Bailan. "Do you think that you could give us a little sunshine?"

"We'll see," replied Bailan, vanishing into thin air.

The Arch Chancellor turned back around, observing the

five friends. "You five have done very well," said Tanier. "You have all made me proud, and tomorrow, you will make the world proud." He stepped to the side and made his way over to one of the enormous tents along the beachfront. "Follow me!"

The five adventurers followed Tanier to the tent, with Thorstein listening from the outside, crouching. Inside of the tent, were nearly fifty men, all suited up in different types of armour.

"Tanier!" shouted Crag from the front of the room. The entire tent of people turned around to witness the Arch Chancellor's presence. Crag made his way around the crowd, hopping from person to person. "Everyone, this is the honourable, Tanier Frost; Arch Chancellor of Arlbega!"

"I'm glad that many of you have volunteered your armies for this purpose!" shouted Tanier. "The Black Allegiance may not concern you now, but without your help at this time, it wouldn't take long to reach your lands." He stepped away from the doorway and held out his hand, presenting the five younger adults. "These are the generals of our armies."

The men in the room looked at the four adventurers in the doorway, with Thorstein behind and out of view. There was a brief silence before an up roar of laughter and dismay.

"You cannot be serious, Tanier!" yelled one of the men. "These *kids* are going to die!"

"They are some of the greatest warriors that this world has ever seen!" yelled Tanier. At first, it seemed as though the entire room was against the Arch Chancellor's idea. The

[385]

pressure in his stomach began to increase, feeling like he was about to burst, until he saw a familiar face, make his way through the crowd.

"My name is Silus Kane; emperor of Arad!" He stood next to Tanier, yelling over the assembly. "I have seen these brave souls fight; watched them fight for their lives!"

"I have witnessed their abilities as well!" yelled Grakken, stepping out from behind of the posts holding up the tent. "Lena, here, is the best archer in all of the known lands!" The men in the room quickly became silent, not a word being shed.

"Thorstein defeated over ten giants, single handily, when my city was attacked!" yelled Archus from the other side of the tent.

"Even though he has caused numerous problems at the university," said one of the men. "I have to say that Guin is possibly the brightest young wizard, and one hell of a quick learner."

"What about the other two?" demanded one of the men. "Who are they?"

"This is Kailan, the greatest swordsman to live!" shouted Geamille, standing off to the side.

"Who's he then?" said another man, pointing at Viktor. "How come no one's ever heard of him?"

"Viktor can hide from sight in full daylight," said Kailan, chuckling. "That's why no one's ever heard of him. If you do hear him, you're most likely about to die."

Viktor laughed, patting Kailan on the back. "Thanks."

"We will attack tomorrow," said Tanier, arms crossed. "We will march at midday, but be prepared for battle immediately. We cannot be sure of what to expect from our enemy." Tanier turned around, facing the five friends. "I will speak to all of you in a couple of minutes. I need to first brief the officers." The four companions that were inside, quickly stepped out of the tent; walking away from it with Thorstein.

They made their way down to the beach, walking along the shore. The wind was cool by the ocean, and the water was even colder. They were only about a month away from the first signs of winter, and the lands were getting much colder.

"Thorstein!" yelled a large man, running over towards the giant.

The boy quickly turned to face the man. "Father!" he yelled in Feltsch. The giant boy hurried over to the man and lifted him into the air like a child. "What are you doing here?" He slowly lowered the man to the ground.

"The men and I are fighting with you," said Thorstein's father. "We're being called heavy cavalry."

"You are riding your dornbeast into battle?" questioned Thorstein.

"They are being fitted with some amazing armour," replied his father. "I'm sorry, but I must get back to work. We are supposed to be ready for battle by tomorrow." Thorstein watched his father wave, then run away, back towards the other soldiers.

[387]

"Thorstein!" yelled Tanier. "We're ready!" The giant turned away from his father and headed towards the tent. When he reached it, Tanier stood outside, with notes in his hands. "Most of you already know your stations, but I will go over them again. Kailan, you are in charge. Lena, you are the one in charge of every bow that is out there. Guin, if someone uses magic, they are under your orders. Thorstein, you have the dwarven berserkers and heavy cavalry. Viktor, you will join in the fight later on, but we have a special task for you to do first."

*   *   *

Kailan awoke; a strange feeling within his gut. He was full of fear, and more nervous than he had ever been before.

"We're moving on early," said Lena, picking up her bow from the ground. "Are you coming to save the world?" The look on Lena's face confused Kailan. It was either that she didn't care about the battle ahead, or that she was very good at hiding her emotions.

"Yes, I'm coming," Kailan replied, hopping to his feet. Tanier quickly ran over, two horses in his hands.

"These are yours," said Tanier, handing the reins over to Lena and Kailan. "I might not see you until the end of the battle." He paused for a second, staring at both of them. "I bid you luck." He ran past the two companions, moving from soldier to soldier.

"We might need more than luck," said Kailan.

"Kailan," said Lena, holding the reins tightly. "Is there any way to back out of this?" She looked up at him, as her feelings started to show.

The boy placed a hand on her shoulder. "Don't worry," Kailan said, now smiling. "We will win this." He helped Lena onto her horse, holding her hand for a moment. There were suddenly horns, sounding about; they were not from the forces of good though. Kailan hopped onto his horse and looked ahead. "I will find you when this is over." Kailan dug his heels into the horse's side and ran amongst the soldiers to the front lines. Across the fields, he could see the enemy amassing. The Black Allegiance was much bigger than what he had hoped for. Thousands of beasts were on the other side of the field, with the castle just behind them. The only thing separating Kailan from them was an open field, with a distance that he could run on foot in under two minutes. He hurried his way in front of the swordsmen, awaiting the others as they marched on. He quickly searched for Thorstein, galloping from one side of the massive army to the other.

"Thorstein!" Kailan called out. "I need your cavalry out in front. Have the men from Achland in the centre. They can do the most damage and hopefully split their forces in two." The giant nodded, riding his dornbeast ahead. Thankfully, Lena was not too far off from Kailan. "I need the archers just in behind the cavalry."

[389]

"Why?" questioned Lena. "Tanier told me to have them out front at first."

"I have a plan," Kailan replied. "Trust me, it'll work." When everything was ready, Kailan waited with his men. The others could not figure out what he was waiting for, but they trusted him, even though it seemed like a horrible idea. Kailan gave no great speech; he had no amazing presence over the men. To Kailan, this battle didn't feel as spectacular as it really was. To him, it was just another mess that his friends and he needed to get through. It was the sound of the explosion by the castle, shaking the earth that signalled the start of the great battle. "Thorstein, charge!"

The giant burst forward, his soldiers keeping rank with him. "To war!" he shouted.

"Lena, aim for the front lines!"

The girl dipped her bow into the small flame in front of her, igniting the tip of the arrow. She aimed it high into the air, followed by the rest of the archers. At once, they shot into the air, raining down a barrage of hell upon the enemy. The sky went black with arrows, just before Thorstein's men reached the front lines. By the time they reached though, all the arrows had fallen, allowing for a further advance. Kailan's plan had worked perfectly; everyone's job fitting in like pieces of a puzzle. Before the battle, it was explained to Viktor that he was to go behind the enemy lines, along with a few skilled elves, and plant a bomb that the Aradian Wizards' Guild had created. It destroyed a large chunk of the castle walls, leaving an entrance for Kailan's troops. It served a different purpose in Kailan's plan, however. For him, it was meant as a distraction, a device to instil fear. With Thorstein's cavalry going farther into their ranks than originally expected, it broke the enemies' spirits even more. Mowing down goblins and men as they went, Thorstein's cavalry carved a hole in the Black Allegiance's forces. Kailan rode up to Lena, standing beside her.

"Give us cover as we make our way in." He made his way back to the infantry. "It's our turn men!" The first push into the fight stuck in Kailan's mind permanently. He charged in with his horse, not a care in the world. The swordsmen were right with him as he entered the battle, even after taking substantial losses from the attacking goblin archers. The next few minutes were a complete blur to him; he had no true sense of what was happening, but was lost in the moment.

*   *   *

Thorstein charged from the allied lines, with his berserkers this time, sending the cavalry in from the sides. As he broke through the lines, Thorstein sent goblins and hobgoblins flying into the air. With his armour, he was nearly unstoppable; charging through with no fear of anything. A number of ogres made their way up through the ranks, pushing their allies aside, as they tried to get closer to the giant. The Black Allegiance had many giant beasts, but Kailan's army only had Thorstein to stand over everyone. Thorstein quickly made eye contact with the ogres, smiling, and changing his course.

"Mindless beasts!" he yelled, swinging his axe and clearing dozens of goblins from his path. The distance between Thorstein and the ogres quickly lessoned as they charged for each other. As the two forces hit, a number of the ogres were knocked backwards by the sheer force of Thorstein running into them. He swung his axe, slicing at the other few. Within the blink of an eye, Thorstein had already killed about fifty enemy soldiers as he ran on foot.

Archus followed very close behind, swinging his axes wildly. It wasn't long before he was drenched, from head to toe, in the blood of his enemies. The red and purple liquids dripped from his hairs as he spun around, cleaving his axes into his foes. "Is this all you've got?" he yelled out. For the dwarven berserkers, they were fewer in number than the swordsmen, but they were much stronger; doing just as much damage to the enemy army.

For Guin and Lena, they were not fighting as much, as opposed to defending the others from attacks. As Thorstein and Kailan's soldiers were charging in, the enemy sorcerers were constantly casting spells that Guin and his wizards had to counter. Lena was constantly giving cover to the soldiers, keeping their aim on many of the larger creatures that Thorstein was not able to handle. It was as his father fell though, that Thorstein no longer needed any cover.

[392]

The giant raced over to the cavalry, running with little care, through the enemy lines. Upon reaching the cavalry, he looked around, finding a number of the men, and their dornbeasts, mangled and torn apart. His father's head lay on the ground, detached from his shoulders, rolling around in a pool of blood. It was at that point that Archus' training began to dawn on Thorstein; it was that moment when he understood the true power of the suit. As he turned around, Thorstein howled out in pain, creating a sound that thundered across the battlefield. "You will DIE!" he cried. He swatted the goblins and men like flies, casting them into the air as he ran deeper into battle. Thorstein suddenly found his strength, his speed; everything was amplified. A group of ogre's decided to charge him, not knowing what they were about to face. As the giant picked the first up by its neck, he twirled it about, using it as a weapon against the others before throwing it far into the air. The giants that came after that were no problem either. With his axe, Thorstein sliced through five at a time, leaving nothing but mangled torsos and blood across the battlefield. In all of his time living in Achland, Thorstein never expected anything like this; but he enjoyed it, the sense of power.

"Kailan!" screamed Lena, at the top of her lungs as she pointed off into the distance. There was no response as the boy was too far away and so well immersed in the battle. She kicked her heels into the horse's side and charged through her own ranks, heading towards the fighting lines. "Kailan!" she yelled a second time. The boy turned around, and stared at her for a

[393]

second as she pointed up towards the sky. He followed her hand off into the distance, watching as the thick black cloud arose from the ground. What looked like a dragon at first, emerging from it, quickly changed into something that Kailan did not expect.

"Terilla!" shouted Aroculus, in between spells.

Guin looked down at his book, still holding his spells constant. "What did you say?"

"Look up, it's Terilla!"

Guin looked up as the demonic woman soared through the skies, letting out her scream, causing the men to stop fighting and hold their hands to their ears, muffling the screeches.

She was dressed in black armour, leaving only her midriff and arms exposed. Her wings, black as the night, and vast like those of dragons, blocked out the sun as she flew. The two horns on her head curved outwards, and then towards each other, stopping a few inches apart. As beautiful and seductive as she was, she was just as deadly. Terilla looked down upon the battlefield, laughing as the soldiers of the world looked up and gasped, with the Black Allegiance laughing. No more were they to lose; their one true hero had finally arrived. She held out her hands, casting darkness into the men, killing them instantly. As she swooped down, she picked up numerous soldiers, taking them high into the sky dropping them to their deaths below.

"Fall back!" yelled Kailan, watching as the men came crashing to the ground. He hopped on the back of Lena's horse as they quickly made their way back towards their own lines.

Thorstein himself was pushing through, making sure to not have to deal with Terilla's magic. Viktor even popped out of the shadows for once, revealing himself as he made his way back. "Thorstein, Viktor, this way!" Kailan cried out. The four group members quickly converged upon Guin.

"Where is the leader of your army? What leader is he that he runs away from battle?" called out Terilla.

"Stop," said Kailan.

"What?" questioned Lena, with a concerned look on her face.

"Stop the horse."

Lena pulled back on the reins, turning the horse around as her and Kailan looked up towards Terilla.

"Get her attention," said Kailan. He had the same smirk that appeared on the faces of a number of his friends. The problem was this facial expression always meant that there was to be trouble.

Lena pointed an arrow, just above Terilla, and fired. The missile arched through the air, cutting her cheek slightly, causing her to turn and stare at Lena and Kailan.

"It is me that you look for!" yelled Kailan. Terilla smiled, slowly fluttering over with a drop to the ground at the last second. The shake caused the horse to rear, knocking both Kailan and Lena from their seats. Kailan quickly held his sword in front, keeping Lena behind him. As the dust settled, Terilla looked upon the two and smiled.

"How sweet," she said, smiling as she moved her bat-like wings away from her face. "You protect your dearest love, even in certain death." She raised her hands, and just as she was about to cast the spell from her hands, she was thrown to the side by Thorstein, charging in. Terilla skidded along the battlefield, stopping herself as she landed back on the ground.

"Are you alright?" questioned Thorstein. The two nodded, with fear in their eyes.

"I see you have my ingredients," said Terilla, laughing.

"Your what?" questioned Kailan.

"That armour, that sword, her quiver; they are all products of mine. I created them, to summon the greatest warrior ever to walk upon this earth." She slowly walked over, picking at her nails. "That is no problem though; I can take them from you still."

"Run!" yelled Crag and Tanier, standing in the way as they held up their hands. Terilla tried to move forward, but it was no use. As more and more wizards joined in, Terilla only began to laugh more and more. The five companions quickly regrouped, trying to come up with a plan.

"We could try to use magic, attacking her from all sides," said Guin.

"No," replied Aroculus.

"I could get my archers to shoot a wave of arrows for her," said Lena. "There is no way that she would be able to survive that."

"No."

"Let me fight her on the ground," said Thorstein. "I can

kill her."

"Shut your mouths for one second!" yelled Aroculus. Four of the companions looked at the book, and then at Guin.

"He gets like this sometimes," said Guin, joking.

"These five items were not created to fight her, they were created by her," said Aroculus.

"What?" Kailan asked.

"I was there at the first battle," said Aroculus. "Terilla created these items so that she could create the ultimate soldier. The impenetrable armour, the flaming sword, the poisonous daggers, and the never ending quiver. She would then use this tome to bind all of them together into one. All that Terilla needed was a willing soul; one that would be worthy to be her king."

"So how do we defeat her then?" Guin questioned.

"I have been waiting for this moment for over a thousand years," said Aroculus. "Terilla was once my wife."

The entire group looked around at each other oddly. "You married her?" questioned Kailan.

"She didn't have horns or wings back then, you idiot," replied Aroculus. "I was a great page, and she was the sorceress that I worked with. We fell in love and married at a young age. One day, I returned home to find our house nearly destroyed, and she was lying on the bed, in a pool of her own blood. A few weeks later, we received word that the Black Allegiance was amassing on this island. I was sent with the wizards to assist them with their spells. Terilla came forward, just as she is now, but nowhere near as strong. I was told that when she died, she spent time in hell, burning for days on end. Apparently a powerful demon made a deal with her, to give her power and freedom in exchange for her to bring chaos and death upon the world. She accepted, planning to rebel, but didn't expect to be warped by the powers. After being defeated, we found the five ingredients to her spell. There was a message in the book meant for me. Terilla wanted me to bind myself to the book, with the rest of the items and avenge her. She obviously knew that she would lose the battle at first, but she still had a love for me."

"You did as she told you to?" shouted Guin, astonished.

"I did what was right," replied Aroculus. "The power of this book is not within the soul that is trapped inside, but within the pages and covers themselves. This tome has withstood over a thousand years of wars and bloodshed. Terilla made it so that I would be immortal as she is."

"So what are we going to do about her then?" said Viktor, getting frustrated.

"You must bind the book to me," said Aroculus.

"But you just said that that is what Terilla wants," replied Kailan. "How can we trust you?"

"If you guys could hurry and come up with a plan, that would be great!" yelled Crag, straining as the force field slowly began to push back under Terilla's barrage of attacks

"You'll have to trust me," said Aroculus.

"You helped Gorgul destroy kingdom after kingdom," replied Guin.

"One day, you will learn more about Gorgul, and how his stories are not entirely true," replied Aroculus.

"Why not just bind me?" questioned Kailan.

"How can we trust you?" snarled Viktor. "You'd go mad with the power, killing your friends."

"Why don't you shut up!" yelled Kailan.

"Both of you stop!" Aroculus let out a long sigh. "Once someone has been bound, there is no way of returning to their own body. They are forever trapped, unless killed."

The five companions looked around at each other. Their faces were pale, and their eyes wide. "How do we bind you then?" questioned Guin.

"Everyone, hold hands," said Aroculus. "Guin, place me in the centre of the circle and read the words that appear on the pages within."

"Ok!" The five companions each held hands as they stood up. Guin quickly began reading the pages out of the book as the barrier slowly began to fade away. "AROCULUS FIN GALA NOC TORNA MALPHET RENTRAK!" The five companions looked at each other, surprised that nothing had happened.

"Stupid children!" laughed Terilla, breaking the wall of magic completely. "It won't work for you!"

The adolescents were thrown back as their items disappeared from their sides, and their backs. In the centre of the circle was a bright, white light that slowly lifted into the air, then shooting up through the clouds as a beam. Amidst the beam of

[399]

light, something made its way towards the ground, crashing into the earth. As the dust settled, Aroculus stood up, smiling. He spread out his magic wings of fire as he stretched, raising his sword towards Terilla.

This was the first time that her face had filled with such fear since arriving back on the surface. "You can never defeat me Aroculus!" she yelled. "I am, and always have been stronger than you!" She reached to her side, pulling a whip from her belt.

"Back down now, Terilla!" shouted Aroculus, sheathing the sword. He was wearing the same armour that Thorstein wore, except that it was now a gold colour instead of silver. There was a cloak on his head, keeping his face hidden, with a quiver on his back, and a bow in his left hand. Aroculus pulled an arrow from the quiver, and notched it on the flaming bow. "You have one chance to come back," said Aroculus.

Terilla looked to her sides as the creatures of darkness stared up at her. "Never!" she cried, cracking the whip to the side. The remaining army of goblins and men charged for the humans, screaming as they advanced.

"Attack!" cried Kailan at the top of his lungs, picking up a sword from the ground. Even more intense than before, the two armies crashed like opposing waves in the sea during a storm.

Aroculus shot the bow for Terilla, missing her by a hair. "You'll never get me from there," Terilla giggled, cracking her blade tipped whip again.

"Fine, have it your way," said Aroculus. He dropped

the bow to his side, and unbuckled the quiver from his shoulder. "I'll fight you, face to face." He darted across the battlefield, his sword glowing with fire. As they clashed, Aroculus blocked her whip, using it to grab the robe, ripping it from her hands.

She looked up at him with astonishment before raising her hands and casting out magic. The black darkness hit Aroculus, sending him to the ground, knocking the sword from his hand. As he stood up, he too held out his hands, shooting flames from his hand. He made his way up, into the air, trying to get close to her. Aroculus was no match for Terilla when it came to magic, but physically, he was greater than her by many means.

He flew higher into the air than she had expected, crashing down upon her from above. As they plummeted to earth, Terilla smiled, not letting Aroculus go. They crashed into the earth, taking out numerous men from either of their own armies. Aroculus stood up from the dust, leaving Terilla on the floor, lying still. He quickly turned around, watching the battle, but when he turned back, he found Terilla standing straight up.

"Don't think that I will give up that easily," said Terilla, wiping the dirt from her armour. She shot straight into the air, with Aroculus in hot pursuit, chasing directly after her. Again, they clashed in the heavens, punching and kicking at each other. It was as they slowly started to make their way back down to the earth that Aroculus made his finishing move. He grabbed Terilla by the feet, lifted her higher into the air, and threw her towards the ground. For a moment, all of the fighting

[401]

ceased as Aroculus slowly floated down towards her body. He landed near Terilla, slowly moving towards her.

"End this now, Terilla!" yelled Aroculus. "Come with me!" No one was sure if it was arrogance, or if Aroculus just didn't know about the dagger that she held in her hand, but as he stood over her body, she stabbed him through the chest.

"Aroculus!" cried Guin at the top of his lungs, shedding tears.

The mighty warrior crashed against the ground, his arms to his sides as Terilla slowly crawled up, on top of him.

"You bitch!" screamed Lena.

Aroculus looked down at his chest, noticing the dagger sticking out of his ribcage. He looked around for his friends, but he could not see them. All that he could see were bodies, and weapons. The only things that were familiar to him were Terilla, and the arrow that lay at the tips of his fingers.

"You could have had life," she said, pouting, playing with the blade. "You could have had freedom. You could have had me."

"I had you once," Aroculus whispered. Terilla removed his hood and slowly brought her face in towards his, licking his cheek.

"You could have had me again," she said with a seductive smile.

"I loved you once as well," said Aroculus, bringing his hand in close, stabbing Terilla in her unarmoured side with the arrow.

[402]

"What do you expect that to do?" laughed Terilla.

"The arrows are poisonous, even to you, my love."

The demonic queen quickly felt the poison take effect as her skin began to grow black around the wound. As she dropped upon him, Aroculus embraced her, with his last strength, for one last time as his essence disappeared.

What came next was considered one of the strangest, yet most beautiful things that ever happened within that world. The spirits of both Aroculus, and Terilla slowly floated up, out of their bodies. They were not the creatures that everyone was used to, but were the spirits of the humans that lived over a thousand years prior. They slowly floated up towards the sky, causing the dark clouds above to disappear, creating light upon Trekta. The two bodies that lay on the ground quickly dissolved into the sand below them, leaving nothing behind.

Kailan looked up from the pile of dirt, facing towards his enemies for one, final charge. "To the death!" Kailan shrieked. They drove the remaining army into the sea, causing most of them to drown, many of the others being slaughtered, and only a few were taken as prisoners.

*   *   *

"Kailan!" yelled Tanier running up from the boats. "Come, they are preparing a feast for us!"

[403]

Kailan patted Thorstein on the back as he held up his father's axe. "I didn't know him, but to raise someone like you, he must have been a great father," said Kailan.

"He was the best," replied Thorstein, shedding only a single tear.

Tanier stopped by the two friends, only realising what was happening as he was near them. "I'm sorry about your father," said Tanier. "He was a good man, and a brave warrior."

"Thank you, Tanier," Thorstein replied.

"I know that this may not be the time, but there is a feast being prepared for us on the beach," said Tanier with a slight smile on his face. "If you interested, you can come and join us."

"Where I come from, Tanier, there is no time for mourning," said Thorstein. "We have a time for honouring them." He paused for a second, looking back at the beach. "My father always loved a good meal," he laughed.

"Come then," said Tanier. "Guin is already waiting for you two."

Kailan cocked his head to the side. "Just Guin? Where are Lena and Viktor?" questioned Kailan.

"I think that they went to inspect the castle for any further enemies," said Tanier.

"I'll be down in a couple of minutes then," said Kailan, walking over to one of the horses. "I think that they should know about the food." Kailan hopped on the horse, and started across the battlefield, dodging countless bodies as he made his way

[404]

towards the fortress. He made his way through the rubble that used to be a wall, and towards the towering doors. As he made his way off the horse, he stared at his sword for a second and shook his head. Kailan opened one of the doors, straining because of its massive weight. Upon entering, Kailan found a great hall, with a set of stairs at the far end by the corner. At the top of the stairs, there was a long hallway, with doors on either side cascading down the hall. After that, there was another set of stairs, with light coming from the top. Red drapes were hung across the stairwell, from wall to wall as Kailan slowly made his way up. Upon removing the last curtain, he came upon a large balcony room, with a view of the entire battlefield. Standing in the one corner of the room, by a group of large pillows, were both Lena and Viktor.

"Ah, Kailan, I was wondering when you would show up," said Viktor, smiling.

"We're having a feast on the shore," said Kailan, huffing his breath after running through the castle.

"We won't be joining you," said Viktor.

"W-What?" said Kailan, confused.

"Me and Lena will be staying here."

Kailan looked at the girl as she stood in the corner, motionless. "Lena, are you coming?" Kailan stepped forward with his hand held out.

Viktor smacked the boy's hand, standing in his way. "Listen, Kailan, there is something that we need to tell you," said Viktor, grinning the same grin that he had at the assassins' guild. "Lena no longer has any feelings for you."

"Viktor, shut up, and get out of my way." Kailan tried to push by, but the other boy was much stronger. He was pushed back and thrown to the ground.

"There are some things that maybe you never guessed about me," said Viktor. "You see, Kailan, my mother was a bit of a whore; something that my father never really knew about. I was not my father's son, but the offspring of something greater. Or so I at least thought. My mother became very friendly with a vampire name Raol. Quite the handsome man, but still undead none the less. I never understood it, but when I man impregnates a female vampire, the child is born dead; after a few drops of blood are given to it, it lives and becomes a vampire. When a male vampire impregnates a woman, they create what is called a half breed. We have all of the abilities that vampires do, but with none of the weaknesses. I can lift things of immense weight, even move like the wind, yet I can live in the sunlight. I have a reflection, and best of all, Lena can feel the warm touch of my skin against hers."

"You are mad!" yelled Kailan, trying to push back Viktor a second time. This time, the boy twisted Kailan's arm behind his back, forcing him to the ground.

"There is something about Lena that I think you have always wondered," Viktor chuckled. "How come when you and Thorstein first entered her village, there were no men around? Not a single male was in the village." Viktor turned his head to the side as Lena slowly approached him, standing in front of

Kailan, smiling. "You see; the women in Lena's village are sirens. They seduce, and make love to an unsuspecting victim, then kill him, leaving nothing left but a new born child in its place."

Kailan looked up at Lena, who in turn, smiled, almost letting out a slight giggle.

"You see, Kailan; we are freaks, both of us. It was with your help that we were united."

"The other night," said Kailan. "That meant nothing to you?"

Lena bent down beside Kailan and closed in to his ear. "Oh, yes, I now have a child to call my own, but too bad you won't be able to see it," said Lena, smiling.

"Now Lena, it wouldn't be nice to just kill our friend," said Viktor. "We'll let him go free." Viktor looked down at Kailan, tightening his grip on Kailan's hand. "Now you have one chance, Kailan. Don't mess this up and get yourself killed." He released Kailan's arm, kicking him down the stairs. The boy quickly darted towards the exit, making sure not to look back. As he made his way across the battle, Viktor looked at Lena. "Kill him."

With a look of surprise, she turned to him. "You promised him that he would be spared."

"I lied!" Viktor smiled as the boy quickly made his way back to the horse. "Shoot now or I'll kill you too."

Lena held up her bow, aiming the arrow directly at Kailan. As he rode away on the horse, Lena pulled back on the

[407]

string and released, firing the bow into the air. It was oblivious to Kailan that the shot was being made until he saw the arrow land a couple yards in front of him. "I'm sorry, Viktor," said Lena. "He was too far out of range."

"Ah, well, I guess he gets to live," the vampire continued to chuckle to himself.

As Kailan neared the camp, he called out. "Thorstein, Guin!" The giant and wizard looked towards the horseman in the distance and smiled.

"You're missing some of this great food!" yelled Thorstein.

"Roasted potatoes and pork!" Guin called out, laughing with the giant.

Kailan ran up on the horse, panting as he grabbed onto Thorstein for support.

"Where's Lena and Viktor?" questioned Thorstein, stuffing his mouth.

"Viktor is a vampire, and Lena tried to kill me!"

"You sound hungry, here try some pig snout," said Guin, passing Kailan a plate.

"Dammit, this is serious!"

"What happened?" Thorstein asked, dropping the food from his mouth.

"I went to the top of the castle, and found Lena and Viktor there. Viktor told me to leave, and that he was a vampire. Lena is also a siren, her whole village is. That's why there weren't any men when we went there. She said that she was

[408]

going to kill me, but Viktor spared my life. As I was running away though, Lena shot at me with her bow, but she missed."

"She missed?" said Thorstein, rubbing his chin.

"She aimed too high, thank goodness for that," said Kailan.

"Where's Viktor?" said Tanier, appearing out of nowhere.

"He's in the castle with Lena."

"Get her out of there!" yelled Tanier. "We just received reports that the entire assassins' guild was slaughtered, many of them were poisoned to death."

Thorstein and Guin quickly jumped from the benches that they were sitting on and quickly ran for the horses, and the dornbeast. As the three ran through the field, Thorstein looked over at Kailan.

"Kailan, do you remember something that Lena said about her abilities?" said Thorstein.

"No, what?" questioned Kailan.

"Lena could never miss, not unless she tried," replied Thorstein. "She must have been forced by Viktor to shoot. He probably has her under a spell."

"He has her under a spell?" said Kailan, almost jumping out of his seat.

"I forgot to mention that he could do that, didn't I.

"Dammit Thorstein!"

The three boys quickly made their way over the rubble of the wall, and into the castle grounds. They quickly ran into the great hall, running past the pillars that held the ceiling up, and towards the staircase. As they neared the steps, they heard the door burst open, with the doors flying off their hinges.

"It's too late Kailan!" yelled Viktor with the same mad grin on his face.

"You two go ahead!" yelled Thorstein, looking back at the other two. "I'll keep him from getting any farther.

Viktor smiled as he ran at Thorstein, tackling and knocking him to the ground. It was the strangest feeling that Thorstein had ever felt. Never before had he needed to gasp for air so hard, never had he thought would he need to.

"Get up!" yelled Viktor. "You can't give up that easily." He let out a chuckle as he advanced upon the giant. He smacked the tall man on the face, flipping him on his side.

Thorstein let out a swift kick, launching Viktor into the stone wall behind. "Just knocked the wind out of me, that's all," said Thorstein as he picked himself up. Viktor pulled his head out of the rubble and gave the giant a dirty look, only to find him leaping through the air, hoping to land on Viktor. The half-breed quickly dodged the attack, sliding on the floor.

"That was a good try," said Viktor. "Let me show you a few tricks that I learned over the years." He jumped in the air, flipping backwards, and bringing his foot under Thorstein's chin as he did so. The giant fell backwards, but quickly regained his stance afterwards. He picked up one of the stones from the pile of the wall and threw it at Viktor, who quickly dodged it. "Hey, you keep up at that, and someone's going to get hurt." Viktor's

[410]

smile quickly disappeared as he saw the second stone fly through the air, missing him by a hair. He hid behind one of the pillars, but it wasn't a good enough cover, crumbling to the floor as the stone hit it. Viktor picked up one of the smaller stones and threw it at Thorstein, hitting him directly in the face. "That looks like it hurt."

Thorstein wiped the blood away from his upper lip, and cracked his nose back into place. "Ah!" he yelled at the top of his lungs, charging at the vampire. Thorstein sprinted across the room, leaving two more piles of rubble that were once pillars, on the floor. He hit Viktor with serious force, sending him all the way through a wall. "Don't piss me off!" yelled Thorstein with a smile on his face. He turned around, only to hear a slow clap, followed by laughter.

"I'll tell you what, Thorstein," said Viktor. "You are strong; at least, stronger than me. The problem is that where you beat me in brawn, you fail in brains." Viktor held out his arm and brought it back, against the centre pillar within the room. As the ceiling slowly collapsed, Viktor used his immense speed to make a getaway before it fell completely, trapping Thorstein underneath. "Don't worry," Viktor chuckled. "I'm sure that they have many uses for bulls in the afterlife."

Guin stood waiting, smiling, but filled with fear as Viktor entered the corridor.

"Not another one!" said Viktor, panting from the running.

"End it here Viktor, and I won't have to kill you!" Guin

took the same stance that he would if he were fighting with his fists, ready to make a move.

"Fine." Viktor held out his hand, releasing a fireball at Guin, which was quickly stopped mid-air. "I know a lot more magic than I let any of you know." Guin's mouth was wide open in awe. "What did you think I did for so many years with no family, take up gardening?" Bolts of lightning, balls of fire, and spurts of water were cast back and forth with no advance of either of the young men.

"You're not stronger than me!" yelled Guin, shooting a burst of light from his hands, blinding Viktor for a brief moment.

"I don't plan on winning like that," replied Viktor. He kicked a hole in the wall, and walked through to a side room. It was a large room, much smaller than the great hall, but still quite large. As Guin stepped through the hole, he found Viktor standing at the other end of the room, looking about for an escape. Guin smiled, remembering a spell from the tome. He held out his hands and tightened his arms.

"ANGKALA!" Guin screamed, belting out the magic words as loud as he could. He didn't wait this time as he had with the boy at the University in Kelenath. Guin cast the greenish orb towards Viktor as fast as he could, trapping him inside. A slight smile appeared on his face as he made his way over to the orb. "I bet you didn't expect that one."

It wasn't until the dust settled, and Guin was picking himself up that he realised that the orb had burst, releasing

[412]

Viktor. "I bet you didn't expect me to know the counter for that," said Viktor, chuckling out loud, with his palms pointing at Guin. Suddenly, fire burst from his hands, shooting across the room. The young wizard held out his hands to stop it, almost stumbling back as he did so. Guin quickly changed his blocking magic, to a gust of water, pushing back on the fire, and gaining ground.

"It's no use!" yelled Guin.

Viktor could feel the fire being extinguished, his power slowly coming to an end. With a last effort, Viktor let out all of his might at once, engulfing the room in flames. Guin used his water to swiftly snuff out the flames, creating a thick cloud of steam. As he looked back at Viktor, however, he found that the vampire had disappeared. It was within that instant that Guin had realised his defeat as he was thrown to the opposite side of the room and into the wall. He slumped to the ground, motionless.

"You know?" said Viktor. "There are times when I almost pity people like you." You spend almost all of your life inside a room, never experiencing the world around you. When you do finally break free, you are too weak to handle it. Viktor stepped back through the hole in the wall and continued down the hallway to the final flight of steps. As he rounded the corner, he found Kailan, arguing with Lena. "It's no use," said Viktor, slowly making his way towards Lena.

"Get away from her!" yelled Kailan, holding the tip of his sword up to Viktor's throat.

[413]

"You had your chance, Kailan," said Viktor, walking closer, slowly. "You could have lived, but you decided not to." Viktor held his hands, pulling a sword out from behind his one hand, using magic that Kailan had never seen before. "I bested Thorstein's brains, something that he held so proudly about himself, even above his muscle. Guin's magic was weak, and easy to get around. I could have beaten him nearly five years ago." Viktor held the sword up and pointed it at Kailan. "Now, I will defeat you at swordplay." With one clean motion, Viktor struck Kailan's blade, knocking it to the side, but not out of his hands. Kailan used this momentum to spin around, meeting Viktor's blade again in front of him. He brought the sword up, and then back down upon Viktor's sword. For every attack that Kailan did, it seemed that Viktor had a very useful counterattack. It was now that Kailan wished so much for his flaming sword, but it had disappeared, along with the other items.

"Lena, wake up!" yelled Kailan. "Please, snap out of it!"

"What are you talking about?" laughed Viktor. "She doesn't love you anymore." The vampire swung his sword to the side, knocking Kailan's sword out of his hands, and off the edge of the balcony.

"Lena, help me!" yelled Kailan.

"Shut up already!" Viktor demanded, holding out his hand as he cast a ball of fire at Kailan.

"Lena!" Kailan screamed, burning as he fell over the

edge of the balcony.

She wasn't sure whether it was Kailan's scream, or her own will that snapped her out of Viktor's spell as she raced over to the edge of the balcony. She wept, watching as Kailan plummeted to the ground, hitting the earth in a fiery explosion.

"You monster!" cried Lena, punching and kicking at Viktor. He did not expect her to be as good of a fighter as she was, but he was still much better, and much stronger on top of that.

"What are you doing?" said Viktor, giving Lena a look of concern. "He doesn't love you. Well... at least not now, seeing as he's dead." Viktor grabbed Lena's wrists and threw her to the side of the room. Suddenly, there was a flash of light, blinding Viktor for a second, as Kailan rose up and over the balcony, the flames slowly diminishing.

"I guess that the sword lives within me," Kailan chuckled, stepping onto the floor.

"Great," said Viktor sarcastically. "Now I have to figure out how to kill you!" Kailan held out his sword towards Viktor, who tried to move it out of the way with his, but found that it was immobile. He took a swing, specifically at Kailan's sword, but it did not move, not unless Kailan willed it to.

"I am going to give you the chance to run for your life," said Kailan. "And don't worry, I don't like to lie."

"I'll take my chances," said Viktor, smiling. The two clashed swords again, like before. This time, however, it was Kailan who had the upper hand. Each swing of his knocked

[415]

Viktor's sword farther and farther away as he began to lose control of it before it completely left his hand.

"You have been defeated," said Kailan, thrusting the sword into Viktor's stomach. He pushed the sword almost all of the way in, letting out a sigh as he let go of it. Upon looking up, he found himself to be confused seeing Viktor smiling.

"I'm a vampire, you idiot," laughed Viktor. "This won't kill me." Kailan held the boy down with one hand as he reached for the dagger on his right side.

"Dagger of a thousand suns," he uttered to himself. "Let's just hope it works." Kailan raised the dagger into the air, stabbing it into Viktor's heart.

"Again, you have failed at trying to kill me," laughed Viktor. "Only a…" The boy looked down at his chest, slowly pulling his shirt, watching as his veins turned a dark colour.

"I think you are dying," said Kailan as he stepped away and walked towards Lena.

"Kailan!" she screamed.

As the boy turned around, he saw the blade flying towards him. It was by some great miracle that Kailan was able to dodge the attack, or was it? He turned around and smiled as Viktor slowly let out his last breath by calling out Rina's name.

"You missed," said Kailan, smiling as he turned around. Suddenly he was filled with fear, anxiety, anger, so many emotions. Lena was lying on the ground, with the knife, sticking out of her chest. Kailan rushed to her side, holding up her head. "No, no!" he cried.

[416]

"Kailan," Lena whispered. "I have to tell you. What Viktor said about me; that was true."

"You don't need to justify yourself to me," said Kailan, dripping tears from his face.

"I am a siren, but from the first day I met you, I wondered if it was the right thing to do," replied Lena. "It wasn't long before I had fallen in love with you, calling off my destiny."

"You're going to be alright, Lena."

"Kailan, I love you with my whole heart; I always have. Even when we argued, I still loved you."

"D-don't give up, Lena. You can fight it." Suddenly, Kaela flew in the balcony, landing directly beside Kailan, nuzzling against Lena's side.

"Do you have any water?" the girl said, licking her lips.

Kailan patted his shirt and belt for his wineskin. "I'm sorry, I must have left my water at the camp," Kailan replied.

"The glass vial," whispered a distant, but familiar voice Kailan. He felt a strange warming feeling against his cheek, watching a leaf slowly flutter in the wind by the opening of the balcony. "Love is not lost."

He reached into his pocket, pulling out the small bottle of water that he and Thorstein found near the beginning of their journey. "It's not much, but it will help." He popped the cork from the top and gently held it to Lena's lips, pouring the clear liquid back.

"It tastes sweet," said Lena, smiling. She looked over at

[417]

Kaela, and waved. "You're going to stay with Kailan now. He's going to take care of you. The bird moved forward, rubbing her beak against Lena's cheek. The girl looked back up at Kailan and spoke. "I wanted to spend my life with you," said Lena. With those last words, Kailan looked deep into her eyes and kissed her on the lips.

"Me too," said Kailan, pulling away. As he looked into her eyes again, he noticed her green eyes glazing over as her head tilted to the side and dropped.

*   *   *

In the time since the battle against the Black Allegiance, Arlbega had become one unified country again. For his loyalty, Silus Kain was offered to rule Arad as a separate country, but he gave up the offer, and continued to run it as a territory of Arlbega. Kailan, Thorstein, and Guin were offered their own positions as rulers of the remaining countries, but all of the companions turned the offer down. Kailan decided that it was too much for him and that he wanted to continue his life in peace and quiet. Guin was too preoccupied with his studies as a wizard. He was now the newest member of the wizards' council in Kelenath, and living a life with his new wife, Tateena. Because of his father's death in the battle, Thorstein took over the village of Schtein. It was always in his mind that men had to work for their own worth. A good, honest day's work would give much better results than running the country. After the battle at Trekta, Tanier and Bailan were reunited with Dolci Grabote and Finn Clayse. Tanier, Bailan, Crag, Dolci, and Finn, all had Master Scholton removed from the wizards' council in Kelenath and had him jailed until the end of his life. He was found to have sent numerous boys to their deaths on journeys just like the one he sent the five boys on.

*   *   *

When Bailan and Tanier returned to Harlem, Bailan walked into Tanier's office and place a piece of paper on the Arch Chancellor's desk.

"What's this?" questioned Tanier. "Are we still receiving letters from Silus?" Tanier laughed and slowly read down the page. The more that he read though, the more his smile went away. "This is your resignation?" Bailan nodded as a tear rolled down his cheek.

"I'm sure going to miss everyone," said Bailan. He walked over to Tanier and threw his arms around the Arch Chancellor.

"You make it sound like you're going to just disappear," said Tanier, laughing. Bailan stepped back from the desk and walked towards the door slowly, closing it behind him.

[419]

"Bailan?" There was a sound, like that of rushing wind that rang through the Hall for a second or two before fading away. "Bailan?" Tanier called out again, running for the door. As he opened it though, there was no Bailan to be found. Machesney Hall was empty, except for Tanier standing in the doorway of his office, oblivious to what happened.

*　　　　　*　　　　　*

Thorstein raised the glass of beer to his mouth, blowing the foam over the rim. He guzzled down the beer and smiled. "You know, I haven't had a good beer like that in such a long time," said Thorstein, with a look of satisfaction on his face. "You Helforts make some good drinks." Guin laughed uncontrollably.

"You think we should have shared some of that 'water of life' with him?" said Thorstein.

"I don't know," replied Kailan. "We'd have to get some for Tateena then, as well."

"Ya, but the people here are a different story," said Guin, trying to ignore the conversation. Kailan laughed as he walked over and sat in the chair.

"You know, I can't thank you guys enough for coming to visit me in my new home," said Kailan. "It must've taken you a number of days to get to Helforth." Thorstein and Guin looked at each other before chuckling. "What, did I miss something?" questioned Kailan.

"Guin finally learned how to teleport," said Thorstein with a smile on his face. "I was at my village an hour ago." The three friends began to laugh again before a brief silence.

"I miss the good old days," said Guin, looking up at the ceiling and smiling. "All of the adventures that we used to have, the trouble we got into." Kailan and Thorstein smiled as well.

"You call those good times?" said Kailan, jokingly. "I'm pretty sure that we nearly died a number of times."

"Well, at least we made it," said Guin. The room quickly went silent again and the smiles disappeared. Thorstein dropped his head forward and whispered, "Most of us." The feeling of sorrow filled the hearts of all three young men for a short moment as they thought back on that night atop the castle. In the almost full year that had passed since then, they had thought of it very little, and when they did, they tried to forget. How could they though? Their whole adventure lead up to that one night, and the biggest tragedy happened when they least expected it. Kailan raised his beer glass into the air.

"To the ones we've lost," said Kailan. The other two men smiled and raised their glasses as well. The three of them took as drink before putting their glasses back down. As a shadow passed in front of the house on the street, Kailan stood up.

"What is it?" questioned Thorstein.

[421]

"Oh, nothing," said Kailan. In his mind though, he knew that he was longing for the one that he loved, hoping that she would return to him. Kailan sat back down on the wicker chair, placing his beer on the table next to him. He leaned in the chair and tossed his head backwards, resting it on the top of the chair. Suddenly, there was a knock at the door. "Now who could that be?" said Kailan, bothered by the interruption. He tried to look out the window, but he couldn't see the person standing by the door. There was another knock. "Go away!" yelled Kailan.

"Ya!" Guin agreed. "We're drinking!" The knocks continued until Kailan walked over to the door and opened it. There, standing in the doorway, looking almost the same as she did when he first met her, except for her protruding baby belly, was Lena.

"Sorry, dear."

*   *   *

Kaela soared through the skies, passing over Kailan and Lena's home, cruising from the small village, over hill and dale until reaching an old elf on a hill. It was Drast, the same elf that taught Lena how to use a bow. He held out his arm allowing Kaela to perch on it.

"Are you ready Kaela?" said the old elf, smiling. He laughed as he looked into the white eagle's green eyes. "They

[422]

never realised what their destiny held for them before those pesky letters. They never realised the true value of friendship until they left their homes and went on a journey that had them going from country to country. Ah, but another adventure is afoot for them soon in the future. They'll continue on with their lives in happiness." Kaela flapped her wings and flew up into the air beside Drast, hovering for a brief moment before landing next to him. Suddenly, Drast began to glow, and change shape. Within a few seconds, it was Bailan instead, who was standing on the hilltop next to the bird. "And they never knew that we were with them the entire time, watching them, protecting them, guiding them." The young man smiled and turned to face off into the distance as Kaela changed from eagle to a young woman. Lena's sister stood atop the hill, next to Bailan, smiling, but with tears in her eyes.

"Where are we off to now?" questioned Kaela.

"Another world," said Bailan. "It is a strange world, very different from your own." The young man smiled as he walked forward and into the portal that appeared before him. He grabbed Kaela's hand just before walking through. "Don't worry, we'll return… when you're ready." The portal closed behind them as they left for the new world, hoping to return someday.

Made in the USA
Charleston, SC
01 December 2014